Choices

As Fate Would Have It

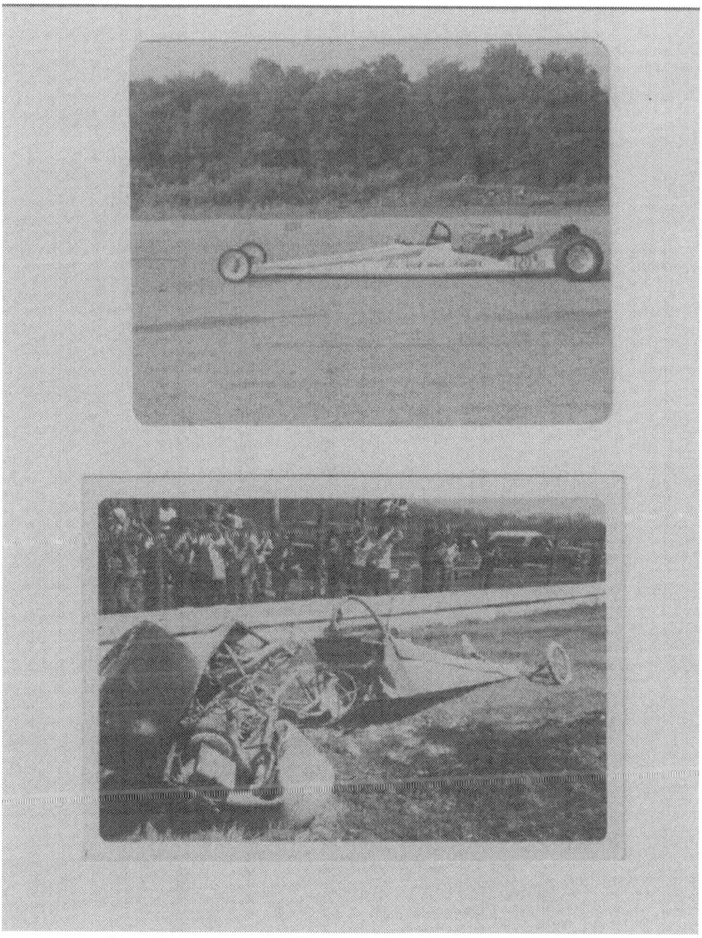

Arts Dragster before and after the accident

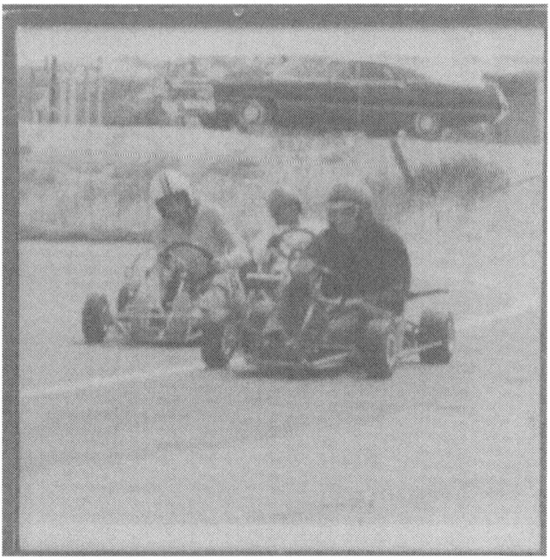

Art In Kart Race Ahead Of Pack

Art in Exxon office just before the crash

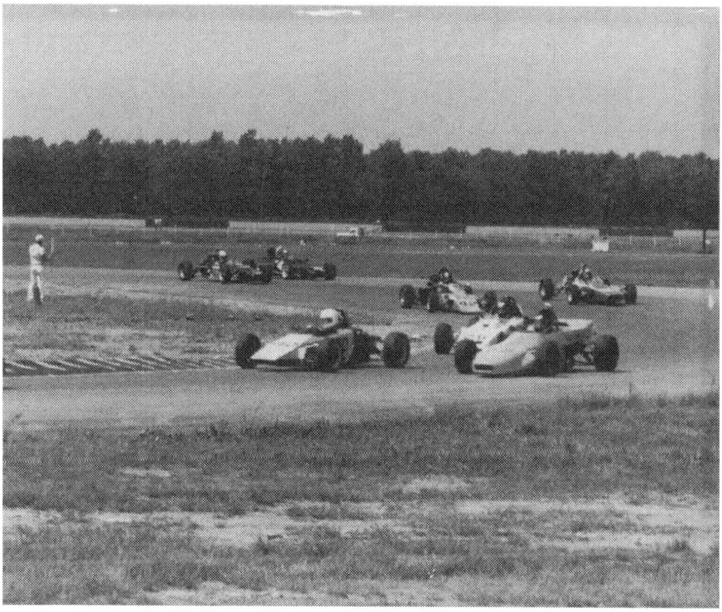

Art's Yellow Formula Ford in second place

SUPER ENGINEER

Cracking Reactor

About the Author

Art recovered from his accident after spending six months in the hospital for 3rd-degree burns and other injuries. Several years later, he remarried and now has six grandchildren.

Art has approximately twenty US patents. He won the Exxon's most valuable patent award twice and received numerous non-US patents. He received the Marquis Who's Who lifetime achievement award for his engineering accomplishments.

After the accident Art returned to drag racing for several years and then raced boats to win many awards. He earned a pilot's license and built an experimental plane.

From 1965 to 1999, he served as head of the Cracking Reactor Design Group and Lead Specialist for Exxon. His group did the process and mechanical design for most of Exxon's Cracking Reactors. He invented and co-developed over 90% of Exxon's Cracking Reactor technology. He co-invented two low resident time cracking coil designs which significantly-improved ethylene production (a major component in plastics). These designs are the premier designs used by Exxon today. He invented Low NOx (Flue Gas Recirculation burners) to meet EPA requirements. He also co-invented a device which permits cracking heavy garbage feeds containing high asphaltites. Many of these developments are kept as Exxon trade secrets.

Since 1999, Art has served as a consultant for a major oil/chemical company where he developed new designs for cracking reactors. He also solved numerous problems with their existing Cracking Reactors and solved a flameout problem to prevent a major explosion in a plant that was having problems with their low NOx burners.

He developed the hydrodynamic/aerodynamic and structural design for 3 high-performance boats currently being built by American Offshore Powerboats. He did failure analysis consulting for two high-performance boats outdrive manufacturers?

He developed a method for recovering 700 times more Geothermal energy from abandoned subsea oil wells than any other existing OTEC system. He consulted with Knighthawk Engineering to develop a shock-resistant rough sea boat for the US military and working with Knighthawk engineering developed a system to convert waste streams to clean hydrogen and carbon monoxide.

As the owner of American Offshore Powerboats, he designs and builds family-oriented performance boats. Website is http:// www.american-offshore.com Art wrote a partial draft of his book several years after his accident. After friends had read portions of his draft they prompted him to write this book so that others might learn something from his experiences.

Contents

Introduction

Sometimes we made choices which we think were a mistake. Some of the choices were made by free will and some by fate. We don't realize that a higher being deemed that these choices were necessary for us to reach a higher goal that is only known to Him. We do not have the ability to see the ultimate goal planned for us..After reading the author's story you may come to realize that the poor choices you think you made in the past were necessary to guide you to where you are today, If you are not happy you should not dwell on those choices because they cannot be changed and you should move on and pursue your dreams, even if your acquaintances tell you that you will not be successful

Chapter 1
The Beginning

When death is imminent, your entire life flashes before your eyes. In just a few brief seconds, you get to relive your life. In that twilight zone between life and death, the past and present merge, and time stands still.

The choices you make in life are real. With death hovering over you, you understand in an instant what it took you a lifetime to learn. You judge yourself with the wisdom of ages. The fact is that when the time comes for you to leave this world, you look at your life from so far away. Everything is ending, and nothing you could change will matter anymore.

You wonder if the choices you made were determined by fate, or did you really have the ability to change them. That moment itself teaches you more about life than anything else. Unfortunately, though, you cannot and maybe should not benefit from what you think you have learned as a direct result of your choices and painful experiences.

April 17, 1977

It was a beautiful, sunny spring morning. The peaceful sleep of the lazy New Jersey countryside was rudely disturbed this Sunday morning. The ear-splitting roar of the thunderous engines emanating from two dragsters running down the quarter-mile racetrack pierced through the trees and rolling hills. The race was almost neck and neck. Any bystander looking on would just see a blur of colors as the cars roared past.

The sleek patriotic red, white, and blue rear-engine dragster in the left lane of the track were barely ahead of the black dragster in the right lane. The red, white, and blue ones were capable of speeding up to 180 miles per hour on the quarter-mile track. It was built specifically for the purpose of drag-racing, and every part was as good as could possibly be.

Art, the driver, and his partner, Bill, had designed and fabricated the car themselves. They took great pride in saying that they built the car with their own hands. They had worked hard in making the car one of the best ones in their circle. These guys were those who loved cars on another level. The majority of their paychecks were spent in procuring that one part, which would make their car faster. Right now, as Art sped down to the finish line, nothing was on his mind except complete focus on his goal. It was these moments that he lived for. That quarter-mile left behind every single worry he had. It was all so euphoric. He had nothing to focus on except the finish line. Art felt the air rush past his helmet as he sat in the open cockpit of the car. However, the only thing he could focus on was how he could make his car go even faster.

The shattering roar of the engine and the vibration of the roll cage were muffled only by his helmet and the wind buffeting of the car's streamlined body. Art glanced at the speedometer; it now showed 140 miles an hour and was further accelerating. The spectator stands that lined both sides of the track were now a mere blur.

Art looked out to the track, memorizing it subconsciously, and glanced to his right. He caught a glimpse of Jim Warren's ominous-looking black dragster in the right lane. Art barely led the race. Within a second, his eyes were back on track, his fist tightening around the steering. Jim’s entire car, including the huge Chevy motor, was painted black. The only exception was the ghostly silver lettering on the sides of the car, proclaiming in front of the world that he was "THE GRIM REAPER."

Art, like most race car drivers, was a little superstitious. He knew that the difference between life and death in racing was a moment's mistake. Everything could go wrong instantly and fully. A single nut could come loose and break hell loose. He wished now that he had not looked over and seen the GRIM REAPER. He, like most drivers, did not like to think about death and continuously tell themselves that they are invincible. He was very well aware of the fact that accidents happen. Yet, like most others, he also thought that they occurred to others only.

Ever since he was a little kid, Art had looked up to famous racers he read about in car magazines. Somehow, the worst accidents happened to the best drivers, but he always convinced himself that it was their own fault. He was not going to make that mistake, and he would be safe, he thought. However, he couldn't help but feel a slight uneasiness creeping in, racing against "*THE GRIM REAPER.*"

Jim, a funeral director by trade, was a pleasant fellow who pleased the crowd with his theatrical antics. That, along with his impeccable timing, had made him a well-liked member of the community. In keeping with his theme of death, Jim dressed entirely in black. As a crowning touch, a long black Hearse carrying his pit crew always followed Jim's dragster down the track. His antics unnerved Art. He was playing psychological tricks on the other racers, and that alone was shallow, trying to get in their mind and hoping to get them to make a mistake. However, that was a cheap tactic, and it was useless because it tended not to have any effect on experienced drivers like Art. These guys' entire personalities were built around their instincts and ability to act fast and right in a moment.

Art blocked any thought of death from entering his mind. However, with the race going neck to neck and the sight of 'THE GRIM REAPER', it seemed like an impossible task. He was ahead by a narrow margin, but "The GRIM REAPER" was chasing him down the track and closing the gap. Art glanced down at the tachometer and shifted to top gear almost without thought as he had done hundreds of times before. He glanced at the finish line, which was only

400 feet ahead. In a mere two scant seconds, it would be all over. All he had to do was pull the parachute release handle and hang on until the car came to a stop.

Murphy's Law dictates, *"Anything that can go wrong, will go wrong."* Even though Art checked everything himself and made sure the car was up for the race, there were still things that could go wrong. It is the case with everything, and the only thing you can do so that things do not go wrong is hope and pray. Someone had once told Art that there is a nut on a helicopter called the 'Jesus nut,' which holds the main rotor to the main body of the chopper. It was named so because if the nut came loose, the only thing that was left to do was pray to Jesus to save you.

Art heard a bang and immediately cursed. The left rear tire blew. The rear of the car jumped to the right, and the car veered sharply to the left. The sudden jerking of the car at almost 160 miles per hour startled Art. His mind immediately fell back on his instincts, and he tried to ascertain what was happening. Art's mind raced into action, trying to compute cause and effect logically. In the heat of the moment, he questioned if he had done something wrong or if something on the car had broken. All this while, he was trying his best to get the car to stop and steer away from crashing. He had no answers. Desperately, he tried to steer and correct the heading of the car, but his efforts were in vain. He tried his best to steer the vehicle away from crashing, but it just would not respond. That did not stop Art from trying his best to get the crazy ride under control. His right hand pulled hard on the brake handle and his left-hand firm on the steering wheel. Nothing seemed to be working properly. He felt utterly helpless and did not know what to do.

Before, whenever he had driven or raced, he had always been in control. This time around, it was different. In fact, it was the exact opposite; he had no control. The car he had built with all his heart was acting on its own accord, subject to the laws of physics. All those laws and stunts it was showing were gunning for a crash. He knew physics would win; it was inevitable. His mind showed him images of the greatest drivers crashing. He visualized the images he had seen of his childhood heroes dying in fiery crashes. One moment, they could be winning, and everything could be going their way. In the next, there was nothing. He was going to be one of those drivers.

Panic settled in as everything slowed down. The cockpit was still intact, but he knew it would break soon. He saw everything in slow motion, but he knew that he would remember nothing when asked to recount it later if he got out alive, that is. Art began to panic as thoughts of dying enveloped in flames ran rampant in his mind. The car was hurtling towards the edge of the track at 140 miles per hour. It slowed down from the friction of the frame scraping on the track surface, and now, it was entirely out of control.

The lower part of the frame dug into the rough asphalt near the edge of the track, flipping the car over. The rear end went over the top, and this resulted in a violent, uncontrolled roll. The windshield broke away, and instinctively, Art's hand flew off the steering wheel. He covered his face. The car was now upside down, and Art was enveloped in the dark shadows between the car and the track surface.

A single thought was in his mind, *"Oh my God! I'm upside down. I'm going to die."*

The only thing between Art and death was the roll cage and his seat belt, keeping him in place. The roll bar scraped on the asphalt surface beneath it. In his peripheral vision, he could see the friction generate a shower of sparks like those from a thousand birthday sparklers. He wished now that he had built **a** better roll bar because this one was barely up to standards. He knew now that the only thing that stood between him and death was the flimsy roll bar. The crashes he had seen on television and in real life went through his mind. He knew all too well that if it broke, he would resemble an egg hurtled into a brick wall. He knew that in many cases, there was not enough left to bury.

Art wondered now if he would end up the same way; cleaned up and discarded somewhere. It wasn't the way he wanted to go. He did not want to die. His vision was now blurry from the violent movement of the car and the inevitability of death finally setting in his mind. He did not know how much time he had, but he tried to make peace with himself. There was not enough time, and the only thing he could think was that he was alone.

He was all alone. At this time, it was just him and the machine that he had built himself that would ultimately become his coffin. He thought about all of his friends and family, but none of them were there to help him or give him advice. Irrationality led him to believe that there was something they could do, but logic knew there was nothing there. He began a conversation between himself and his God, which was just about all he could do. He knew God was the only one who could save him now.

"What should I do? I can't think clearly. I can't seem to do anything, can't get the car under control. I'm helpless. I'm going to die, and there's nothing I can do about it." He pleaded with God. He wanted some peace at that time, but it was just too much. He wished God would Himself descend to save him, but no such miracle happened.

Millions of thoughts and images now rushed wildly through Art's mind. Images of his friend Billy Nansen, who had crashed his dragster and died at this very spot last year, flashed before him. He continued his conversation with God. It had taken him a very long time to convince himself that what happened with Billy would not happen to him.

Never before had he let his car get so out of control, but again, all it took was a single thing going wrong. It was going to result in his death. Against all the odds, he hoped that he would survive. That's what every human naturally does and hopes for in situations like those.

"Was Billy conscious? Did he know that he was going to die? What was he thinking about? Did he ask You to help him?" He asked God.

No answer. No sudden sense of peace enveloping his heart, no peace of mind. He tried again.

"How did I get myself into this situation? I shouldn't have been driving today, too many problems in my life, can't think clearly. My life is all screwed up. How did my life get so messed up? My marriage to Joy was a failure. Windy no longer loves me. I've messed up everything. Maybe I should just give up and die. There's no reason to live. Nobody will give a damn if I die. No one will miss me." He shouted.

Immediately, he regretted what he said. He did not want his last thoughts to be those where he was cursing his life and was not happy. He wanted to die, believing that someone was going to miss him and cared about him. He wanted to believe that he was a good person. *"No! Someone has got to care. Joy will miss me."* Yet again, the reality of his life hit him hard, and he started rationalizing with himself. *"No, she won't, she's still angry and bitter. She blames me for our marital problems."*

Art intensely wished to believe that he was a good person. He gave all that he had to justify that to himself. A man who had walked through life with his head held high was now reduced to a fearful, helpless human, rolling on the ground. There was almost nothing standing between him and death.

"I didn't want to hurt her. We've been through so much together, we've shared so many of the joys and sorrows of life. I wish things could have turned out differently. Windy won't miss me either. I love her, but she doesn't love me. We've had our good and bad times, but it seems that she only remembers the bad times."

After a lot of self-talk, battling, and struggle, Art finally came to accept the inevitable. He accepted that this was the end. His entire life was flashing before his eyes, and time had slowed down to a crawl. It was scary that his death was taking so long. His mind stopped at an image where his two sons stood.

"My sons Mike and Pat will miss me. No, no, they won't. They're too young; they'll forget me. Joy will remarry, and they'll get a new father and forget that I ever existed. My death won't make any difference to anyone," Art murmured in fright. This thought hurt him more than anything else. He

may have wronged people in his life, but he had never wronged his sons. He loved his sons more than anything in the world. He had done everything he could to be a good father to them until now. He had almost gotten himself killed, and because of this, his boys were going to grow up without the shadow of their father.

He knew that no man would be able to love his sons as much he loved them. His entire world had changed when he first cradled his little boys in his arms, and they held his finger. He could never forget how he felt when he looked into their eyes. In that moment, he knew that he would do anything in the world for them.

He lied. He could not do anything in the world for them. He could not even be around for them anymore. Internally, he regretted everything. He regretted not spending more time with them and not giving up racing when they were born. He regretted so many things, but he could not do anything to compensate anymore.

"Life will go on as if I had never been born. I'll never ever see them again. I hope life is good for them. Dear God, please let them know how much I loved them. Let them understand why I had to leave their mother and that I never

meant to hurt them,"

Art prayed. He was on the verge of giving up.

At that point, he knew that he was clinging on to life. If he wished, he could let go right now, and it would all end. Just as the thought entered his mind, it felt like God intervened. It is weird how strongly people will cling onto life when all it takes is letting go. Maybe it was God, or maybe it was just stubbornness. Whatever it was, Art chose to believe that it was God. It was like He steeled Art's heart and will to live took over his heart. He continued his conversation with God.

"No, I've got to do something. I don't want to die. I want another chance. I've got to put my life back into order. I can't give up, got to keep trying, got to protect myself, got to try to pull myself up into the body of the car as far as possible." He thought.

Art knew that God could listen to whatever his heart said. He believed that truly. God had listened to him now and had given him courage. Still rolling around in the cage, he could hear the roar of steel clashing against the asphalt. The roar of the engine being splintered and the exhaust going off. Yet, eerily, everything seemed quite at the same time.

"Dear God, help me. Blessed Mother, give me the strength. Don't let the roll bar break, protect me. Don't let me die here." He whispered.

In desperation, he even asked his Dad for help. His Dad had died several years before, but he had always come to Art's rescue when he was a kid. Even though everything around him roared in protest against being subject to the cruelty of asphalt, he could still hear himself. *"Please, Jesus, help me. Give me another chance. I haven't accomplished anything important yet. I am supposed to accomplish something important, aren't I? I must have meant something to someone. I had to have touched someone's life for the better. I must have done something worthwhile in life. Maybe I mean something to that homeless guy I helped? Maybe I mean something to that guy I helped who was stranded on the road."* He whispered again, still able to hear his own voice. He pleaded with God, thinking of all the good he had done in the world.

Art knew that he was not a bad person, and he deserved another chance to live.

"Did I choose my destiny, or is it as fate would have it?" He inquired, but unfortunately, that was all he could say. Suddenly, something seemed different. It was almost like there was nothing. Art was unsure if he was alive or dead, but all he saw was darkness. It was all dark, and he was enveloped in darkness entirely. Art could then spot gravel, sparks, and stones flying everywhere. *"When will it stop, when will it stop?"* He thought.

Chapter 2
The Early Years

Childhood

Little boys and girls sat at wooden desks. All of them had blank expressions on their faces. None of them even pretended to listen to the teacher who talked on and on without making an impression on any of the little children. However, they knew they had to sit still and not make a single noise.

Their teacher, a Dominican sister, was known to lose her temper. She was much like any of the other sisters who taught them. The Dominican sister was dressed in a white robe, black scarf, and cape that covered her head and back. The children consensually believed that her garments made her look like a big fat penguin.

The room was painted a gaudy yellow, which sharply clashed with the green tile floor. Most children had to cover their eyes in the morning when they came in because the paint would hurt their eyes. They collectively thought that whoever painted the room wanted to hurt them. The sun shone brightly through the partially frost-covered windows of St. James Catholic School, casting ominous shadows on the floor and walls. Icicles on the window ledges were beginning to melt as was evident by the slow dripping of water from their tips. The force of winter was easing. The children were all excited that they would get to play outside in summers. It wasn't that they did not play in winter, but they shivered throughout, and the snow made them feel even colder.

The classroom was stuffy and hot. The hissing of steam could be heard as it escaped from the traps on the large brown cast-iron radiators that lined the walls. They all shed their huge jackets, coats, sweaters, and gloves in a huge pile at the back of the classroom as soon as they entered. An old 1952 Coca Cola calendar hung on the wall next to the American flag. The large, circular clock over the blackboard ticked away monotonously, attracting the attention of one or two children periodically as they mentally calculated how long it was until the class ended. The hands now struck two o'clock. Art was sitting in the middle of the room next to his friends Ron Kashon, Gary Cross, and John Daoud. He liked his place in class. It was a good place to sit.

His place was close enough to the front of the room to see the blackboard easily, but far enough away from the teacher so she could not hear his running commentary on her lesson or the constant jabbering with his friends. Art liked school, even though he did not like sitting in class listening to the sister droning monotonously on and on about something trivial.

He liked it because his friends made it fun for him, snickering behind their hands and coughing to conceal laughter when he said something too funny. Of course, if he were causing too much of a ruckus, they would be given a swift reprimand. For someone studying in a catholic school, such behavior resulted in a slap on their palms or spanking in front of the whole class. While Art and his friends had gotten more or less used to it, they still dreaded it whenever it happened.

Rocco, a stocky, muscular twelve-year-old, sat in the last row in the desk closest to the door. Curly black hair framed his rather flat moon-like face. His little beady eyes sent threatening chills down the spines of his school mates. Despised and feared by all but a few, Rocco was a bully and pushed everyone around. It seems he always had a nasty, threatening comment and specifically went out of his way to pick on Art, frequently forcing Art to give him candy and baseball or boxing cards.

The entire class hated him unanimously. He would try to make smart ass comments like Art did, but he would never be able to get a single child to laugh, yet when Art spoke, more so than not, everyone would erupt in laughter. Of course, that meant that Art would be at the receiving end of his teachers and Rocco's brutality, but he loved it nonetheless.

Art had the easy-going personality and impeccable sense of humor that endeared him to most of the class. Even though he was labeled a troubled child by the sisters, he was smart and would achieve good grades in almost all his subjects. Yet, that was not enough for the sisters who insisted that he needed to be disciplined to the maximum extent.

Nevertheless, the sisters did not make Art as afraid as Rocco did. Fearful of him, Art thought that if he gave Rocco what he wanted, he would eventually leave him alone, but he was wrong. Rocco seemed determined to make Art's life as difficult as possible. Art did not realize that what Rocco really wanted was to see Art squirm and give in to his demands. Seeing the fear in Art's eyes made him feel stronger. Art could see the enormous pleasure of Rocco seeing Art grovel in cowardice.

He really did not want the baseball cards, boxing cards, or the bubble gum. His sick ego required feeding. It had an insatiable appetite for the feeling of control and power that he exercised over others by his threats. He received some sick satisfaction when others submitted to his demands. He ruled unchecked and unchallenged in the fifth grade.

Art wished that he was stronger so he could take on Rocco, but while Rocco was big and bulky, Art was more lean and agile. Sure, he was strong, but when it came to facing off against Rocco, he was scared of getting hurt. He, along with his friends, had been hurt in the past for trying to stand up to Rocco. The other class fellows might not have liked Rocco, but they did nothing when the time came to intervene. He knew that reporting Rocco to the sisters was a mistake because he would not get expelled from the school. The only thing that would happen would be that his life would get considerably worse.

"What's your hand up for, Arthur?" The teacher asked, looking at Art.

"Sister, can I be excused? I have to go to the bathroom." He asked, in the politest voice he could muster.

"Okay, but don't stay too long or you'll miss the entire spelling lesson." The teacher said in an admonishing tone, and Art nodded solemnly.

A boring hour of school was still left. Art stood up to go with the intention to stay out as long as he could without arousing suspicion. He hated spelling lessons and was doing everything possible to keep from falling asleep.

He thought that spelling a waste of time, and he wished more than anything that time would pass by more quickly. His friend, John, had already nodded off a couple of times only to be awakened by the prodding of Art's sharp pencil, which he skillfully but gently jabbed into John's chubby behind.

That was perhaps the more lenient option rather than getting caught nodding off by the sister. The sister seemed to be in a good mood today for some reason, and this was an opportune time to be excused from class. Once safe from the watchful gaze of the sister in the confines of the boys' room, Art reached into the back pocket of his brown corduroy trousers and took out his collection of Bazooka bubble gum boxing cards.

He started looking through them and paused wistfully when he reached the Jersey Joe Walcott card. It was his favorite. Last summer, he met Jersey Joe at Nick's candy store, which was on the same street as his grandfather's restaurant. That had been one of the best moments in Art's life, and he had told everyone about it enthusiastically. Of course, that meant that he was once again on the receiving end of Rocco's bullying. That alone was enough to ensure that he never talked about it again.

He looked at the card, fondly remembering the time he met Jersey Joe. He was with his family, but he took time from his hectic schedule to chat with all the kids. Art remembered the interaction as one of the best conversations he had ever had. He had been star-struck and fumbled over most of what he wanted to say, but Joe had been a good sport about it. He gave Art his autograph. In those days, there were many good white boxers like Rocky Marciano, but Jersey Joe, a kind and gentle black man whom many considered much too old to be fighting, was Art's hero, and he idolized him. Everything about him amazed Art, and he wanted to follow in his hero's footsteps.

Art's daydream and fantasy, however, was soon broken by a loud menacing, and much-dreaded voice of the most loathed person Art could think of. *"Give me that card. I want it!"*

'Oh my God, it's Rocco, and he wants my Jersey Joe Walcott card.' He thought as he closed his eyes, trying to gather up the courage. *"No, Rocco, you can't have it. I can't give it to you, please, it's my favorite card."* He pleaded. Deathly afraid of Rocco, Art was squirming again. Rocco saw that he was groveling, and a cruel smile spread on his bullish features. *"I'll give you my Rocky Marciano card."* Art tried to negotiate, but Rocco was not having any of it.

Supremely pleased with himself already, Rocco spat, *"No! I want your Jersey Joe Walcott card."* He came to Art and pushed him against the cold gray steel partition wall, which separated the toilets from the rest of the room. Art's fist closed tightly to his Jersey Joe card. He would not part with it. It was his hero's card, and he knew that Rocco would probably just throw it away or tear it up in front of him.

Art's resistance in giving Rocco the card resulted in grave

circumstances. Rocco pulled him closer to himself and shoved him again towards the cold hard gray steel wall. Art's head bounced against the wall, and his grip on the card loosened. Rocco then took the chance to snatch the card from him. Now that the Jersey Joe card was safely in his hand, he bellowed out a sickening laugh and did exactly what Art thought he would do. He ripped it in half, all the while laughing and spewing curses at Art.

Seeing Rocco tear his card made Art angry, angrier than he had ever been. Something snapped inside him. Rocco had destroyed his prized possession - a card autographed by his hero. His hero was strong, unlike him. The only thing that Art wanted to do was be like his hero, and now he could be. Aided by his anger towards Rocco, months of welled up emotions and resentment finally erupted, and Art forgot for a moment his fear and subservient role. He forgot that Rocco was the master. He saw that Rocco was too busy laughing and was not paying attention to Art. Using all the strength he had, pulled his fist back and punched him as hard as he could. Rocco lost his balance momentarily. He would have recovered if Art had not charged him again. He punched Rocco again and kept going on. After the fifth punch, Rocco was down on the ground, covering his face under the parade of punches that rained down on him. Art was not done, though. Without breaking the parade of punches, he knelt over him and kept punching him.

Blood gushed from Rocco's nose, and he tried to fight back. He was big and powerful, but he was slow while Art was lithe. Even though Rocco occasionally managed to land a crushing blow to Art's mouth but Art barely cared. Blood now rushed from Art's lacerated lip. It hurt him a lot, but he was driven with pure anger and adrenaline.

Art's rain of blows thundered down on Rocco's thick face. He kept punching him again and again. Soon, even Rocco's occasional punches stopped. He now began consuming all his energy in cowering and saving his face. Art curled his fist around his arm and pushed it aside, exposing his face and hitting him with his other hand. Neither of them could now tell whose blood was whose. Art was bleeding from his lacerated lip and fist while Rocco was bleeding from his nose, mouth, and forehead. His arms now flailed wildly in the air as he tried desperately to protect his ugly face.

"Give up! Give up!" Art shouted, year's worth of resentment spewing from him. *"Stop bullying me. Stop*

pushing me around! Don't push me around anymore, Rocco! No more pushing me around; no more! I won't take it anymore!" Art cried, tears streaming down his face of repressed anger. He wanted to go on, and he would have if Rocco had not given in.

"Okay, okay!" Rocco shouted. *"Stop, stop, please. No more, please. Stop, Stop hitting me, please. Stop hitting me. I can't take it anymore."* Rocco cried.

Art stopped punching him and stood up. His bully was finally beaten. He dug deep into the reserve of energy he had and breathed in deeply, regaining his strength. For a moment, Art stood over Rocco, trying hard to restrain himself from shaking.

The fact that it was Rocco he was standing over and the fact that he had longed badly for this moment made his victory even sweeter. He watched as Rocco cowered on the ground at his feet. Looking down at the pathetic cowering figure in front of him, Art now pondered why he had allowed Rocco to push him around for so long. Silently, Art vowed to himself that he would never again let anyone push him around even if it meant suffering the consequences of being physically beaten. In his imaginary world, he had made his hero very proud and was impressed with himself. He always had the strength in him to do that. He was just too scared to see it. It was freeing to know that he would not have to be scared now. Even if Rocco wanted another go at him, he would go again, and again, and again until he came out on top. Whimpering, Rocco crawled away to sanctuary behind the gray partition wall.

The sight of it inspired nothing except intense satisfaction in Art, even though the boy looked pitiful. The evil bully was no more, at least as far as Art and his friends were concerned. His beating had had the desired effect, and Rocco never again pushed them around. Art learned that he could not let his fears govern his life no matter what the outcome might be. However, once in a while, Art would hear stories of how Rocco had pushed and bullied some kids around. He was not too surprised.

He promised himself that if he ever came across Rocco bullying anyone, he would intervene. One good beating taught Rocco a lesson, but it was not enough to completely transform him. Art had learned to not let bullies to continue to bully even if it meant taking a beating and getting hurt.

Life at school henceforth was completely different than it

had been before. It was much more enjoyable now without the looming threat of being bullied.

Eventually, the chilly winds of winter gave way to the warm breezes of summer. Spelling lessons were forgotten, and school books were setaside. At the Jersey shore, a boy's life in the summer revolved around the water. For most boys, it was time for fishing, swimming, or if they were lucky enough, they went boating.

For as long as he could remember, Art had dreamed of having a boat. He had built numerous unsuccessful rafts from old scraps of wood. The best of his designs slowly sank when he climbed aboard them while the worst of them would tip and pop out violently from under him. Despite his efforts, he couldn't seem to master the art of designing and building a successful simple raft.

However, he was sure that this summer would be different. He had accomplished a lot this year, taking down his bully being the biggest of them. His dreams would finally become a reality. Art and his friend Gary saved up the nickels, dimes, and quarters they earned delivering groceries for the local A&P supermarket. They would walk miles in the hot summer sun carrying heavy bags of groceries for a nickel, or on some lucky days, they got a quarter. It was laborious work, but at the end of the day, it was a means to an end. That's all they were looking for.

After months of hard work, they managed to accumulate the forty dollars needed to buy a small wooden boat, which was in a sad condition. Nonetheless, they didn't care. All they cared about that day was having fun to their heart's contentment. The khaki green paint was peeling, and it leaked badly. With hard work, a can of caulking compound, and some paint, they transformed it into a seaworthy craft, or at least something they thought was seaworthy.

It was now bright red, and a white paint scheme made it something that two thirteen-year-old boys could be proud of. It was a small boat, only seven feet long, and could barely seat the two of them. Every morning at nine sharp, they would rendezvous at the overgrown weed lot on the east shore of the lagoon where they kept their little boat.

All their friends who couldn't afford to rent a dock kept their boats there since no one ever took anything or borrowed anything from that lot without permission. No need for chains or locks. It was the 50's, and the world was a safer place. No one would dream of taking something that didn't belong to them, especially in this small town on the Jersey shore. Here they would go rowing in their little boat. It was fun at first, but soon boredom set in, and the urge to go faster struck them. Of course, since all the kids were adrenaline junkies, nothing was ever going fast enough, and no sport was rough enough for them. The boys didn't have enough money to buy an outboard motor, even a used one. One day, however, as luck would have it, they found an old motor that was relegated to an ignominious death on a trash heap. After taking it home and cleaning it up, they tried in futility to start it.

After working on it for about a week, however, Art managed to get it to run good enough to propel the little boat faster than they could row it. One day, Art decided it was time to take his father for a ride in the new boat. Now, to take his father out in the boat, he had to inform his father first that he had a boat - a secret that he had carefully guarded from his parents. He knew that his father loved the water and boats, but he also knew that his mother was deathly afraid of both boats and water.

Since he really wanted to take his father boating, he decided to risk his mother's wrath. Upon learning of his boat,

Art's mother worked herself into a nervous frenzy.

"Blessed Virgin Mother Mary! It's dangerous. You're going to turn over. You're going to drown. Please get rid of the boat, give it to Gary. If you really love me, you won't go out on the boat again. Please don't go out on the boat. Boats are so dangerous." Art's mom said, as he listened patiently and tried to convince her that the boat was fine, and even if it did turn over, they knew how to swim - something he should've kept to himself. That didn't inspire confidence in her, or his father, at all. All mothers worry about their children.

It was part of her nature, but Art's mother worried excessively. She was a compulsive worrier. She worried that he would get hit by a car when he rode his bicycle or played in the street. She worried that he would get caught in an undertow and drown when he went down to the beach. According to her, just about the worst things that could happen to a child when he set foot outside their mother's reach would happen to her son.

Art's mom was even worried about useless things like the weather. If it rained, she worried that Art would get wet and catch a cold. If it was sunny and hot, she worried that he would get sunstroke or succumb to heat prostration. Now, she worried that he would drown if he fell overboard or the boat turned over. Being a brave kid with a boxer for his idol, Art was sure that her fears were unfounded. He knew that it was virtually impossible for this boat with its low center of gravity to turn over, and the idea of falling overboard was out of the question. He was no klutz; how could she even conceive such an absurd idea. Art knew that this was just another unfounded concern on his mother's part. Her suggestion resulted in a resounding 'no' from Art. Giving up his new boat was simply out of the question.

Art's father was on his side, however, and on repeated occasions during the next several days, he tried to calm her down and convince her that it really wasn't dangerous. So, after a few days of worry and repeated pleadings, she calmed down. Every Saturday morning, however, just as Art and his dad would be leaving the house to go down to the bay, she cautioned him, *"Arthur, please be careful. Boats are dangerous."*

Today was no exception. She cautioned them to be careful at least four times before they left the house. *"You know boats are dangerous. They can turn over so easily."*

She cautioned, her face etched with worry and doubt on her son's and husband's abilities.

"Don't worry, I have the situation under control, nothing can possibly happen, we'll be careful," Art's father reassured her as they left the house and went off to the boat.

Upon first sight of the boat, Art's father was shocked by its small size. *"It's so small! Are you sure we can both fit in it?"* He asked, his eyebrows raised in concern. However, he did trust his son enough not to announce judgment that the boat was unworthy.

"Sure! No problem." Art replied with great confidence and authority.

They dragged the boat to the water's edge and launched it. After a few minutes of pulling the starting cord, they managed to start the sputtering motor and then headed out to open water. From the calm waters of the lagoon and into the mile stretch, a 500-feet wide by a one-mile-long channel cut through the marshland that connected the lagoon to the Lake's bay, a large open body of water.

Due to the weight of both of them, the little boat sat very low in the water, barely above the water level. Both of them had to exercise great caution not to jostle about, or else they would be showered with a spray of water. Things were going smoothly until they neared the end of the mile stretch and were about to enter Lake's bay. Suddenly, a forty-foot long yacht streamed pass them at full throttle.

The wake and turbulence kicked up in the water behind the yacht by its powerful motors, and great speed was too much for the little boat to handle. For a second, it bobbed around like the cork in a stormy ocean, and then over it went, dunking Art and his father into the water. After recovering from the shock of being thrown into the water, they managed to swim the 100-foot distance to shore dragging the small boat behind them.

Once they were on the muddy, swampy shore, they righted the boat, bailed it out, and then waited patiently for someone to come to their aid. After what seemed like an eternity, Vinnie, Art's friend, passed by in his boat. Waving frantically, they caught his attention. Coming to their assistance, he towed the little boat back to the lagoon.

"What's your mother going to say when she finds out what happened?" Art's father asked, bemused that her words had turned out to be true. *"You know she'll be upset. She'll never*

let us go out in the boat again." He added, sounding almost disappointed. The thought of never being able to go out in the boat was one that Art found extremely distasteful. *"Don't tell her,"* Art replied, almost immediately. *"It's for her own good. All she'll do is worry. You know I'll go out again no matter what she says."* Art said, making up his mind.

"She'll know something is wrong, we're all wet," Art's father countered, sensing something wrong with Art's logic. *"Tell her we went for a swim if she asks."* Art replied, sticking to his guns.

"No. We can't lie to her." His father responded.

Art thought for a second, and retorted, *"It's not exactly a lie, maybe an exaggeration of the truth, but not exactly a lie. We did swim to the shore, didn't we?"* Art retorted.

"That we did," his father conceded, *"I guess it would be just stretching the truth just a little. No sense giving her something else to worry about.* I don't want her to worry, but I don't want you to use this boat again. It's dangerous." His father decided.

"No!" Art's anguished cry escaped. *"Please, Dad, I can handle it, I'll be more careful, it won't turn over again. I can*

fix it so it won't turn over. I can make some outriggers. I can't give it up. All my friends have boats." He pleaded.

Art's father looked at him sympathetically, he understood where Art was coming from, and after all, he too was once a boy. He also had dreamed of having a boat, but because of one thing or another, he never pursued his dream. He wanted Art to continue his passion for boating, but his fatherly instincts took over.

"I know how hard you worked to buy this boat and fix it up. I also know that you'll be tempted to use it even though I don't want you to." He said, staring at the small boy standing on the balls of his feet in anticipation. After a long pause of silence, he smiled at Art and said, *"So, I guess we'll just have to go out next week and buy a real boat and motor, one that's safe for the both of us."*

Art stared at his father in complete disbelief. Finally, after the shock wore off, he was beyond ecstatic. Art's father kept his word. In a week, they had a real boat, a sleek 14-foot-long redone with a brand new fifteen horsepower outboard motor. His father knew that he would be sneaking off and that he could not be there every time to save him, so he might as well ensure his safety by other means. He understood him, and sometimes things worked out for the best.

A Boys Dreams

Most boys have heroes whom they admire and emulate. Only a lucky few, however, have any special talents and or abilities that aid them in their journey to become like their idols. Most can only dream of performing great feats like their heroes.

It is every boy's greatest wish to be respected and appreciated by their friends. That feeling of awe when a boy does something which everyone sees and goes, 'ohhhhh!' Yeah, that is what every boy dreams of. Art was no exception. He dreamed of performing heroic acts, which he thought would gain him the respect and admiration of his friends.

"Mr. Keating, Mr. Keating! Can I play the quarterback position in today's game?" Art asked hopefully, painting out the whole scenario in his head where he crossed the finish line in record time.

"No, Art, you can't. John is going to be the quarterback today. You have to play the end position." Mr. Keating, Art's coach, said in a knowing tone. Jeff Keating, the older brother

of one of Arts friends, was a physical education teacher at one of the local Schools. Jeff, on Art's request, had agreed to coach their team. He practically dealt with kids like Art every day.

Somehow, he didn't understand why he was being given the third degree. *"But why can't I be the quarterback today and John the end?"* Art questioned, sick of John getting to play the quarterback every time while he was stuck in the end position.

"John can throw the ball farther and more accurately than you, but he can't catch as well as you. His talents are better suited for the quarterback position. You can run faster, and you can catch better than him. That's why your talents are best suited for the end position." He explained patiently, after all, he had a soft heart for Art.

"But why? Why can't I play quarterback?" Art questioned again.

Finally, Mr. Keating's rational side got put out of commission. *"Because I said so. I'm the coach, and I know what's best for the team. We're playing a really tough team today. They're undefeated. We have to play our very best, or we won't stand a chance against them. Do you remember when you asked me to be your coach?"* He asked.

"Yeah..." Art replied sheepishly. He had secretly asked Mr. Keating to coach so that he could be the star player.

"You said you would always listen to me, so listen to me now. A champion team utilizes the talents of its members to work together, but a team with a lot of individuals that have talent isn't necessarily a champion team. What's really important to you?" He tried reasoning again. *"Do you want to play quarterback, or do you want to win today's game?"* That was the end of the conversation.

Art's head hung low, and he nodded. Art wanted the team to win more than he wanted to play quarterback. Their team, The Ventnor Angels, was a ragtag sandlot football team that Art had organized. It was made up of all the misfit thirteen and fourteen-year-olds who couldn't make the sponsored, uniformed teams.

What they lacked in talent, and Lord knows, that was a lot. They made up for, well, almost made up for, in spirit and enthusiasm. Halfback position was played by *"Crazy Charlie."* At 16, he was by far the oldest on the team.

Mentally challenged since birth (Downs Syndrome), the neighborhood kids poked fun at him and called him ‘Crazy Charlie.' No one would play with him, but Art and his friends treated him as an equal and accepted Charlie as one of them. Art knew firsthand what it was like to be bullied, and he would go as far as he could to make Charlie accepted. They had even changed the connotation of Crazy to mean something positive.

Art was also quick to recognized Charlie's potential. Although he wasn't too bright and had difficulty distinguishing his right hand from his left, he was strong and fast. If Art or one of his teammates managed to put the ball into Charlie's hand and head him toward the goal line, they had it made.

Almost no one could stop him or would want to stop him. He was so much bigger and stronger than all the other kids. Fat Johnny Daoud played the center position. He was one of Art's best friends. He was chubby and slow, but he tried very hard. Because he was so large, he was difficult to get around.

He made a good center because all he had to do was to

pick up the ball at the appropriate moment and pass it through his chubby legs to Johnny Fetter, the quarterback who would then try to figure out what to do with it. Johnny Fetter was a few inches taller than Art. They were both the same age, but because he failed reading last year, he was now a year behind Art in school. John couldn't make snap decisions. He had to ponder long and hard before taking any action. When he opted to run with the ball, he would always manage to run a few yards before being stopped. He had a good arm and could really throw the ball. The only problem was that it often took him so long to figure out who to throw the ball to that he was frequently tackled with his arm in the cocked position with the ball still in his hand.

Gary Cross was their tackle. He was stocky and strong, a natural for the position, but he had a small problem. He couldn't see very well without his glasses, and he couldn't wear his glasses in the game. So, sometimes, not often, though, he would tackle the wrong player.

Ron Kashon played the other end position. He was the most agile and talented of them. He could've made one of the other sponsored teams if he wanted to, but he chose to play along with his less talented buddies.

The Ventnor Bulldogs were a uniformed team, and like their namesake, they were built like bulldogs. They were tough and mean. They were the number one team in the sandlot league, and they were the team to beat. The Bulldogs team was composed of all the tough guys from Ventnor.

Marindino, a big ugly kid, was their quarterback. Tony Santamaria and Tony Bull, his inseparable buddies, played the backfield with him. Rocco was one of the more sedate players on the Bulldogs. They took great pleasure in kicking ass. In fact, they took more pleasure in knocking the daylights out of the opposing team than winning, but usually, for them anyway, the two went hand in hand.

As such, they were a very tough team to go up against, especially for Art and his buddies. However, Art knew that if they got their act together, they could beat them. He was a living example of that. He had beaten Rocco to a pulp back when he had lost his cool. He was sure that all other team members had it in them to beat them, given they could channel that inner anger and precision.

It was difficult, if not impossible, for a battered and beaten up team to win. On this day, however, the miracle of miracles was unfolding. The Angles were holding their own by using evasive tactics in avoiding as much physical confrontation as possible. It was just as Art had imagined it. They were playing with their minds instead of using brute force, and most of all, they looked cool as hell.

With only minutes to go in the game, the score was 7 to 6 in favor of the Bulldogs. Art knew that it was the make or break point of the game. The Angles had possession of the ball with only 30 yards to the goal line. Fat Johnny Daoud snapped and slowly handed the ball back to Johnny Fetter.

Art was in the clear on the ten-yard line. It was his chance to become a hero, a once in a lifetime opportunity. No one was around him. He could score easily if Johnny Fetter would only throw him the ball. Johnny Fetter had his mighty right arm cocked, ready to throw the ball in bullet fashion to his target. For some strange reason, the Bulldogs weren't able to get to him. John was looking around. He was trying to decide where to throw the ball for what seemed like an eternity. All he had to do was give the shot to Art, and they would win.

Art was in the clear; two Bulldogs covered Ronny Kashon.

Finally, unable to take it any longer, Art yelled, *"John, here, throw it to me."* Nevertheless, John could not react to Art being unexpectedly in the clear. It just didn't register in his mind.

Puzzled, Art couldn't figure out what John was doing. Suddenly, John handed the ball to Charlie. Dread gripped Art's heart. A sickly feeling of disappointment swept over him. He now had no chance of being a hero and becoming a legend in the minds of his friends, but at least the team would win the game. No one can stop Charlie.

Suddenly, Murphy's Law took hold. Anything that could go wrong will go wrong. *'Oh, no! Oh, no!'*

Art realized that Charlie was running in the wrong direction. The Bulldogs were cheering him on. Art yelled quite futilely at the top of his lungs. *"Charlie, Charlie, turn around, turn around, you're running in the wrong direction."* And all the Angels yelled along with him, *"Charlie, Charlie, you're running in the wrong direction. Turn around, turn around!"* But, to no avail.

Since Charlie was single-minded, he was too engrossed in what he was doing. He didn't realize he was running in the wrong direction. Ron and some of the other Angels started the chase after Charlie, but the very fact that made him an indispensable member of the Angels now made him their undoing. They tried in vain to stop him. The crowd was going wild, half of them jeering while the other half laughed and cheered. Art was sure that Charlie was having his own delusions of becoming a hero.

Charlie smiled as he ran across the goal line - the wrong goal line. The whistle was blowing, and the Angles once in a lifetime chance to beat the Bulldogs was all gone. It was all over, all over

Art clutched his head in his hands and knelt, trying his best to understand that Charlie was slow, but he was having a very tough time. The sight of Marindino and the Bulldogs snickering and making wisecracks made his blood boil with rage. They had beaten the Angles and now were going to rub it in.

Ron threw his helmet to the ground. He was distraught. Gary and fat John were disappointed too, but Charlie was all smiles. He had no idea that he had made a mistake. In his mind's eye, he thought he had won the game for the Angles. He was a hero.

He ran up to Art and asked, *"I did good Art, didn't I?"* He believed that he had once and for all won his teammates' approval.

Art was upset and hurting inside. Charlie had blown their chance to beat the Bulldogs and Art's once in a lifetime chance of being a hero. However, seeing the big bright smile on Charlie's face, he couldn't bring himself to tell Charlie that he had made a serious mistake.

Art, despondent, reached up and patted Charlie on the back and said, *"Yes, Charlie, you did well."* Charlie was his friend. At the end of the day, they had performed very well, and in a way, the victory was theirs.

Chapter 3
Lifetime friends

Off the coast of southern New Jersey lies an island, ten miles long by one mile wide. Its eastern shore is lined with white sand beaches, which are washed by the pounding waves of the Atlantic Ocean. Sandwiched between the island and the mainland is a five-mile wide stretch of marshes and wetlands with- inland waterways known to the locals. The bay meandered through the marshes and connected the ocean at the northern and southern tip of the island.

At the northern end of the island lies the town of Atlantic City, and at the southern end lies Longport. In between these lay the cities of Ventnor and Margate. During the winter months, the island population is a scant 60,000. Soon after the schools in Philadelphia, Pennsylvania, close their doors for their summer recess, families pack up their households and flock to the island for their summer vacation. The island population swells to 250,000, and the deserted beaches of the winter months become overcrowded with vacationers swarming to enjoy the good life and get the perfect tan. Come Labor Day; the crowds evacuate the island as if it were a sinking ship. They pack up their belongings, load their family members and pets into their cars, and make the sixty-mile journey back to Philadelphia for the winter. Many of the shops and businesses hibernate for the long winter months. The major attraction of the island is the beaches and boardwalk. The boardwalk is a 50 foot wide elevated walkway that runs along the beach through the towns of Atlantic City and Ventnor.

When it was constructed in 1896, it ran the entire length of the island, but a hurricane in September of 1944 destroyed significant sections of it in Margate and Longport, which were never rebuilt. In Atlantic City, stores and small shops front the edge of the boardwalk opposite to the ocean. Everything from ice cream to the world's finest jewelry is available in these shops. One can spend an entire day wandering in and out of them as they amble down the boardwalk for a Sunday stroll.

For the cost of $1.00, one can be pushed down the boardwalk in luxury in a wicker carriage known as a "*rolling chair*." Easter Sunday, you will find entire families decked out in their exquisite new wardrobes walking down the boardwalk, women wearing the latest fashion in hats, and men wearing pin-striped suits and derby hats. They participate in this Easter parade and compete for the approval of their peers and the chance to be mentioned in the local newspaper as one of the ten best dressed.

The world's best amusement parks found their home on these piers: The Steel Pier, Young's Million Dollar Pier, and the Steeplechase Pier compete for the crowds. Every type of ride imaginable was available for a mere 10 to 25 cents. For the cost of a two-dollar admission ticket to the Steel Pier, one can see two first-run movies and a first-class stage show featuring top name performers like Franky Avalon, Paul Anka, and Ricky Nelson.

Ballroom dancing with a live big band is available for the older crowd in the grand Marine Ballroom. Crowds of all ages are thrilled by the water show featuring the world-famous high diving horse. One can watch a beautiful woman mounted on a horse jump off a diving platform into an Ocean pool forty feet below. There were also several free exhibits on the boardwalk in which you could spend your idle hours.

Among the more popular was the General Motors exhibit, which featured the latest model cars and the car of the future, and the Goodyear Tire exhibit, which displayed the largest tire in the world. The island was home to two High Schools, Atlantic City High and Holy Spirit High. On Thanksgiving Day, the focus of the entire island's population was the traditional football game between these two rival schools. Houses were spaced close together, and yards were small. Kids played in the streets and on the beaches. Trolleys ran down Atlantic Avenue, the main street, from one end of the island to the other.

Hills were nonexistent on this flat island, but winter sledding was provided by ice and rare snowfalls on the boardwalk entry ramps. In the '50s, The Island was an ideal place for a kid to grow up.

Growing Up

The lagoon in Ventnor was about a mile long and a hundred yards wide. At the south end and all along the east shore were boat docks jutting out into the water. At the mouth of the lagoon was Weepers Dock. Weepers was a rundown wooden dock that jutted out 150 feet into the lagoon. At the main entrance to the pier was a small store that sold soda and candy. Art and his friends hung out at the dock during the summers of their teenage years, making memories that would last them a lifetime. The boys would often get into arguments but makeup quickly and let go of bad blood between them. Most of his friends had boats, and it was the jump-off point for all of their adventures. It was a place for friends to hang around to talk of girls and boating adventures. It was a place for sibling rivalry and boyhood bonding, a place where their characters developed, and they grew from boys to men.

A place where one makes friends that are remembered forever. They were a fairly close-knit group of boys ranging in age from about 13 to 18, and of mixed religious and ethnic backgrounds. Any prejudices that their families or previous friends had imparted to them were soon washed away by the cleansing waters of the ocean, which entered the lagoon with each incoming tide.

There was Vinnie Fumo, a lean, curly blond-haired fifteen-year-old kid. Like most teenage boys, he was going through the awkward stages of puberty that boys go through on their path to manhood. He waddled like a duck when he walked. Some who were close to him would say that looked remarkably like an ostrich; his long spindly legs awkwardly protruded from his shorts.

Every summer, Vinnie came down from Philadelphia with his parents. His parents owned a Savings and Loan in South Philadelphia. He didn't have any brothers or sisters. What Vinnie wanted, he usually got from his doting parents. Being spoiled by his parents, however, didn't seem to affect his relationship with his boyhood friends. He was never one to flaunt his belongings over them to make them jealous, nor did he ever have a problem with sharing his stuff with the other boys. He was immensely down to earth and an all-around awesome guy to hang out with. He wasn't the least bit stuck up or snooty, and everyone liked him.

Ron Cutler was a stocky fifteen-year-old boy from 'Phillie.' His parents were in the real estate business. They made a comfortable living owning and operating low rent apartment houses. Ron's pale green boat was called the Shy Shark. Ron was well-liked by them all.

In the early morning hours before Art's friends descended on Weepers, one could find Ron sitting on the dock by his boat playing his guitar. There was Joe, who was sixteen at the time, and John Celione, who was twenty-two. During the summer, they, along with their older brother Anthony, lived with their parents in a large white house just about midway between Art's house and Weepers. On his daily bike ride to Weepers, Art would often see Joe's mother and father sitting in the rocker on their front porch watching life go by. Their home during the winter was in south Phillie. Across the street from their red-brick row house, in the heart of the Italian ghetto in south Phillie, was the family grocery store that their older brother Anthony ran with some assistance from his parents.

To earn some spending money, Joe would often help out after school. John was a budding and successful Real Estate agent. During the summer, he and Anthony would make the daily one and a half-hour commute back and forth to Phillie. Theirs was a close-knit family. Their parents immigrated from Italy only three years before Joe's birth. They raised Anthony in the traditions of the old world.

John, on the other hand, was brought up in the traditions of the American culture. He loved fishing. Every Saturday morning, he, Joe, and their father, equipped with a picnic lunch, would set out in the family boat for a day of fishing. Evenings would find Joe, John, Anthony, and their father taking their constitutional stroll through the neighborhood with a traditional stop at Weepers to briefly chat with Art and his friends. Richie, a wiry nature local sixteen-year-old, was quick to temper and somewhat of a loner. With a dark complexion and straight jet black hair, he looked devious even though he wasn't. In fact, he was rather handy with good carpentry skills, having built his own boat from plans in Popular Mechanics magazine.

Art's younger brother Steve hung out there too. He was fifteen and a few inches shorter than Art. He had curly dark brown hair while Art's hair was light brown and straight. He was always dressed very neatly while Art's dress bordered on very casual, or in Steve's opinion, sloppy. As most brothers are, they were at each other's throats every chance they got, but when it counted, they always had each other's backs. Their taste in boats and almost everything differed. Steve thought boats should look good while Art thought it was more critical for them to go fast.

When they weren't arguing, they shared a bedroom and the family boat. Sibling rivalry was intense, and they fought often, but if anyone else were to start a fight with either one of them, the other one would, without hesitation, come to the other's defense. It is a peculiar, almost universal experience between siblings that they are the only ones who could be mean to each other. They would beat each other up to the point where their parents would have to intervene, but God forbid someone said anything to either of them. They would have hell to pay. Since they couldn't agree on a boat's primary function, Art had his own small, fast race boat in which he spent most of his time either working on or riding around in.

Johnny Little was a stocky, muscular kid who lived down the street from Weepers. Although usually good-natured, he was often quiet and forlorn. He carried a heavy burden around on his shoulders, which haunted him and affected his life. One summer evening, several years earlier, Johnny was heading back to the Weepers in his little boat after a long day of fishing.

He was only twelve years old and had just lost his father during the winter. His vision was blinded by the setting sun. His boat was jarred abruptly as he heard a loud thud against the side of the boat. Immediately he stopped to investigate. Spotting something or someone in the water, he jumped in.

"Oh, my God!" He yelled when he realized it was a young girl.

He yelled for help, but no one came. He swam with her unconscious body to the shore and tried to revive her, but he failed. This young seven-year-old girl had been swimming in the channel. She shouldn't have been there, but unfortunately, she was. No one ever called Johnny to the task or blamed him for this tragedy, but John held himself accountable. He was too young to understand what 'survivors guilt' meant. When someone dies doing the same thing you do every so often, you always feel that you could've done something to save them even if the situation was completely out of your control. However, you just cannot stop feeling guilty, and it takes a toll on your life.

Ray Gilborne was also a local. He lived across from the street from Weeper's and could see the lagoon and the docks from his bedroom window. A freckle-faced, fifteen-year-old kid with curly black hair and a severe case of acne, Ray was probably the most normal and stable one of the guys. Every Sunday afternoon, Ray could be found by the side of his house washing and waxing his father's 1950 yellow Chevy. He waxed that car so often that he wore the paint off. Albie Bat was a stocky kid whom Art had known since he was a baby. Art first met him on his daily walk home from school when Art was in third grade as Albie played on his front lawn in his diapers and offered to share his toys with Art. He didn't have a boat but followed Art and his buddies around. Jerry Creech had a fast yellow jacket boat that Art easily beat in in his Pen Yan Swift that he shared with his brother. He got a fast 61 Pontiac when he turned 17, but he still couldn't beat Art's old 50 ford.

Voodoo, his real name, was Michael Vender, but everyone except his mother called him Voodoo, was one of the youngest members of the group. He was a tall, incredibly skinny, thirteen-year-old. Short brown hair framed his long narrow face from which his rather large nose, which had developed prematurely, awkwardly protruded. However, he was extremely sociable and friendly, always ready to lend a helping hand.

He didn't have a boat of his own, but he usually tagged along with one with Art or one of his friends.

There were also a lot of other boys in the group, and most were nondescript teenagers who shared a common interest in boats and water sports. Some wandered in and out of the group like driftwood with the ebb and flow of the tide.

Crusaders

At the young age of sixteen, Vinnie's talents as a politician and organizer began to emerge. He convinced Ron and Steve that they should officially form a club. They then convinced the rest of the guys that it was a good idea. So, the gang that hung out at Weepers formed a club with rules, regulations, and 30 registered jacket-wearing members. They chose to be known as the *"Crusaders."* Now that they had reached official club status, they, of course, had to have officers just as every self-respecting club did. It was one of the things they took great pride in, given that they were part of such an exclusive club.

Several of the guys, including Vinnie, volunteered to be officers, but other members had someone else in mind. They unanimously settled for Art as the president. They had always looked up to him, and he had been the unofficial leader of the gang that hung out at Weepers. Hence, Art was now going to act as the official leader. He didn't want to be the president, but after coaxing by the guys, he reluctantly agreed. That was just something that he wasn't interested in, but he knew that it would be a good experience, and he did feel that he would be well suited to it.

Even though Vinnie didn't get the presidency, for which he vigorously campaigned, he did get to be treasurer. He was in charge of the funds for the jackets and the few bucks he managed to squeeze out of the guys for dues. The official club jacket was a fire engine red with white trim. "*CRUSADERS*" was emblazoned in large white letters across the back.

In the imperfect but carefree period of the late 50s, every self-respecting club of teenage boys had to have a rival or enemy club. If they didn't, there would be no reason to have a club. The arch-enemy of the 'Crusaders' was the 'Pistons.' The Pistons wore black jackets with "*PISTONS*" scrawled across the back in large silver letters. Above their logo was a set of crossed automotive engine connecting rods and pistons which resembled the crossed bones on bottles of poison.

They were the bad guys, and of course and the Crusaders were the good guys. Compared to the savage violence commonplace in today's world, it was a harmless rivalry. The Crusaders would cruise their cars in the Pistons territory, and they would travel in the Crusaders territory. The Pistons territory was the area around Carama's Pizza parlor in

Margate. Up to this time, confrontations had been limited to games of wit and showmanship. The Crusaders would drive by the Pistons favorite haunt with 15 to 20 members decked out in their club jackets just to feel their oats, and the Pistons would drive by Weeper's to feel theirs.

Words and vulgarities would be exchanged, but that was the extent of the confrontations. One late August afternoon in 1959, while a couple of the Pistons were cruising in the neighborhood of Weeper's, a fight broke out between Ray and one of the Pistons. The Pistons were outnumbered. Ray and his friends, being the good guys, agreed that the showdown should be postponed until that evening when both clubs could summon their troops.

Word leaked back to the Crusaders that afternoon that the Pistons were joining forces with a gang from south Philadelphia, a gang that was known by reputation to carry and use weapons. The problem in this was just that they could ruffle up each other just fine, but when it came to weapons, that was a bit too much. At the same time, their pride was at stake, and as much as they would have liked to call it off, they just couldn't. All the Crusaders were notified that there was going to be a showdown with the Pistons and a South Philadelphia gang that would probably have weapons. The guys were told that they were to bring whatever knives, chains, or baseball bats that they could get their hands on to Weeper's at 8:30 that night.

Richie and Johnny were both home on leave from boot camp. Richie was now in the Special Forces, and Johnny was in training for the Green Berets. As loyal Crusaders, they were summoned to the cause. At 8:00 PM, Art picked up Ron at his house. Ron had a sizeable rusted machete that he had found in the corner of his garage and a highly polished shark knife that hung as a decorative on his bedroom wall. Both of them did feel that they were a little out of their depth for this particular showdown. However, this was something much more significant than either of them. It was the reputation of their gang that was at stake.

Art brought a pair of brass knuckles (they were lead knuckles, but nobody's ever heard of lead knuckles) that he spent the afternoon making by melting lead fishing weights into a plaster mold. He really tried to find something else to carry, because that was just pathetic, but they would do the job, and they were handcrafted, so that was another thing to be proud of.

By 8:15 PM, about 20 of the club members had assembled at Weeper's and were busy trying to bolster their courage and planning their strategy. It was unanimously decided that they had too many weapons. There was a strong possibility that their weapons might be used against them. Besides, if the cops learned of the fight and stopped by to break it up, they would be thrown in jail with the knives in their possession.

They were low-key hoping that they wouldn't have to fight. However, at the same time, they didn't want to end up in jail. They managed to gather their wits about them and eventually make way to the place that was set. All the knives were piled into Art's car, and he and Ron drove the car a couple of blocks away from Weepers and parked it on a dimly lit street.

As they walked back to Weeper's, they tried to convince each other that probably nothing would happen, and even if by some chance there was an actual fight, they would be able to handle it. It was like that mentality that they didn't want to entertain the genuine possibility that they could be in the middle of a firefight. Once back at Weepers, they took their positions with the rest of the guys and began their vigil. The guys were now armed with only a few baseball bats and a couple of pieces of pipe. Art stuffed his trusty new lead knuckles inconspicuously into the back pocket of his jeans. Since Voodoo was too young to participate in this action, he was set up as a lookout. Tension grew as dusk turned to darkness. To everyone's relief, it began to look as if the Pistons were not going to show up. Their relief was short-lived, however.

At 9:30 PM, however, Voodoo came streaking past Weeper's on his bicycle, shouting at the top of his lungs like Paul Revere, *"They're coming, they're coming; the Pistons are coming!"* and, off he sped into the safety of the darkness. Suddenly, five or six cars drove up and stopped by the empty lot next to Weepers. Just a glance at the vehicles told him that they were filled with guys, most of whom were probably carrying some type of weapon. Art's heart sank to the pit of his stomach.

There were about thirty of them, and the Crusaders were severely outnumbered. Most of them were from the South Phillie gang, and that was bad news. This was no longer a kid's game of wits. It was now a serious situation; their worst fears were now about to become a reality. Four of the South Phillie gang surrounded Richie. Richie, not being stupid, realized that the four of them armed with knives and pieces of pipe were too much for him to handle. Quickly summoning all the skills he had learned in his recently completed Special Forces training, he took off like a jackrabbit into the black water of the lagoon and swam away into the safety of the night.

Pushing, shoving, threats, and vulgarities concerning nationalities, religion, parents, and relatives ran rampant. It seemed like mass chaos. Isolated fistfights were breaking out. Johnny was engaged in an all-out battle with two Pistons but was managing to hold his own. Bull and three of the guys from Phillie came up to confront Ron and Art, who were standing by the dilapidated wooden store at the front of Weepers. They slandered Art's and Ron's nationalities, parents, and everything else they could think of, but Art and Ron were quick to return the barbs.

They shoved Art and Ron against the store's wall, but Art pushed them back. One of them threw a couple of punches at Ron, and he threw a couple back. When it came down to it, they weren't just going to act like the bad guys. They had to prove their manliness. Bull swung at Art, his fist glanced off the side of his head, fortunately just grazing him. Art turned back, with all the power he could muster, and hit Bull squarely on his big ugly nose. Several more punches were exchanged. Art's lip was now cut and bleeding, but he managed to knock Bull down.

Suddenly someone grabbed Art around the neck and began choking him. His reflexes took over, and Art walloped him in his gut with his elbow and managed to break loose. All things considered, it was going pretty well. The Crusaders, or at least the ones who were left, were putting up a fight. And that, in their book, was admirable. One of South Phillie guys then threatened Art with a three-foot-long pipe while another one pulled out his knife.

This was the point where the reality of the situation hit them. It was now somber; they were ready to bash his head in and stab him. Art was now terrified and didn't know what to do. He was in over his head and wanted to surrender or run, but he couldn't give up. He had learned from his experience with Rocco that if he gave up now, he would never have any peace from the Pistons. Besides, he was the leader of the Crusaders, and the guys looked up to him.

How would it look to them if he gave up or ran away in cowardice?

How could he ever face them again?

Art's pride was at stake. He had to take his chances, however slim, and fight them. He knew he had only one small chance against their knives and pipes. He slowly and inconspicuously reached into his back pocket and grabbed his lead knuckles. He began to pray for a miracle as he slowly withdrew them - hoping to God that his reflexes would be good enough to keep him safe in an outright fight.

Suddenly there was a lot of commotion and shouting. *"The cops are coming. The cops are coming!"* Instantly, Art breathed a sigh of relief, his prayers were answered, he was still alive, but relief lasted only a second. He thanked God that he didn't get stabbed or have his head bashed in, but now he could get into serious trouble with the cops. They would all go to jail if the cops caught them with the weapons. It was like God was laughing at them for showing up.

Nonetheless, this way, they could at least join in on the joke a couple of years later, perhaps. This was the better alternative anyway. They would much rather be in trouble with the police and live to see another day, rather than die at the hands of the Pistons, anyway.

Of course, when push came to shove, the Pistons jumped in their cars and sped off. The pipes, bats, and the few small pocketknives that some of the guys had; were discretely thrown into the tall weeds. Some of the Crusaders managed to escape before three Patrol cars came to a screeching halt and aimed their searchlights on them.

"What's going on here, Dinick?" a voice from behind a spotlight bellowed.

Art breathed a sigh of relief. It was Sergeant Kennedy, the father of one of Art's friends. *"Nothing, nothing at all. We just had a club meeting. We were going to play baseball with the Pistons."* Art lied through his teeth, trying to look innocent. The gang surrounding him tried to cover up any marks of them having been beaten up.

"Dinick, come on, it's pitch dark out, don't bullshit me." Said Sargent Kennedy, exasperatedly.

"Well, okay, Sarg. The Pistons and their buddies from South Philadelphia came around here looking for some trouble, but nothing happened. Really, nothing happened." Art replied truthfully. He knew that it was pretty obvious from looking at them what happened. It would be useless and

just infuriating to lie.

Sargent Kennedy looked at him incredulously and sighed, *"Okay, guys, but go home now. It's late. Don't hang around here anymore."*

Art and his buddies quickly scattered off into the darkness before the Sergeant could change his mind. Sergeant Kennedy and the other cops stayed behind to make sure the Pistons didn't come back. Sergeant Kennedy didn't buy Art's story, but he figured that he had established his point. He knew nothing further could be gained by forcing Art and his friends to admit that there was a scuffle between them and the Pistons.

He knew the boys and their families. He knew that they were good kids who liked to rough it up now and again. They would all grow out of it in a few years; no need to apply force to correct something that would correct itself in a little time. He had learned that if you apply too much force too quickly, you could break what you were trying to straighten out.

Art accompanied by Ray, Ron, Johny, Steve, and a couple of others, headed off to retrieve the car. Fearing that some of the Pistons might be lying in wait for them or that one of the cops might try to follow them, they took the most indirect root possible. Up one dimly lit street, down another, through a dark alleyway, and back up another street. Art's car was now in sight, only a few more yards to go. They looked around, no cops in sight. *"Phew!"* Art breathed a sigh of relief; they were safe.

At the very instant, they reached the car. However, Connie Gaskill cruised around the corner in his big black police car. Art's heart almost stopped beating. A sickening feeling of fear came over him. Connie was a real bastard. To say he disliked Art was a real understatement. He derived his greatest pleasure in life by issuing tickets to Art for the slightest infringement of the strictest interpretation of his law.

According to him, justice be damned. Connie envisioned himself as the avenging angel enforcing his law. He behaved like a World War II Nazi SS Gestapo. Art and his friends intensely disliked and feared him. Connie flashed the red and white strobe lights on the roof of his patrol car. Bringing his car to a halt in the back of Arts Ford, he directed his spotlight onto the car. He then threw open the door of his car, slowly and dramatically got out, and sauntered over to Art's car with his right hand on his holstered pistol. Connie was a giant of a man. He stood six- and one-half feet tall and weighed approximately 250 pounds. He looked as if he should have been a heavyweight boxer rather than a cop. It was pitch dark out, but Connie was still wearing his dark green wire-rimmed sunglasses. According to a rumor that Art heard, he thought they made him look tough. He was right; they did.

Connie's eyes finally settled on them, and Art's heart sank. He could feel the hand of God working on this day being the worst possible choice for something like this to happen. Connie walked forward, and even though he was supposed to protect them, he was kind of a bully. He gestured for Art and his friends to get away from their car.

"Why is your car parked here, Dinick? I know you're up to no good. Your 'friendly' little meeting with the Pistons was blocks from here. What are you hiding?" Connie said in his heavy voice. It was infuriating for Art, and he just kept his mouth closed. *"Come clean, you know I'll get the truth out of you. Sergeant Kennedy isn't here to protect you."* He said.

He interrogated them for ten minutes and then ordered Art to open the doors and trunk of his car. Art knew that he could not refuse a 'request' made by an officer, he could, but

Sergeant Kennedy wasn't here to save his ass. Connie then proceeded to search it.

To his great satisfaction, Connie discovered the stash of weapons. *"The jig is up, Dinick."* he snickered. *"Why are all these knives in your car? Were you planning to use them during your friendly little meeting with the Pistons tonight?"* He almost sounded delirious with pleasure instead of worried about Art.

On the other hand, Art was speechless. He feared that the jig really was up. He had to think fast and come up with a plausible explanation that Connie would believe. He knew that Connie believed in the letter of the law, in it' strictest interpretation. Justice and mercy be dammed.

Art concluded that telling Connie the truth, that they originally brought them to protect themselves against the pistons but had decided against using them, would only get him and his buddies in deep trouble with Connie. After all, even if they did finally change their mind, they did have the intent to use them. That would be an infringement of the law, according to Connie.

"No, no, Connie. We're going on a fishing trip tomorrow.

We needed these knives for filleting fish." Art replied, hoping to God that Connie would let this go.

"Well, I might believe that you could use this knife for fishing if you were fishing for sharks." Connie said as he picked up the three-foot-long machete off the floor of the car and held it in his hand, *"But I don't, even for a second, think that anyone would ever believe that you could use this knife on a fishing trip."* The knives were confiscated, and the boys were stuffed into the back of Connie's big black patrol car and hauled off to the police station.

They were taken to a room with a long wooden table in it. Art and his friends sat on one side of the table, and Connie paced the floor on the other side. The interrogation lasted about an hour. The boys stuck together, but Connie wasn't buying their story, and he was not about to cut them the slightest break.

He wanted to book them for carrying concealed weapons. He wanted them to serve time in a correctional institution. Art's and his friends' lives were about to be ruined, and Connie would take great sadistic pleasure in doing that.

Chief Mouer was finally called in. The Chief was an older

man in his late fifties or early sixties. He had been on the force his entire life and had a reputation for being fair and honest. Connie paced the floor nervously while the Chief talked to the boys. They all knew that a fair punishment for the boys would be to lay them off or give them community service. However, Connie wanted them to go to jail.

They told the whole truth to the Chief. Their parents were summoned, and discussions continued into the wee hours of the morning. Chief Mouer then released the boys to the custody of their parents on the condition that the Crusaders meet at the police station every Saturday morning for the next year and do public works for the benefit of the community under his direction.

All in all, Art and his friends were pretty happy that they weren't going to jail. However, they still couldn't believe their bad luck that they would run into Connie of all people while getting Art's car back.

Connie was disappointed, to say the least. He wanted the boys punished. The jig was not really up for the guys now. They would be free again to roam the streets and break Connie's laws. As the boys left the station, a wicked glimmer came to Connie's eyes. He must have realized that he would be able to continue to play his game. He, once again, had a lot of chances to continue his sick pursuit of the Crusaders and be free to harass the boys for breaking one of 'his' laws.

The guys that hung around Weepers looked up to Art since he was their friend and their leader. They had had equal shares of good and tough times together. He affected their lives, though not always for the best.

Everyone took great pride in the fact that they had such fond stories for their next generation to come. Their boyhood adventures with their buddies in the Crusaders and Art and his friends will live again in the memories of their children and grandchildren.

Chapter 4
The Challenge of Competion

Art thrived on competition and was always pitting himself against a real or imagined competitor. Everything was a competition for him, no matter if it is a friendly match in his own gang or an actual altercation between two opposing gangs. Nothing was ever too small or too insignificant, and there was no way that losing was ever an option. Everything required his constant effort.

Although it was not obvious to his friends and acquaintances, he was very insecure, and he lacked confidence in himself, hence the constant need for wins to reassure his own self. A constant struggle raged within him. It was the kind of struggle that drove people to greatness, even though it is not apparent to themselves. The constant need to go above and beyond in everything made them excellent, as it did to Art. Driven to test his abilities to the limit, Art was obsessed with the desire to do something better or faster than had ever been done before.

He strived for constant improvement in everything he did, never content to do anything the same way twice in a row. Each time he did something, it had to be better than the last time. Giving up was just not in his blood. On the off chance that he did fail at something, it was back to the drawing board, figuring out a way to win. However, the constant internal struggle plagued him to his core. He was constantly trying to convince himself that he was doing well, especially when it came to racing.

The time between the beginning and the end of a race was enthralling in its own way. In that time, nothing else mattered to Art, not his gang, not even his issues, nothing except the thrill of winning. That feeling when he pulled ahead of his competition and finished first; the euphoria and the excitement was unlike anything else he ever felt. It was almost an addiction.

The feeling and the sound of the wind rushing past his face and body was exhilarating. The sights and feelings experienced when racing over water in a small boat stimulated his senses in a manner that cannot be expressed in words. Art often found himself wondering if that feeling was akin to a Grand Prix racer in an open car or a downhill skier taxing his abilities to the limit while racing down a slope. At just fifteen years of age, he started racing boats professionally. The boat races were held on various lakes and rivers located within a 200-mile driving distance from his home. The American Power Boating Association organized these races. During the summers, there were at least one or two races a month. Being too young to drive to the races himself, his father would load the racing boat onto a rack on top of the family car and drive Art and his brother to the races.

Their race boat was eight feet long, powered by a 25 horsepower Mercury outboard motor. The boat and motor together weighed only 150 pounds. The streamlined hull, known as a hydroplane, was designed to run on a cushion of air. The boat was so designed that it spent more time in the air than on the water. Capable of the high speeds of 70 miles per hour, coupled with its lightweight, made it extremely unstable.

If proper driving techniques were not exercised, the boat would become completely airborne, take off like a kite, flip over in the air, and come crashing back to the water upside down. What Art lacked in driving skills, he more than made up for in fortitude, but no matter how hard he tried, he was always a bridesmaid and never a bride. If some overzealous maneuver did not flip the boat over and toss him into the water during the race, he would end up finishing in the middle of the pack.

He took some small satisfaction in the fact that he could, most of the time, stay up with or even beat the best boats on the straight sections of the racecourse. The winning drivers, however, usually managed to get a better start than him or were able to outmaneuver him in the turns.

Most of them were in their mid-twenties or early thirties had the advantage of the experience on their side.

John, Art's friend, and Joe's older brother, was always among the winners. He was a skilled driver and was among the high points winner during the previous season. Up until two years ago, however, John thought that the only reason to have a boat was to go fishing. His entire life changed one day when Art let him drive his small race boat.

Instantly the speed bug bit him, and there was nothing he could do to cure himself of this terminal illness. Since this disease was only curable by going out and buying the finest equipment money could buy in hopes it would ease the pain, John did exactly that. Racing now consumed all his spare time, and he lived, ate, and drank speed. Art had been looking forward to the race being held at Collingswood, New Jersey, on the Delaware River. It was the fourth race of Art's second season of racing. The water was smooth, and his motor, tuned perfectly. The warning gun fired, signaling that the race would start in five minutes. His dad and brother lowered the boat into the water as Art donned his helmet and life vest.

The motor sprung to life as he pulled the starting cord for the second time. He drove out to the course where the other boats were driving around awaiting the one minute gun and starting flag. Art took inspiration from John and spied on his boat, driving alongside him. They started to play around, racing each other.

Art would drive alongside John and then speed up ahead of him testing to see if John could catch him. Being so engrossed with staying ahead of John, Art lost touch of time and what was going on. Whenever he saw John speed up to catch him, he just squeezed his throttle harder to stay ahead of him. He was so caught up in the moment that his previous shortcomings in the turns did not even register, and thus he managed to beat John. Around and around the course, they went — each course adding onto Art's wins.

After what seemed like an eternity of playing around, Art started to worry about running out of gas before the race ever got started. He could not understand why it was taking so long for the one minute gun to signal. Suddenly, out of the corner of his eye, he spotted his father and brother standing on the shore, waving frantically.

"What do they want?" Art wondered. *"Maybe they're signaling me to come in and get more gas before the start of the race."* He thought.

Art turned the boat off the course and headed toward the shore. Art's father and brother were now waving even more frantically. He could not for the life of him figure out why they were waving so frantically. He decided to shut down the motor and coasted into the shore. His father and brother rushed into the water towards him, waving frantically and yelling.

"Art, Art, what in the world are you doing? Why did you quit the race and leave the racecourse?" They said, quite

obviously flustered.

"What race?" Art replied, taken aback.

"The race! The race!" Steve, Art's brother, exclaimed. *"You were in the lead. You and John were way ahead of the pack. You only had one more lap to go. You were beating everybody. You got a terrific start. You really blew it; you could have won easily."* He almost yelled, exasperated at his brother.

"But, but, you were waving your arms for me to come in." Art replied, feeling let down.

"We were cheering you on, not signaling you to come in." He retorted, incredulous at the stupidity of his brother.

Being so engrossed in trying to stay ahead of his friend, Art had not realized the race had started. He did not hear the one minute gun and never saw the starting flag. Unfortunately, there was nothing Art could do now. He had blown his big chance. In fact, blowing chances had sort of become his forte.

No matter how hard he tried, something always went wrong. Be it his self-confidence, some peculiar condition, or any of the thousand other things that could possibly go wrong, did go wrong. And now, he blew yet another opportunity. Disappointed, he walked off to a secluded spot by the river bank and sat down to ponder his plight.

"Why can't I seem to get anything quite right? Why can't I put it all together? Well, at least I showed John that I'm faster than him. If I ever get a good start in a race again, I could probably beat him. I do not think he was purposely letting me beat him around the course, even if we were just playing around. I proved that I could do it. I can be a winner. John and my father now know that I have all the right stuff to be a winner. I'll just have to put it all together in the next race." The flurry of thoughts raced in his mind, simultaneously consoling himself and berating himself for not winning.

There was a silver lining somewhere there though, John and his fellow racers took him more seriously after that day. Unfortunately, Art could never put it all together and win a professional boat race.

Digger', Art's friend, collected junk. Anything that did not run, digger would buy and store in his father's garage.

Digger's friend Bob got a new boat that actually ran well almost. So, Art decided to talk to him.

"Hey Bob, when did you get that boat?" Art asked.

"I just got it yesterday. It's a brand new racing runabout. My dad bought it from Ruby Skull. It's really fast, but it does not turn very well." Bob replied, looking distastefully at the boat.

The boat, sleek and fast looking, sat low in the water from the weight of the large, powerful motor. It had a red deck and white hull.

"What do you mean it does not turn very well?" Art questioned.

"It slides sideways, so I have to slow it down to make it turn, but even then, it feels like it wants to turn over," Bob explained, which left Art even more confused.

"You're probably not driving it right. You have to drive it like a race boat. You have to put all your weight to the side you're turning. Never ever let off the throttle in turn." Art argued.

"No, Bob replied, if I do that, it will turn over." Bob

retorted, sticking to his original argument.

"No, it won't, Bob, trust me, I know what I'm talking about." Art said, after reconsidering his stance. He worked out the physics in his mind and decided that he was right.

"Art, you may be used to driving fast boats, but I'm not. Do you want to try it out to see if you can make it turn?" Bob asked, making up his mind to try out what Art was saying.

"Sure, let me try it out. I bet I can make it turn on a dime." Art replied.

Art lacked confidence in his ability to do anything well but his ability to drive a boat and make it do what he wanted it to do. He was almost famous for this specialty of his, and his friends admired this skill of his. This would be an ideal opportunity for him to capitalize on his skill and hopefully get a sorely needed boost for his frail ego.

He started the motor, which hummed to life easily enough. Art pulled away from the dock, leaving Bob behind to watch Art demonstrate his driving skills and perform his wizardry. He knelt down on the floorboard and assumed the normal driving position for this type of boat.

The boat accelerated quickly and smoothly across the

glass-like water towards the south end of the lagoon. Kneeling forward, he shifted his weight as far to the left as he could. The throttle locked in a fully open position as he threw the fast-moving boat into a left-hand turn. To his dismay, however, the boat started sliding across the water just as Bob had warned. His pride and reputation were now at stake. He had driven boats a lot faster than this in many races. How would it look to his buddies when he failed to make this boat turn. At the moment, his ego got the best of him. He was not going to back off and slow down. That would be too embarrassing. He kept the throttle open and shifted more of his weight to the left.

Art's body was almost entirely hanging over the left side of the boat, but the boat was not responding. It continued to slide. It was making an extensive, sloppy turn. Art was looking down and concentrating intensely on the water that was slipping under the boat. He had not noticed that the boat was rapidly sliding towards the boats and the docks that lined the east shore of the lagoon.

Suddenly, out of the corner of his eye, he caught sight of a large object looming out of the water. *"Oh shit! It's the back of a big yacht. Shit! I'm going to hit it. It's too late."*

The thought raced past his mind as he tried to slow down to lessen the force of the impact. The speeding boat slammed into the back of the yacht-like a torpedo shot from a submarine. Careening off the splintered stern of the yacht-like a billiard ball, Bob's boat shot into the air only to come smacking down on the deck of the dock three feet above the surface of the water and shearing off the top of one of the support pilings. It then slid across the dock and back into the water. Now, with a huge gaping hole in the front of Bob's new boat.

Art, half-dazed, sped back towards Weepers dock at full throttle in an attempt to keep the front of the boat above water to keep it from sinking. As he approached the dock, he drove the boat up onto the sandy beach next to the dock.

Bob rushed over, *"What happened? What happened? There's a big hole in my boat. It's ruined! My new boat is ruined! What am I going to tell my dad? What am I going to do?"* Bob said hysterically.

"Bob!" Art, glad that he had made it back alive, exclaimed *"You were right; this damn boat just won't turn."* Art added, deeply ashamed that he had stuck to his point.

"But, but my boat's ruined," Bob said, almost reduced to tears.

"I'm really sorry about your boat, but don't worry about it, I'll fix it, I promise." Art said, trying to calm Bob down in front of the spectators. With Bob's help, Art crawled out of the beached boat. Blood streamed down his legs as he sat down on the ground, wincing in pain. Bob ran off to find someone to take Art to the hospital. As Art sat on the grassy shore waiting for Bob to return, a man came running up to him, completely out of breath. He seemed irritated and upset.

He pointed at the damaged boat and asked Art, *"Do you know who was driving this boat?"*

"Why?" Art asked, already nervous.

"Well, son, I know it's hard to believe but, the idiot that was driving that boat smashed into the back of my $40,000 yacht and put a hole in it the size of a watermelon. Then he flew across my dock and sheared off a couple of pilings. In all my life, I never have seen anything like it. I do not for the likes of me know how he could have done so much damage and survived." He said loudly, equally angry and amazed.

Even though Art knew how much trouble he was in with

Bob, he decided to be honest and maintain his integrity. In great pain and embarrassment, Art replied, *"Sir, I'm the idiot, I did it, and I'm sorry, I'm really sorry I damaged your boat and dock. I'm hurt and have to get to a hospital. Please don't worry; my father will take care of it."* Art said, supremely worried now about the damages his ego had given way to. Art could always rely on his father to take care of things that he could not handle himself.

Now upside down in the dragster, Art cried out.

"Where are you now, dad? I really need your help now. Can't you help me?" Art called out, hoping beyond hope that his dead father would hear him.

Chapter 5
Teenage Years

Follow Your Dreams

Growing up, most teenagers that hung around Weepers didn't date. It wasn't that they didn't like girls, but that they were shy and too afraid of rejection. Their mentality was something akin to not even approaching girls, fearing they will get to hear the word that all teenage boys fear hearing; "no." Of course, they thought about girls, they talked about girls and fantasized about them, but when the time came actually to approach them, they made up some excuse or another to not speak to them. On occasions when one of them was lucky, a girl would approach and talk to them, and that was about all the conversation they would have.

Art had several crushes on girls in the neighborhood and his high school class. He had them in his daydreams and fantasized about making out with them. However, talking to them was a whole different matter. He could never muster up enough courage to even strike up a conversation with any of them, let alone ask one of them out. The fear of rejection was too much to handle. It would be too embarrassing for him if any of his buddies ever found out that he asked a girl out and that she shot him down. Many warm summer nights of Art's seventeenth year were spent cruising the streets with his buddies in his trusty blue and white 1950 Ford. It was 1958, and the world was at peace. A bunch of his buddies would pile into the Ford, and they would each put up twenty to twenty-five cents for gas. The radio would be turned up, windows rolled down, and 50's rock-n-roll music emanated from the car.

Set for the evening, they would cruise the streets looking for girls to holler at, or someone to race. Hollering seemed like a better option than actually talking to them; that way, at least, they wouldn't be getting rejected straight away.

It was safe to attempt to pick up girls that you met while cruising in your car. There was no fear of rejection. The guys expected to get shot down and, most of the time, they did. It wasn't embarrassing for them since, the way they saw it, it was always the group that was shot down and not any one of them as an individual. Long hours would be spent at Weepers reminiscing about the great looking girls that they met the night before and almost picked up. It was always 'almost picked up' even when they didn't have a chance.

With every encounter, they grew more confident that they would be more successful in their next attempt. Many a warm summer day was spent prowling the waterways in their boats looking for someone to race and hoping to find some beautiful girl who wanted to go for a ride with them in their boats.

"Hey Art, look at those two girls on that dock over there. Look at the knockers on them. Wow! They're really hanging out of their bathing suits. Swing the boat over there by the dock; maybe we can get them to go for a ride with us." Joe Cilione, Art's buddy,exclaimed. Joe had gone to Southern High School in south Phillie. Standing over six feet tall, weighing 175 pounds with neatly groomed straight black hair, Joe was strikingly handsome and had a way of enchanting girls with his smile and smooth talk.

Joe had a special way with them, as evidenced by his reportedly high pickup rate. Now, of course, if Art was with him, his chances of picking up girls increased as well. He was confident that Joe could talk the girls into going out with them. Two beautiful looking girls in bikinis were sitting on the edge of the old wooden dock by the Albany avenue bridge, looking out at the water. Art fantasized that they were looking at him and Joe and that they wanted to go for a ride in their boat.

"How about it, I'll take the blondie," Joe said.

"Sure, you can have her, I like the brunette better anyway," Art replied hesitatingly, even though Art really thought the blond was better looking. After all, having the second-best was far better than having nothing at all. He was not about to challenge Joe. He knew that without Joe's talents, he didn't have a chance.

They pulled the boat alongside the dock. Like a pro, Joe went into action and started his smooth patter with them.

"What are you two beautiful girls doing sitting here on this dock all by your selves?" Joe opened, smiling his charming smile.

After the small talk and introductions were out of the way, Joe popped the one hundred dollar question.

"Why don't you girls come for a boat ride with us?" He asked. Art, meanwhile, held his breath in anticipation, expecting to get rejected.

"Sure, okay," Responded the brunette, *"but first, we want to try out your boat by ourselves."* She added, smiling broadly. Almost immediately, Art got a flashback of him crashing a boat.

"Do you know how to drive a boat?" Art asked, a bit apprehensive.

"Of course we do," they replied in unison, a little too quickly. *"Judy's dad has a boat, and we drive it all the time."*

Art was, of course, still skeptical.

"Go ahead, Art, let them have a short ride," Joe urged.

Being a trusting soul and eager for the chance to go out with them, Art reluctantly agreed. They climbed into the boat, and Joe and Art got out. The girls threw the motor into gear and pulled rapidly away from the dock. They made several passes by the dock.

The more they drove, the more apparent it was to Art that they had no driving experience. His apprehension grew as he waited for them to return. He realized that his fear was now becoming a reality. Even more fearful was the fact that the boat that also belonged to his brother Steve.

After about five minutes, Joe and Art signaled for them to come back to the dock. As the girls sped past the dock, they shouted, *"We can't slow down."*

"What do you mean, you can't slow down!?" Art yelled back in panic.

"We don't know how to stop the boat!" Art heard them from afar.

With all he had in him, Art yelled out, *"Pull the throttle lever straight back!"* Communication was difficult, if not impossible, with the girls swinging past the dock at 30 miles an hour. *"Pull the big lever back,"* Art shouted, *"pull the big lever back."* He yelled again.

"What?" the blonde yelled.

"The big one, the big one!" Art yelled, making it as simple as it could be.

"Which one!" she yelled back.

By now, Art was in full-on panic mode, having nightmarish visions of never seeing the boat again in one piece. What was he going to tell his brother? Steve would be pissed if he found out that the boat had been wrecked because Art was so gullible and stupid to let some inexperienced girls drive his boat. Art was getting nowhere, shouting at them. They couldn't hear him very well over the roar of the motor, and what they did hear they didn't understand. Now, he had to take drastic action if he ever wanted to see the boat in one piece again.

"Swing the boat over closer to the dock on the next pass!" Art shouted. As they swung the speeding boat close to the dock, he leaped into the boat just as he had seen stuntmen do in the movies. Art, however, lacking their skill, nearly capsized the boat as he ungracefully landed with a loud thud between the two startled girls. After several violent, uncontrolled maneuvers, he managed to grab the steering wheel and eventually got the boat under control.

After recovering from the shock of Art's wild unorthodox arrival into their midst, the girls were grateful for his rescue and very apologetic for their inability to stop the boat. Art, trying to act cool while recovering from the excitement of the instant, responded to their apology in a John Wayne fashion *"That's okay, it was really no problem."*

Now, at last, he and Joe would be able to get down to business and go for the long-awaited boat ride with them.

Maybe, just maybe, if they were fortunate, this impromptu date would end in one of those heavy make-out sessions that he had heard so much about but hadn't yet experienced. He calmly drove the boat over to the dock to pick up Joe. As he pulled up to the dock and stopped alongside it, Judy climbed out of the boat before Joe had a chance to get in. Art was surprised.

"I'm really sorry, but I have to go home for lunch now. I'm already half an hour late, and daddy is waiting for me." The blond said.

"So do I!" Jill chimed in, *"I'm late too, and my dad's waiting for me!"*

"But, but... What about the boat ride?" Art asked apprehensively.

"Oh! We'll meet you back here after lunch in about an hour," they promised. Art and Joe watched them as they walked off down the street and disappeared around the corner. Joe and Art were still full of hope and great expectations. They came back in an hour, but the girls weren't there. They waited for another 15 or 20 minutes, but the girls never returned.

To those of little self-confidence, it might have looked as if they were shot down again, but Art tried not to let it bother him. After all, they had a good excuse. Art and Joe somehow managed to convince themselves that the girls' parents wouldn't let them out after lunch because they were late. They concluded that the girls would probably be back at the dock again tomorrow. They promised themselves that they would drive by in the boat to see them tomorrow.

Art and Joe never saw the girls again, though. Art tried to convince himself that the girls' vacation was probably over, and they probably had to go back to Philadelphia with their parents that very night. It had to be so; he couldn't have been rejected, especially when he was with Joe.

No Musical Talent

High school graduation time had arrived, and in the tradition of all graduating classes from Holy Spirit High, members of the graduating class had to entertain their family and friends at what was known as Class Night.

"What are we gonna do for Class Night?" Art asked Ron Kashon. *"I haven't been able to think of anything."*

"Neither have I," Ron replied. *"We better come up with*

something quick. The auditions are on Friday. How about forming a band and playing a song?"

"A band!" Art said excitedly.

"Yeah!" Ron said.

"Fat Johnny Daoud can really play the piano, and I just got a new electric guitar. I've even taken a few lessons. Didn't you use to play the guitar?" Ron asked. *"Well, I have an old guitar that I bought in a pawnshop for $10 a couple of years ago. I've never taken any lessons. I bought a book on how to play it, but the book wasn't very good, and I didn't learn anything, so I really can't play very well. In fact, I'm really terrible."*

"Don't worry, Art. All you'll have to do is stand in the background and play softly. John will play the piano into the microphone, and I'll turn my amplifier up, we'll drown you out. Nobody will be able to hear you. Let's get together for practice at John's house Wednesday night." Ron said.

So, with only one practice session, they formed their band and went to the audition Friday afternoon in the high school auditorium. Sister Olivia, dressed in her black robe and habit, looking very stern, sat in the audience. She was to be the supreme judge of the talent. When the time arrived, Art, John, and Ron proudly walked up on stage while their classmates cheered and gave them an encouraging round of applause, which irritated Sister Olivia. John sat his fat body down at the piano, Ron plugged in the amplifier on his guitar, and Art stood in the background, trying to look inconspicuous behind fat John.

Now ready at last, they started to play 'Rock Around the Clock,' the song that was made famous by Bill Haley and his Comets. Fat John pounded away on the keys of the out of tune on the grand piano. Ron, oblivious to the audience, blasted cords through the amplifiers while Art strummed softly on the strings of his guitar. To them, it sounded fine, certainly better than it sounded in their practice session.

Sister Olivia, however, had a different opinion. Her sisterly ears were too attuned to choir music and weren't ready for their strange new sounds.

"Stop, stop!" she yelled. *"Stop that racket! It's horrible! That's not music! You're all tone deaf! You boys have no talent, absolutely no talent at all! Get off the stage immediately! Dinick and Kashon, you're absolutely terrible! I can't allow you to play on Class Night. John, if you want to*

play your piano on Class Night, you'll have to play it as a soloist. Under no circumstance can I allow you to perform with those two stooges. They're terrible, absolutely terrible. They have no talent whatsoever." She said, a stream of insults pouring from her mouth.

"But... but Sister, I want to do something with my friends." John rebutted.

"Well, they can't play their guitars. If you want to perform with them, you'll have to come up with something else, and you'll have to do it quickly. As you well know, Class Night is next Friday night." Sister replied.

"What are we going to do?" Art asked.

"How about lip-syncing to a record?" John suggested.

"Yeah, okay!" Art said excitedly. *"But what record?"* He queried further.

"How about the song 'Twenty six Miles' by the Four Preps?" Ron suggested.

"Sounds good to me." Art said.

"Yeah, me too!" John echoed. *"I'll get the record, and we'll meet at John's house on Monday night to practice."*

Ron offered.

Monday night's practice went pretty well. It seems they were a natural at it. They were good, or at least they thought they were good. They were now ready for their final audition and practice on Wednesday in the auditorium. On Wednesday, much to the displeasure of Sister Olivia, who disliked Art and Ron for some unknown reason, the boys passed the audition with flying colors and cheers from their classmates.

Friday night arrived. Gary Cross, their friend and classmate, was put in charge of managing things backstage. Gary was going to operate the record player for them while they were out on stage. Ron, John, and Art were dressed in white sport coats and red bow ties, which they rented at the local uniform rental store. The faded yellow curtain on the stage opened, and, after what seemed an eternity of silence, Gary started to play the record, and the boys started their lip-sync act.

Twenty-six miles across the sea,

Santa Catalina is the place for me

Santa Catalina, the island of romance, romance,

romance, romance

Twenty-six miles in a leaky old boat, any old thing that will stay afloat

Things were going really well when the music stopped. It later transpired that someone backstage tripped over the record player and knocked the record off. It was very embarrassing because Art and Ron were using this music to get by on their average voices. Art looked at Ron, and Ron looked back in bewilderment. They both looked at John, and after a long obvious, ominous silence, they were inspired and started to sing without the record.

Any old thing that will stay afloat, Santa Catalina, the island of...

Z I P!

Twenty-six miles across the sea

Z I P!

Whatever they lacked in their singing abilities, they more than made up for in their enthusiasm.

"Shit!" Art cried aloud.

Gary had put the record back on but in the wrong place.

The boys reacted quickly and started to lip-sync it again.

Santa Catalina is the place for me

Santa Catalina, the island of

Z I P!

...any old thing that will stay afloat.

"Shit! He did it again!" Art cried.

Finally, Gary realized his mistake and tried to correct it. He moved the record player's arm to where he 'thought' was the correct location, but Murphy's Law started to take effect; everything that could go wrong did go wrong, and he goofed up again.

One thing that did work for them was that Gary was not stupid, and he quickly realized his mistake. Once again, he tried to correct his error. However, in his excitement to get it right, he knocked the record player arm off the record once again.

Again, the boys started to sing without the record.

Santa Catalina, the island of romance, romance, romance, romance

The crowd started to roar. Gary didn't know when to quit.

The boys up on stage had their gig under control, doing fine without the interruptions. He tried his best to reset the record, which resulted in two more failures. The boys finally reached the end of the number under their vocal power, singing with enthusiasm that caught on to the whole crowd. They couldn't believe that the boys were going to acapella. The crowd went wild; they gave them a standing ovation.

Art was baffled by this reaction of the crowd and learned that things don't always turn out the way you plan them. Sometimes we have to be thankful for small favors. By sheer accident, their mediocre but serious lip-sing act turned into a great comedy act — the best comedy act the audience had ever witnessed at any Class Night. Everyone was doubled over laughing themselves. They were jubilated that they came there.

After the epic performance was over, everyone surrounded the guys to congratulate them individually. The exception was Sister Olivia, who decided to sulk in the corner. The crowd even congratulated Gary, who, through no effort on his own part, became part of the act. He was solely responsible for the hilarity that ensued, which resulted in them getting the standing ovation.

Some Kids Are Jerks

West End Avenue connected Ventnor Heights with the Blackhorse Pike from Atlantic City. It started as a four-lane highway but quickly turned into a narrow, two-lane road. At night it was dimly lit and rarely patrolled. Of course, it didn't take long for young boys with cars to find that highway and start using it as a drag strip.

Clark was a pompous, stuck-up eighteen-year-old kid. He was a whopping six feet and four inches tall and somewhat lean with slicked-down black hair. He was always passing demeaning remarks to others who were less fortunate than him. He had more money than brains and was spoiled rotten by his parents. He was the kind of guy you would find in country clubs who were always complaining about one thing or the other. Nobody really liked hanging out with him. However, since he had money, he always had people around him.

Another reason he was so famous was that he had a new 1958 Studebaker Golden Hawk that his father bought him for his birthday. It was a fast, good-looking car, the kind of car that attracted the attention of all the teenage girls. Art's nine-year-old 1950 Ford was definitely not a head-turner, but it meant everything to him. He and his father had bought it for $200. Art spent $100 of his hard-earned money to fix it up. It was light blue and white and had a white vinyl top, which was rare at that time. Powered by a flathead V8 motor, it had all the latest hot items that were the rage at that time. From the rearview mirror hung two large sponge rubber dice and a set of rosary beads.

The Black tires were dressed with wide imitation whitewalls. These fake whitewall rubber rings, to his disappointment, would flip-up onto the sidewalk if he parked too close to the curb. The front hubcaps were equipped with spinners, which sparkled in the sunlight when the car was driven slowly but were nothing more than a blur at high speeds.

White fender skirts hid most of the rear tires. Art installed a set of chrome-plated side pipes that directed un-muffled exhaust to just ahead of the rear wheels whenever he activated the cutouts from inside the car. The roar of the exhaust from the open cutouts made the engine sound like a real race car, and Art was convinced that they gave the car a surge of power when needed. The motor sported a chrome generator cover and chrome air cleaners.

They didn't do anything to improve the car's speed, but they impressed the other kids whenever he lifted the hood at the local drive-in. It had a full-race cam and twin two-barrel carburetors on an Offenhauser manifold. This inexpensive old car was no slouch, and he could win more than his share of street races. It was Art's pride and joy, like a car is for a young boy, no matter how old. He would often go for long drives, and that would serve as a therapeutic experience for him.

One warm July evening, Art was sitting on the fender of the Ford in front of Weepers. He and his friends were engaging in their typical idle conversation about their adventures during the day. They were planning what they were going to do for excitement later that evening.

Oblivious to the rest of the world, they were unaware that Clark had shown up and had pulled his car alongside the Ford. They were startled when he made a tire screeching burnout, which kicked sand and dust from the gravel road on them. While they were recovering from the shock and brushing the dust and sand off themselves, Clark backed his car up, and poking his head out the window, he shouted.

"Hey, Dinick, why don't you and your buddies take a bath once in a while?" He sneered, like the jerk he was.

"You're an asshole, Clark!" Art retorted.

"You really impressed us with that burnout," Ron piped in a while, brushing the road dust off his new sky blue shirt from Cowboy Bobs and looking at him angrily.

"I wish I could do a burnout like that," Art said sarcastically, internally cursing him even more. *"Do you think you could teach me how?"* Art asked, scratching his eye with his middle finger.

"Yea, probably I could, but first, you'd have to get rid of that piece of shit you drive and buy yourself a real car like mine." He said, knowing that he would hit really close to home if he said that.

Obviously, what Clark lacked in between his ears, Art had in ample supply. Art quickly came up with, *"Clark, if I had the bucks your father spent on your car, I wouldn't waste it on a car like yours."* He retorted, setting his friends laughing. He could see the perplexed look on Art's face and had just one more trick left up his sleeve.

"Well, Dinick, my Hawk could blow the doors of that

refugee from a junkyard you drive any time of day or night." He said, clearly angry that Art had insulted his car.

Alarms went ringing in Art's ears. He saw everything red, and that was it. He had insulted Art's pride and joy. He had thrown down the gauntlet, and Art had to accept his challenge.

"I'll meet you at West End Avenue at 9:30 tonight, and we'll see who can blow whose doors off." Art dared, seemingly keeping his cool, although all his friends knew that he was fuming inside. Clark, on the other hand, sneered, accepted the challenge, and raced off.

The time and place for the race were now set. They had to wait until dark because they both knew that there would be less chance of getting caught by the cops at night. Just as the last rays of sunshine were slipping over the horizon, Art drove out to West End with Ray and Ron.

Clark was waiting there for them on the shoulder of the road. Confident of his imminent victory, he brought two girlfriends with him to witness his racing prowess. Art pulled into the left lane alongside him. Their little challenge had entirely blown out of proportion, and they had an audience by the time they reached the start line. One of the girls came up to the start line and counted down the seconds to the start of the race.

Immediately there was the smell of tires burning and sounds of screeching tires. Since Clark was up against a car that was nine years old, he had a slight lead, but Art started to pull on him.

Art shifted to second gear and pulled ahead of him.

When Art shifted to third, he had about a car-length lead on Clark.

They were quickly coming up to the point where the road narrowed, and the right lane ended. Art watched in his mirror for Clark to pull his car behind, but his pride was too hurt. He was staying in it, and he was trying in vain to catch Art.

Art, realizing that Clark wasn't aware that the road was narrowing, blew his horn to signal him, but it was to no avail. Art watched in dismay as Clark drove off the road into the grass and weeds.

"Keep going, Art," Ron urged, sitting in the seat beside him. *"We'd better get out of here before the cops come. He deserves what he gets."* He shouted over the roar of the

engine.

However, Art wasn’t going to do that. He slammed on his brakes and turned his car around to see if anyone in Clark's car was hurt. Art couldn't leave Clark, no matter how rotten he was. Miraculously, Clark and the girls were unscathed and standing outside of the car in the overgrown weed field off the shoulder of the road. He parked his car, doing a handbrake turn where they had gone off the road.

"Are you alright?" Art shouted after Ron and he got out of the car.

Clark looked up, dusting off his jeans. *"Yea, my car is banged up a bit, but we're okay. You beat me. I didn't think you had a chance with that old car of yours."* He said, smiling humbly now that he was beaten. At least he had that going for him; he wasn't a sore loser.

"Sorry about your car. Need any help getting out of there?" Art asked, also being polite now that his prowess was proven.

“No thanks, I think we can manage by ourselves. You better get out of here before the cops come by, or they'll get the both of us for drag racing." Clark replied, nodding

somberly.

After that day, Clark was a different person. He was no longer the cocky wise-ass, stuck-up, bastard that he was before. He and Art even shared a cordial relation after that day. Art knew that you have to stand up for yourself and even take risks to get respect from those that don't respect you.

Joy

Joy was a fifteen-year-old freckle-faced, red-haired little girl who lived down the street from Weepers. Art had often seen her in the neighborhood tagging along with her older sister Ronnie whom he had known since second grade. On warm summer days, Joy and her girlfriend Rosie would go swimming off of Weepers dock. Art and his buddies rarely paid any attention to her or her girlfriends, as they were much too young to socialize with. Any conversations with them were extremely limited and brief.

"Hey, little girl, could you swim over here and pull my boat over to the dock?" Art or one of his buddies would say.

"Yea, but if I do, can I have a ride in your boat?" She would reply.

"Yea, but not today, I'm too busy now, and I have to fix the motor. Maybe tomorrow." Art would make up an excuse. Tomorrows came and went, and with each tomorrow, Art always had a new excuse for not taking her for a ride in his boat. After all, what 18-year-old boy wanted to be seen with a 15-year-old girl?

Art was tall and ruggedly handsome. Looking into his deep-set brown eyes, you would feel as if you were looking into the very depths of his soul. He had a reputation for being a maverick and a rebel. To the neighborhood kids, he was extremely kind and helpful. They respected and emulated him. His exploits with the Crusaders were the main topic conversation of the neighborhood kids and Joy's teenage girlfriends. Of course, that was enough to make Joy develop a serious crush on him.

After all, Art was handsome, daring, and had his own car and boat; what more could a teenage girl want in a boyfriend?

Joy couldn't get him out of her mind. She dreamed and fantasized about being his girlfriend. Thus, she set her mind to it; she had to have him. To her dismay, however, Art wouldn't even acknowledge her existence.

He seemed to ignore all of her advances simply because the possibility never even registered in his mind.

Nevertheless, that wasn't enough of a reason for Joy to back down. She had to get him to notice her. As time passed, she became bolder in her approach. She and her girlfriends started to show up at Weepers at all times of the day. Most of the time, they just stood off in the distance and giggled amongst themselves as they watched Art and his friends while fantasizing about being with him.

Frequently, Joy would come up to him and his friends, jump uninvited into the conversation, and boldly ask Art for a ride in his car. Art, nonetheless, was always quick with an excuse why he couldn't take her or her girlfriends for a ride. He would never outright reject her; instead, he just chose to make an excuse that would get him out of giving them a ride for the time being.

When summer turned to fall, the boats were put away. Art's friends from Philadelphia returned home for the winter, and he went off to college in Pennsylvania. Often during the winter months, he would return to the shore to spend weekends with his family and friends. On Friday nights, Art would walk from the corner bus stop to his Mom's house, and often find Joy and her girlfriends sitting on the sidewalk of the two-story brick duplex where he lived. Just for the sake of being sociable, he would say *"hi"* to them and run up the back stairs. After that, he would go into the house to get changed to go out with his friends, who had usually lined up a date for him. Joy and her friends would patiently wait for another glimpse of him as he rushed down the stairs and jumped into his car.

They would sit and stare as he drove off into the night, hoping for a miracle that would make him forsake his date and return to ask her to go out with him. Saturday afternoons were usually spent playing football with his friends on the weed overgrown corner lot by Weepers or on the now deserted beach. Art would often notice Joy and Rosie standing on the sidelines watching him and the guys play ball.

They sure did seem to be running into him a lot, and he knew that he wasn't the one following her. So the only logical assumption he could make was that she was following him. She seemed to show up everywhere he went. He usually ignored her and went about his way. On Saturday nights Art and his buddies would go to the Ventnor dance. It was the social event of the week. Held in the gym of Saint James School, the place was packed with high school kids from all over the island and college kids' home on weekend leave. Art would often run into Joy and her girlfriends at the dance. It seemed that Joy's only mission in life was to follow Art around and watch every move he made. He had to admit to himself eventually that he liked the attention he was getting from her, even though he knew that nothing would ever happen between them.

Sometimes, after the dance, she would come up to him and ask him to give her a ride home. However, Art always had an excuse.

"No, I can't, tonight. There's no room in the car," Or, *"We have to go someplace, and we're already late,"* were his go-to excuses. On Joy's part, these refusals never seemed to discourage her; in fact, she seemed to persist in asking him on every possible occasion.

Growing tired of the relentless pursuit of younger girls, Art's buddy Ray often arranged a date for him with someone his own age. One of the dates Ray arranged for Art was with a girl named Cookie. She was a senior in Atlantic City High School, and she was in several of Ray's classes. Cookie was tall and slender with long brown hair and large brown eyes. She was beautiful and sociable, and Art quickly fell for her. They dated almost every weekend for a couple of months. Soon Art gave her his high school ring, and they were officially going steady.

Things seemed to be going smoothly for them, or so Art thought. One Saturday night at the Ventnor dance, Art asked Cookie, *"Hey Cookie, Ray just told me he saw you driving around with my brother Steve in my car on Wednesday night. Were you and Steve driving around in my car?"*

Freshmen at Villanova University weren't allowed to have a car on campus, so Art would leave his car at home in Ventnor during the week and take the bus to college in Philadelphia on Sunday evenings. During his absence, Steve, who was a senior in high school, would often use the car.

When he asked her the question, he could already see her getting skittish. Art knew that answer well before he heard it.

"Uh, well, mmmm, yes, yes," she stammered. He had caught her off guard, and she didn't know what to say.

Not being one to get rude with her, Art decided that the best approach would be to just ask her politely what she was doing. *"Why were you out with him?"* He asked, his voice getting low, and his gaze intense.

"Well, we met by accident at the basketball game, and he asked me to go to the Dairy Queen for ice cream after the game." She replied, refusing to look Art in his eyes.

Art sensed that something wasn't right. Neither she nor Steve had mentioned anything about it to him before, and they had plenty of opportunities. Now Art wanted the whole story, so he probed further. He could already see the loophole in the story.

"I'm confused. The game was in the Atlantic City High Gym, wasn't it? Dairy Queen is just down the street from the high school. Ray told me that he saw you in Longport." He told her, his voice still low, and what he hoped was polite. Longport was the city at the southern tip of the island, while Atlantic City High School was located at the northern end. *"What were you and Steve doing in Longport? The only thing of interest that I know of in Longport is Makeout Point. Were you there with Steve?"* He asked straightforwardly.

Art had asked the $64,000 (popular TV Quis Show in The Late 50's) question, but he was hoping she had a good explanation and hadn't really gone there with Steve. He had even considered not bringing it up at all. However, he needed to know.

"Uh, well, uh, yes. Uh, but only for a little while," she replied.

A sickening feeling came over him. He was hurting inside. Art felt his brother and his girlfriend had betrayed him. Beyond all hope, he found his heart hoping she had a good explanation.

"What do you mean 'only for a little while'?" He growled, not caring anymore about keeping his voice polite.

"Well, uh, we only parked there for a little while," she said, *"Steve talked me into it."* She explained, still refusing to look him in his eyes.

"What do you mean he talked you into it?" Art asked.

"Well, well, he did. He said he just wanted me to judge if he could kiss better than you, and so he started kissing me, and one thing led to another. But I don't like him nearly as much as I like you. We didn't do anything; really, we didn't.

We didn't do any serious making out; we just kissed a little." She explained as if that would make it better.

Now Art was agitated and hurt. All he could manage to do at that point was stare blankly at her, wondering how he was even supposed to react to that. He felt as if he had been kicked in the gut. The fact that hurt the most was that she had gone out with his brother and made out with him in the sanctity of his very own car. That was as low as anyone could go, and the fact that it was his own brother who stabbed him in the back. It was more than he could handle; his heart was broken. All the walls he had built up to restrain his anger tore down. All the rage he had in him let loose.

"That's it. It's over between us!" He shouted. *"I could never trust you again. Give me back my ring!"* He shouted, holding out his hand for the ring.

Art didn't really want to break up with Cookie, but he felt that he had no choice. He was too hurt, his pride was wounded, and to accept her actions would be a sign of weakness. He could never show any sign of weakness in front of anyone. His line of thinking was pretty simple. If she could do that once and get off lightly, she would definitely do it again, thinking that she would be able to get off again.

Knowing that he was not going to budge on his decision, Cookie reluctantly handed the ring to Art. He saw a tear spring up to her eye, and the sight of that moved him. He felt compassion for her. He didn't want to hurt her. He now wanted to make up with her and end his pain, too, but his pride was hurt. He was too hurt to forgive her. He fought back his own tears.

Unknown to Art, all of this action was being carefully observed by Joy and Rosie. As soon as Cookie handed Art back his ring, Rosie and Joy rushed up to him.

"Forget her. She's no good for you. You can do a lot better." Joy said. Art was too confused to wonder why Joy was even there.

"Yeah, forget her!" Rosie piped in.

"Don't worry," Art said, trying his best to cover his expressions and not let the hurt show through, *"She's forgotten. I don't need her."* He said, more to himself rather than anyone else around him.

"Yeah, you don't need her," they both chimed. Here she saw an opportunity to get him to be friends with her, and she could then build her way from there.

"Can I see your ring?" Rosie asked.

Before Art knew what was happening, Rosie snatched the ring out of his hand. With the ring tightly clutched in her little fist, Rosie ran off through the crowd in the dimly lit hall. Art ran after her with Joy hot on his heels. The crowds were too thick, and he was too far behind to catch her. He stopped just short of the door.

"Don't chase her anymore." Joy said. *"She'll give it back to you later. Why don't you dance with me now?"* She suggested, her eyes wide open.

"I don't feel like dancing." Art said stoically, still looking out for Rosie.

"Oh, come on," she said. *"It'll be good for you,"* Joy insisted.

Art was hurt and really didn't feel like dancing with her or anyone else, but he reluctantly agreed to dance with her. It was good for him. It helped him get his mind off of his problems with Cookie.

After the dance, Art took Joy to the Dairy Queen for some ice cream, and then they sat outside her house and talked for a while. For the first time, he realized that she was a female, a member of the opposite sex. Before this, he had always thought of her as a pesky little kid, a neutral person, and not really a guy or a girl.

The following weekend, as Art was driving past Joy's house on his way to Weeper's, he spotted Rosie. Rosie, upon seeing Art, darted down an alley, which lead to a courtyard behind Voodoo's house. Art brought his car to a screeching halt, jumped out, and ran after her.

"Rosie! Rosie! Give me back my ring!" He shouted as he pursued her. He was gaining on her, but she was booking it.

"I can't!" she yelled as he caught hold of her just as she reached the courtyard.

"Why?" Art panted.

"I don't have it." She replied, doubling over and clutching her ribs.

"What do you mean you don't have it?" Art asked, slightly angry now.

"Well, well, I gave it to Joy," she whimpered.

"Why did you give it to Joy?" Art asked, flummoxed.

"Because she wanted it."

"But Rosie, it's mine, I want it back. It's my ring."

"You'll have to get it from her!" She yelled, jerking her arm and running away.

Later that day, Joy showed up at the corner football game as she had many times in the past. Upon spotting her, Art dashed over to her and asked for his ring.

"No!" she replied adamantly. *"I'll only give it back to you if you promise to go to the dance with me tonight."* She said with a sly smile.

"No, I can't go with you. I'm going out with my buddies." Art made an excuse, as he always did whenever it had anything to do with Joy.

"Well then, if you can't go to the dance with me, I can't give your ring back." She retorted. She had been waiting for a long time for this to happen.

"That's stupid. It's not your ring, it's my ring, and giving it back to me should have nothing to do with me going to the dance with you. Come on, give it back." Art said, now getting infuriated.

"No! Not unless you go to the dance with me." She said,

determined to get him to take her to the dance. She knew he wanted the ring, but she was not about to give it back to him. She was desperate, and it was an excellent opportunity to get him to go out with her. She was not responding to his reasoning.

Art couldn't force her to return the ring. Joy had a reputation for being stubborn, and she was now demonstrating it to him. At the end of it, he had no choice except to take her to the dance. So, he reluctantly went to the dance with her that Saturday night. Even though he was not expecting it, he had a good time. Through persistence and perseverance, Joy finally weaseled her way into his life.

After that day, whenever there was a spare seat in his car, Art let her tag along with him and his buddies. Gradually and expectedly, he grew fonder of her, and soon enough, they began dating without the company of his buddies.

One summer evening, Art drove up to the front of Joy's house, stopped the car in the middle of the street, and blew the horn twice. He had picked her up this way dozens of times during the past couple of years. In a matter of seconds, Joy ran out of the house and jumped into the car. Off they went. That night, they caught the early show at the Ventnor movie. The movie ended at approximately 9:30, and they sauntered to the car.

"What do you feel like doing now?" Art asked, looking down on the street.

"Well, it's still early. We could drive over to Bater Field and listen to the radio while we watch the boats." She said, tucking her hair behind her ear. In Art's peripheral vision, he could see that she was blushing hard. That was it.

That was the invitation that a twenty-year-old sex-starved virgin boy needed.

Bater Field was one of the local Atlantic City make-out spots. Art drove over to Bater Field quickly as he didn't want to waste any valuable time. The night was young, and there were plenty of desirable parking spots still available.

Art parked at the far end of the field, which had a good view of the water. The area was dimly lit, and they were at least 200 feet from the nearest car. It was the perfect spot. He hastily put up the convertible top on his new 1961 red sports car and locked the doors. He then rolled the windows up to keep out the mosquitoes and ensure that their conversation, or lack of conversation, would not be overheard by their neighbors. The radio was tuned to their favorite rock and roll station. Soon they were going at it hot and heavy and were oblivious to the world around them.

Bang! Bang! Bang!

The worst thing that could happen to two teenagers almost having sex in a car happened to them. They were brought back to consciousness with a loud pounding on the hood of the car and some violent shaking.

"What's that?" Joy exclaimed.

"Get out of the car! Get out of the car immediately!" A heavy voice boomed.

"Shit, it's the cops!" Art exclaimed, his heart growing heavier by the second.

Suddenly, common sense took hold of him, and realized that there was no way it could be the cops. They wouldn't be pounding on the car and shaking it.

He peered out the fogged-up window, squinting to see into the darkness. The shaking and pounding continued. He could barely see four figures clad in Piston jackets. He recognized one of them; it was Marandino. He was a rich spoiled nineteen-year-old kid from Ventnor. His father was a doctor, and as reputation had it, a kind and considerate one. However, Marandino had the reputation of being a good-for-nothing, mean kid who would just kick a dog lying in his path and then step over it. He was stocky and muscular, standing at a whopping five feet and ten inches tall, and weighed about 200 pounds. He had a chip on his shoulder and was always looking for someone to pick a fight with.

"Cut it out, Marandino!" Art shouted, losing his temper. After all, he had a girl in the car, and it was necessary to protect her honor too.

"No!" Marandino, being a piece of shit, yelled back. *"Get out of the car now!"* He shouted again, angrily. For some reason, he seemed to think that he was entitled to be doing this. *"Or we'll rip the top off and kick the shit out of you!"* He shouted again, shaking the car again.

Art realized that they were not going to stop, and even if they did get out of the car, they would probably still beat the shit out of him. Discretion being the better part of valor, he quickly started the car, shoved it into gear, and took off like a jackrabbit knocking Marandino and one of the other guys down to the ground simultaneously, just like bowling pins.

Art was enraged. They weren't going to get the best of him. Who the freak did they think they were anyway? They had no right trying to push him around, but he was only one, and there were four of them. Art didn't need to be too bright to figure out that he was outnumbered. He could fight, but he certainly wasn't James Bond, and he couldn't take on four guys at once.

Art's priority at the time was Joy, so he hurriedly dropped Joy off at her house and set off to find some of his buddies. He managed to round up Johnny, Ray, and Ron, picking them up at their houses. The odds would now be even, he thought. They all climbed into Art's car, which in and of itself was a major feat as it was only a two-seat sports car. They set off to find the Marandino and his boys. Ray was riding shotgun when he spied Marandino and his four cohorts walking down Ventnor Avenue.

"There's five of them now. Marandino, Weed, Bull, and two other guys I've never seen before." Ray yelled from somewhere inside the car.

"Yea, I can count too, genius. One of their friends must have crawled out of the sewer to join them," Art replied, furious. They were outnumbered, but since justice and right

were on their side, they had a moral edge.

Art brought the car to a screeching halt by the curb directly in front of them and jumped out.

"What kind of shit were you guys trying to pull back there?" Art shouted, getting up in Marandino's face.

"Nothing much, we were just trying to have a little fun. We just wanted to scare you a little. We weren't serious. What's the matter, can't you take a little joke?" Marandino laughed.

"Yea, I can take a joke, but it didn't seem like a joke to me," Art replied.

"Aw, too bad," Bull said, stepping from Art's side and shoving Art against a street sign.

Not one to take kindly to being shoved, Art pushed him back. He swung at Art, hitting him in the mouth, and without missing a beat, Art punched him back.

A full-blown fight had now broken out. Art knocked Bull down to the ground and jumped on top of him. Kneeling over him, Art and Bull were furiously exchanging blows. Some of Bull's punches were striking Art, but Art was managing to get the best of him.

BAM! BAM!

From seemingly out of nowhere, Art's head was being battered by crippling blows. Art didn't know what was happening. Looking up momentarily, he managed to catch a glimpse of Marandino standing over him, furiously punching him on the side of his head and nose.

Art didn't know what to do. He was caught in between a rock and a hard place. If he turned his attention to Marandino, Bull would be all over him.

"Stop, Marandino, stop!" Art yelled. His hands were fully occupied, trying to contend with Bull. He was all Art could handle.

Art needed help. In a panic, he cried out, *"Johnny! Johnny! Get Marandino off of me. He's punching me in the head."* Johnny, however, was totally engrossed fighting the one known as Weasel. He couldn't help Art.

Ron and Ray couldn't help either as they were totally engaged in battle. Art gave Bull a couple of more punches while trying to dodge Marandino's blows to his face and head.

With each punch, Art shouted, *"Give up, give up!"*

"Yeah, yeah! I give up!" Bull cried, covering his head with his hands.

Art then got up to take on Marandino, but, by this time, the brutal pounding had taken its toll on Art's battered body. Blood was streaming down his nose, and his head felt like it was run over by a truck.

Using every bit of energy left in his body, he managed to land a few good punches on Marandino's ugly face. Luckily for Art, who was fighting using his last reserves of energy, Marandino suddenly realized he wasn't having any more fun and decided to run off with his buddies. Art was staggering now. Johnny, Ray, and Ron came over to him. They were in much better condition than Art.

"Get in the car," Ray ordered, *"You look terrible. I'll drive you to the hospital emergency room."*

"No, I'm alright, just drive me home." Art insisted, getting his bearings. He was lightheaded, but there was no way he was going to get his reputation torn down because he couldn't take a beating.

They looked at each other apprehensively. However, Art

had the final say in it. They decided to drive Art home and helped him up the stairs to the house. Art's mom, seeing the blood streaming from his nose and mouth, almost fainted.

"Oh, my God! Blessed Virgin Mother Mary; there's blood all over you, your face is swollen, what happened to you?" She exclaimed, clutching her son and looking for the source of the blood.

"Nothing, Mom, I'm alright. I just got into a little fight." He said, sighing. In hindsight, he should've known that this was going to happen.

"Pat, Pat, come here quickly, your son's hurt. We've got to take him to the hospital immediately." She yelled for Art's Dad.

"No, Mom, I'm alright, I really am." Art insisted. *"I'm alright, just get me some wet towels and some ice. I'll be alright."* He said, looking sternly at his mother.

Art was stubborn and refused to go to the hospital that night, no matter how much his mother insisted. His head was swollen, and he had a tremendous headache. He thought he could have a concussion. His face looked like it had been pounded by both Rocky Marciano and Jersey Joe Walcott in a 15 round fight. After a couple of days of suffering in silence, Art succumbed to the demands of his mom and dad and went to the doctor. The doctor informed Art that he had a broken nose, and to set it correctly, he would have to re-break his nose because, by that time, the bone had reconnected, but in the wrong way. Art flatly refused. No way was he going to let the doctor break his nose again.

Art couldn't take any more pain. Now when Art looked closely at himself in the mirror, he could still see the results of the facial rearrangement that was done by the skilled hands of Marandino that night. Eventually, he started daydreaming of someday paying Marandino back. However, the way things look now, he might never get that chance.

'I guess some people do get away with the wrong they do,' Art thought ruefully.

My Brother

Steve was a freshman at Villanova University when Art was a sophomore. During evenings when Art was studying in his dorm room, Steve was usually cavorting around with his friend Vinnie. To get around, Steve and Vinnie needed wheels. Freshmen were prohibited from having cars on campus, so during the week, Steve's car was left at home in Atlantic City, but Steve and Vinnie always knew where they could borrow a car.

Big brother's car was always reluctantly available.

"Can Vinnie and I borrow the car tonight? We lined up a couple of hot numbers from Harcum College." Steve said to Art.

If you lined up a date with a Harcum girl, you had it made. Harcum girls had a reputation for being easy. Of course, he wasn't going to deny that opportunity to his younger brother.

"Yeah, you can borrow it, but be careful with my car. You know I need it on the weekend." Art said, holding the keys over his head, about to throw them to him.

"Yeah, yeah, don't worry," Steve asserted, holding out his hand. *"If anything happens, you can use my car."* He offered.

"Yeah, but then I won't have any transportation to get home on the weekend. I'll have to take the train to Phillie and then take the bus from Phillie to Atlantic City. That's a real pain in the neck. Just be careful, will you?"

The next morning when Art ran into Steve and Vinnie at

breakfast, he greeted them with, *"Where's my car key?"* he asked while sticking his hand out eagerly. The face Steve and Vinnie of them made when he asked them about it; he already knew that something terrible had happened.

"Uh, they're at the gas station in Brynmawr," Steve stammered.

"What do you mean, at the gas station in Brynmawr?" He said, already a sinking feeling in the pit of his stomach.

"Well, we, uh, sort of had some trouble with the car." He said, averting his eyes.

"What do you mean you sort of had some trouble with the car? Did you wreck it?" Art asked, fearing the worst.

"Well, no, uh," Vinnie piped up. *"Uh, the car's okay, but the transmission's broken, but it's being fixed right now. It'll be ready in a week."*

Instantly, Art was livid. *"How did you break the transmission?"*

"Well, Steve had a girl sitting on his lap, and she was shifting for him and...?"

"And what?" Art asked, cutting them off. *"Well, we were*

racing another car and uh, instead of shifting into third, she shifted into reverse. You should have seen the look on Steve's face. Transmission pieces went everywhere." Vinnie said, his face red from trying to control his laughter.

"Aw shit! That's great!" Steve sighed, looking down.

"You'd better make sure it gets fixed, right!" Art then demanded the keys for Steve's car and promised to give them back only after his car was repaired and delivered to him. Art didn't enjoy the train and bus ride home that weekend, but, once he was home, things began looking up. He had Steve's car and Steve's gas. He lost some and won some, so it was okay.

The car was a bright red 1957 Plymouth in mint condition. It had brand new plush red carpets and white vinyl seats. It even had little white twinkling lights surrounding the front grill. It was immaculate as Steve always took great pride in the looks of his car. It was something which he had learned from Art, so he thought he could trust him with his car. What was done was done, and there was nothing he could do about it except wait and, of course, not trust Steve again.

The following Saturday afternoon, Art picked Joy up. He liked exploring, and they often spent all day Saturday riding around the country looking for some new roads or places to see. This Saturday was going to be no exception. They had a full tank of Steve's gas at their disposal and a car to explore with.

On the road which ran between Atlantic City and the mainland, one could see a deserted haunted-looking building looming out of the marshes several miles away from the main road. Rumor had it that it was the old Atlantic City Electric Company, which had been abandoned about 20 years ago.

There were other rumors about the buildings as well, such that it was a secret government UFO research center. However, Art set no store by them. He had had a thing about this building for a long time; but, up until this point, he never really had a chance to go in and explore it. He wasn't going to miss this opportunity.

Art could never figure out how to get to the building through the marshland. This day, he was determined to find a way to get there. He drove along the side of the road very slowly for several miles. Soon, he spotted a dirt road that meandered into the marshes.

"Do you think we should try to drive down that path?" Joy asked, looking a bit concerned. *"It looks awfully narrow and broken up."*

"Don't worry. Steve's car can take it." Art reassured her, sounding confident in his abilities as a driver and Steve's car. It was a golden opportunity for Art. Even if something happened, it wouldn't have been to his car.

Art drove off the road onto the old dirt road. It appeared to wander around aimlessly through the marshes, and after what felt like hours, they seemed to be approaching the deserted building. Art had successfully navigated several washed out sections of the old dirt road and now had every confidence of successfully completing his journey.

Maybe he had a bit too much confidence as he started to navigate the last washed out section of the road.

"What's the matter?" Joy asked as the car came to a dead stop in the middle of a rather shallow stream of water that crossed the road.

"Uh, nothing, we're just stuck for a second," Art responded, knowing that he screwed up. He hesitatingly got

out of the car to size up the situation. The car was stuck in the mud, but it was nothing he couldn't handle, or so he thought. He found a pair of old snow chains neatly packed away in the trunk of the car and somehow managed to get them on the rear tires. He tried again and again, his confidence fading after every failed attempt. Finally, after numerous attempts, he came to the sad realization that they were stuck. The ground was clutching to the car securely, and there was no way they were going to get out of there without the help of another car.

It was now late in the afternoon, and the sun was beginning to set. Both Art and Joy decided to abandon the car and head across the marshes on foot towards the main road as it was much shorter that way than trying to backtrack down the road they had driven. They trudged through water up to their knees to get to the road. Darkness set in, and the cold engulfed them. Joy complained of being wet and cold.

Finally, after what seemed like an eternity, they made it to the road. They managed to hitchhike a ride and arrived home at 8:00 PM. Art explained the situation to his father, and his father convinced him to wait until morning before attempting to rescue the car. Art spent a very restless night.

Every moment seemed to be stretched out to an eternity.

When the morning finally did arrive, he immediately went to his dad.

"Dad, can we go now? Can we go now to get Steve's car?" He asked, almost standing on the balls of his feet. Art's father agreed it was time to go after the car but insisted they first get a tow truck. They drove to several gas stations before they finally found someone willing to drive down the old dirt road with their tow truck.

When they finally reached Steve's car, Art got the shock of his life.

"Good job, Art, you really did it this time," his father said. *"You managed to drown your brother's car."* He added, standing beside Art, who seemed to be having a lot of trouble closing his mouth.

The only thing visible on Steve's car was the top of the roof and the raccoon tail hanging from the antenna. The shallow puddle of the night before had now been turned into a 3-foot deep pool of water by the tide, which frequently flooded the marshes.

After several attempts, the tow truck was hooked up, and Steve's car was pulled out of its watery bed. The inside of the car was a mess. The beautiful white upholstery and plush red carpets were covered with mud and reeked like the inside of a fish market.

Art felt terrible; he had wholly wrecked Steve's car. What could he do to make up for what he had done? What was he going to tell Steve? Remembering how he felt when Steve told him about his car, Art knew how pissed Steve was going to be.

Art now resigned himself to the fact that since he was responsible for ruining Steve's, it would only be right for Steve to have his car. He would just have to use his thumb to hitch rides.

"Dad, what can I do about Steve's car? Do you know anyone who can fix it?" He asked, nervous that his father would get angry.

However, his father was a man of almost no anger and replied, *"Yes, Art, I'm sure Brownie can fix it."*

Art's father came to his rescue again and made arrangements to get the car fixed and cleaned up. When they finally got the car back after a couple of very long weeks, it looked as good as new. Steve never really ever forgave Art, and Art never did get to explore that old deserted haunting looking building and discover its secrets.

Why Go To College

*"A dream is your creative vision for your life in the future." –**Denis Waitley***

All our dreams can come true if we pursue them passionately and relentlessly. Aaah! The sheer joy of imagining yourself on a pedestal and then following through with your goals is something only the most devoted dreamers can feel! The feeling is inimitable to any other feeling in this world and fills your whole being with a sense of self-worth and amour propre.

This self-confidence is what takes you to places. Remember reminiscing your childhood days? When you used to be this over-enthusiastic ball of energy ready to take the world by storm. That invigorating spark in you that would want to plunge into every new thing you came across and your inquisitive mind is having a gazillion questions popping up in your mind whenever you read or learned something new. The spark in your eyes that would never dull owing to the innumerable learning opportunities out there. That is the beauty of innocence and naivety that we possess in our childhood days. We are nothing but a blank slate, ready to be filled with words of wisdom and intellect and all those wondrous ideas that would give wings to our dreams.

We are far beyond the misgivings and insecurities that hold us back as adults, setting new standards of bravery and valor, challenging the status quo, and breaking the norms to set more inspiring precedents.

Most kids dream and fantasize about what they will be when they grow up and enter the adult world. They all envision themselves to reach a certain point in life where they can own their individuality. Be the person they are and truly and deeply love what they are doing. People who dare to dream are the ones who accomplish great things.

College life is one major phase of our life where we give way to our qualms only to be replaced by stronger and loftier goals. All of Art's friends had a dream which they wanted to pursue. Vinnie wanted to be a politician, Ron wanted to be rich and build skyscrapers, Ray wanted to be a pilot, and Johnny, a CIA agent. Art wanted to have an impact on the world and make a contribution to society - something so substantial and value-adding that the world would remember him for all time to come. His philanthropic dreams had him chase any means and resources of accomplishing his long-awaited dream.

"For better or worse, our future will be determined in large part by our dreams and by the struggle to make them real."

- Mihaly Csikszentmihalyi

However, irrespective of all the efforts he put in, luck was not on Art's side. Some lucky kids get to realize their dreams, but Art, unfortunately, was not one of those kids. He dreamed of becoming a research doctor and developing a cure for cancer or one of the other multitude of diseases that ruin the lives of so many people.

His dreams shattered when he got nausea dissecting the frogs and worms in high school biology class and realized that he was too squeamish about being a doctor. So, reluctantly, he gave up on his dream. Art was a dreamer, and he was no way going to let this come in the way of achieving greater things in life. So what if he couldn't pursue his career in the medical field? It was not the end of the world. He channeled his negative emotions of despondency and failure into something more productive and discovered his new-found love for engineering. Yes! From dissecting into body parts and organ systems, he had shifted his interest to get to know the intricate parts of a working machine. He had a versatile mind, and he believed that he was accomplishing whatever he set his heart and mind to.

Art enjoyed racing and building motors and thought that with a degree in engineering, he might be able to develop a better, more efficient type of motor or work for a company designing and developing new innovative equipment for race cars. Although it wouldn't cure any of the illnesses of the world, he thought it might be an interesting career.

It was a great way of turning around his destiny in his favor and not letting life's disappointment come in the way of his dream of being a well-renowned and famous man one day and giving back to society. Having lived a highly ambitious life throughout his childhood days, always having a vision in mind, he knew that he had to develop a go-getter attitude to get connected to his dreams. By the time the senior year in high school rolled around, Art had had enough of school and decided to make his fortune in the world without any more formal education.

Why not? What did he need to go to college for? He was smart; school work was extremely easy for him. He could learn almost any subject he wanted to just by reading a book about it. He was the number one student in his high school class. He thought that there must be someone out there who would appreciate his talents and give him a position of responsibility that would pay more than the minimum wage, a position where he could have an impact on their business.

From his out-of-the-box and radical thinking, he believed in defying the norms. He did not want to enter the job market just like any other graduate would and start at a minimum wage and struggle to rise up the ranks. Art being Art wanted to do something different and earn a competitive advantage over other colleagues.

After beating the bushes for several weeks looking for this ideal job, Art came to the sad realization that no one other than himself had any faith in his ability. People's lack of faith in him was beginning to weaken the little faith he had in himself. No one would give him a job with any responsibility. Everyone demanded a formal degree before employing him or even considering him for a suitable position in their company.

It was soon dawning upon Art that he would have to pursue a formal degree or accept odd, menial jobs, which was never his vision, to begin with. Art was offered a job pumping gas at the local service station, but he couldn't get a job as a mechanic because he had no previous work experience or formal training from a technical school in that field.

They didn't care that he had some experience building racing engines for boats. That didn't count. He was offered a job as a sales clerk in a department store but couldn't get the vacant assistant department manager's job. He was also offered a job inspecting the galvanized plating on washers but couldn't get a supervisory job in the plating department.

The pièce de résistance was that no one, absolutely no one, would even consider giving him a tryout driving their race car. Art had basically sensed the market and gauged the demand for high school graduates like him. It was the time that he did the needful to bag a position of his dreams and not be left behind in this race.

Reluctantly, Art realized that either he had to start at the very bottom like everyone else and try to work his way up the ladder or else he could go to college and study engineering as he had originally planned. The guidance counselor at school assured him that with an engineering degree, he could get a reasonably good job since there were currently more jobs for engineers than there were engineers to fill them. This was the only hope that Art had to regain his confidence and faith, which the unresponsive market had gnawed at. He was adamant about making sure that he would do his best and live up to his dreams.

During the senior year in high school, about two months before graduation, testers from the New Jersey Department of Labor descended on Art's high school to administer a new test that they developed. These tests were supposed to be able to determine what type of career the students were best suited for. Art's class was to be an experiment.

They had never administered these tests before to any high school class, but they were confident that with these new tests, which they had spent millions of dollars developing, would be able to accurately tell the students what career to pursue and what careers to avoid. Art thought this was a one-of-kind opportunity to get his knowledge and skills set tested and get expert advice on his career goals. He was fervently looking forward to it.

An entire day was spent taking the tests. Students had to put nuts on bolts, washers on pegs, square pegs in square holes, round pegs in round holes, identify tools, add numbers, subtract numbers, read stories, answer questions about stories and even tie knots in small pieces of rope. All of this was done under the scrutinizing eye of the testers with the time clocks. The comprehensive methods applied to test the students were not only interactive and engaging but also made the testing process smoother.

When the testing was over, and everyone waited with bated breath for the results. Art and his classmates wanted the answers to their questions as to whether or not they had chosen the right career for themselves. If they hadn't yet been able to choose something for themselves, they wanted them to help them decide.

In a couple of weeks, the testers again descended en masse on their class. This time, they had the long-awaited answers.

Art was summoned into the auditorium to the makeshift office of one of the testers. He introduced himself.

"Hello, I am Mr. Jones from the New Jersey Department of Labor. You're Mr. Dinick?" he asked.

"Yes," Art responded.

"Let's discuss your test results. Based on your performance on our comprehensive tests, we think you should choose a career as either a pipefitter, a mechanic, seamstress, or a plumber. Were you planning on pursuing a career in any of these fields?"

Art was taken by surprise.

"Well no, I am not," Art answered in a rather defensive tone

"Well, what are you planning on doing?" He asked inquisitively.

"I'm, I'm going to college to study engineering."

"Engineering?"

"Yes, engineering. Why?"

"Well, based on your test results, we do not believe you should become an engineer. We do not think you will be able

to pass the courses in college. Yes, definitely not."

Why not?" Art asked, rather disappointed and in total awe of the situation.

"Because the courses are difficult and our tests indicate you won't be able to pass them," the evaluators said without a trace of compassion.

"But I think I will be able to pass them," Art insisted, "and I think you are wrong."

"Well, I wish you luck, but our tests are never wrong," he said. *"Only time will tell."*

The session ended on this note, and Art was left in a state of apprehension. He couldn't understand what had just happened, and he felt this sudden urge to prove the test results wrong. How would they come to such abrupt conclusions without actually gauging him on the field? He felt helpless at this point but did not let the comments overwhelm him.

As usual, Art had the mental energy to sail through this, like every other challenge that he had done in the past. Art was shaken up by the testers comments. He was overcome by doubts spawned by his own insecurity. What if the tester was right, and he didn't have the ability to make it through engineering school? Art didn't want to believe him. His competitive spirit struggled against his feelings of insecurity. He had to prove that the tester was wrong. He believed that if he tried hard enough, he could do anything he really wanted to do. He thought he might have a few failures and setbacks in the process, but if he persisted, he would be able to accomplish whatever he set out to do. It was this conviction and unwavering determination that ultimately led him to keep pursuing a career of his dreams.

Villanova University is located in eastern Pennsylvania, about 20 miles North West of Philadelphia, in an area known as the Main Line. Its vast sprawling campus was laid out on the rolling hillside. Large, neatly mowed grass fields separated the buildings.

It is not exactly sure why Art chose to go there, but the fact that his father and uncle Don had both gone there probably had something to do with it. It was a legacy that he wanted to continue and make his family proud. Art was a grounded personality and had a family orientation – such that acceptance from his family meant a great deal to him.

It was a blistery cold February day in 61. Six inches of

snow covered the ground. English Literature class had just ended. Art glanced down at his Timex wristwatch. *'Shit! It's 9:50 a.m., only 10 minutes to get to the physics class in Vasey hall,' he thought.* Vasey hall was a fifteen-minute walk on a good day. To make class on time today would require a mad dash through the snow. Vasey was a huge lecture hall. The room was already crowded, with over 500 engineering students.

'Where am I going to find a seat?' Running and panting, he finally made it to the hall in the nick of time. Art was in luck; the seat next to his buddy John Voelmicke was still vacant. Art sat down and took off his coat and stuffed it under his chair. On the stage were professor Driscal and his staff. He began his lecture on the magnetic effects of electrical currents.

The lecture hall was hot and stuffy, and Art was cramped in his seat. Driscal had a habit of lecturing in a monotone voice, and the lecture today was incredibly dull. The hissing of steam issuing from the radiators had a hypnotic effect, and it was taking every last bit of Art's energy to resist nodding off. His mind was beginning to drift. He was starting to conjure up visions of Weapers dock on a hot, summer day.

The sun was beating down. Ron was sitting in his boat, eating a bag of chocolate chip cookies. A beautiful girl in a skimpy bathing suit was motioning for him to come over to her boat. She wanted him to go for a boat ride with her. She was gorgeous; how could he refuse?

"You there, you there in the eighth row, you with the red and black sweater."

Art was shocked out of the land of nod

"Uh, me?" He stammered

"Yes, I mean you. What's your name?"

"Dinick, sir."

"Well, Mr. Dinick, you don't see any beds in here, do you? If you want to sleep, you should do it in your bed. Since there are no beds in here, I suggest you go back to your dorm now. Go on, get out of here and make sure that you get enough sleep before you come to my class next time," He said rather aggressively.

Driscal couldn't be reasoned with. He had sent many others before Art off to their dorms and would send many others after him. So off to his dorm, he went muttering to himself about the injustice Driscal had done to him. What could he do if the lecture was so boring? Art didn't like sitting in huge stuffy lecture halls crammed in with 500 students, listening to some professor standing up on the stage trying to teach a subject which he wasn't interested in. He didn't like all the seemingly useless and meaningless homework assignments. How were they going to help him in his practical life? How would any of these assignments prepare him for the tough job market out there, which relied heavily on interpersonal and soft skills which nobody ever taught them? This was the very reason that Art was never in favor of going to college because he did not feel that bookish knowledge could ever get him anywhere.

He was always of the opinion that if he leveraged his intelligence, analytical skills, street smartness, and quick problem-solving and decision-making skills, he could land a job at a reputable place. Art didn't really like college, but he wasn't a quitter. Once he started something, he had to complete it no matter how hard it was or how much he disliked it. He decided that as long as he was in college to get a degree, he might as well get the most out of it. He was determined to work his butt off to learn the subjects and get the best possible grades.

He did not want to leave any stone unturned when it came to proving his competency and ability to materialize his dreams in the face of adversity and setbacks. If he dared to dream, he also had it in him to accomplish it. There was no power on earth that could stop him from working hard towards his dreams – not even pessimism and the demotivating environment.

Mondays through Thursdays, he concentrated on his studies until 9 p.m. At the stroke of nine, he put away his books and began socializing with his friends. He wouldn't deviate from this ritual no matter how much pressure his buddies put on him or how much they tried to distract him. He was a man of principles, and it was showing.

On Friday afternoon, after his last class, he would close his books and forget about school until Monday morning when his ritual would begin all over again. He knew how to strike the perfect balance between academics and leisure. He did not give up his extra-curricular activities to become a full-time nerd and not enjoy life. He knew that to be able to concentrate and be productive, his mind and body needed to de-stress as well, and he wasn't going to burden them unnecessarily.

At night, in the dorms, there were the usual bullshit sessions. A group of guys would gather in someone's room and discuss class, girls, ball games, or what they did over the weekend. This was their way of lightening up their spirits and divert their minds from the everyday drill and gruesome, monotonous routine. Sometimes to break the boredom, they played games or hurled jokes on each other. One of the more popular games was called "sneak attack."

It was originated by Art's buddy John Voelmicke who lived in the room next to Art. John, a lean 6'3" tall kid who grew up in a small rural town in north Jersey, had a fantastic sense of humor and loved to play practical jokes on his buddies. The floors of the dorm rooms were white and black vinyl tiles, and none of the rooms were carpeted. Two-inch thick oak doors barred intruders and insured privacy.

To initiate the sneak attack, one of the guys would bang on their neighbor's door to be sure someone was in the room. They then would squirt lighter fluid under the door and ignite it with a match and run to the shelter of their own room, locking the door behind them. If the attacker had the presence of mind and some of the intelligence he was born with, he would block off the bottom of his door with a wet towel to prevent a retaliation attack, but you would be surprised to find out how many of the supposedly brilliant college kids in their dorm didn't. The person whose room was attacked would almost always try to retaliate after he finished stomping out the flames in his room.

Art developed a slight improvement in this game. After retreating to his room following an attack, he didn't use the customary wet towel stuffed under the door to prevent the retaliation attack. Instead, he would lay in waiting for the retaliator to bang the customary warning on his door, at which time, using precise timing, he would swing his door wide open and soak the attacker with a trash can full of water. It was all in good fun, and no one ever got really pissed off or upset.

The last tag was another game they would play to spice up an otherwise boring day. The object of the game was to run up to one of your buddies, punch or tag him very hard and run off to the safety of one of the buildings on campus considered 'safe sanctuaries.' Tagging back was absolutely taboo within the confines of a designated sanctuary. The master and inventor of this game was none other than John

Voelmicke. On graduation day, after receiving his diploma, John came up to shake Art's hand and say his last good-byes. Instead of shaking his hand, however, he punched Art on the arm, yelled *"the last tag,"* and ran off to the safety of his parent's car, never to be seen again. He was the all-time winner of the last tag.

Heat transfer was a tough subject. The three-hour final exam was worth 70% of the grade for the semester. Flunk the final, and you flunked the course. Mr. Murphy, the instructor, liked asking trick questions on tests. He figured that if you could answer the trick question correctly, you really understood the subject. He had given several quizzes during this semester, and most of the class was doing miserably. McWinkle was no exception. He just couldn't see or understand the trick in Murphy's questions. On the other hand, Art was doing okay with an 85 average but needed to ace the final to get an A in the course. This would also help him win a scholarship that would help pay some of his expenses. Art never aimed low; he was always a high-achiever and gave his 100% when it came to acing his courses. He never slacked or gave in to temptations no matter how hard his mates tried to lure him into involving him in other activities.

"Uhh, Art. Uhh. Art. Wha..wha..what ty...ty...type of questions da..da..da..do you think Muh.. Muh... Muh... Murphy will ask in the fi...fi...fi...final?" McWinkle asked.

He stuttered a lot when he was nervous.

"Trick questions! He always asks trick questions," Art answered. *"Study all the homework questions and make sure you know them inside and out, and you should be able to pass the test. Don't pay any attention to the questions at the end of the chapters. They're too straight forward."*

The day before the final, Murphy held a review class and went over the type of questions he said he would ask on the final. He told the class that the questions would all be a slight variation of the questions at the end of Chapters 1 through 15. This was paramount to saying 'know everything in the book.' He ended the review session by saying, *"Well, class, now that I have let the cat out of the bag, none of you should have any problem passing the final."*

For some reason, Art didn't believe him, it just wasn't his style, and Art again warned McWinkle to watch out for the tricks. At last, the test day came. Nervously, the students sat down at their desks. The blue test booklets were passed out. Murphy then gave the signal to open the test booklets and start the test. Dead silence fell over the room. It was exam time all over again - the most dreaded time of the year when even the best of the students would go blank or not be able to perform as well as they did throughout the year. Exam pressure is evil on its own, and nervousness can just turn over things for an otherwise well-performing recording as well.

It was so quiet you could hear a pin drop as they read over in horror, the test questions to themselves. The questions were brutal. Each and everyone had a trick to it. Any similarity to the questions at the back of the chapters was purely coincidental. Suddenly, the dead silence was broken by a voice from the back of the room.

"Ca...Ca...Ca...Cats out of wha..wha..what ba..ba..ba..ba..bag! Fu...fu...fu..fuck you, Murphy!" and out of the room, stormed McWinkle. No question in anyone's mind what he thought about the test. He flunked the course in style. Art admired him for speaking his mind and saying what he thought. Many others in that class who suffered and struggled through the test in silence also flunked. Art

struggled through the test but passed. This was insane. Murphy had yet again been successful in intimidating the students and get them to flunk. That's just how some teacher's psyches operate, and there is not much that you can do about it. It's the very reason they are notorious, and trying to make them think in a different direction would be like banging your head against the wall.

Some teachers derive this inexplicable sense of pleasure from tormenting and torturing the students. Little do they realize that this undue pressure can be mentally taxing for someone's health. It is not these gruesome exams that prepare us for the ultimate, but the series of lessons on humanity, compassion, considerateness, and other values that build our personalities.

Art didn't believe what the tester from the New Jersey department of labor him told him about his abilities and didn't take their advice. Art's self-belief was not that flaky that he would give up on his life plans based on some testers' results. He believed in the far-sightedness of his dreams, and he wouldn't let anything bring him down. He went to college and studied engineering as he had planned and tried to prove that the tester was wrong. Graduation day from college came, and Art got his engineering degree.

And, despite what the New Jersey Department of Labor test showed, he graduated number one in his class. Art had done it! YES! Not only had he proven his worth to himself but also established the fact that no paper can determine his worth and also that barriers exist only in mind! Had he been let down by the tester results and given up on engineering, he wouldn't have made it to this day.

Here he was standing proud on the podium, ready to receive his degree and feel this feeling of accomplishment that no other achievement could compare. He had set an exemplary precedent, that acting in due course of time can do wonders for your personal and professional growth. Art did not have an engineering mindset, to begin with; however, upon finding out that biology was not his cup of tea, he did not let that discovery bog him down.

He exercised practicality and, after weighing his options, decided to change his academic trajectory only in the hopes of making something out of his future. He did not let his setbacks consider himself a failure. He did everything that was in his control to gain clarity of his vision and make sure that things work out in his favor. I guess tests aren't always right, and "experts" don't always know what they're talking about. If you really want something bad enough, you should go for it regardless of what anyone else thinks. Pursue your dreams. Believe in the power of your dreams, because if you give up on them, then there is nothing that anybody else can do to make you pursue them. You are your biggest strength, and only you can keep yourself motivated to climb the ladder of success. Nobody else can do the needful for you, and you need to fetch for yourself.

Vinnie's, Ray's, and Ron's dreams were fulfilled. Vinnie got to be a Senator and is frequently in the news. Ray is flying freight around the world. Ron didn't get to build skyscrapers, but he did make a fortune building three and four-story office buildings. Johnny never got a chance to pursue his dreams. His hopes and dreams came to a swift end one night in a dark and lonely field in Vietnam.

Chapter 6
Grown Up and On His Own At Last

Goodbyes are one of the hardest and dreaded things in life. A place where you've spent the most transformative years of your life and made so many indelible memories is hard to leave behind. However, goodbyes are part and parcel of life, and you can't have a special edition of life where you get to skip this part. You've got to go through it and deal with it maturely. Life is but an amalgamation of phases, each one embedding certain core values into our system and helping us grow into beautiful, self-reliant individuals.

Graduation day finally came. School books were put aside, and goodbyes were said to college buddies. The time had come to bid farewell, and there was no evading it. Colored sweaters and worn-out jeans were replaced with conservative grey polyester suits. The time had finally arrived for Art to start supporting himself and take his place in the adult business world. His first few years would determine his entire success trajectory in his corporate life.

He accepted a job with DuPont in Wilmington, Delaware, as a design engineer. All his valuable personal assets, including his model car racing set, were moved to a newly rented apartment in Wilmington. As we go through life's stages, we realize that to proceed to the next stage, we have to leave certain things behind. We have to understand that we cannot stay stuck at one point in our lives because that would simply mean shutting out other opportunities from reaching you. Here was Art ready to embark on a new journey of life, sending ripples in all directions.

One warm August evening, Art and his friend George were having dinner at their favorite restaurant and pondering what they were going to do for entertainment that night. Joy and Art had an argument four weeks ago, and they hadn't seen or talked to each other since. What do 22-year-old males who have just recently moved into a strange city do in the evenings? On Wednesday nights, they would go to the dance at the DuPont Country Club, and Thursdays, they would go see the trotter's race at Brandywine Race Track. This, however, wasn't Wednesday or Thursday. It was Monday. Based on a statistical analysis of past Monday night activities, they would probably go for a walk and end up in the local bar where they would have a few beers, participate in some idle discussion and watch the little dramas of life unfold around them. They would see who was picking up who and who wasn't, and after a couple of hours, Art would walk back to his apartment. He then used to watch the news on TV and then go to bed - not a very exciting prospect, of course.

In short, life had happened to the friends, and even the prospect of having fun on a Monday evening seemed bleak. They had to think of ideas to have fun because now they were not a bunch of college boys who could go around fooling with people and acting childish. They were now grown up, mature adults who needed to exercise some sense of control and observe a particular code of conduct.

That, my friend, is what we call life.

Just as the boys were contemplating life and rummaging through their mind for some fun ideas while at the corner diner, two gorgeous ladies seemed to approach them from a distance. Clad in body-fitted cocktail dresses, accentuating their curves, they were an accurate picture of any man's fantasy.

"Hi! My name's Charlene, and this is my friend Becky. The diner is very crowded tonight. Do you mind if we sit with you and your friend?"

Art was startled. *"Well, uh, uhh. No," he stammered, "You can sit with us. We don't mind."* They didn't mind, indeed. It was a miracle, the answer to their prayers. Not one, but two gorgeous looking girls wanted to sit with them. How easy it was, and they didn't even have to work at it. It certainly felt like destiny presented the solution to these men's boredom on a plate. They didn't have to come up with awkward pick-up lines. The girls came to them. What else could they have asked for? Art and George sat and talked with them as they ordered dinner.

Charlene was a 25-year-old divorcee. She worked in a real estate office downtown. She was a tall girl, about 5' 6", with a great body. Long brown hair hung halfway down her back; her low cut pink blouse showed off her huge boobs. In fact, they were so large they looked like they were going to fall out of her blouse on to her dinner plate at any moment. They were the kind of boobs that you couldn't keep your eyes off of, and she knew it. She talked incessantly through dinner. By the time dinner was over, she had told the boys her entire life history. Charlene was born and raised on a farm in South Carolina, had learned to ride horses at an early age, and loved to go skinny dipping in a secluded pond nestled on one wooded corner of their property. At 17, she ran off and married a merchant seaman. Being an extremely jealous man, he suspected her of fooling around on him while he was away at sea. Often upon returning home from a long voyage, he would tie her to the bed and beat her. After several years of this abuse, she left him and got a divorce.

When dinner was finished, George and Becky made their excuses and split for parts unknown. Charlene suggested that she and Art go for a ride in his car and become better acquainted. That was a great suggestion. Art couldn't have come up with a better one himself. Acting upon Charlene's suggestion, they ended up at a secluded parking spot along the banks of the Brandywine River.

She snuggled close to Art and kissed him as they gazed at the slow-running stream. Her kisses quickly became very passionate. He didn't want it to be this way with a stranger, although she was a beautiful gorgeous stranger. This wasn't love. It was a raw passion with a girl he had just met.

Art's years of Catholic education told him that this kind of sex was wrong, but he worried that she would think that there was something wrong with him if he stopped her. He was confused about how did he get himself into this situation. He wanted to stop but was mentally and physically too weak. He resisted but for only an instant. In the heat of passion, he gave in and had sex with her. He submitted to her and finally lost his virginity; it was taken from him. He would now have to live the rest of his life with the memory of being raped by a gorgeous, beautiful older woman.

Dating Joy was an on and off event, just like the changing of the corner traffic light. Their friends never knew if they were or weren't going together a particular week. They would go out for a couple of weeks, and everything would be fine, but, as always happened, Joy would start an argument over something insignificant and break up with Art forever or stay away for a couple of weeks at least. This had made their relationship lose the charm and momentum on which they had started. Nevertheless, the two always got back at one point in time or another and had more or less become accustomed to this.

It was a typical early autumn Saturday afternoon. Art was

working under his car repairing a clutch, which was damaged during the Friday night races. Joy was standing over him by the side of the vehicle handing him the tools and parts that he needed. Art gave her the old parts as he removed them from the car. They were engaged in idle conversation when she brought up her favorite subject. It was in her nature to go over some topics again and again until she got her way. She just did not give up on certain things, even if that meant incessant bickering and nagging.

"When are we going to get engaged? All our friends are engaged. Your own brother, Steve, got engaged to Peggy last week. I'm going to be an old woman before we get engaged. You know that I'm going to be 18 on my next birthday." She was relentless and constantly brought the topic up. When she set her mind on something, she nagged until she got it.

"*Alright, alright, if you really want to, I guess we can get engaged.*" Art responded. A big grin spread across Joy's face. She looked like a kid who is let loose in a candy store.

Art had finally given in to Joy's constant nagging as there was no other option but to appease her. He knew that she wouldn't leave the topic until she got her way.

"When, when can we get engaged?" she queried desperately as if she couldn't wait another moment.

"*Just as soon as I give you a ring*." He said, trying to keep it subtle.

"When, when will you give me a ring?" she asked, getting impulsive with every passing moment.

"*Soon*." He said with a sly smile

"How soon?" she exclaimed as if expecting something at that very moment.

"Soon," repeated Art and reached into the right pocket of his jeans and from under the car handed her the engagement ring that he had purchased a couple of weeks earlier from the same jeweler that Steve bought his ring from. This sure happened unexpectedly and out of the blue, but Art and Joy were now going to start a new chapter in life, and Joy specifically was ecstatic about it. Art, however, was not entirely present to imagine what was in store for them. He and Joy were together for a long time now, and he respected her feelings and sentiments for him, and he didn't want to hurt her in any way. Her constant insistence left him with no option but to do as she said. He had to ultimately get settled;

why not with the one who loved him so much.

No marriage date was ever set, but Joy had the understanding that they would get married someday. She would frequently broach the subject of marriage, but Art would always panic and say he wasn't quite ready yet. This, in itself, would often lead to arguments ending with her storming off in a fit of temper yelling

"Well, if you're not ready, I'm not going to wait around for you and waste my life. There's a lot more fish in the sea. You're not the only one buster; I can catch a lot better than you."

And, off she would go in a huff. She never seemed to catch anything better, though. This had become an everyday thing, and Art had had enough of her tantrums. No matter how much he tried to keep things calm, Joy would come around the same topic and spark this unwelcome debate. Obviously, both of them were at an age where a commitment was not an easy thing. They were both struggling personally and professionally, and marriage was the last thing on Art's mind. Joy, however, refused to understand his situation and kept on eating his mind whenever she got the opportunity. After a week or two of being separated, she would phone Art on some excuse, and one thing would always lead to another, and they would reconcile their differences.

In November of Art's first year of working for DuPont, he was living alone in an apartment in Wilmington and surviving on Gino's hamburgers and milkshakes. Early snow was on the ground, and it was cold, freezing cold. The heater in the apartment didn't work properly, and Art caught a cold. He was too ill to go to work or shopping for food; he hadn't eaten in a week. He was too independent to ask one of his friends for help. A high fever was making him delirious and emotional. One evening the phone rang.

"Hi! It's Joy. How are you doing?"

"*Not so good. I'm pretty sick*," Art blurted out in one of his more lucid moments.

"I'll come up and get you," she said without a second thought.

"No," he insisted, *"I'll be alright,"* he said with the last ounce of strength that was left in him and blacked out.

Several hours later, he was awakened by a loud banging on the front door. Art managed to drag himself out of bed and open the door. He was shocked to see his mom, dad, and

Joy. Joy knew Art needed help but would never ask for it, so she notified his mom and dad. They had driven up from Atlantic City. Quickly they called the doctor, who then gave Art a shot of penicillin and prescribed bed rest. Against his protest and insistence that he would now be ok, they bundled him up, loaded him into the car, and took him home with them to Atlantic City, where he was put to bed.

By Sunday afternoon, which was a week later, and Art was well on the way to recovery, Joy came over to visit.

"Hi! How are you feeling?" she asked with warmth and compassion in her voice.

"*Much better*," Art replied without any trace of emotions in his voice. The illness had taken a toll on him, and he was deprived of energy.

"You were pretty sick," Joy said with extreme concern.

"Yeah, I know," replied Art without sounding apologetic for not asking for help. He was as relaxed as he could be, and nothing was taking that away from him.

"I'm really glad you're feeling better now. I'm sorry I didn't get a chance to get over to see you the past couple of days as I have been very busy," told Joy, unable to contain

her excitement.

"Busy? Doing what?" Art asked.

"Making all the arrangements and sending out the invitations," she replied casually.

"What arrangements? What invitations?" Art asked.

"The arrangement and invitations for the wedding," replied Joy.

"*Who's wedding*?" Art queried.

"Our wedding, silly," she replied. "*We're getting married on February 4th, and we have the reception at the Morton Hotel."* Art was stunned. It took him a while to register what Joy was saying until it dawned upon him that Joy was actually pretty serious about planning their wedding.

"*What do you mean we're getting married on February 4th? I never agreed to get married.*"

Was he in a dream, or was this actually happening to him in reality? Everything started to fade in the background, and he was the gravity of the situation began to settle in.

"Yes, you did," she said. "We talked about it last week in your apartment when we were waiting for the doctor to

come. You said we could get married any time I wanted to and that I should make the arrangements, so I did," Joy said, sounding hurt and sad.

"*I don't remember saying anything like that*! Exclaimed Art in a somewhat irritated and fed-up tone.

"Yes, you did," she said. *"You said we could get married."* She started to cry. *"I sent out all the invitations and made all the arrangements." "We have to get married now. I can't call it off; it's too late. I'll be too embarrassed to tell my friends,"* she sobbed. She was getting hysterical as Art's last-minute denial was putting her in a state of frenzy, and she was losing her calm.

"*All right, all right, stop crying*," Art consoled her so that she wouldn't lose her calm and sanity. He felt terrible and didn't want to see her cry because he was so fond of her. Seeing her cry tugged at his heartstrings, and he did not like it one bit. He didn't remember agreeing to get married and didn't really think he was mentally prepared to get married. His memory seemed to lose him, and he could vaguely recall what must have happened—being under the state of fever.

He had agreed to get married while being delirious from

the illness, but she didn't know that. He didn't want to hurt her as he cared too much for her. He didn't also want to embarrass her in front of her family and friends, so he reluctantly agreed to get married.

"All right, all right, stop crying. We can get married," Art told Joy.

"Are you sure?" she asked.

"*Yes, yes, I'm sure, I think, I'm sure, I guess, I'm sure.*" He wasn't really sure, but he didn't have the heart to say no.

When one thinks of weddings, they conjure up visions of a warm, sunny spring or summer day. The wedding was on a cold rainy day in February. It was far from the typical day of a wedding. It was a near-to-miserable day for a couple to start a new life together, but guess that is what was destined for Art and Joy. The weather was so lousy that Art wondered if anyone was going to show up for the ceremony, but to his surprise, no one stepped back. Ron drove down from Phillie with Lynn, but Art always knew that nothing would ever stop Ron from getting a free meal.

Vinnie, Joe, and John also made the long trip from Phillie. All of his buddies from the crusaders managed to make it.

Their wedding was both a joyous and sad occasion as it marked the beginning of a new life for Joy and Art, but the end of the Crusaders. It was the last occasion where they all got together as a group. Naturally, everyone gets busy after marriage, and things do not remain the same.

Life as a young married couple wasn't easy. During the day, Art worked as a design engineer for DuPont in Wilmington, Delaware. Three nights a week after work, he took the long train ride into Philadelphia to take graduate courses at Drexel Institute towards a master's degree. He didn't enjoy spending three nights a week riding the train and sitting in a crowded class. He didn't enjoy the prospects of spending the next eight years this way, but he wanted the degree. There had to be a better, less painful way. Life hadn't unfolded the way he had planned; it was way too hectic to manage with a sane mind. With time, his mental fatigue just gave way to anxiety, and he was desperate to find a way out of this uncomfortable and mentally draining situation.

Joy and Art discussed the situation, and they agreed that she would go to work while Art went to school full time to get a doctorate degree. He contacted Dr. Long, the chairman of the Mechanical Engineering Department at Lehigh

University, and he offered Art a National Science Fellowship, which would pay all his tuition and give him $3000.00 living expense. From the money Joy would make as a secretary and the money Art would get from the fellowship, Art figured they could make it during the next three years of full-time school.

He thought he had his next three years conveniently planned out. Little did he know that life had other plans for him. Art turned in his resignation at DuPont, and the couple made plans to move to Bethlehem, Pennsylvania, to attend school full time, but the best-made plans of mice and men often go astray. Art didn't know it, but Joy had secretly devised other plans of her own. She had her own ideas of what she wanted, and working while Art was in school wasn't what she wanted. Married life wasn't easy for them. It brought with it its fair share of struggles and ups and downs. Marriage is definitely not a bed of roses, and both of them got to know that in the first year alone. Not only did they have to adjust to each other's temperament, but the two also argued frequently, and as usual, they disagreed on just about everything.

One thing that Art thought both of them agreed on was

not to have any kids until Art was finished with graduate school, and they were better established. They were using the only method of birth control that the Catholic Church permitted, the rhythm method. They had sex only during Joy's cycle when they were absolutely positive she couldn't conceive, and then they were extremely careful to have sex only during the safest times.

Around July, just two months before school was to start, Art noticed that Joy seemed to be putting on some weight. She said that she was eating a lot because of depression and that she would soon go on a diet. In August, however, only weeks before they were scheduled to move, Joy announced that she was pregnant and that the baby would be due in December.

"Pregnant? Baby due in December? What do you mean? It can't be! We were cautious! We only had sex when you said it was safe. Are you sure? How can it be?" Art asked in dismay.

"Yes, I'm sure," she said. *"I thought that a baby would help our marriage, so I lied to you about being safe."*

"Help our marriage? How can it possibly help our

marriage? What am I going to do about graduate school? You won't be able to work."

"Don't worry, you'll think of something. You'll be able to work something out; you always do," she said.

In late August, they moved to Bethlehem, Pennsylvania, and rented a run-down apartment on the fourth floor of an old brick building on Fourth Street, which overlooked the Bethlehem Steel Plant. From the vantage point of their apartment, they got an excellent view of the steel plant through the high red and black clouds of smoke, which billowed forth continuously from its stacks. Not to be outdone by the breath-taking view, and I do mean breath-taking, they were serenaded 24 hours a day by the loud ringing and clatter from the pounding of its mighty forges. Windows in this non-air-conditioned apartment had to be tightly shut to muffle the loud sound of the forges and to keep out the voluminous amount of soot-vomited forth from the belching stacks. That was all they could afford on the meager pittance Art was receiving.

Art and Joy made the best of it, however, and survived on corn flakes, bread, and spaghetti. Their big treat was a walk down to the corner store for an ice cream cone on Friday nights and a drive through the surrounding countryside on Sunday afternoons.

In October, they were surprised by the early arrival of a 5-pound baby boy. The doctor blamed his premature birth on the stress of climbing four flights of stairs several times a day.

Art, however, told everyone that the baby had his personality, and he just didn't want to waste time lying around in his mother's womb any longer than he had to. They were able to take little Pat home after only a week of special care and treatment in the hospital's incubator.

Being a colic baby, little Pat cried incessantly. This put a serious cramp on Art's ability to study as there was no refuge in their small one-bedroom apartment. Nights brought no relief as Pat would wake up frequently and bellow forth until Art got up and rocked him back to sleep with a warm bottle. His crying didn't seem to bother Joy; she appeared to enter a deep coma every night. Art, however, couldn't sleep through his unmelodious serenade. On rare occasions, when Art was really exhausted, he would ask Joy to get up and rock him.

"No," she would snap, *"let him cry. It won't hurt him. If*

you want to shut him up, you get up and rock him."

"Please, Joy, I have to sleep. I have class in the morning," he would plead.

"So what," she would snap, *"he's bothering you, not me."* And off she would go back to sleep, leaving Art to tend to their baby. It was as if Joy was drugged.

It would usually take an hour or two for little Pat to drink his bottle and fall back to sleep while Art held him in his arms. This was an hour Art couldn't afford to spend with him and still be alert for a class in the morning. Somehow he had to speed the process up so that he could get back to bed sooner. On several occasions, he tried to lay little Pat in his little white wicker basinet and prop up the bottle with a rolled-up towel, but it would only fall over, pulling the nipple out of little Pat's mouth, leaving him to suck air and cry. There had to be a better way. Using his creative abilities, Art fashioned a holder for the bottle from a wire coat hanger. The holder was fastened to the giant pink bow on the hood of the bassinet in such a way that the bottle swung from it in pendulum fashion. It held the bottle nipple securely in little Pat's mouth until he had his fill and drifted off to baby dreamland. The device worked so well that Art could now return to sleep minutes after preparing the bottle and inserting it into the holder.

By December, it became apparent to Art that they couldn't survive another 2.5 years like this. Poverty had taken its toll, and a lack of sleep was wearing his nerves thin. He could endure a lot of discomfort for a short period, but 2.5 more years didn't seem like a short time to him. He had to give up on the idea of getting a doctorate. He salvaged what he could of his courses and entered a crash program to finish up with the master's degree by June so he could go back to work and start living like a member of the human race again. Where was he going to get a job? He didn't want to go back to DuPont. The work there was too restrictive. At DuPont, a mechanical engineer was a mechanical engineer, and he dare not try to do any work in the chemical engineering area or any other area that was not mechanical engineering. Art wanted to be free to work in any area where he felt challenged.

He didn't want to be constrained by someone telling him what he could or could not do. He would decide that for himself. They preferred to live in the northeast and not in the south or west. Art interviewed several companies, and after careful deliberation, he accepted a job with Exxon's Engineering Department in Florham Park, New Jersey.

Chapter 7
Marriage Problems

Rolling hills and green woodlands abound the northern part of New Jersey in contrast with the flat countryside of south Jersey was where Art grew up. The northeastern sector of the state, which borders on New York, was highly industrialized, but the rest of the state was rural with its countryside dotted with small towns. New Jersey is known as the Garden State, but the residents of the region of North Jersey where Art and Joy lived affectionately called it the Garden Apartment State. All Garden Apartments had a similar layout as if they had the same master architect as a father.

There was impeccable synchrony amongst them as if they had been built with extreme precision, even calculating the distance between them. All had a porch or patio which faced onto a central courtyard. One or two-story apartment buildings were set uniformly around the perimeter of a neatly manicured courtyard. One apartment was indistinguishable from the next, and if you weren't paying strict attention to what you were doing and where you were walking, you would occasionally find yourself trying to enter your neighbor's apartment. Garden apartments were everywhere, and it seemed that everyone, including Art and Joy, lived in one.

It was a clear, crisp day in early April 1966. The snows of winter had all but disappeared, and lush green foliage was slowly returning to the trees. Art had been working for Exxon for almost a year. The nature of his work was something that demanded responsibility, and Art was determined to give his all.

While he was at work, Joy spent her days socializing with the neighbors and watching after little Pat. Joy was a social butterfly, and she loved to spend her free time socializing around the courtyard so that she could spend her free time unproductively. Pat, now seventeen months old, with a full head of curly strawberry blonde hair, was walking under his own power, climbing on everything, and babbling partial sentences which only his mother and father could decipher.

It is these moments that make you want to stop time and not let it slip by like grains of sand from your fist. The pace at which children grow up can be very overwhelming, and seeing them get all independent can be the most beautiful feeling in the world. It was 5:30 P.M. when Art parked his bright yellow Mustang in the parking lot behind their apartment complex. The problems of work were now tucked away for the evening, and Art eagerly awaited spending a pleasurable evening with Joy and little Pat. Walking up the path through the courtyard surrounded by the two-story red brick apartments, Art wondered what Joy would be preparing for dinner. Opening the front door of the one-bedroom apartment, Art braced himself as he prepared to be attacked customarily by little Pat, but to his surprise, there was no attack.

"Hi, I'm home!" reverberated Art's voice in an inquisitive tone.

"Where is everyone?"

Lady, their little brown and white collie dog, scampered out of the kitchen and stood by Art wagging her bushy tail.

"Joy," Art called again with a tinge of concern in his voice, but there was no response.

"That's strange," he pondered. *"Where could they possibly be?"*

"Joy and Pat should be home at this time of day," he said

with his forehead showing signs of apprehension now.

He contemplated for a moment and then concluded that they must have gone to the store to pick something up for dinner. He casually walked into the kitchen. In the middle of the barren wooden table was a single sheet of white notepaper. Curiously he picked it up and read the message scrawled across the paper.

"So long, sucker." The note wasn't signed. His mouth dropped, and his heart momentarily slammed to a stop.

What did it mean, "So long sucker." It had to be a joke, a bad joke.

In a panic, Art ran into the bedroom and threw open the closet door. All of Joy's clothes were gone, not even a crumpled dirty pair of shorts remained. Now his heart was pounding like the drop forges from the steel plant. Pat's diapers were gone. Art ran to Pat's crib. His tattered and well-chewed little blue security blanket and his companion, the little doll called "Bebe," were gone.

The sight which Art beheld was something that he had not even thought of in his wildest imagination. How could Joy just make this one-sided decision and leave the house unattended and that too suddenly? Who gave her the right to walk out on him, and that too, along with their child? Art was in a state of complete shock, and his vision was getting blurry. It was now sinking in. Joy had gone, but why and where? What had he done to deserve this? His head was spinning in all directions, and he couldn't figure out what had just happened. It was just too much to digest at once.

Lately, Joy had been extremely moody and bitchy. They had argued on numerous occasions, but Art loved her and believed she loved him. Their life together wasn't that bad, at least not bad enough to end a marriage. She had never given him even the slightest indication that she was thinking of leaving. What was Art going to do? His world had fallen upside down. He felt as if someone had reached into his chest and ripped out his heart. He was hurting badly.

Yes, it was not a perfect marriage. Art wasn't the best and most perfect husband either, but who is? Every marriage is exposed to insecurities and certain ups and downs that may cause the relationship to falter. These ripples are meant to be taken as challenges, and there's nothing that cannot be resolved with negotiation and dialogue. If Joy, for once, would have brought up the matter with Art, things wouldn't have deteriorated to this extent.

The fact that Joy had taken such a huge step out of the blue made Art furious, and if he could just see and meet her once, he would make her realize what a grave step she had taken. It was just not him and her in the relationship, but they had a life attached to them as well. Did she not think of Pat even once? How heartless was she as a mother to expose their little kid to the darkness of a broken family. Is the future she wanted for her child?

A thousand questions now rushed through Art's mind. Where did she go, and why did she take little Pat with her? What was he going to do? Momentarily, the hurt turned to anger. *"She can't take my kid away from me. If she really wants to leave, that's okay, but she can't have my son."* A state of panic overcame him. He was shaking. His hands were cold and clammy. *"Okay, calm down. You've got to calm down; you've got to get a hold of yourself. She's gone. You have to find out where."* Art racked his brain to figure out where Joy could possibly have gone.

Not able to come up with anything, he decided to call her mother in hopes she might know something.

"Hi, it's Art. Is Joy there?" he asked in a flat tone, in an attempt to hide his apparent anxiety.

"Joy? What do you mean? Why would she be here? What's the matter Art, is there something wrong? Isn't she there with you?" her mother bombarded Art with all sorts of questions.

"No, she's gone, and she took Pat with her, and I don't know where. Did she say anything to you? Please tell me if you know something," heaved Art with a sense of urgency and irritation in his voice.

"No, honestly, she never said anything to me," her mother replied, trying to pacify Art. said Joy's mom in one breath, trying to sound as convincing as possible.

"No, I don't think so. Nothing happened that would upset her so much. I thought everything was all right. She won't be back; I know she won't come back. She took all her things. If she had any intention at all of coming back, she wouldn't have taken everything." Art exclaimed in an exasperating voice. He couldn't keep his calm anymore. The crucial step that his wife had taken was so fool-proof that he had no hopes of her returning.

"I'm so sorry for you! I really am! I know how difficult and demanding she can be at times. She's my daughter, and I love her, but I'll be the first one to admit that she has a nasty temper and can be a real bitch at times. She doesn't confide in me, and I doubt that she will call me, but if I hear anything from her, I'll give you a call and let you know what I find out," said Joy's mother in a rather anxious voice. She realized the gravity of the situation and could sympathize with Art. She knew her daughter really well, that once she would have her bitchy mode on, no force on earth could make her go back on her decision.

Now it was time for Art to check with Joy's friends. There was no place that Art wanted to leave to check for Joy. His fury had filled him with an extraordinary level of energy, and he was adamant about finding Joy. One of them might know something.

Diane and her husband, Bob, lived three apartments away. Art and Joy had socialized with them on several occasions, and Joy spent a lot of time with Diane during the day while Art was working. Diane had a passion for animals. She had a huge lazy Saint Bernard, which roamed the courtyard unleashed and left huge dumpings along the path of his daily journeys. The cabinet under their kitchen sink was the home for her pet, Skunk.

Art knocked on their apartment door. Diane greeted him with the Skunk cuddled in her Arms like a sleeping baby. He asked if she had seen Joy anytime today. *"No, I haven't. Why do you ask?"* she asked inquisitively

"Joy left this afternoon and took little Pat with her. Do you know where she could have gone?" inquired Art, trying to take out information that Diane might have.

"No, I have no idea." "Did she ever tell you that she was thinking of leaving?"

"No, she never mentioned it," said Art in a sulky voice. He was starting to lose hope. He realized that getting mad was not really the solution.

"I knew you were having some problems, but everybody has problems. She never mentioned anything to me about leaving you," said Diane in an empathetic tone.

"Well, she may not have mentioned it to you, but she left, and I have no idea where she went," sighed Art.

"I'm sorry, Art, but I don't know anything. I really don't.

If she contacts me, though, I'll let you know. If there's anything I can do for you, please let me know. Why don't you ask some of the other neighbors, someone has to know something?"

"Thanks, Diane. I'll check with some of them." Art was expecting Diane to know something as she was the one Joy spent most of her time with. If she didn't know of her whereabouts, then it was highly unlikely that anyone else would know.

In desperation, Art began to check with all the neighbors that he thought might possibly know something, but to no avail. Stanley lived two apartments away, and of all the neighbors, he was by far the strangest and most unconventional. He was a 23-year-old free spirit who never worked but always had plenty of money.

Good looking girls and strange-looking guys were always cavorting around his apartment. His apartment had a reputation for being a haven of sexual freedom. His front drapes were usually open, and his friends were very uninhibited. In the courtyard in front of the apartments, you could witness sexual gymnastics of partly clad or nude females and males cavorting about in his apartment. When you knocked on his apartment door at any time of day or night, you were usually greeted by a charming and scantily clad female. Although Stanley was a self-professed bisexual, he was a pleasant, likable guy. He was always sociable and a good neighbor. He was always inviting Art to one of his impromptu parties.

Their daily interchange, however, was usually limited to exchanging the pleasantries for the day, and on certain occasions, a shallow conversation about the Yankees or Art's racing activities. With no other option left and rule out any discrepancies, Art decided to approach Stanley and ask him if he knew anything at all about Joy's disappearance. Still, he really didn't expect Stanley to know anything.

Art was shocked when Stanley informed him that Joy had left for California early in the day with Kim, one of the girls that had been camping in Stanley's apartment. He informed Art that Joy had often spent the afternoons over at his residence and that she and Kim had become good friends. She and Kim had been planning the trip for several days. He also said that he had advised Joy not to go with Kim, but she was too excited to stay, especially with the prospect of the carefree lifestyle in California promised her by Kim.

"Where are they going to stay? How is she going to take care of the baby?" Art queried, unable to take in what he had just heard. It was like a bomb dropped on him. Tears welled up in his eyes, and his voice became shaky. Maybe they were tears of relief, you never know.

"I don't know," Stanley replied, "but I'm sure Kim will call me when they get there. When I hear from them, I'll let you know where they are," he said reassuringly.

Art was both upset and relieved by this revelation. He felt like a great stone had been lifted from him. He now knew where she was going, but he didn't know how he was going to get her or his son back. His senses felt numb, and he couldn't figure out what the next step should be.

Should he go after them, looking for them, or should he just wait for Joy to get in touch. His fatherly instinct was getting the best of him, and he felt helpless in the face of fate. While Joy was spending her days basking in the California sun and nights fighting off the overzealous advances of the sexually liberated California party time boys and enjoying every minute of it, Art was spending his time fighting off depression and loneliness. Racing became his primary interest in life and his only escape from all problems in his life. Art was racing two to three nights a week - an almost impossible schedule for someone holding down a full-time job. To accomplish this feat, he had to race at some pretty strange and rundown tracks located in remote areas all over the northeast. Harmony was one of these tracks.

It was a poorly paved drag strip tucked away in the farmlands of northwestern New Jersey. It couldn't be found on any map or in any racing publication. You had to know someone who raced there before to get directions on how to get there. In those days, a regular pit crew was hard to come by, so Art relied on catch and recruited friends and neighbors to help out when they were available.

It does sound messed up, but sometimes people develop strange coping mechanisms to help them come to terms with certain emotional voids in their life. On this Wednesday night, his next-door neighbor, Johnny Kohler, agreed to come to the track and help him. This would be a new experience for John. John and his wife, Irene, were avid stock car fans. Every weekend they would drive hundreds of miles to see their favorite drivers do battle on the oval tracks.

Tonight would be his first time at the drag races. His main assignment tonight would be to drive the push car. To have a competitive race car, every extreme to reduce unnecessary weight had to be exercised. Therefore, dragsters, which were the fastest type of drag race car, didn't have any cooling system for the motor, so they could only run for short periods of time.

Just prior to the start of the race, the push car would get behind the dragster and push it down the track until its motor started. It was part of the show. The push car would then follow the dragster back down the track and wait behind the starting line. After the start of the race, the push car driver would follow the race car down the track. Just beyond the finish line of the racetrack was a shutdown area. It was usually about a quarter-mile long.

After crossing the finish line, the race car driver would deploy the parachute and jam on the brakes to stop the car within the confines of the shutdown area. Since dragsters had no cooling system, they could not be driven back to the pits. Therefore, once the dragster was stopped in the shutdown area, the driver had to wait for his push car to come and get him and push him back to the pits.

The next race would start only after the push cars had cleared the race cars from the shutdown area as no one wanted the next set of race cars to collide with the race cars from the previous race. Art and John had some difficulty in finding the track and arrived late. Once the admission fees at the entry gate were paid, they drove the car and trailer with the race car on it into the pits.

The dragster was quickly unloaded and taken through technical inspection. However, it was now too late to make any time trial runs to test the car and get the feel of the track. The time came for the first round of racing. Donning his helmet and fireproof jacket, Art climbed into the cockpit of the dragster, and Johnny strapped him in. He then pushed the dragster from the staging lane in the pit area to the racetrack.

At the appropriate moment, Art signaled him, and Johnny pushed the dragster down the track to start the motor. As the motor fired and came to life, Art pulled quickly away from him. The race car was back upped to the starting line as Johnny followed in the push car. Art carefully staged the car in the staging lights, revved the motor up to 7000 rpm waiting for the signal to start the race. In the left lane was Andy Boye.

Art had never raced against him, but Andy's reputation as a great driver preceded him. Andy had raced here often, and it was his track favorite. Being the friendly and sociable fellow he was, he and Art exchanged racing stories in the pits earlier this evening, but now, on the track, he was his arch-enemy. The adrenaline rushed through his veins, and he gave an intense look to his rival as if conveying the message that he better be on his highest level of alert.

With the toss of a coin, Andy won lane choice, and he, of course, chose the lane with the better traction. The starting light flashed. Instantly, with lightning-quick reflexes, Art let the clutch out, his rear tires spun violently on the slippery track surface-emitting great clouds of smoke. Andy's car, however, got better traction and shot slightly ahead of Art's. He was still within striking distance, and with some luck, Art could catch him.

Art shifted to top gear. At 100 mph, the finish line was coming up quick, but Art was catching him. His front wheels were only inches ahead. Now Art was wholly engrossed in watching the position of Andy's car against his own. Art was gaining on him. 'Just a little more and Art will have him.' Art was inching upon him, 'just a little more.'

Suddenly, Art's car shot ahead of Andy's. 'What happened?' Then, like a bolt of lightning, it dawned on Art that he must have crossed the finish line, and Andy must have hit his brakes. Looking up, Art saw the fence at the end of the shutdown area coming up fast. He braked as hard as humanly possible and pulled the parachute. 'Not enough room to stop! God, I'm going to crash!' Suddenly Art crashed through the wire fence at the end of the racetrack.

It tore like tissue paper. The car went careening off the end of the track, hurtling through the air over the four-foot embankment, and came to rest in a freshly plowed field, about three feet from a country road. 'Whew! I'm all right, thank God!' Art climbed out of the car, expecting to have to wave off the ambulance and emergency fire truck, which usually wait with bated breath at the side of every racetrack for just such an emergency

'Where are they?' he pondered. It's a good thing I wasn't hurt. 'I could've died in the time it's taking them to get here.' Art thought and climbed up the embankment to the track expecting to see pandemonium and panic. It's not every day a dragster flies off the end of a track at 100 miles per hour. To his surprise, they were still running the races as if nothing had happened. What was even more surprising was that there was no Johnny. 'Where is he?' Art waited, but still no signs of Johnny. 'Maybe he saw me go off the end of the track and saw that I was okay. So he's got the trailer, and he's going to drive down the road to get me?' Art rationalized.

Art went back to the race car. To his surprise, there was very little damage. The steering bar on the front was bent, and a couple of the body panels were torn and ripped, but no major damage. He waited and waited for Johnny, but he did not come. A man and his wife were walking down the road. They saw the car and came running over. *"You okay,"* they asked. *"You okay?"* They tried to contain their panic and were relieved to see Art was fine.

"Yea, thank you, I'm all right. Can you help me push the car onto the road?" Art asked. *"Sure!"* they said. With some difficulty, they managed to get the car onto the road. Art straightened the steering bar with the aid of a wooden plank, which he found by the side of the road. After waiting for another ten minutes or so, Art deduced that Johnny wasn't coming. He had to get the car back to the track. But how? It was too far to push. Art felt the motor, and it was cool to his touch. He figured that he could probably drive it back to the track without having it overheat too much. Art started the car and drove over to the front gate. He was expecting to get

greeted with open arms, but, to add insult to injury, the man at the gate wanted him to pay an admission fee again. Art was livid.

"What? Are you crazy?" Art shouted. *"This is a dragster. This isn't a streetcar. Can't you see that? I didn't drive it here from home. How do you think I got here in a dragster? Why do you think I'm driving a dragster on the street? Do you know why you idiot? It's because I drove it off the end of your stupid track. In other words, I crashed! Where's your fire truck? Where's your ambulance? Somebody should've come to rescue me, even if I didn't get hurt! They didn't know that I wasn't hurt. Doesn't anyone around here watch what's going on?"* His temper was on a hair-trigger. Even the smallest thing could set him off into a frenzy of flaring emotions, shouting and yelling, saliva coming out with each jagged word. By the time he was done yelling, his voice had turned hoarse, and he could hardly speak.

"Sorry, sorry, calm down. You can go in for free." The man said.

"Well, thanks a lot, pal!" Art sarcastically shouted back as he restarted the dragster and drove it into the pits.

Johnny came rushing over. *"Art! Art! Where were you? I've been looking for you all over! Where did you go?"* his voice filled with frenzy and confusion. What took you so long? I was worried about you.

"What the hell are you talking about, Johnny? Where did I go? I crashed off the end of the track. That's where I went! Where the hell did you go? You were supposed to follow me down the track." He was out of breath now, and the fury had reached his brain. What sort of professionalism is this that nobody was there to attend to him when he met with an accident? Even if someone did not see him crash, there should be some sort of security or rescue team posted there to ensure safety.

"Art, I drove the push car down to the end of the track to get you, but I didn't see you. You weren't there. So, I figured you drove the race car back to the pits by yourself." Johnny tried to calm Art down as he could see that he was losing his calm.

"I guess you figured wrong that time, Johnny." Art was angry and frustrated, but he wasn't really upset with Johnny.

After all, what could he expect? If he were in Johnny's

shoes, he wouldn't have expected to see his friend go crashing off the end of the racetrack the first time he went to the races with him.

Always Give It Your Best

Long black frizzed hair stuck out six inches from his head in all directions. He had a thick black mustache and a husky beard. A long ominous scar ran from his cheek to the corner of his mouth. On his right arm was the tattoo of a snake. He wore a dirty white tee shirt with a pack of cigarettes rolled up in his left sleeve. The sight of the likes of him on the streets of New York would send a chill down your spine, and you would swear that your life was in danger. But, the rough menacing appearance was only the cover of a book and not the contents, and everyone knows that you can't judge a book by its cover.

Jerry McTagggard was a little wild and, some would say, a little crazy for driving his race car the way he did. But, he was a nice guy who had grown up in a rough section of the Bronx in New York. He raced a bright yellow fiberglass replica of a 1923 Model T Ford convertible powered by a supercharged, alcohol burning 396 cubic inch Chrysler Hemi

Engine. It was a fearsome and exciting site to see his car thunder down the track, followed by billowing clouds of smoke from the burning rubber of the spinning tires. A very difficult car to control, it launched like a rocket and wandered down the quarter-mile track in a snake-like fashion reaching speeds of 180 miles per hour in a scant 7 seconds. He was the car to beat when he was able to control the car.

"Hey, Jerry! It looks like you're having a good night." Art shouted over the noisy crowd and buzz on the racing track.

"Yeah, I! So far, I beat Dee, Boye, and Crow." Replied Jerry with his gruff hoarse voice.

"Yeah, I know, Jerry. Looks like I'll have to run against you in the final." He said it with a little smirk. It showed that despite their differences, they both got along pretty well. It's not necessary that making friends requires more similarities than differences because friendship is all about accepting the other person the way they are.

"Look Dinick, I'll tell you something, I broke the high gear in the transmission on the last run, and I don't have the parts to fix it. You've got the win in the bag, so save your

engine and take it easy on the run against me. For me to collect runner-up money, I have to stage against you. When I get the green light, I'll start just like it's a real race, and only we know it isn't. I'll burn my tires across the starting line, but then I'll shut it down. All you have to do, Dinick, is to just make an easy run across the finish line to collect the win money. If I tell the tower that I'm broke and can't make the final, they'll reinstate Boye on the break rule, and I won't be able to collect the runner-up money. Did you get it?"

The broken rule was a rule used by the local track. This would permit the loser of the previous round to race again. That was if the winner of that round broke and could not race again. Art thanked Jerry for telling him. He had known and raced against Jerry on many occasions during the past seven years and had no reason to not trust him, but Art had never made an easy run in his life.

He only made full out runs. Every race he had ever made was at full speed, stressing the car and his driving skills to the limit. Art only knew how to give his best effort on each and every run. The tower summoned them to the starting line. It was not in his nature to underperform, but he would make an exception for his friend. After all, friendship over everything.

"Dinick and McTaggard, report to the starting line for the final round in competition eliminator!" the announcer proclaimed on the loudspeaker. As Art pulled his dragster into the staging lanes, he was still wrestling with himself. Should he take it easy on the run against McTaggard, or should he make a full-out run and risk blowing his motor or breaking his transmission or rear end? As Art pulled up to the starting line, he glanced over at Jerry. Jerry gave him the okay signal with his right hand.

Art was now confused. He wondered if the okay sign meant that Jerry's car was okay and that he had fixed the transmission or if he meant it was okay for Art to make an easy run as they had discussed. Art thought for a second and concluded that most likely, Jerry couldn't have fixed the transmission, but what if he did.

What should he do? Art brought the engine revs up to 7000 rpm. The huge 427 cubic inch motor was screaming. The starting lights started to come down. Amber, amber, and then the green light flashed, and he let the clutch out and floored the throttle. Instantaneously, Art decided that he had to give it his best and make the full-out run. Art was even with McTaggard for a few seconds. McTaggard's tires were burning wildly, and so were Art's. Suddenly, Art shot ahead of McTaggard but hit a slick spot on the track.

Before Art regained control of his car, his left rear tire just kissed the center dividing line. Art crossed the finish line, pulled the parachute, and came to a safe stop.

It was a fast run - his fastest of the night. Russ, his partner, pulled behind him in the push truck. Art unstrapped his helmet and climbed out of the cockpit of the car.

"What happened to McTaggard?" Art asked.

"His car stopped about halfway down the track, and he got out of it. Then he started pushing it across the finish line".

"Why?" Art asked.

"He doesn't have to push it across the finish line to collect runner up money. The tower disqualified you for touching the center dividing line and declared that McTaggard would be the winner if he could get his car across the finish line."

"They can't do that; I didn't cross the center line." Art argued.

"I know," said Russ, *"but they still disqualified you, and there's nothing you or I can do about it."* He said solemnly.

Art knew there was nothing he could do about it. Jerry got the win money, and Art got runner-up money. When they got back into the pits, Jerry ran up to Art—panting frantically. He seemed to be in fury and rage, charging towards Art with a vengeance in his stare.

"What the hell did you do, Dinick? I told you I was broken. All you had to do was make an easy run to get the win money. You had it in the bag."

"I know Jerry," Art replied, *"but I just couldn't make a slow run. I had to give it my best."*

"Well, giving it your best cost you the win," Jerry said with a sigh.

"Yeah, I know, but you would've done the same thing if you were in my place, Jerry. I've never seen you take it easy on a run."

"Yeah, I guess I would've," he admitted.

That was the last time Art ever saw Jerry. A month later, Art learned that Jerry was killed when his race car crashed at a track in upstate New York. Jerry was probably giving it his best. Was it destined for his life to end this way? Was Art's life going to end today the same way on a race track?

Big Black and Bad?

Art had just spent the evening at Steve's welding shop, working on the race car. Steve's shop was located in a run-down section of Passaic, New Jersey, a section of town where you really didn't want to be by yourself after dark. It was now eleven o'clock, and Steve was closing for the night. Art walked through the dimly lit parking lot to his car and got in.

He started the motor and backed down the long dark alleyway to the street. As he was just about to back into the street, out of the corner of his eye, he spied someone standing at the back of his car, waving his arms furiously. For an instant, Art thought it was someone from Steve's that he knew. He stopped backing up. The fellow stepped quickly to the side of his car, yanked open the door with lightning-quick speed, sat down in the passenger seat next to Art, and slammed the door closed. Art's mouth dropped open. The fellow was a huge black man about 6'6" tall who weighed at least 250 lbs. He was ugly and extremely tough looking. He had a large scar across his cheek. Art's heart started pounding. Was this it? Was he going to be stabbed or just brutally beat to a pulp? Art tried to muster up some confidence.

He had just completed an evening course in karate at the local high school. Would he get the chance to try out what he learned now? Would it work? Art tried to convince himself that if he could give him a karate chop in the right spot, he would be all right. But where was the right spot? He was towering over Art. He was massive. He was gigantic, and he was ugly.

Fear was beginning to get the better part of Art. He could feel the sweat drench his skin, his eyes throbbing with the influx of blood, and the thumping of his heart against his chest like it was caged, trying to escape. He curled his fingers into a wrist, and the nails were digging into his palms with nervousness. Although he wasn't breathing rapidly out loud, he could feel the oxygen flooding in and out of his lungs. He tried to maintain his cool and let no signs of trepidation overcome me. He tried not to show any fear so that the stranger wouldn't take advantage of the situation. The black man opened his mouth and started to talk.

"Hey man, you got anything to drink?" "Drink? *No. No, I don't have anything to drink.*" Art tried not to let his fear show through. He expected him to next ask for money, but he didn't.

"Well then, man, how about giving me a lift to Willie's Bar?" he said casually.

"*Willie's bar? Yea, sure,*" Art said while waiting for him to draw a knife, pursing his lips to contain his apprehension.

"*Where is Willie's Bar? How do I get there*?" Art asked suspiciously. He did not want to rule out the possibility of no imminent danger lurking around the corner.

"Okay, man, I'll tell you how. Just follow my directions, and you'll do okay," he said, acting totally normal as if he had not invaded anyone's private space, whatsoever.

Up and down the dark, deserted side streets they went. Art kept one eye on him and one on the road. Where are the cops when you need them? Art kept looking for an opportunity to jump out of the car, but none came. Art kept telling himself, "*just give him a shot in the nose if he starts to make a move,*" but his mind told him that probably all he would end up doing would be to injure his hand in the attempt. The fear traveled up Art's veins, and he could feel his whole body become numb and his nerves freaking him out. He managed to let it reach his skin or facial muscles. He tried to keep a calm demeanor and had his eyes fixated on the road ahead.

They finally got to Willie's. Art expected to be greeted by a bunch of the man's cohorts who would surely beat the shit out of him and then fight among themselves for what little money Art had in his wallet. The possibilities of him being mugged were high, and he was mentally prepared for it. He was just trying to maintain this poker face to keep his emotions from translating onto his face.

"*Thanks, man,*" he said. "*You're okay for a white dude. Come on in with me, and we'll get a few drinks and some pussy,*" he said.

Art's heart stopped pounding. He wasn't going to be maimed. All the man wanted was a ride to the bar. The fear that had previously overtaken him vanished into thin air, and he heaved a sigh of relief. He wiped the drops of sweat from his forehead and made peace with his situation. He had indeed been over-thinking a lot, and the images that he was building in his mind were all a figment of his imagination. The guy did not have any malicious intentions and was only looking for a lift to the bar along with some fun

"*No, thanks,*" Art said. "*I have to go home,*" trying to get out of there as soon as possible

"Ah, man, come on. You ain't had anything until you had some black pussy," he said with a sly smile.

"*No, that's okay,*" Art said. "*I really have to go.*"

"Well, okay, man. It's your loss. I really do thank you for the lift," he said as he popped out of the car and slammed his door shut.

Art breathed a sigh of relief as he pulled away. I guess big and black doesn't necessarily also mean bad.

***

Meanwhile, in another world – Joy's side!

Joy moved into an apartment with three of Kim's friends in Los Angeles. She managed to get a job as a waitress in a go-go bar and was learning to live the carefree lifestyle of a bimbo with no responsibilities in life. One of her roommates kept a partially closed, sleepy eye on little Pat while Joy was working, or more often, cavorting around. Now, for the first time in her life, she was free to do whatever she wanted when she wanted. No parents or husband was there to place demands on her time.

Her only burden was little Pat, but, for the time being, her girl-friends served as full-time nannies. She had always wanted to live a life of freedom and not be bound by any cultural or family restrictions. Now when she was finally living her dream, everything seemed to materialize in front of her, and she was a free bird ready to take the world by storm.

Art tried to get custody of little Pat, but it went in vain as Joy refused to give him up. After several months, however, her newfound freedom was brought to an abrupt end by a court order obtained by Art's attorney. Forced to return with little Pat to New Jersey, she reluctantly settled into her mother's house to take advantage of having another full-time nanny for Pat. She slept days and spent evenings hanging out at the Melody Bar in Atlantic City. This arrangement was short-lived for obvious reasons. Joy's mother didn't relish the idea of being saddled with the full-time responsibility of caring for a baby. She was at a stage when she herself was in quest of some support. Living at home was also cramping Joy's pursuit of pleasure and happiness. Her mother started giving her a scolding about dancing and partying all night and dragging her ass home in the wee hours of the morning like a stray cat in heat.

Her culpable negligence and evasion of duty was now unbearable for her mother, and she refused to put up with her carefree attitude. Her actions were nowhere close to being a mother, and if she didn't turn over a new leaf, it wouldn't be long enough before everyone gave up on her because of her attitude.

Joy soon saw the light and decided her life would be much easier if she gave Art the custody of little Pat. Now free of all burdens and responsibilities, she moved out of her mother's house and into an efficiency apartment in the Ventnor Motel. It was a long hard struggle, but now Art finally had custody of his little boy. However, now that he had Pat, what was he going to do with him? How was Art going to raise him? He couldn't afford a maid, and he couldn't even find a baby sitter to take care of Pat during the day while he worked. Art's job required him to travel frequently to refineries all over the world. What could he do with Pat when he was away on a business trip? Art found himself in a position which was a tough nut to crack. As much as he loved his son, he was in a fix when it came to juggling being a businessman and a father.

Art now came to the sad realization that he couldn't raise Pat by himself, so he turned to his mom and dad for help. The only problem was that mom and dad lived in Atlantic City, and Art lived 115 miles away from them in North Jersey. They readily agreed to raise Pat, and every possible weekend Art made the tiring trip to Atlantic City to visit him.

Sometimes, life puts us in a situation where we are forced to make some decisions for it to keep going smoothly. Art wanted to give his son the comfort of a real home where he would be looked after by his blood relations, so he had to take this decision of having his parents raise Pat with a heavy heart. No love can be compared to that of a loved one. Even though Art had to take this cumbersome journey every week, it was worth it.

Tony, a Fork in the Road

Art was 25 years old. His wife had deserted him, and for all practical purposes, his little boy was gone. Arts parents were raising little Pat, and Art could only get down to Atlantic City to see him on the weekends. He was in the middle of a custody battle. He was hurt, depressed, lonely, and feeling sorry for himself. Loneliness was like a vice on his heart, squeezing with just enough pressure that it persisted like a constant prick in the heart.

Every day the pain would increase just a little bit more, and he would be struggling for fresh air. Even his old buddies, most of whom were now happily married, couldn't seem to cheer him up. When you're down, you're really down, and nothing seems to go right. The one or two dates he managed to get were with real losers. He was beginning to feel that that's all there was out there.

All the women of his choice were either married or engaged. No one that he was attracted to seemed to want to go out with him. Art thought he was doomed to be a lonely bachelor for the rest of his life. Loneliness is something that chips away at your liveliness and swallows you in one hole, depriving you of every ounce of hope that you once exercised. It feeds off your happiness, leaving an empty void inside you, full of despondency and certain memories that you cannot keep inside you anymore. It's like keeping your heart tightly clenched into claws, squeezing the very energy out of you, sucking the very energy out of you, and constricting blood flow. You crave a warm embrace and a supporting shoulder to cry on.

One Saturday night, Art and his old buddy Voodoo were sitting at the bar in Gables Night Club on the Gold Coast in Margate, New Jersey. If you were young and single, it was the place to be on a Saturday night in the summer. The place was packed, and everyone except Art was having a great time. Young, good looking women were everywhere, but what good was that. In Art's mind, they were all probably going with someone or, if by chance, some of them weren't, they wouldn't be interested in him anyway.

He was a loser; He was worthless, and nobody would ever be interested in someone as worthless as him. He was a boiling pot of sadness and hopelessness. Every other emotion seemed to be pushed out of his body. Every inch of him that was formerly filled with the light, the love and the laughter of his wonderful life, was now aching in hollowness. A good looking woman pushed her way through the crowd and paused next to Voodoo. She seemed familiar. Art knew her but couldn't quite remember from where or when.

"Hi, Voodoo. How are you doing?"

Turning to Art, she asked, "*How have you been? It's been a long time.*" She said with an easy-going, friendly tone. No girl had talked to Art like that in a long time.

Suddenly the cobwebs which clouded his memory were swept away. How could he have ever forgotten her?

"Hi, Tony. It has been a long time," he reciprocated with equal enthusiasm and fervor in his voice.

Art first met Tony when he was 19 years old. She was a pretty girl with long blonde hair and big blue eyes, and now she was a beautiful woman. They had dated a couple of times, but for some reason or other, never got serious.

"I'm okay, I guess, but things haven't really been going well for me. Joy left me and took my little boy with her."

I know she replied, *"I ran into Ray a couple of weeks ago, and he told me about it. I'm so sorry for you,"* She said nonchalantly.

"What about you, Tony? How have you been?" "Oh, I'm fine," she said. *"I'm working in a hospital."*

"You and Tom ever get married?" Art queried hesitatingly, fearing the answer.

"No, we were engaged for the longest time, but it just didn't work out," she admitted in a 'matter-of-fact' kind of *way.*

"Are you going with anybody now?" asked Art in an undertone to not sound very nosy.

"No, not seriously," she said. *"Once in a while, I go out with a fellow from the hospital."* She seemed to be quite chill about it, and it didn't seem to bother her much. Maybe she had gotten enough time to get past this stage in her life, and she had moved on.

Sometimes, it's only about taking that one leap of faith that will liberate you from ruminating on your past and finally find your true self in the process. She sat down next to Art, and they talked about old friends, old times and new. Time passed quickly. Art soon forgot how bad things were and how miserable he was. He hadn't felt this way in a long time. Something about her presence was calming and soothing for Art's soul. The good vibes helped calm the inner storm inside him. Even though they were just making casual conversation, there was something about the time spent that made him feel at home. A person who had been lonely for so long had finally felt the warmth in someone's company. It was like his old self had been ignited, and he wished he could feel that way more often.

At 2 A.M., he drove her home. She was still living at her parents' home a couple of miles away. They parked outside just as they had done years ago and talked for hours. Time seemed to be fleeting by, and he didn't want the moment to stop existing. Everything was so pleasant and straightforward for a change. Just as the first rays of sunlight broke over the horizon, they kissed good night and made a date for Sunday afternoon. Art went home to his mom's house; he was a much happier man now.

Tony and Art dated regularly every weekend. Saturday and Sunday afternoons were shared with little Pat. They swam and frolicked in the rough waters of the ocean and built sandcastles on the beach. They took long walks in the woods, enjoyed quiet picnics by smooth mirror lakes and babbling brooks, or shared breathtaking adventures on the wild rides of the amusement piers on the boardwalk. Saturday evenings, however, were reserved for just the two of them, quiet candlelit dinners, slow dancing to romantic music in one of the little out of the way clubs, romantic walks on the deserted beaches, or rock and roll to the loud heart-pounding music of one of the Gold Coast clubs.

The two were young and falling in love. Art was in love all over again; Tony would never leave his mind. She was always there mentally, if not in person. The feeling was inexplicable and incomprehensible. She seemed to be the only constant in her life and the ray of sunshine that had given him hope to start fresh. In a world full of chaos, she was something he desperately needed in his life. He believed that life had given him a second chance in the form of Tony.

She was a ray of sunshine in his dark, troubled world. The weekends were great, but the weekdays were the pits. Art dreaded the arrival of Sunday nights and the long drive to North Jersey, where Art lived and worked. It was just too far away. A long-distance romance over the phone was difficult and painful, but she had her job, and he had his, and neither one could readily move. Art was legally separated from Joy and well on his way to getting a divorce. All the necessary legal papers were filed. He already had custody of his son and only had to wait for the formality of a court hearing for the Judge to grant a legal divorce.

Art was seeing Tony every weekend and was falling in love deeper with her. What more could he ask for? Too many long and lonely weeknights, too much time to think. His conscience started to play a number on him. All of the years of his Catholic education went to work on him. What good was a legal divorce? In the eyes of the Catholic Church, he would still be married.

From the very early days of his Catholic education in a Catholic grammar school, it was drummed into him that you could only get married once and only once. He couldn't escape. Over and over again in his mind, he reflected on his wedding and the struggle he went through to make his wedding vows.

"Do you, Arthur, take this woman, Joy, to be your wife for better, for worse until death do you part?"

"Well, no, not for worse. I don't know. Maybe, I'm not sure," he thought.

Art didn't know how to answer. He knew he was supposed to answer with a loud, clear 'yes,' but he couldn't. He started to think of all the ramifications. What's she going to be like in five or ten years? She's impulsive and has a nasty temper. It seems like she always has to have things her way; we never seem to agree on anything.

'She could be a really difficult person to live with, and I'll be stuck with her until I die. How can I be expected to live with someone for the rest of his life that I don't get along with? I don't know, I just don't know, we're friends, and I love her, I think. I'm so confused. I'm just not ready to get married. What am I going to be like in five or ten years? How do I know I'll want to stay married to her for the rest of my life? That's a very long time. We may drift apart and have nothing in common. We may get completely bored with each other. Maybe I'm just scared now; perhaps it's too big a commitment to make now. Maybe everybody feels this same way when they get married.'

All these thoughts storming in made Art's mind take spins. Art never talked about this with anyone and did not know if it was normal to feel this way. How could he agree to stay married to her for the rest of his life? Too many things could go wrong. Why do we only get one chance for this thing? We could be making a big mistake when choosing someone, he thought. *"Shit! The priest is looking at me and waiting for an answer. Joy is waiting for an answer. Everybody in the church is waiting for an answer."* His silence was beginning to be obvious. What am I going to do? He wanted to say, 'no, I'm not ready! I'm not sure. I need more time to think about this.' But he couldn't. It would be too embarrassing. He came this far; he had to go through with it. He had to say yes and hope for the best.

Well, the best didn't come about; the worst did. His worst fears were realized, and now, he could never get married again. He believed he was doomed to lead the lonely life of a single person or else stay married to someone he didn't get along with, and all because he was born a Catholic and made a vow to stay married for the rest of his life. He pondered, *"Why does the Catholic Church want me to live with someone I don't get along with? Why do I have to live with her or else live by myself for the rest of his life? It doesn't make any sense to me. Why wasn't I born a Presbyterian or Methodist? If I was, then I could get married again. They get a second chance, but I don't. It's not fair. It's just not fair."*

He struggled with these thoughts in his mind, but he couldn't make peace with himself even though he believed that the church was just plain wrong. Too many years of blind, unquestioning obedience to the rules of the church had to be overcome. He couldn't really convince his conscience that the church was following archaic rules it developed centuries ago to hold a family together in times when women and children would have been destitute and helpless if their husbands left them.

That was the situation 2000 years ago, but that was not the situation today in the 20th Century. Women are no longer helpless. The husband no longer has to hunt for food for the family. Women today can survive quite well without husbands, and with alimony and child support, they can even survive much better than their ex-husbands. Art, however, was fighting a losing battle with myself.

So, if he didn't want to live by himself for the rest of his life, he had to patch things up with Joy. No matter how difficult it would be, he had to patch them up. He had no other choice. Sometimes in life, you have two paths – the right and the left. It might be a struggle between your heart and mind, and the outcomes can be drastically different. Just like in Art's case, he could either choose to mend ways with Joy and stay true to his vows that he made to her as a Catholic. The other path would require him to go with his heart and live with the woman with whom he was happy with. He would give himself another chance and live his life to the fullest. However, choices cannot be undone.

Like they say, time heals everything. Even though things had deteriorated between Art and Joy to the extent that there was no going back, Art was left with no choice but to accept whatever fate had decided for him.

Irreparable damage had been done, but if they were to raise Pat as a healthy child, they had to meet midway and unanimously decide upon how they would take things ahead from now. Parents have a big responsibility to shoulder when it comes to their kids, and they have to act as mature adults if they do not want the mental health of their child to suffer.

Enough time had now passed. The bitterness and anger he had felt over Joy's leaving without warning had gradually subsided. She had given him custody of Pat, and he no longer felt any animosity towards her. Pat was living with his parents in Atlantic City, and Art only got to see him on weekends. Art missed not being able to see him during the week, but without having a wife, he had no way of taking care of him. Even though his parents gave little Pat all their love and care, Joy was the only one that would enable little Pat to grow up in a normal family environment. Art did not want Pat to have a disturbing childhood and internalize these feelings to become someone rebellious and stubborn in the future. Hence, for the sake of his child, he was ready to make things work between him and Joy. Life doesn't always give chances, but when it does, you need to have the maturity to avail it and make the best of it.

Mentally confused and lonely, Art began to think more fondly of Joy and started to wonder how much he really contributed to the failure of their marriage. He was no longer sure. Time had changed a lot between them. Just like your anger subsides and you start thinking clearly, the same had transpired between Art and Joy.

Realization is something that can completely change the way you think as you start seeing things in a totally different light. He began to think of times gone by, and the little girl that used to follow him around when he was a teenager. He began to remember the good times' Joy and he had together in those carefree days of long ago. Going down memory lane had been quite overwhelming. The rush of bitter-sweet memories enveloped him in a blanket of reminiscing, instantly making him realize what he had lost. He wondered how it would have been, had their marriage not fallen apart, and they would still be sharing a life together. Nostalgia hit him hard, but all he could do was bask in the memories.

Art phoned Joy one day and asked her if she would like him to bring Pat over to her apartment for a visit. Art had given in to his heart and mind who kept urging him to bring back those sweet, dreamy days when love was what held them together, not Pat. But their son was his only excuse left to spend quality time together as they both let go of those bitter-sweet times.

She said: *"Yes, sure! Why not? You're most welcome. I would love to have both of you over."*

"Okay! Then I'll be there by 12 noon," said Art ecstatically.

"Sure, what would you like to have for lunch? Your favorite cheese Bolognese and apple pie?" she asked casually.

That moment hit like anything. Art spiraled into thinking about all those times Joy cooked for him and some of the good times they had shared. He wished he could go back in time somehow and restart his life with Joy.

While they were visiting, they started to discuss their problems and what went wrong with their marriage. They reminisced about the past. In time, his visits became more frequent, and they even went out on a few dates. They seemed to be getting along much better. They stopped arguing and actually managed to have good times during their dates. After several months, Art and Joy agreed that for the sake of little Pat, they should try again to live together as a family.

They had been seeing each other for quite some time now and were more accepting of the changes that had come with time. Maybe, the time that they had gotten apart from each other had helped them understand where they were going wrong. Absence really does make the heart grow fonder. Spending time with each other had rekindled the spark within them, and they were ready to give each other another chance. For old time's sake and for the feelings that they once harbored for each other! Young first love and a lovable little child is an inexplicable feeling that makes a man do things a rational person would not do, but the hope that in the end, it may be all.

The last vestiges of crimson and gold leaves had all but disappeared from the trees, and there was a chill in the air. With sadness in his heart and tears in his eyes, Art told Tony of his decision to patch up his marriage with Joy. She was hurting as much as him. She pleaded with him and even offered to give up her job and move to North Jersey, but Art couldn't be swayed.

He loved her, but too many years of Catholic education with blind obedience to the church had to be overcome. His conscience dictated that he had to try with Joy again. Did he really have the ability to change his decision, or was it decided for him by fate? He was adamant about keeping the past behind him and embarking on a new journey for the sake of their son, Pat. Sometimes, in life, you've got to make a conscious effort to turn things in your favor.

Chapter 8
Bottom of the big Corporation Totam Poll

Joy moved back to the apartment in North Jersey, and they managed to live together as a typical young family. Art and Joy still had arguments but managed to survive them. Every once in a while, her temper would flare up, and she would go stomping out of the apartment only to return in a few hours after she calmed down, back to where she felt at home. Just like most young married couples, they too were smitten with the great American dream.

The typical idea of a well-settled and happy family seemed too good to be true. They had longed to have their very own home in the country. Skimping and saving, they eventually managed to scrape together the $2000.00 needed for a down payment on a small house.

With bittersweet memories, they packed their possessions, bid adieu to their crazy neighbors and the carefree lifestyle of garden apartment living, and moved into their new house in the beautiful rolling hills of northern New Jersey. Joy, who had been dreaming for these days, easily settled into the role of the suburban housewife. She occupied her spare time with gardening and long chats over morning coffee with the other housewives in the neighborhood. While she was busy with domestic chores, socializing, and taking care of Pat, Art was busy traveling around the world, solving Exxon's problems. Clearly, being the breadwinner of the house wasn't easy, but he had to make ends meet. This was his second chance at his marriage, and he did not want to blow it up like that.

He did not want to go through the emotional turmoil of letting it all go down the drain after making concerted efforts to build it all up again. After a couple of years' boredom set in, and Joy got tired of the routine household chores and morning chats with the neighborhood women. The perfect idea of having another addition to the family popped in her head.

The thought of it alone sent a wave of excitement down her spine. She started imaging all that could improve with the entry of another baby into their life. And so, without discussing her thoughts or desires with Art, she took control of the situation, stopped taking the pill, and managed to become pregnant.

Hurry Up and Wait

With the cold breeze and golden hues, Joy had really been feeling under the weather. As she took care of Pat while staying at home in New Jersey, waiting for Art to come back so that she could surprise him! Meanwhile, Art was in Stenungsund, Sweden, finishing up an inspection job on a reactor that he had designed.

He had been working there for about three weeks and couldn't wait to go back home to his supportive family. One after noon at 3 o'clock, Al, his boss, called him down to his office. Art had sensed something was wrong, and whenever his boss called him up, it was nothing but trouble. It made him upset and nervous. *"What's the problem now, Al?"*

Al didn't waste another minute and upsettingly stated: *"Our plant in France has a serious problem. They have to shut down their reactors every few days to clean them out. It costs the company millions of dollars in lost production."*

Art was confused, *"I know that, Al. But, there's already a task force there studying the problem. They've been there for over three months. They must be making some progress. Why the sudden panic?"*

And what Al said after that shocked Art, *"Headquarters wants it solved now. They think this thing has dragged out too long. You have to get the 7 o'clock plane to Paris tonight. They want you to be in the plant in Gravenshon, working the problem by 8 a.m. tomorrow morning."*

Art felt trapped and anxious; he was expecting to spend the next couple of days finishing up what he was working on in Sweden and relax with Joy and Pat by the weekend. Heat rose to his cheeks as he turned red with frustration.

"Holy shit, Al! Thanks for all the warning! You sure didn't give me much time!" he shouted back.

"Sorry, but I'm only following orders. I want Headquarters and the back seat managers in Florham Park, New Jersey off my back."

Art had no time to waste if he was going to make the 7 o'clock flight to Paris. He made a quick call to a travel agent and a trip to the plant cashier for a cash advance. With a heavy heart, he called Joy to tell her that he was going to France for a couple of weeks and wouldn't be able to make it home on the weekend. She was upset, but there was nothing Art could do about it other than feel guilt and regret.

Rushing back to his hotel, he quickly stuffed all his possessions into his suitcase. He then made the forty-mile mad dash to the airport in Gothenburg in his rental car through the rush hour traffic. Arriving at the airport with no time to spare, he rushed through customs and sprinted to the gate just in time to get onto the plane during the last call for boarding. Life had been pretty much a race for Art for the past few months.

He was expected to make sudden business trips, and he couldn't turn them down because that is where he was getting the money to the run house. With the recent down payment made for the new house, the couple did not have any space to make a mistake or lose their source of income. They had built their dreams from scratch, and they wanted no piece of the puzzle to go missing.

The plane landed at Orly Airport in Paris at about 9 p.m. After clearing customs, Art took a cab into Paris to the train station. Since he had been told to rush over as soon as possible, he could only hope for things to go smoothly. And you could say he spoke too quickly. It was about 11:30 p.m. when he got there. And to his despair, the station master informed him that the last train of the evening to be Rouen had just departed. The next train would be at 6 a.m. in the morning. Exasperated, Art ran his fingers through his ruffled hair and limply dragged them over his tired face. *"What am I going to do?"* he thought as he rummaged through his jumbled thoughts. He couldn't very well spend the night in the train station.

He didn't know any hotels in Paris either. After he gave it some thought, he remembered that a friend had once mentioned that he had stayed at a hotel called the Prince DeGaulle Hotel off the Champs de Elysee. With some difficulty, Art managed to communicate the destination he had in his mind to a taxi driver who refused to speak any English. The cab arrived at the hotel at about 12:30 a.m. Art registered at the front desk and ordered a 5 a.m. wake-up call.

Now, however, although extremely exhausted, he couldn't get to sleep. His sleepless night was filled with longing and disturbing thoughts; even the doors down the hall were banging as people were coming and going like it was the middle of the afternoon. Art was drained but wide awake when the wake-up finally came. He caught the taxi cab to the train station. Again to his dismay, he was informed by the station master that today was some sort of holiday and that the 6 a.m. train to Rouen would not leave until 8 a.m. Art, totally fatigued, had no energy left to throw an annoyed tantrum instead stretched out on a hard wooden bench in the station and managed to catch a 'cat nap.' It was around 10 a.m. when the train pulled into the old red brick station in Rouen.

The plant, however, was located in Gravenchon, a small town in Normandy approximately 50 miles from Rouen, and the only transportation available was a cab. Art was stuck with using a combination of body language, a few French words, and scribbling diagrams on a piece of scratch paper. At some point, he succeeded in communicating his desired destination to the cab driver.

He finally reached the gate that leads to the plant when he was faced with yet one more setback. The guard didn't speak any English, and Art couldn't communicate with him. His arsenal of a few French words, body language-hand gestures, and writing were of no help. After several minutes of writing and pronouncing his contact, John Pierre, an infinite number of times he managed to find out that John Pierre wasn't there because of the holiday.

At this point, he felt like pulling out all his hair from his head. Had he known what he was getting himself into, he would not have agreed in the first place. Depressed, Art now took the cab to the Hotel De La Petite Campagne, fondly known to everyone as the Celibataire. It was a hotel owned and operated by the company. There the plant male bachelor employees lived a celibate existence in solitude.

It was also where male company visitors, like Art himself, who didn't know better, would stay. When he arrived, the hotel was just about deserted. The only person to be seen was Gunther Hillman, an engineer from Exxon's plant in Germany. He was there as a member of the international task force that was working on the problem. *"Where is everybody?"* Art asked, emotionlessly.

"Today is a holiday, the Feast of all Saints, so everyone's gone. They won't be back until Monday morning."

"Monday! Its only Thursday," Art replied in a panic.

"Yes, and there is nothing we can do about it," Gunther replied rather calmly. *"When the French take a holiday, they really take a holiday,"* he added with a slight chuckle. Art was furious would be an understatement. A turmoil of mixed

emotions was eating him up from inside. All the rushing, planes, trains, and cabs and missed sleep to get here. Now, all he could do was sit and wait for four days while the French were off vacationing or playing in their houses. It wasn't worth anything, especially when Art hadn't seen his family in weeks and desperately missed them. *"Come on, don't be upset, man,"* Gunther said. *"We'll go to Paris for the weekend, and I'll show you a Paris that you have never seen."*

Gunther had a flair for the theatrical. He liked that extra emotion and drama in life that undoubtedly gave Art some consolation. Everything was done in a grand style with lots of pomp and ceremony. They left the hotel and the sleepy little village of Notre Dame De Gravenchon at 2 p.m. in the afternoon and headed for Paris.

Art was so emotionally and physically worn-out that he didn't even protest. Perhaps it was life's way of giving him a break because there are never enough breaks to compensate for all those expected or unexpected hurdles that may come in your way. Gunther was only a source with whom he could just stop and take that much-needed breath of fresh air - a breath that could instill a feeling of rejuvenation and harmony. Gunther drove down the winding roads and through the little villages at an astonishing speed of over 100 miles per hour. He must have thought he was driving in the Monte Carlo Grand Prix. Nonetheless, they miraculously reached Paris by 3:45, unscathed. Like an expert, he continued to drive through the crowded streets and around the Arc De Triomphe.

It reassured Art since it seemed like he knew exactly where he was going. Even the crazy French drivers and their blaring horns didn't faze him. He was in total control as if he was the Red Baron of the highways. Soon he drove to the top of a hill in the center of Paris, a place known as Montmartre. Gunther showed Art around "his Paris," which surprisingly felt like being accompanied by a very close childhood friend who could oddly make you feel at home.

Art was confused yet enjoyed as if he just hadn't had a crisis and felt like murdering someone. Notre Dame Cathedral in Paris is a popular tourist spot because of its grandeur and breath-taking state of the Art monuments. It also depicts the whole controversy about Catholics and Protestants but on the hill was the Church of the Sacre Couer, which is known for its beauty and cultural value. In the streets and alleyways surrounding the church, the starving young French artists spent their days developing their artistic skills painting scenes from the surrounding area. This made Art realize about the countless blessings that were bestowed upon him, without him even asking. If he hadn't chose to patch things up with Joy, he would have never understood life more practically and maturely. If he didn't have this job, then he wouldn't be here.

This part of Paris made him appreciate and be grateful for the immense opportunities and joys (pun intended) life had thrown his way. Gunther stopped the car in the plaza in front of the church. He threw open the doors of the vehicle, rushed around to his side of the car, grabbed Art by the arm, and took him over to the wall on the precipice of the hill, which overlooked the city. Then, in a dramatic theatrical gesture, he threw his arms into the air like an ancient conqueror and said, *"Here, Dinick, I give you all of Paris!"*

"You gave me all of Paris, indeed!" Art laughed. As a matter of fact, his grandiose gestures made Art forget all the frustration of his futile rush to France. The bright orange sun shone over the mesmerizing city of love. It felt like every day Paris came to life with its people and extraordinary

features. It was almost as if he could hear Paris humming a melodious tune that sends a wave of peace and bliss all over the land. Standing here on the hill weirdly gave him confidence. Earlier today, he had felt defeated and tiresome. But somehow, just a few hours later and a change in the atmosphere had completely uplifted his spirit. *"I can do this,"* he thought.

After all, how often in a lifetime do you get to meet a character like this? It made him laugh at how easygoing, and comfortable Gunther had made him feel. Back in his school days, he had been a quiet, shy kid who would not speak in front of the class despite knowing the correct answer. After roaming around a bit for about an hour and Gunther exaggerating at how Art had never seen the Eiffel tower, it was already dinner time.

Gunther, yet again, left Art speechless with his knowledge about Paris and the French language. Art had observed and concluded that either Gunther had stayed in Paris for a considerable time, or it's clearly his dream place. He had such clear pronunciation while speaking French as well as had knowledge about almost everything from its cuisines to the holidays. They drove to a small but crowded restaurant on one of the out of the wayside streets. No empty tables available, but that didn't faze Gunther. Instead, like always, he had some tricks up his sleeve as he made his way towards a table of four that was occupied by two young French ladies. With little fluent French words and his versatile nature, he managed to get him and Art the remaining two seats. The show wasn't over, and Gunther played along, trying to impress the women.

Art, as usual, was dumbfounded since he only knew a handful of French words, not even enough to read the menu. Being a local restaurant, the waiters didn't speak English at all. So obviously, Gunther translated for Art, and being the lively, fun personality he was, decided to act fancier.

While Art was relieved to recognize at least one word, *"tornados"* written in the menu, which meant steak, he also chose a flavor that seemed more familiar than the others. With that being said, Gunther called over the waiter to give their order except in more Germanized French. Which confused the waiter, but it made the ladies on the table giggle. While they waited for dinner, Gunther kept reassuring Art that he shouldn't worry about such trivial things. However, he failed to kill two birds with one stone, and what they got served was far from what the German French had anticipated. A well-done steak for Art was not the issue but a rabbit cooked in red wine sauce was.

After returning to the Celibataire, and eating that rabbit, Gunther was stuck in his room with a severe case of dysentery that made him take trips to the restroom more often than he wanted to.

I guess the mighty German wasn't really as fluent in French as he thought he was. Time seemed to fly by, and Monday morning came all too soon. The weekend of French food had taken its toll on the mighty German system. Gunther had contracted a severe case of dysentery and had to spend the next week in his room close to a toilet.

The French member of the task force was next to useless. After he spent most of his time arranging his lunch, dinner, and social schedule, Art decided that he was going to have to work by myself to solve the problem if he was to ever get out of there. Art inspected the reactors but found nothing physically wrong with them. He then had the feed analyzed for several contaminants, which could cause this type of problem, but there was none present. He was puzzled but not ready to give up. After an intensive study of the data and some calculations, he concluded that the operators were shutting down the reactors prematurely because of some changes in operating conditions. In fact, they really didn't have to be shut down, but the operators were reacting to fear. Instead of normalizing the operating condition, they shut the reactors down in panic. After only a week of intensive work, Art managed to solve the problem that the entire task force hadn't made a dent in after three months of study. Now we know why Art was given the position that he was in, and his availability at the last moment was more important than ever.

His intellectual and analytical mind made him the go-to person to brainstorm problems and advice sustainable solutions for the longevity of the firm. Art explained his analysis of the problem and his solution to Messieurs Pascal, the plant manager. That established his position in the eyes of the management, stronger than ever.

Pascal, a kindly natured distinguished-looking older gentleman, questioned Art intensively. After showing him the data which supported his position and answering all his questions, he was satisfied that Art had drawn the correct conclusions. Art had the knack of doing things with extreme precision and left no stone unturned in making sure that his claims and analysis were backed by proper stats and figures. His eye for detail and ability to manage things to the tee gave him an upper-hand over the other employees. His findings were never misleading and made sure that he proved his credibility.

"Thank you, Dinick. You have done remarkable work. I am convinced that you are right, but I am a bit surprised that you have developed such a simple solution to what appears to be such a complicated problem. You may leave France at your discretion, but we must first call Florham Park and explain your conclusions to the managers there." Pascal told Art with a grateful smile.

He commended him for his hard work and commitment to work out a palatable solution in an attempt to solve the problem that had halted production and was impacting the bottom-line of Exxon drastically. As a responsible part of the organization, he worked with a holistic perspective in mind.

And as much as Art was relieved, his instinct kept bugging him that something might go wrong. For the time being, he concluded that following his instructions was the best he could do. At last, he couldn't wait to return home to his wife and son, which gave him the drive to take care of such uncalled and hasty business trips.

They called Florham Park NJ, and Art explained his conclusions to Don Gard, the manager, and his boss, Pat Bardi. One cannot get everything easily in life, even if you are correct. So try accepting the challenges in life as teach you indelible lessons for life. In Dinick's case, even though he had acted so responsibly and worked hard to locate the flaw in the system, his solution was viewed with skepticism. Both men were very skeptical and started to question the viability of the results.

They argued that Art couldn't possibly have solved the problem so quickly. In their opinion, it had to be much more complicated; after all, the international task force of experts had spent months working on it. His solution was too simple. He surely must have made a mistake in his observations and calculations.

How could this looming problem just disappear into thin air? There had to be some aspect of it that Art was overlooking. The feedback infuriated Art to a degree he couldn't put into words. How could they possibly contest a solution which made sense and was actually solving the problem? This was only a way of creating roadblocks in his approach and deterring him from achieving recognition for his genius.

"I am right, I know I'm right, I haven't made any mistakes in my calculations. I am sure I have the correct solution." Art insisted and then impatiently told them that he was coming home next week.

"No, you can't come home. You have to stay there and check your calculations and observation. You have to watch their operation longer and take more data," they insisted.

"I don't have to take any more data; I haven't made any mistakes. I've finished my work, and I'm coming home." Art held his ground and spoke with utmost conviction and confidence.

"You had better be right, or else you'll be out looking for another job," they threatened.

Art was young, but Exxon management should have had more faith in him. Employees often reach the burnout stage because their contributions are not acknowledged and given proper recognition. He thought that they would have been pleased that he solved the problem so quickly, but they weren't. The attitude of the management was a big disappointment for Art. All his brainstorming seems to go in vain as he met with this backlash. What did the management want from him? What more could they want than a surefire solution to the problem hanging like a sword over their heads? Gunther wasn't too happy either; he wanted to be the one who solved the problem. The Frenchman on the task force was happy; however, as now the only problem he had to concern himself with was what wine he should order for lunch.

Sometimes, problems that seem complicated have a simple solution. It's about applying the right technique and strategy to get you through. That's what people that can think outside of the box and have conviction do. Instead of beating around the bush, they bring a unique perspective to the problem at hand and get down to solving the problem dexterously.

Art was right and saved Exxon millions, but he didn't get any of the money. They never even thanked him, but if he was wrong, they would have fired him. Is it worth giving it your best? The corporate world is wrought with such dilemmas. Companies that discredit the invaluable contributions of employees lower employee morale drastically. Why is that when something goes wrong, the employee is totally responsible, and when the same employee saves the company millions of dollars, it is considered his duty? Why do so-called multi-national corporations not understand and give employees their due right and acknowledgment? It was a sad state of affairs that Art, despite giving his best, had to face such discrimination, and have his recommendations reluctantly accepted..

Mike

Deep in thought, Art's concentration was broken by the loud ringing of the phone in his office. He picked it up on the third ring.

"Dinick speaking." He spoke into the phone, sitting upright

"Art, Art, come home right away. It's time! Hurry! The contractions are coming every three minutes. You've got to get me to the hospital soon." Catching her breath, almost on the verge of a breakdown. Her squeals and moans made it evident how much pain she was in.

"No, Joy, it can't be. The baby isn't due for another six weeks," he replied, unable to understand what was happening. He couldn't register the conversation as it seemed really bizarre. He was inexperienced, obviously.

"I don't care when the baby is due; it's coming now. Hang up and come home immediately." She said frustratingly. She didn't understand why Art was wasting time on the phone and not listening to her.

"It's going to take me at least 45 minutes to drive home.

Maybe you had better get a cab." He said, freaking out.

"I'm not getting a cab. Just hurry home as fast as you can." She screamed into the phone and shut it in anger.

Art hung up and rushed out to the parking lot. He jumped into his trusty 1966 Ford Mustang, thrust the key into the ignition, and began cranking the engine. No Matter how much he cranked it, the engine just wouldn't start—what a time for this to happen.

Art jumped out of the car and threw open the hood to see if he could find the problem. Feverishly he looked but couldn't find anything wrong. Art was beginning to panic. His mind seemed to go blank for a moment. Sweat had beaded his forehead as he paced about the engine.

While fidgeting, he tried reconnecting some wires that might have caused trouble. But to no luck, the car seemed to have a low battery. The thundering rain pelted on the ground like stones, clouding Art's ability to think rationally. He couldn't waste time on repairing the car as he dashed back inside.

"Dubie, Dubie, my car won't start," He managed to say between pants.

"Can I borrow your car? Joy just called, and the baby is on its way. I have to get home to take her to the hospital."

"Yeah sure, just be careful with it," Dubie replied, slightly taken aback.

"Thanks a lot, Dubie, don't worry about it, I'll be careful." Art grabbed the key from his hand and ran as fast as his legs could take him.

The car engine ignited effortlessly as he reversed from the parking space, and with a sharp turn, the car screeched out from the parking lot. The traffic was at its peak, and the rain was copiously pelting on the windshield, but that didn't slow him down as he pressed on the gas pedal firmly. The 45-minute ride took only 30-minutes as he came to a sharp stop.

He hastily opened the front door and noticed his very pregnant wife squirming on the staircase, trying to come down with a plain duffel bag in her hand. He acted without giving it a second thought, and within a flash, helped her get to the car. He asked Pat to close up everything behind him. Despite the rainstorm, Art dodged and skid through the traffic carefully.

About 15 minutes of wild driving, he pulled in front of

the hospital. The past few hours seemed like a race against time, but Art was relieved that he had made it in time, and now his wife was safely at the hospital. His mind was flooded with so many thoughts that he felt it would explode anytime. But he needed to keep his calm. If not for himself, then for his wife, who needed him badly at this time and only his emotional support and reassurance would help her get past this.

He had to be there for her, as promised, through thick and thin. Soon they would be blessed with a new life, and nothing could compare that feeling. He was positive that life would change for the better. He and Joy would together make this the biggest blessing of their life.

Tears rolled down his cheeks as he thought of the roller coaster ride that he had with Joy in the past few years and how destiny had ultimately reunited them. This was God's way of rewarding him for his undying spirit and support. Love and family had indeed prevented them from drifting apart, and now he was going to become a father again. His heart warmed up with warmth and compassion for the little bundle of joy who would very soon be in his arms.

He would love him with all his heart and soul and do

anything to give the best possible life. After all, he was a sign of their love.

Chapter 9
Super Engineer

Exxon's chemical plant in Kawasaki, Japan, needed five new cracking reactors. One day in early November, Pat Bardi, Art's boss, called him into his office. The walls of the office were painted grey, with the only outlet to the external environment in the form of a floor-to-ceiling window. The décor was also matching with the walls with hues of lavender uplifting the aura of the office space.

A large gray calculator lay atop the grey desk, with an abstract-cover notebook lying open, and an untidy pile of files kept in place by a turtle-shaped paperweight. A swivel chair was placed in the middle of the room, and the air-conditioner in the corner kept the room airy.

In the corner, you could spot a bookshelf oozing with books, like a boiling pot of knowledge. Yet another pile of random papers lay on the bookshelf, which resembled a tuft of grass. A few stationery items lay around. When Art was summoned to the office, Pat was fidgeting with his pen and was making some notes in his notebook. Looking at his expressions, Art knew that something was awaiting him. Something substantial that would require him to own responsibility and get down to work. After all, that's what the management of Exxon—Chemical was notorious for. Whenever they would be faced with a dilemma or technical difficulty, Art was the first person whom they would call out to.

It was like Art was the go-to option by default, who would always be ready to render his services, even if that required him to travel internationally. However, whenever it was time for acknowledgment or appreciation, Art would always feel left out. He never felt that he was given due credit for his contributions to the firm.

Even the last time when he trouble-shooted the solution to the crisis which the technical people weren't able to solve in months, the senior management reluctantly accepted the solution in such a short span of time. It was a sad state of affairs, how employees were not valued at this Company, and were slaves to capitalism.

Before Art could say anything, Pat dropped the bomb on him and told him to pack his bags for a two to three-month assignment in Japan. Art's most profound fears had come true. He had a gut feeling that this Christmas would be spoiled, and he hated to break this to his wife every time he would have to go away for work. Art was to work on the design for the new reactors for the plant in Japan in the contractor's office. One to two weeks in Japan would be okay, but two to three months without his family was going to be a drag. Just the thought of it sent a huge wave of sadness over him. It felt like he was plunged deep into an abyss of loneliness.

As much as he loved to flaunt his command over his job and his polished skill set, he hated to go away from his family! Every few months, he would be sent away for work, and it would take a toll on him mentally and emotionally. He would find himself distracted at work, staring at his family photo placed on his desk. Could he have refused to take this assignment? Did he really have the freedom to refuse to go, or was he destined to accept it?

Pat had just turned six, and Mike was now ten months old and crawling everywhere. He wanted to enjoy every moment of his kid growing up, and these uncalled for urgent trips were a huge hindrance in his fatherhood. Every time it was time to say bye to his children, his heart would swell up with mixed feelings. Art felt torn between his professional responsibilities and that of a father. While his profession called him to be there on duty, being a father always made it hard for him to stay away from home. Art didn't want to miss Christmas at home with his kids. It was one of the most auspicious occasions of the year, and he wouldn't miss it for anything. Yet, every time he promised himself he wouldn't go away for work, something would turn up and leave him with no choice! It was worse than any existential crisis he had ever been in.

"Pat, do I have to stay there for two to three months? What about Christmas?" he asked sheepishly, wondering if Pat had some ounce of compassion left in him.

"Art, you have to stay long enough to get the job done. If that requires staying there over Christmas, I'm sorry, but there's nothing I can do about it. You can come back when you're finished, but, based on all the past jobs like this that I have ever had experience with, I know it will take you a minimum of two months and most likely three," he stated nonchalantly. Pat was very professional and strict about following the code of conduct that was laid down to get things done, whenever any technical fault rose.

"I know you're a very good engineer, but I also know that it's not humanly impossible to finish in less than two months. So, don't even try, you'll just make life miserable and frustrate yourself," he said assertively, to make sure that he had gotten his point across. His tone made it clear that Art had no option but to stick to the plan and prove his mettle once again.

Sadly, Art said his farewells to Joy and the kids. As much as Joy had grown weary of Art's sudden business trips, she knew there was no point complaining about it. She knew that her husband had some duties that he needed to cater to, and that was what was helping them make ends meet. These moments made Joy realize how carefree her life was before marriage, but now since they were sharing lives, they were inevitably dependent on each other.

Also, the way their lives were entangled could justifiably be called a beautiful mess. If you want the good, rewarding parts of being a family, you've got to keep up with the hard times and know for a fact that it's not a one-man show. When Art used to be away, Joy would have to tend to the kids, be there for them emotionally and physically, all the while juggling the house chores. She couldn't just throw a tantrum and give up on everything. These were the moments that were a real test for both Art and Joy and a display of how well they had matured over time. As he drove off in the long black limousine to JFK airport, the kick-off point for his long journey to Tokyo, Japan, he couldn't help but wonder when he was going to see them again. He was missing them already.

If it was in his jurisdiction, he would go running back to his family, or ideally, finish off his work as soon as possible and book a return flight. It was the grueling two to three months that haunted him. Exhausted, he arrived at Haneda airport on the outskirts of Tokyo at about 10 a.m. in the morning after traveling a grueling 20 hours. Landing in an alien city at this hour was peaceful as well as weirdly unsettling.

He wasn't able to get any sleep at all on the plane. It was crowded, not one vacant seat, and he was constantly being disturbed. He would go in and out of short bursts of sleep, only to be woken up by the same old drill of being herded out like cattle. It seemed every time he would start to doze off, the plane had to land for fuel. He and all the other passengers were herded off the plane into a crowded airport lounge where they had to mill around like cattle in a holding pen. The plane stopped in Los Angeles, Anchorage, Alaska, and Honolulu. Just to ensure that everyone on the plane stayed wide awake between stops to experience the joy of flying, the captain made blaring announcements every thirty minutes over the loudspeaker such as "*we are now crossing the international dateline, or the temperature in Alaska is a warm 40 degrees".*

The confusion and chaos had frustrated Art to the brink of losing his sanity, and he was highly frustrated. Is this the way you treat your passengers that you do not even allow them to stay in one place for some while and herd them like cattle? He abhorred the inhumane behavior of the flight attendees, and he couldn't wait to get off the flight and get some sound sleep.

The plane took off from New York and landed in Los Angeles, Anchorage, Alaska, Honolulu, and finally Tokyo. After getting his suitcase, Art spent another grueling hour in line for immigration and customs. The airport felt like a sea of faces with people going about their destination in all directions. An unknown current seemed to be drifting them in the form of a flowing river. Sometimes, a small group would stop in their way, but the others seemed to flow without caring about others around them. The walls of the airport were full of plasma screens with an influx of arrival and departure times changing slots. The check-in desk had its usual duty to perform and patiently attend to the passengers, lined with their baggage and suitcases. The floors were sparkling white and clean, reflecting the rays of the morning sun.

A couple of Japanese friends met him at the airport and escorted him to the hotel in Tokyo. It was about 1 o'clock in the afternoon when he checked into the hotel and went up to his room. Art was so tired he didn't even know his own name and had trouble writing it on the hotel registration. He could barely keep his eyes open, and lack of sleep had blanketed his mind like a grey cloud.

He couldn't make sense of his surroundings, and his hand and eye coordination seemed to have lost it. It was like he was on the verge of zoning out, but his last trace of senses had kept him awake. Yes! He was jet-lagged! The jet lag had taken the form of some giant leech, sucking the very energy out of him. He was so drowsy that he felt drugged up to his eyes, ready to fall asleep any instant. When he got to his room, before he could even lay his head on his pillow, he was already in a transition phase, and his body became floppy as he hit the bed. His eyelids had felt heavy since he was on the flight, and they couldn't bear the pressure anymore. As he sinks into the comforts of the hotel bed, his face muscles relax, and he finally meets the state he was craving for.

A Loud knocking on the door awakened Art from his brief sleep. Half dazed, he sprang to his feet and opened the door.

"Hi, Vinnie, what are you doing here?" with his eyes half-open, holding his head which was pounding with a splitting headache

"Vinnie!" the fellow said, *"What's wrong with you? It's me, Chuck, your old buddy. We work together in Florham Park! You know I've been working in Japan for the past six months! What's the matter with you? Are you all right?"* he exclaimed in over-exaggeration.

Art felt really stupid and embarrassed. Exhausted from lack of sleep, he had hallucinated that Chuck was Vinnie Fumo, his boyhood friend that he hadn't seen in six years.

Now shocked to consciousness, Art responded.

"I'm awake now, and I know perfectly well who you are. I can't imagine how I could ever have confused you with Vinnie." No one else in the world has such flaming red hair and a nose as big as yours, he responded humorously.

"From the way you're talking, I can see you're awake now," Chuck said, putting his arm on Art's shoulder in a friendly manner.

"Judy and Hanzawa-san are down in the lobby and would like to have dinner with you if that's alright," he said, extending a gesture of goodwill.

"Yeah sure, I'd love to. Just give me a couple of minutes to wash up." He added, rubbing his eyes. His tummy was growling with hunger. He had just not been able to notice these hunger pangs in the midst of his sleeplessness.

Art, now recovered, joined Chuck, his wife Judy, and his Japanese friend Hanzawa for a pleasant dinner.

The next day, Art quickly settled into work and set about doing the design job at a record pace. As usual, Art was a pro at this, and his track record was quite impressive. The very reason he was summoned on an urgent basis was his nimbleness, quick-wittedness, and attention to detail. He knew how to approach the problem with an analytical viewpoint and brainstorm several ideas that would crack the code and prove his superiority over other engineers in the Company. He never failed to surprise himself, and neither did he let down his supervisors in any way.

Lunch at the office in Kawasaki was a new and unique experience. The Japanese, being very gracious hosts, didn't feel that their cafeteria was up to American standards, so they arranged a special lunch and brought it up to the office every day. Every day at exactly 12 noon, Chuck and Art had three special little sandwiches, and a Coke delivered to them. They each got a little cheese and lettuce sandwich, a little cucumber and lettuce sandwich, and a little ham cucumber and lettuce sandwich.

Each sandwich was about the size of a silver dollar. After a couple of weeks, Art really began to hate those special little sandwiches and began having dreams about a fairy godmother appearing at lunchtime, bringing them thick juicy hamburgers and French fries, but it wasn't to be. All he ever got were those special little sandwiches. It was a very inconsequential thing to crib about, but nonetheless, it was something that bothered Art! He had gotten weary of eating the same meal, monotonous meal like a zombie, but he had little choice. He was on a work trip and not a leisure activity that he could make indulge in luxurious behavior. After all, the sentiments of the Japanese also had to be kept in mind. Art worked at a feverish pace. He wanted to get home to his family and couldn't bear the thought of a couple of months of those special little sandwiches.

The Japanese were working like bees to keep up with him. At four o'clock every day, Art would give them numerous drawings with dozens of design changes marked in red, and every day at exactly 9 a.m. in the morning, they would give him back a set of perfectly corrected drawings. To accomplish this, they had to have a group of engineers and draftsmen working on them all night long. In exactly four weeks, Art had accomplished what Pat Bardi said was impossible.

He had completed his work and was ready to return home. Yes! He had done it once again. He was super proud of himself, and a sense of accomplishment and empowerment overtook him. His chest swelled with pride, and just the thought of being able to go back home for Christmas made him ecstatic.He would now get to spend Christmas with Joy and the kids. He wouldn't have to miss them from afar and wish they were near. Art was a passionate and determined individual, and he left no stone unturned in ensuring that his targets were met in the minimum possible time. He worked with utmost dedication because that was his tried and tested technique to strike the perfect balance between professional and personal life.

He knew that if he would propose a viable solution and fix the problem for which he was called on-site, there was nothing that could stop him from going back home. Discharging his duties as a responsible employee would allow him to act like a responsible father, and he did everything under his discretion to make things work.

The protocol, however, required him to telex(telegram) Pat and inform him that he was coming home. Art sent the following brief Telex to him:

"Job completed in record time, Super Engineer will fly home tomorrow," he wrote with profuse confidence. After all, he had every right to call himself a super engineer.

When Art arrived at the office in Florham Park on Monday morning, he got the surprise of his life. Across the back wall of his office was stretched a computer-printed banner with the words *"Welcome Home Super Engineer"* printed across it in ten-inch-high letters. On his desk was a copy of his Telex. The words 'super engineer' was underlined in red pen. A note from Pat telling Art to see him immediately was scrolled across the bottom of the Telex.

What could he possibly want? What was so important that Art had to see him immediately? Art's mind was flooded with questions of all sorts, and he couldn't help wonder what Pat was up to this time. Would they ever let him bask in the glory of his own victory?

Quickly Art went down to Pat's office, dying of curiosity.

He greeted Art with a smile and said, *"Good job, Art! I'm proud of you. Nobody could have executed this project better than you!"* and then said, *"Dinick, you're a shit!"*

Pat was like a pseudo-father to Art. He always called Art a shit whenever he did something that wasn't exactly to his liking. The sudden shift from one end of the continuum to another threw Art out of place. What was Pat up to? Had he lost it? Why was he praising him and calling him shit at the same time? Art always kept himself mentally prepared for something unexpected whenever he returned from a business meeting.

"Don Gard, our eminent manager, is really pissed off at you. Didn't you know that your super engineer telex to me would be sent to all our plant managers around the entire world? Don is worried about their reaction when they read it." He said as if it was the end of the world. The urgency in his tone made Art wonder what was so wrong about his Telex. Exxon's management was surely self-obsessed and only cared about themselves.

"Well, Pat, I really didn't know that it would be sent to anyone but you. But what difference does it make? Who cares anyway about a simple little telex?" said Art indifferently. He wasn't foolish to take this concern to heart. After all, it was just a candid telex which he had written out of pure ecstasy and joy of having completed the task in record time. More than that, he was overwhelmed to be back home for Christmas. Nothing could beat that joy, and he wasn't going to let such an inconsequential matter spoil his mood.

"Don Gard does, and so do some of the other managers. It's too bold. It shows you don't conform to their conservative image of a Company engineer. I'm worried." Pat said, *"that a simple little thing like this might have a big impact on your career with the Company, and that would be a shame. You're too good of an engineer."* He added with concern. Pat did not want Art to come off as an overconfident engineer who had no respect for the protocol. He was one of the most value-adding resources at Exxon, and Pat couldn't lose him at any cost.

Art didn't care if he fit their image. He was a very good engineer, probably the best they had, but an impact it did have. For the next six months, every time Don would pass Art in the hall at work, he would shake his head and mutter *"super engineer, indeed."* Art really did not know what to make of this, and he never really reacted so that things would not blow out of proportions. For the most part, it was in his favor only, as he was only getting publicity this way. Being called a 'super engineer' was in no way embarrassing or degrading for him. The super engineer telex and its ramifications, however, seemed to ignite a spark of enthusiasm and imagination amongst Art's fellow employees. One of them made up a character drawing of him in a Superman costume, cape blowing in the wind with the insignia of 'SE' standing for super engineer emblazoned on his chest. Copies of the Super Engineer drawing quickly found their way around the world, and engineers in Exxon's plants worldwide began to refer to Art as 'Super Engineer.' Even now, on occasion, they still introduce him as Super Engineer.

Even though most have now forgotten the origin, a drawing of Super Engineer will sometimes show up on some engineer’s office wall. I guess it was a rather funny incident than a serious one, as it only exposed the senior management's insecurities and their inability to create a work culture that empowered its employees and encouraged opinion sharing.

If Art had refused to take this assignment and not sent a telex around the world, many young engineers would not have been inspired to become a “super engineer.” The hustle of working and living in a foreign country may seem exciting to some, but to Art, it was lonely and tedious, especially if he was traveling alone. He always thought that there was an allure to going abroad and working, but that only remained until he was there over there. It might be very new and exciting in the first couple of months, but then homesickness sets in. For Art, however, homesickness set in way earlier than that. During the weekends, he would entertain himself by traveling around and sight-seeing, but in the evenings after work, there was usually nothing to do.

Having dinner in a restaurant, even a good restaurant, by himself was lonely and seemed rather pointless. He would often think about what his friends and family were doing back home, but that would make him even more homesick. Even sitting in the hotel room and watching television lost its appeal. All the shows were in a foreign language that he didn't understand and certainly could not enjoy.

All the forms of entertainment which he had enjoyed back home weren't available. He couldn't go to the movies or see a night club show because of the language barrier. His only source of entertainment was to wander the streets, browse through the open shops, and watch the actions and dramas of the crowds. While working in Japan, Art was living in the Imperial Hotel. Ginza, Tokyo's famous shopping district, was only a few minutes' walk from there. Neon signs and glittering lights abound.

This section of town was one that never slept. Hundreds of thousands of people crowded the streets until the wee hours of the morning. In the evenings, to ward off death from boredom and keep his sanity, Art would walk the streets of the Ginza. He couldn't walk the short distance from his hotel to the Ginza without being accosted ten to twenty times by someone wanting to hustle him off to their night club. According to them, their clubs featured the most beautiful girls in Japan. Neatly dressed in suits, the hustlers stood in every little alleyway and in front of almost every store. When they spotted a potential customer, they would brazenly walk alongside them and held a running conversation trying to persuade their mark.

"Hey, Joe! Want to see a good show? I take you to a nice club. You see the most beautiful girls in Japan."

Art's reply would never waver from a resounding, *"No, I'm not interested."*

However, they were not ones to give up so easily and would usually respond, *"Why you not interested? It not expensive."*

"No, I'm just not interested." Art would reply for the twentieth time that day.

"Why? You no 'likey' girls? You may be likey men?" They would ask, wondering if their approach was wrong from the beginning.

"No, I don't 'likey' men. I'm just not interested." Art would say before giving them a stern look that told them to walk off.

It got to be extremely annoying. The same guys tried to hustle Art night after night, making him wonder if there was anything which he was doing on his part to invite this behavior. Art thought that after a couple of refusals, they would have left him alone and tried to hustle someone else, but they didn't.

To them, maybe Art looked like the kind of guy who would pay well once they got him to their nightclub. They must have gotten some pleasure out of pestering him nightly and asking him if he 'likey' men. Art decided that enough was enough, and one day, however, Art decided to make the best of a bad situation and make a game out of it.

"Hey Joe, you want to see a good show? I take you nice place. You see most beautiful girls in Japan." They began again. Part of Art was now wondering if they thought persistence was the key to success.

"Okay, I'll go see the show, but I'll only pay 300 yen," Art said, which was about one dollar, *"for a beer, and I won't buy any hostess drinks."*

Art assumed that no club would let him get away with paying only 300 yen for a beer or without buying a hostess drink. It only seemed logical to him that upon hearing his ridiculous terms, the hustlers would leave him alone or, at the very least, they would stop asking him if he 'likey' men.

"You crazy, Joe. You have to buy hostess drinks. It's standard practice in all clubs. Hostess drink only cost you 10,000 yen," The guy said, putting a price of about $30.00. *"Beer, it cheap, it only cost you about 5,000 yen."* That was approximately $15.00. *"You can afford it, Joe. You rich American."*

That made Art laugh out loud. *"No, I'm not rich. I can't afford it. I can only afford to pay 300 yen for a beer, and I won't buy a hostess drink. That's it. Take it or leave it."* Art said, mocking him.

"No!" "You crazy! You no find any club for that money." The guy said, his face showing that he realized that he made a mistake.

"Good! I don't care if I do." Art said forcefully and walked off.

The guy then walked away in discontent and approached the next sucker they came upon. That interaction with the guy kept the hustlers off of Art's back for a while. However, one evening, one of the hustlers thought he could outsmart Art and figured he could get the best of him. Art had seen him before since he had tried to hustle him at least three times. As usual, Art told him that he wouldn't buy the hostess drink and that he would only pay 300 yen for a beer.

To Art's surprise, this time, instead of regarding him as crazy while walking off, the man replied, *"Okay, you come with me. You see show; you only have to pay 300 yen for beer."*

'Wow,' Art thought, wondering what he had gotten himself into. A few more moments of thought brought Art to the conclusion that either the hustler must really be desperate

or he has arranged a scam to get some money out of him. Art really didn't want to go to his club, but now that he had said he would, he had no choice. The hustler then led him down the crowded street and up to several alleys. The air was filled with pungent aromas from the cooking of fish on charcoal grills in the little restaurants that lined the alleyways. The night was alive with the sounds of buzzers and bells, which echoed from the pachinko parlors dotted among the tiny restaurants and shops.

Here, the Japanese businessmen dressed in their suits crowded over the hundreds of pinball-like pachinko machines trying feverishly to win a few yen before going home to their families for the evening. Art and the guy finally got to a place called *'Club Dream.'*

He parted the black curtain in the open doorway and led him in. He spoke in Japanese with who appeared to be the boss, a short, stocky sinister-looking Japanese man dressed in a blue double-breasted pinstriped suit, sporting a thin black mustache. The hustler then disappeared out the door, leaving Art alone. After waiting for a little while, a young Japanese woman dressed in a pink and white flowered ceremonial kimono came up to Art and took him by the hand, escorting him through another curtained doorway into an adjacent dimly lit room. After seating him at a table in the corner of the room, she brought him the beer he had promised to pay 300 yen for.

Shortly thereafter, another young Japanese girl clad in a red kimono showed up and sat down beside him.

"Hi! You American?" she said.

"Yes," Art said, already wanting to leave.

"You come from New York?" She asked, flashing him a dazzling smile.

"No. I came from New Jersey." Art replied, taking a sip from the beer.

"New Jersey nice place? You on vacation in Tokyo?"

"No, I'm not on vacation. I'm working here."

"You 'likey' Japan? You 'likey' Tokyo? You 'likey' Japanese girl?" She asked, firing the questions off one after the other.

Art rolled his eyes, knowing that the girl wouldn't be able to see that in the room. *"Yes, they're okay."*

"I sit with you now. I keep you company. You buy me drink."

"No, you don't have to sit with me. I'm married; I'd rather be alone. I'm sorry, but I don't want to buy you a drink." He said, as politely as he could. He already felt sick to his stomach.

"I no care you married; I keep you company. You buy me drink, and I show you good time. It only cost you 10,000 yen."

"No, I don't have 10,000 yen." Art replied again. Art wondered where they got the idea that all Americans were rich.

"You rich American. You must have 10,000 yen," the lady said.

"No, I don't, and even if I did, I really don't want to pay for you to sit with me." Art said.

"You have to buy me drink," she demanded belligerently.

"No, I don't. I don't have to buy you a drink. The man that brought me here said I didn't have to buy a hostess drink." Art clarified, trying to keep his cool.

"You have to buy hostess drink. Everybody here buys hostess drink." She said again.

"Not everybody. Not me. Here are the 300 yen for my beer."

"No, No! Beer cost you 5000 yen, not 300. You mistaken, you have to buy me hostess drink, and you have to give me 5000 yen for the beer." She said, getting in Art's face.

Art held his ground and said sternly, *"No, the man that brought me here clearly said the beer would only cost me 300 yen, and he said that I didn't have to buy a hostess drink."*

Art was really frustrated now, knowing that he didn't have that kind of money to spend on a beer and a hostess drink. He could tell by her expressions that even she was getting frustrated and very perturbed. After Art's adamant refusal to buy her drinks, the woman went to get the boss. Art didn't think it would be a good idea to leave, so he sat there and waited while she returned with him.

He was a bit more reasonable, to begin with, and informed Art that if he wanted to stay to see the show, he would have to buy the hostess drink for 10,000 yen and would have to pay 5000 yen for his beer. Knowing that this wasn’t a man whom Art could just say no to, he tried a more reasonable approach. *"Sir, the man that brought me here gave me the assurance that I would not have to buy a hostess drink and that the beer would only cost me 300 yen."*

The boss replied, *"No, you must pay 5000 yen for the beer, and you have to buy a hostess drink."*

Art had had enough now. He decided that calmness go to hell and flatly refused to pay another penny to them. He even offered to leave. The boss was so frustrated and angry that his scam wasn't working. Of course, Art knew that at some point, this was going to happen, and now it did. The boss threw his arms up in the air and waved them violently, motioning for him to sit back down. He stormed off only to return in about 5 minutes with the hustler that brought Art to the place.

"Hey, Joe!" the hustler said. *"I wrong. You crazy. You different than everybody else. Everybody I bring here buy hostess drink. You only one who refuse to buy. You okay, Joe. You come with me. I buy you drink."* The hustler said, sounding impressed.

This made Art wonder if the guy was crazy. However, he didn't dwell on it since the hustler was handing him the 300 yen back, which he had given the girl for the beer, and then led him out of place. Art then followed the hustler down the crowded smoke-filled alleys of Ginza as he led him from club to club.

One after the other, Art and the guy went from one club to another, and the hustler paid all the bills. Every place they went, he told the people in the club, *"This my friend Joe. He crazy American. He okay. I not able to fool him. I like him."*

Even though Art was very annoyed at first, he concluded that the guy was fair. He was trying to earn his living, and people did get what they were paying for. That day, he learned that sometimes it is best to stick to your guns and not give in to the hustlers you meet in life. Sometimes, some of them may just respect you for it!

One up Manship

Exxon's plant in Sarnia, Ontario, Canada, was having operational problems. Typical of their modus operandi, Exxon management assembled a task force of experts to study the problem and develop a solution. Art's buddy,

Chuck Nogy, and Art himself were full-time members of the elite group. Art would spend hours every day just looking at the reactor. Most of the task force members thought that he was wasting his time, but he thought that they were wasting their time just sitting in the office making meaningless calculations.

To Art, it was evident that the office wasn't having any problems, the reactor was. After several weeks of wasting time, Art made a unique discovery. He discovered that the operators were accidentally and unknowingly shocking the reactor every day by dumping raw cold fuel from another unit into their reactor. This was shock-quenching the reactor and causing it to crack when the temperature dropped from 2000 F degrees to 200 F degrees.

Art was sure he found the cause of the problem, but he still had some doubts deep down in his mind. He, however, decided to take the risk and managed to convince management that his conclusion was the only thing that could be the cause of the problems. After working the problems for about six months, several of Art's recommendations were beginning to pay off. They were finally beginning to make progress, and the plant was starting to make some money. Ralph Lepard, the General Manager of the plant, decided to throw a celebration party for his department managers and some visiting executives from the Toronto office. It was a huge deal for Art and Chuck, the only engineers to be invited since the management regarded them as peons.

Because they were on the task force and had done all the real work, they were extended an invitation to the party. Several suites in the Sarnia Holiday Inn were rented for this occasion. It was a stuffy affair with all the executives neatly dressed in their charcoal-grey worsted wool suits standing around, sipping their Martinis, and discussing the company's financial affairs and business strategies.

Chuck and Art weren't the least bit interested in their conversations and could think of a thousand other places they would rather be.

After a particularly boring conversation that the engineers were a part of, Chuck had had enough. He turned to Art and said, *"Let's get out of here. I can't take any more of this stuffy bullshit."*

"Yea, me neither," Art agreed. *"Let's go downstairs to the lounge."*

The dimly lit bar was filled with good looking women, and in the corner, a musician pounded on the keys of his piano. Chuck, although happily married, had a roving eye and couldn't pass up the opportunity to tempt fate and test his skills at picking up good looking women. Sitting down at the bar next to several of them, he quickly struck up a conversation.

Art, however, decided that his time would be much better spent sitting quietly and observing Chuck. After about a half-hour of small talk and a few beers, Chuck asked several of the women at the bar to join them at the party upstairs. They accepted his invitation and promised to meet him up in the room in a few minutes.

Art was not at all okay with this, although he waited till they were out of earshot of the ladies. Looking at Chuck, Art asked, *"Are you crazy? Do you know what you are doing? I don't think Shepard and the other exec's will appreciate these women coming to their formal little social gathering."*

"No, don't worry," Chuck said, smirking. *"I am sure they won't mind. It will liven their party up."*

Art didn't really know what to say to that, so he went with what was happening. They went upstairs and rejoined the stuffy, stodgy gathering. In about five minutes, two of the women from the bar descended to the gathering. They poured themselves some drinks, sauntered up to the stereo, turned off the elevator music, and turned up the volume to their local rock station to liven up the dull affair. Lepard, startled from his intense discussion by the glaring music, spotted the girls.

"Excuse me, girls," he said, confused, *"this is a private affair. How did you get in here?"* he questioned.

Art knew that things were about to go really bad for Chuck. Before they had a chance to answer, Chuck piped up, *"Mr. Lepard, Dinick invited them up here."*

Lepard looked at Art in disdain and said, *"Dinick, get those two bimbos out of here."*

Flabbergasted, Art looked at Chuck and said, *"Thanks a lot, buddy."*

"Don't worry," Chuck replied, barely hiding his laughter,

"he'll forget all about it tomorrow." About five minutes later, however, four more of the women that they met at the bar wandered into the room.

This time, before anyone had a chance to speak, Art piped up, *"Ralph, Chuck's girls from the bar just showed up, but don't worry, I'll take care of everything."*

Ice Box Joe
Is Risk-Taking Inherited Or Learned?

Known as Ice Box Joe in the casinos and gaming houses from Vegas to Hotsprings Arkansas, Joe was a professional gambler, and cards were his specialty. Thousands of dollars would be risked every night without batting an eye. A ten thousand dollar bet on one hand of cards was common.

Was he bluffing, or did he hold the winning hand? His opponents never knew. His cold blue eyes would never give the slightest hint. Joe died during his 65th year of a massive heart attack after dropping $100,000 in a 45-hour long card game. Did the pressure of the game finally get to Ice Box Joe, or was it just the consequence of age? He was one of the ten siblings born to a wealthy businessman in Atlantic City, New Jersey, in 1903.

His father had several businesses both in the states and in Italy. Joe left home at the age of sixteen to make his fortune in the world. He drifted from town to town, living solely on his earnings from gambling. Stakes grew larger and larger, but he always managed to stay afloat and afford a good life.

Frank, Tony, and Pete, Joe's older brothers, were in the night club business. Their clubs included the Follies Bergere, the Silver Slipper, and the Palis Royale. Many famous actors and actresses, including the likes of Evelyn Nesbitt, George Raft, and Jimmy Durante, got their start in their clubs during Atlantic City's golden days, before, during, and after prohibition.

In the early 1900's Stefano LaRosa, Joe's father, exported olive oil and lemons to the United States from Italy. He also owned the Mercer Cab Company in Atlantic City, one of the first cab companies in the states. Stefano had a remarkable talent for business and managed to amass a great fortune during the '20s. The failure of the American banking system during the great depression took its toll on Stefano's fortune. All was not lost; however, through talent and some luck, he managed to salvage a significant portion of it. His faith in the American banking system, which had almost ruined him, was now lost. Thus, he invested what was left of his savings in the Italian banks. In the late 1930s, with the threat of war looming in Europe and unrest in Italy under the leadership of Mussolini, a large portion of Stefano's fortune was frozen in the Italian banks. Being an influential businessman, though, Stefano got his records together and managed to get an appointment with Mussolini to discuss the release of his money.

Stefano bid farewell to his wife and children and set sail for Italy aboard the Roma in July of 1939. Because of the war in Europe, communication between the United States and Italy was soon restricted, and during the next several years, his family heard nothing from him.

All their attempts to communicate with him were in vain. They longed for his return and worried for his safety but were powerless to do anything. His family never saw or heard from him again. In 1942, his family learned that he had died. It is unknown whether he ever kept his appointment with Mussolini or what the outcome of the meeting was. The fortune, however, was lost for all time. Ice Box Joe got married but never had any children. In fact, of his entire family of 10 brothers and sisters, only one had children.

It was his younger sister Katherine who had two sons. Joe was Art's uncle, and Katherine was Art's mother. Art's family had failures as well as successes in their ventures, and most people would not have taken risks in businesses that they undertook. Art did not inherit a gene that made him fearless. Every time he faced a challenge that was risky, his insecurity made him fearful of the possibility of failure, but he could not resist the challenge.

The bigger the challenge, the riskier it was, and the greater the fear he had of failure. For some unexplainable reason, he couldn't let fear get the best of him. He always hoped that he could conquer the challenge but believed that no matter how hard he tried for success, the result would be in God's hands, and he would have to live with the consequences because he didn't have the ability to change his decisions.

Cops, Good or bad?

As a teenager, Art had a lot of trouble with cops. Cops like Connie who constantly harassed him, but not all cops were a pain in the ass. Don Rochford was the Chief Detective on the Boardwalk in Atlantic City. He was a very sociable and likable guy who would go out of his way to help people. He was always doing favors for someone, even if it meant looking the other way while they violated some unreasonable or small city ordnance. He did favors for everyone. He got them jobs and got their kids jobs, too. He helped them start businesses and helped them get vending licenses. He was always giving handouts to the poor and unfortunate.

Even Art benefited from his generosity. Born the son of an Irish immigrant family, he attended college on a baseball scholarship. After graduation, he played pro ball for a short time with the New York Giants until an injury sidelined him. During World War II, he was an Army MP. After the war, he patrolled the city as a beat cop until he got promoted to detective. One day he married his longtime sweetheart and officially became Art's uncle.

Don was as Irish as Paddy's pig. Beer and ball games were

the loves of his life. He loved football, baseball, and basketball, but racing wasn't on his list of favorite sports. He had his favorite quotations. Hardly a week would go by without Art hearing one of his favorite quotes. One of his all-time favorites was, *'you're as thick in the head as a pig is in the ass!'*

This he would say to someone he thought was stubborn, and he often thought Art was stubborn about something, but hearing that would always crack Art up. On one of his visits to Art's home in North Jersey, Art managed to talk him into going to the races with him on the outside chance that he just might like them.

It was a cool Sunday afternoon in October. Dressed in his grey pinstriped suit, blue cashmere overcoat, and grey Derby hat, he looked like he was dressed for a Broadway show and not for the races. He was always dressed in a suit and never even owned a pair of jeans or work clothes. He had no mechanical ability whatsoever, and Art wondered if he knew one end of a screwdriver from another. This Sunday was the finals for the Schaffer Beer championship.

Art had qualified fifth, and that day, the top sixteen qualifiers were to have their showdown for the championship. After completing four rounds of the regularly scheduled races and winning runner up money, Art was ready for the competition in the Schaffer Beer championship. Art's Uncle Don, however, was not. It was getting late in the day, and he had had his fill of racing. He was starting to fidget.

"What do you want to do this for?" He asked. *"It's getting cold. Let's go home. We've had enough for today. Your Aunt Jeanette is waiting for us."*

"No, we can't go home now. I have to compete in the Schaeffer championship races. We'll go home soon, though. I don't think I have too good a chance. I have to run against Dee in the first round." Art replied, being self-deprecating since he didn't want to jinx himself.

"Good," he said. *"Lose so we can go home!"*

Somehow, however, Art won and was ecstatic. His uncle, on the other hand, was not. He was missing a good football game on TV. The second round came, and Art faced Andy Boye, and as luck would have it, he won that round too.

"Come on, let's go! It's late. The game will be over by the time we get home," Art's uncle Don complained.

"No, I can't go yet, but we'll go soon. I'll probably lose the next round." Art said, hoping secretly to keep his winning streak going. He could see that his uncle was really fidgeting.

He was pacing back and forth in his pinstriped suit and long dress coat. *"Come on, let's go! Your Aunt Jeanette is waiting for us. We're missing a good football game."*

"But you're seeing outstanding races," Art pointed out.

"Outstanding?" he asked sarcastically. *"All you do is make a lot of noise and smoke; then, in less than ten seconds, it's all over. A football game is good; this is not. Let's go!"*

"This is good. You're watching your favorite nephew race and win. If you can't admit that this is good, you must be as thick in the head as a pig is in the ass." Art said, finally causing him to break in his stride.

He smiled at Art, *"Okay,"* he said, *"but we've seen enough good races for today. Let's go."*

"Just one more round." Art begged.

"You've been saying that all day, why don't we just go? Why don't you just go slow and lose so we can go home and

watch the ball game," he said.

"I can't do that! I want to win." Art said, vehemently.

"What for? You have more trophies than you know what to do with them. You don't have any place to keep all the trophies," Don said.

"No, I want the prize money," Art replied.

"What for? You'll only spend it on the damn car," Don replied again.

He was right, but Art still wanted to win. The time for the final round came. Art was to race against Crow. Out of the corner of his eye, he could see his uncle standing on the sidelines, concentrating intently on Art's prerace burnouts. The lights on the starting tree came down, and Crow got off to a handicapped head start.

Crow's lead was significant, but Art was chasing him down the track and slowly closing the gap. It was only by inches that Art nipped him at the finish line lights.

"Good, it's finally over," Art's Uncle said ecstatically. *"Can we go home now?"* He asked, vaguely reminding Art of a little child asking on a long road trip, 'Are we there yet?'

"Just as soon as I collect my money." Art said patiently.

"Aw, come on, leave it, they'll save it for you. Get it next week."

"I can't." Art said, very patiently.

"Well then, hurry up, or we'll miss what's left of the ball game."

Some people, he thought, *just have a one-track mind.* His uncle was the kind of person who wouldn't spend all day at a cold, noisy, dirty track and appreciate a good race when they're missing a good ball game in the comfort of their warm living room with a good can of cold beer, even if their favorite nephew is racing. Art wasn't sure who between his uncle and himself was really 'as thick in the head as a pig is in the ass.'

Haste Makes Waste

They were having a winning season in 71. The race car was running really well. Art would consistently run slightly below the record for their class of dragsters. The Indy Nationals was the premiere drag racing event of the season.

It is to drag racing what the Kentucky Derby is to horse

racing. This was the year they had their best chance of winning. Never before had they been able to run consistently below the record. Art's starting line reflexes were lightning quick, and he could easily beat the other racers even when their cars were a little faster.

He and Russ Wolfe had been partners for several years. They had built the dragster in his garage. Russ was a mechanic by trade and a valuable member of Art's team. Up until three years ago, he had campaigned his own race car but was pressured into giving up driving by his wife.

Bill Reuter, Art's racer friend, stopped racing his own car for the season after sustaining a broken leg when he was thrown off a horse. He became a partner an active member of their pit crew. Short and slightly chubby, Bill was laid back and relaxed. Nothing could ever upset or anger him; even his broken leg didn't seem to bother him. In contrast to Art, he took everything in stride.

They loaded the car into the trailer and headed off to Indianapolis. There were seven of them, including Art's partners Bill and Russ, Russ's wife Sharon, his brother Bob, Art's old neighbor Johnny, and their friend Jimmy. They towed the trailer with Russ's truck, and Bob towed a small camper with his car. After driving all day and night, they arrived at the campgrounds in Indianapolis, Indiana at noon.

They checked over the race car and discovered that part of the frame had cracked from bouncing around in the trailer during its long 1000-mile trip. They were extremely tired, but they didn't have time to spare. They set out looking for a welding shop to repair the car. By 3 p.m. in the afternoon, they had the car repaired and drove back to the track to get the car inspected and complete their registration for the race. The day they had arrived was the last day for inspection and registration, and they had already lost too much valuable time. The inspection line was extremely long.

"Johnny, you and Russ stay with the race car and push it up to the inspection area as the line moves up. Bill and I will go to the inspection area and try to find out what things they are really picky about and flunking the cars for." Art instructed.

To their surprise, most of the cars were failing inspection because their emergency fuel shutoff valve was sticking. They never used this valve and because they thought it was a useless piece of equipment. They hurried back to their car and tested the fuel shutoff valve. Just like everyone else, theirs was sticking as well.

And work began!

They worked at a feverish pace, taking it apart and freeing it up. Hastily, they reassembled it and bolted it back into the car just in time for inspection. The cable-operated handle now seemed to work perfectly, and the car passed inspection, but Art had to get a new fireproof face mask before he was allowed to race. They spent what was left of the day driving around Indianapolis, trying to locate the mask. The next three days were plagued with rain. It rained so much that they couldn't get any time trials to test the motor and to find out how well the car would run at this track.

Conditions at the campsite were miserable. The camper couldn't handle the seven of them. There was just not enough room for all of them to be in the camper at the same time. Conditions outside were extremely uncomfortable because of the constant rain. Johnny, Bill, and Art had to put their sleeping bags in the mud under the camper.

Friday, the day before their race, the weather cleared up, and they got to make their first-time trial. The car was 30 miles per hour slower than it usually was. Something was wrong. They checked the fuel injectors and the ignition system, but couldn't seem to find anything wrong. The spark plugs indicated that the motor was running lean and needed more fuel. Maybe the injectors were bypassing too much fuel?

They changed the fuel jets in the injectors. As the sun was setting, they made their second-time trial. It was a little better, but nowhere good enough to have the slightest chance of winning. Most of the night and the next morning was spent rebuilding the engine and the fuel injection system. Their final time trial was made under the blazing noon sun on Saturday, but still no improvement.

Art and fellows were hot, tired, frustrated, and irritable. The car wasn't running properly. They had had very little sleep, the camper was overcrowded, and to top it all off, someone had stolen Art's travel bag, which contained his spare clothes and toiletries. Bill, however, didn't seem to be the slightest bit fazed by all of the problems and even seemed to be enjoying himself despite all the aggravation.

In a last-ditch effort, they rebuilt the fuel injection system again and borrowed a new fuel pump from Andy Boye. At about 5 p.m., the car was pushed into the staging lanes for the first round of racing. Art dawned his fire suit and helmet, climbed into the cockpit of the dragster, and settled into the seat.

Russ strapped him in and wished him good luck. The ignition was switched on, and the huge motor fired up. Art drove the car into the burnout area, revved the motor, made his burnout, and carefully staged the car in the staging light photocell beams. His opponent pulled his car into the lane next to him.

The tension was mounting. Hopeful that they had finally corrected the problem, Art was a bit apprehensive as the engine revs were brought up to 7000 rpm while waiting for the starting lights to flash. First yellow, second yellow, third yellow, he quickly let the clutch out and floored the gas pedal. The car lurched forward, great clouds of smoke billowing off the rear tires.

It was a perfect start. Art glanced over to see his opponent. Thankfully, he had a full car length lead on him. Unfortunately, the motor stumbled and misfired. Art quickly shifted to second gear, his opponent gaining on him. The motor stumbled again. He shifted to third gear, glanced over at his opponent, and watched him inch upon him.

As they crossed the finish line, the opponent's front wheels were just barely in front of Art's, but as were the rules, Art had lost. The time slip and the misfire in the motor indicated that they hadn't corrected their problem. Their hopes for victory at the Nationals had been dashed. Disappointed, they loaded the car into the trailer, but at Bill's insistence, they stayed to watch the rest of the races before heading for home on Sunday.

They finally arrived home at noon on Monday, after getting a flat tire on the trailer and one on their truck.

All in all, it was a very disappointing and frustrating trip. Tuesday night, they met at the garage to rebuild the motor and fuel injection systems. They had to find their problem before Saturday's race.

In the solitude of their garage, they were able to think and analyze the problem more clearly. Art assumed command of the team and started directing the work tasks.

"I'll disconnect the fuel lines from the injection pump to the tank and take off the injection system. Russ, Bill, start

unbolting the engine and transmission. Johnny, you take off the body panels." He said.

"Uh, Art!" Johnny said. *"Be careful when you disconnect the fuel line from the fuel tank to the injection pump. Make sure you plug the end of the line or fuel will run all over the garage floor."*

"Don't worry, John. I always close the fuel shutoff valve before I remove the fuel line." Art assured.

"No, that won't work. It doesn't shut off all the fuel," John said.

"Are you crazy," Art said, *"when the valve is closed, it's closed, it has to shut the fuel off. Fuel can only flow through the line to the injection pump when the fuel valve is open."*

"No," John insisted, *"When we were working on the fuel injection system at the track in Indy, I found that to shut the fuel off, I had to put the handle halfway between the open and closed position. When I put the handle in the closed position, fuel would still pour out."*

"Holy shit!" Art exclaimed.

"That means that when the valve handle was in the open

position, the valve was really half-closed. It's no wonder the engine couldn't get enough fuel. Why didn't you tell me that before when you discovered it?" Art questioned.

"Uh, I'm sorry," John said sheepishly, *"you were busy, and I really didn't think it was all that important."*

"Forget it, John. It's not your fault. I'm not blaming you." Art said, actually meaning it. He was their friend and helper.

In their haste to reassemble the valve for inspection, someone had inadvertently put the valve back together with the handle lever in the wrong position. So, even though the handle indicated the valve was fully open, it was only partially opened, and the motor couldn't get enough fuel. Unfortunately, the boys discovered the problem a little too late, and it ruined their chance for a national victory.

Art now knew *"that sometimes haste does make waste."* Bill didn't seem to mind the trip, though. He got to see the races and had a good time despite all their problems. Maybe sometimes a bad experience isn't so bad. It all depends on your nature and perspective on life.

Chapter 10
El Temible

El Temible, Spanish for the fearsome one; how or why someone gets to be known as the 'fearsome one'?

One spring day in May 1972, Don Gard, Art's division manager, called him to his office. He was sitting behind his big, intimidating wooden desk. Apprehensive, Art sat down in one of his large comfortable tan leather chairs. What did he want? He had now fully recovered from the 'Super Engineer' incident, so there was really no reason in Art's mind for him to be here.

"Art, this is your lucky day," he said.

That caught Art by surprise, but he didn't show it. *"Why?"*

"Because you have two choices." He said. Art could tell by the look on the manager's face that he was excited to tell him this, which meant that it was probably good news.

"Two choices? Wow! I can't wait to find out what they are!" Art exclaimed, wondering if this had something to do with his promotion.

"Yes, you can transfer to our new chemical company, which will be moving to Houston in December, and be their lead cracking reactor engineer, or you can take a two-year assignment in Aruba." Don offered.

"Aruba?" Art asked. *"Where is that?"*

"It's a small island in the Caribbean Sea located about 20 miles off the coast of Venezuela," Don said.

"Well, thanks a lot Don for the wonderful opportunities you're offering me," Art said sarcastically, *"but I think I'll just stay here in New Jersey."*

"Sorry, Art, you can't. You either have to go to Houston for the rest of your career or go to Aruba for two years. You don't have the option of staying here." He said, appearing solemn now. Art genuinely thought that he had been excited about giving him the news.

"What happens after two years in Aruba?" he asked.

"Well, you'll come back here to New Jersey," Don replied promptly.

"And do what?" Art asked, for the sake of his own clarity. He didn't want to leave New Jersey for good. It was his

place, after all.

"Well, with your experience, we'll probably be able to get you a promotion into a low-level management job," Don said. Even though you are one of the best engineers that I have ever seen, engineers don't advance as far or as fast as managers, and they do not make as much money as managers.

Art certainly didn't want to live in Houston for the rest of his life. It was too hot and humid, and there were too many bugs. Besides, all of his family and friends lived in New Jersey. He didn't want to go to Aruba for two years either. Living on a 20-mile-long, five-mile-wide Desert Island where the only means of escape was by airplane. It was certainly not on his bucket list.

To visit his family and friends would be an expensive four-hour plane ride away, which was a huge drawback. Aruba had one advantage over Houston, though it was for only two years. Art knew he could stand a lot of discomforts if he knew when it would end.

"Fine, can I discuss this with my wife?" Art asked, knowing that he could not take this decision alone.

"Sure you can, Art, but I'll have to have your decision by tomorrow morning," Don said, in his typical boss way.

"That's not a lot of time." Art argued.

"It's plenty of time. It's an easy decision to make," Don said, in a tone that made it clear to Art that he was dismissed.

Don hadn't given Art a lot of time to make a decision as important as this, but then again, it wasn't important to Don but Art. Art was the one who had to make a painful decision in less than 24 hours, not Don. After arriving home, Art told his wife that he had to choose between the two places that night.

Eventually, the couple concluded that two years in Aruba would be the better among the two evils. After that, Art was sure that he would probably get a low-level management position and won't be hopping around the world.

Thus began the packing of their lives for temporary but substantial relocation. Their furniture and prized possessions were quickly packed by several clumsy and incompetent movers and shipped to Aruba. The responsibility of renting the house out was given to their next-door neighbors. The race car was left with Bill, Art's partner, who promised to take good care of it and drive it very carefully. Art and Joy said tearful goodbyes to their family and friends and boarded the plane with Mike, Pat, and Tinker, their cat. The family landed in Aruba on a hot August day. The wind blew at about 20 miles an hour, as it did there eleven months a year. When they stepped out of the air-conditioned airplane, it felt as if they stepped into a giant clothes dryer. The airport was old and dilapidated and reminded Art of the last outpost in the old western movies. It was a truly depressing sight.

Art and his wife exchanged looks, knowing that they were thinking about turning back right then and going home. However, the prospects of not having a job when Art got back there were not at all inviting. So, they decided that they had to make the best of it for the next two years. The very next day, they moved to their house.

To their surprise, it was a cute, Spanish-style yellow stucco house surrounded with palm trees and a three-foot-high stucco wall fence. The floors were parquet. At one end was the master bedroom and at the other end was what once was a maids quarters, complete with its own private bath. It would now be Pat's quarters. The house was temporarily furnished with the company's standard, cheap furniture.

The day was spent cleaning up and getting rid of the unwanted guests who had taken possession of the vacant house.

"Roaches, roaches everywhere." Art heard Joy mutter in disgust. There were roaches in the cabinets, in the closets, under the sinks, in every nook and cranny imaginable, and they were gigantic - the largest roaches Art and Joy had the displeasure of ever seeing. There were almost like a hydra; if you killed one, two more would sprout from somewhere or the other.

Art and Joy killed at least a couple of hundred roaches on their very first day in the house. The next day, they won the battle, getting every last one of them. Their numbers had dwindled rapidly now that they knew someone was massacring them. By the end of the week, a roach or bug in the house was a rare occasion, and they lived in peace for the next several months.

Aruba is a desert island nestled in the Caribbean Sea twenty miles off the northern coast of Venezuela. The north coast is rugged and untamed, and the ocean is rough and terrain, rocky and barren. Coral reefs protect the southern coast, and the shore bathes in the gentile clear turquoise waters of the Caribbean. Beautiful white coral sand beaches abound on this shore. In Aruba, as said before, the weather is hot and dry eleven months of the year, and the air has a faint aroma of salt and sea. The rocky, windswept countryside known as the 'canucu' is dotted with cactus and scrub bushes.

Intermixed with the cacti are a few strange looking trees known as divi-divi trees, which are bent over since birth by the constant twenty miles per hour wind. The rocky soil and lack of rain have made this island almost devoid of vegetation. Herds of wild goats and sheep roam unclaimed and unencumbered in the wasteland of the canucu.

The native Arubans are descendants of the Arawak Indians intermixed along the way with some Spaniards and a few Dutchmen. They are a light tan skinned friendly people. The official language of this country is Dutch, but the native language is Papiamento, which is 90 percent Spanish and 10 percent Dutch and Portuguese.

Art and Joy lived in a community on the southeastern end of the island known as Sero Colorado. It was built in 1929 by Lago Oil for its employees and was a private community open only to Lago Oil or Exxon employees, which was its parent company. Most of the community residents were expatriates, such as Art, who came from all over the world. Most of the native Aruban employees of the company chose to live in other areas of the island.

Several hotels and casinos were located on the southwestern shore of the island. The largest and most famous were the Sheraton, the Holiday Inn, and the Aruba Caribbean. Located on the south coast, approximately 12 miles from Sero Colorado, is Oranjestad, the capital and largest city. Its architecture is a blend of Dutch and Spanish styles. Stucco buildings painted light pastel shades of pink, yellow, and blue with red tile roofs were common.

Between Oranjestad and Sero, Colorado is the port town of San Nicholas. Small friendly bars filled with women of the night abound in this quaint little town. Patrons of the bars were usually friendly and peaceful. They were rarely any fights, and business solicitation by the women was not obvious.

It was a typical Saturday night in early November. Art and Joy drove to the other end of the island with their friends, Dave and Linda, to have dinner and saw a show at the Sheraton Hotel casino. After the show and a little gambling at about 11:30 pm, they started the half-hour drive home. Something seemed different on the ride home, but they couldn't quite put their finger on it. Then it dawned on them, the aroma of salt and the sea in the air had vanished, and the wind had stopped. Yes, the wind that blew at 20 miles per hour had stopped.

They had become so accustomed to the wind that they were unaware of it, and now, without it, it seemed so strange. Dave drove down the street past Art's house. Something was wrong; our house appeared to be completely dark when it shouldn't have been. Art and Joy had left all the lights on.

The baby sitter should also have been there, but there wasn't any light shining through the windows. It was dark as if the shades were drawn. They were sure that was not the case, though, because they hadn't installed shades yet. As they got closer to the house, they got the shock of our lives.

The windows were completely covered with bugs, every type of flying bug imaginable. They were attracted by the lights in the house and were clamoring to get in. They formed a thick blanket on all of the windows. They quickly made their way into the house, followed by a hoard of flying insects. The walls of the living room were covered with bugs above the few lamps that were lit. They had never seen anything like it before; it was like a scene out of an Alfred Hitchcock movie. The only difference was that it was all real. Quickly, they shut off all the lights in the house. The bugs were then shot with every can of bug spray they had in the house, and Art and Joy began swatting them with newspapers.

They were battling a losing battle with the bugs all night long. The next morning, however, the wind returned, and the bugs vanished as quickly as they had appeared. It was an experience that they did not want to face again.

One day, the following November, the wind stopped again, and again, they were besieged with insects' invading armies. This time, though, it was not as shocking to them and also somewhat easier to bear. They knew that they were only temporary and would be gone again as soon as the wind returned, and when it did, off the bugs went.

There were no dragstrips on this tiny island, so Art couldn't drag-race, but there was a go-kart track. Art wanted to race, and this was his only choice. He knew nothing about kart racing, but he had good coordination and could drive anything with a motor. The only time he had ever driven a kart was at an amusement park in New Jersey, but those karts were mere toys in comparison. These karts were racing around a Grand Prix track like miniature Formula 1 cars at speeds of 80 miles per hour with the driver sitting only inches from the ground.

Once a year, the tiny island of Aruba hosts an international go-kart race. The best drivers of Holland, Venezuela, and Columbia descend onto the island track to test their driving skills against each other and to vie for the championship of Aruba.

The race that year was held in December. It was held on the day before Art was scheduled to go back to the States for the Christmas holidays. Art had raced against the Aruban's in several races and managed to beat some of the best drivers the island had to offer, and he was confident that he could win this.

He had the opportunity to meet and race against the drivers he had read about in the international karting magazines. The Aruba Karting officials decided that it would add to the international flavor of the race if he represented the United States in this race rather than representing Aruba.

The Arubans were competitive but friendly, and Art expected the drivers from the other countries to be the same. However, when Art's Aruban friends introduced him to the drivers from Columbia, Venezuela, and Holland, he found the Columbian and Venezuelan drivers to be arrogant and unfriendly. For Art, it was just another race, but to them, it was as if they were fighting for the honor of their country and didn't want to lose to an American.

They seemed to take great pride in their respective countries and were quite vocal in their sentiments. They clearly proclaimed that the Venezuelan's or Columbians would defeat the United States. Art had never been placed in a position of having to represent his country or to defend it. He had always raced against drivers as individuals.

Never had he run against a country and had no idea how to handle it. However, having gotten the chance to represent the United States on an international forum was a matter of pride and honor for him, and he clearly couldn't contain his excitement. Life was quite uneventful in Aruba with his family, and he had made it a point to keep on going with his passion for racing. Who would've thought that he would be representing his country on a global level? At the thought, his heart warmed up with feelings of pride and nervousness at the same time. He knew he was shouldering a great responsibility and that he would have to return victorious for the sake of his country. Art did not want to let his country down and was adamant about getting the badge of victory.

They drew numbers from a hat for starting positions. This wasn't particularly Art's lucky day, and he had to start near the back of the pack. Slowly but steadily, Art began to work his way up to the front of the pack, passing one or two drivers on every lap. Passing a Venezuelan or Colombian was a risky business. Whenever he got his kart alongside theirs, they deliberately and savagely tried to force him off the track.

It was the most brutal and violent race he had ever participated in. Many of the Aruban drivers weren't as fortunate as him and were knocked off the track and out of the race. The sides of the track were littered with karts, which were put out of commission by the Venezuelans and Columbians. So, after thirty minutes of racing with only ten more minutes to go, with the aid of a little driving skill and a lot of luck, Art managed to work his way up to the fifth place.

From that position, he knew that he could easily overtake the two drivers in front, guaranteeing himself at least a third-place to finish. Both racers in front of him were Venezuelans. One was on his right side, and two were behind him. The two in front slowed down. The driver on his right moved over and was forcing Art to the left side of the track.

The two karts behind him pulled up very close, their karts only inches from his. Now that Art was boxed in, there was no place to go. One of the drivers in the back started to bump his kart into Art's. Suddenly without warning, his kart was flying through the air. The Venezuelan driver on his right side managed to get his front wheels under Art's rear tire and flipped his kart into the air like a penny in a coin toss. *"Oh, my God!"* he screamed with panic.

The kart came crashing down, as Art hit his head and his left shoulder on the concrete track surface, the kart landing on top of him. He had met with one of the most unfortunate incidents of his life. He could see his defeat lurking around the corner. He knew that he had lost his one and only chance to make his country proud, but right now, Art needed to concentrate on whether he had gotten seriously injured or not.

His head was spinning as his kart was hurled across the road. Even though he had competed in several races, it was always a precarious business. The likelihood of even experienced racers meeting an ill-fate was common as you never know when things would turn ugly, and you would have to make do with a crashed kart and a broken limb.

"Shit! I'm out of the race now. The Venezuelan's got their way. Their country beat the United States. I guess it doesn't matter to them how they play the game. To them, winning is all that counts."

He was short of breath, and his lungs painfully squeezed, desperate for some air. He felt light-headed, and from the corner of his eye, he saw a brief flash of light, which made him wonder where he was.

The Aruban officials came rushing over to him and lifted the kart off of him. Two large hands slid under his armpits, pulling him upwards. A little dazed, but he managed to stand.

"I'm alright! I'm all right!" he shouted as he stumbled, trying to walk as straight as he could. His legs felt heavy like someone had tied rocks to them. He managed to maintain

balance. The only thing on his mind was to get away. Go to a place where it's calm and serene. Somewhere he could breathe and digest what just happened. He wished they would leave him alone.

Henry Lockley, the chief official for the race, held on to Art. A jolt of sharp pain surged through his body, and he winced noticeably.

"Art! Art! You're injured, we'll get an ambulance to take you to the hospital in Orangstad! Don't worry; we'll take care of you and make sure you get the best treatment in town." He said with an empathetic tone.

His eyes studied Art's face and scanned his body for visible wounds. He suddenly felt exposed, as if he could see through him, reading his thoughts. Art mentally shook his head to clear the unwanted and anxious thoughts. *Perhaps I was just extremely worried that I had met with such an ill-fate*, thought Art. But right now, Art didn't need that. He needed peace. He needed air.

"No, no! I'm okay, Henry!" he insisted.

"I just need to sit down on the side of the track for a minute. I'm just a little banged and scraped up, but I'm

alright. I don't need to go to the hospital." Art sighed, trying to escape the hustle and bustle of going to and from the hospital.

Joy came dashing across the track holding Mike in her arms and dragging Pat behind her. *"Are you badly hurt? Can I do something to help you?"* She asked.

She was calm and in complete control of her emotions. Her voice had a deep tone of empathy, and she just wanted to be of assistance. She made him feel at peace. She understood.

"No, I'm not badly hurt; I'm just banged up a little," he replied with a not-so convincing tone.

He didn't want the people around him to worry too much. He didn't know why, but they seemed to be freaking out. *I'm fine; I will be in a few days*, he kept repeating in his head.

"No!" Henry blurted out. *"He's injured, he's seriously injured! Art, you're seriously hurt, and you must go to the hospital now!"*

Henry looked at him with concern. Art didn't know what to do. He felt lost and shaken up.

Half dazed, he looked down with a sigh. Strangely enough, he knew he was feeling immense pain, but at the same time, he felt numb. Does that make sense?

As the confusion and panic started to fade away, he noticed that his shirt was wet and sticking to his body. He couldn't figure if it was blood or sweat. He expected his hand to move as he tried raising it. Instead, he felt another wave of excruciating pain. He looked down at his chest, and to his surprise, something was sticking through his shirt around the collar.

What's that? He pondered. Realization dawned upon him sooner than later. His broken collarbone was protruding through his shirt. Thinking about it intensified the pain, and he finally gave in to Henry's offer; he should go to the hospital. At the hospital in Orangastad, the doctor set his broken collarbone as best he could under the circumstances.

Since it was broken in three places, he said that he would have to operate to set it properly; but because it had pierced Art's skin, he thought that there would be a high risk of infection as a result of the operation. He let Art make the decision as to whether to forego the surgery or not. Art obviously opted to skip the surgery. He didn't want to go through all that hassle, and he was sure that it would heal over time.

After he set the broken collarbone, he released him at his insistence against his and Joy's better judgment. The drive home seemed to take an eternity. They had definitely not envisioned their ride back home to be this way. Time seemed to be going by at a snail's pace. He was in excruciating pain. Something wasn't right. Joy took control of the situation and decided that he should be checked out at the Company hospital in El Lago.

At first, Art was hesitant but eventually gave in because he had no other option than to oblige with what his wife said, as she knew best. She was the only one who was there for him, and he felt that the least he could do was make this easy for her. Her proactive approach and compassionate-self did not let her sit in peace until he was completely fine.

The company doctor took x rays and concluded that Art's collarbone wasn't set correctly, so he'll have to reset it. Art groaned in frustration. Wasn't this injury enough? Why don't doctors do their work properly? He hated hospitals. They remind him of the nightmares that he used to have in his childhood - dark, empty hospital corridors, and the horrid smell. Every time he had the nightmare, it would continue from the last one.

Remembering them made a shiver run down his spine. No one used to believe him back then even though his mom said she did, he knew she didn't. Anyway, the doctor and Joy pleaded Art to stay in the hospital after the procedure. But again, he insisted that he would be just fine at home. He didn't want to spend the next few days in the hospital. He wanted to go home to New Jersey for Christmas and spend it with his mom and Dad. He missed them terribly, especially with all the recent events. He wished to be young again and just have fewer things to worry about.

Christmas vacations started as planned. The next day they flew back home to his parents' house. He constantly tried to ignore the pain and uneasiness because of his unset collarbone.

Nonetheless, he was glad to be back in New Jersey, celebrating Christmas with the people he loved.

"Art, what happened to you? How did you get hurt?" This was the first thing his mom asked with worry coating her voice when she saw his arm and shoulder strapped up.

He knew it was not good to lie, but he had to. His mom got worked up easily on the slightest of matters. There was no way he could upset her by telling such a thing.

"Oh, I was painting the house and fell off a ladder," he lied, his voice laced with guilt and sorrow.

Besides, she didn't know anything about Art's racing, and he didn't want her to know anything. Mainly because he knew she'd be very mad at him, but it would also make her worry about him all the time.

By Wednesday, the pain was getting unbearable. At his mother's constant persuasion, he decided to get it checked out by the local specialist.

"The collarbone is incorrectly set," he informed him. "*It will never heal that way. It will hurt a lot, but I will have to reset it,"* the doctor said.

Art sighed. When was this going to end? He felt like running off to a place where no one would pester him. He needed some time off. He was so darn tired.

He had lost track of time that he had spent on these hospital trips. Three doctors and three attempts to set it correctly. When did it get this bad? Will the doctors ever get it right? The pain was excruciating and hadn't gotten any less since the accident. He had no choice but to agree to let him do what he wanted. He just wanted the pain gone and a healed collarbone. He didn't care about anything else.

"Okay, Doc, you can have your shot at it. It's not that I don't believe you or trust you, but how do I know that you can set it correctly when nobody else did?" he asked.

"Trust me. I'm a specialist," he replied. His answer wasn't convincing at all, but it's not like he had a choice. He, like the two doctors, ruled out surgery because of the serious risk of infection even though it was the only sure way of getting the three pieces of bone to heal correctly.

The breaking and resetting procedure took around an hour. He wasn't feeling any pain, but that was probably due to the anesthesia. His body felt numb, and all he could see was a thick chunky gauze wrapped around his chest. The white hospital room made him nauseatic. The risk of injuring his reset collarbone during vomiting was high, but thank God nothing happened.

After that, the doctor took a couple of x-rays; and showed them to him. It still looked like a broken mess to him, but the doctor said it was now setting in the proper place and would heal alright. He wanted to believe him, and he did because he was the third doctor, and three was always his lucky number. Well, that was what kept him going and bear all that pain and discomfort. Also, he didn't want to go to a fourth doctor and experience the pain of a fourth reset. He knew he had to get back into the kart again as soon as his broken bones were healed. What happened may or may not be his fault, but that doesn't matter.

He loved the challenge of racing, but he wasn't too sure anymore. Every time he had flashbacks of the way his kart toppled over, the blood, broken collarbone, and the chaos, he felt horrified. He didn't want to go through all that again. He knew accidents were meant to happen on a race track, but is it worth it? He had to work and be a responsible person, a dad, and a husband. Can he really afford to do this?

He did get back into it in about two months later, but the accident had taken its toll on him. He could never get rid of the fear, and it clearly had an impact on his racing skills.

The other drivers were walking all over him. They knew he was afraid, and they took every advantage of it. They pushed him all over the track, and he let them. He knew he couldn't let fear control his life. He couldn't let it get the best of him. He had to overcome his fears, but he didn't know how. If you break a leg, you need a crutch until your leg heals. He needed a crutch until his mind healed, and he regained his confidence. His crutch took the form of a leather racing jacket with sponge pads in the shoulders and a couple of pieces of triangular-shaped steel tubing, which he welded onto the kart in front of the rear wheels. He hoped his design would stop other karts tires from getting under his own and tossing him into the air as the Venezuelans did to him.

The shoulder pads would take the impact if the triangular bars that didn't work, and he did get tossed into the air. He convinced himself that they would work and prevent him from suffering the consequences of another violent accident.

Benito was one of the Aruban drivers taking advantage of the situation. He felt no sympathy for Art's situation. When he would get alongside him in the turns, he would get on the inside and hook his front wheel just in front of Art's rear wheel. He would then take great pleasure in forcing him off the track or seeing him slow down his pace in cowardice to avoid hitting him. It was Art's fourth race since returning to the track after his accident. He had driven miserably in the last three races. His motivation levels were at their lowest ebb. It felt like somebody had sucked out the passion from within him, and he felt extremely helpless in front of the other racers trying to exploit his situation. Racing was something that sent adrenaline rushing through his veins. However, since the accident, things were a lot different than they used to be. He really wanted the tables to turn and show his competitor racers what it feels to be in this excruciatingly painful situation. He was adamant about showing them who was the real boss!

Today, he started in the fourth position but had dropped to sixth in the first turn in order to avoid the mass confrontation of karts that was typical in the first turn. As he was entering the second turn, Benito was on the inside, trying to pass him. He was up to his old tricks, and he hooked his front wheel in front of Art's as he had done during the last three races.

He started moving closer to him, expecting Art to give way in cowardice as he had done in the past. Only this time, Art was going to test his newfound crutch, i.e., the new triangular tubing welded in front of his rear wheels. He decided he had driven like a coward long enough. He wasn't going to give ground to him. Instead, he floored the gas pedal, and Benito's kart went flying off the track. Art's kart was unscathed; his crutch had worked.

He now started moving up on the leaders of the race and passed them one by one.

And guess what? He won that race! He was the champion of that race! The victory was his. He was ecstatic and couldn't contain the excitement that made him want to jump around.

Yes! He did it. He had finally overcome his biggest fear and stood up for himself. That day he realized that it was in his hands to be brave enough to gather himself and not be demotivated to give up. If you want to turn around your life for the better, you can do it with unwavering resolve and determination to not let anything bring you down.

How long could he let the bullies have the upper hand? He learned from his childhood experience that you had to stand up against bullies like Rocco. He had had enough of their exploitation, and he was no longer ready to be oppressed and mal-treated at the cost of his career.

His fear had gone, and he was driving better than ever.

He was the one to beat, and they couldn't. The Arubans started calling him 'El Temible - the fearsome one.' Advertisements for the kart races in the newspapers and commercials on the radio and television announced to the Aruban population when El Temible would be racing. That year in the international race, he beat the Venezuelans, the Columbians, and the champion from Holland. He had successfully overcome his fear with the aid of a crutch, and he won the championship. He had successfully triumphed over those who had mocked him and tried to take undue advantage of his past injuries.

Yet, he had managed to live through all the chaos and anarchy and all the sabotaging efforts made by his opponents to harm him and his career. It had been quite overwhelming, and a tough phase, which he thought would not end anytime soon. However, when he finally gathered all his courage, he felt an inexplicable sense of confidence and energy rush through him, empowering him to lead with undefeatable valiancy.

The Venezuelan kart racers invited the Aruban kart racers and him to race in the little town of Valencia in Venezuela. The people of the town of Valencia arranged for the airplane to transport them and their karts from Aruba to Venezuela. They also paid all the expenses for their meals, hotels, and transportation. This was to be the first international kart race ever held in the country of Venezuela, and apparently, it was a very big deal to them. Art, of course, was invited only to lend more prestige to this international race since he would represent the United States. When their plane arrived in Caracas, they were promptly met at the airport by government officials from both Valencia and Caracas. There appeared to be a lot of friction and hostility between the two sets of officials.

He didn't understand the reason for this apparent hostility until one of the Venezuelan racers who spoke English explained the situation to him. It seems that Caracas was the capital of Venezuela, and as such, the government officials from Caracas believed they should have the distinction of hosting the first international kart race and not the insignificant little town of Valencia.

It seems that there had been numerous newspaper editorials concerning the impropriety of holding this race in Valencia. They were now the pawns of a South American political game of chess. They were only racing in Valencia because they were invited to race there by the people of Valencia. The officials from Caracas, however, now asked them not to participate in the Valencian race but to participate in a special race that would be held through the streets of Caracas. They, however, refused, since they had already committed to race in Valencia and they were men of honor. When they refused to succumb to the demands of the officials from Caracas, they were promptly branded on the television, radio, and Caracan newspapers as the 'Rebels without a Cause.' During the pre-race ceremonies, the racers were officially welcomed by the Mayor of Valencia and presented with commemorative medals.

Art stood to attention as they raised the American flag and played the Star-Spangled Banner. Art was proud to represent his country. The feeling of being the only one from the United States was something that made him feel like he was on cloud nine.

The actual race in Valencia was anticlimactic for him as the over patriotic Venezuelans again ganged up on him. They knocked him off the track several times during the race by crashing their karts into his, making him finish in the fifth place. The Venezuelans were too proud and couldn't bear the thought of losing to an American in their very own first international kart race. Some people are overzealous and too patriotic. They can't bear the thought of their country being beaten, even if it is only in a little insignificant kart race. They had this air about themselves that made them indulge in a superiority complex, and they wouldn't accept their defeat in their own land. He never understood this attitude of people having this notion that they are superior to others. A sporty spirit is what they lacked in such times as they are unable to rise above victory and loosing and playing the game in a positive competitive spirit.

Pride sometimes causes people to do strange things, both good and bad. It is like a venom that overshadows your ability to think clearly and blurs your judgment. It all becomes a matter of ego and self-respect when it comes to winning a competition or an international challenge or sport for the pride of your nation.

Little did they realize that they all belonged to a unified class and race of human beings, and there is no harm in uniting for a good cause and pursuing something for team spirit and in good faith. Throughout history, people driven by pride have died for even less important causes. Often caught up in the spirit of the moment, Art thought he could do things that were beyond his ability.

Return to Aruba

One Saturday night, Art and Joy went to the local drive-in theatre in Orangastad to see a movie about Bobby Evel Knevel. His ability and his skill in riding a motorcycle intrigued Art deeply. The ease with which he executed dangerous jumps with his motorcycle made a big impression on him. He was bamboozled and in awe of his stunts.

He couldn't help but imagine himself in his place because he always had an attraction to sporting activities – the kind that sets the adrenaline rushing through your veins. Seeing him perform such brave and risky stunts set Art's heart on a spree of wanting to feel the same excitement.

That night, all night long, Art dreamed of riding his motorcycle with his skill and ability and performing the death-defying stunts with the ease that he had seen Bobby perform them on the screen.

The swiftness that he portrayed was literally mind-boggling and something that was playing on repeat in his head. Sunday morning came, and he awoke from his dreams to face the stark reality of the day. Aaah, all that he had seen last night was merely a dream, he thought to himself. He could never be competent enough to display such gallant stunts and leave the audience in awe. He knew he couldn't ride his motorcycle like him, and he probably would never be able to, or would he? These thoughts were continually rummaging through his mind, and he couldn't contain them. He desperately needed an outlet to vent out his over-zealous feelings and control them somehow before they took the better of him. What could he do to give these thoughts some shape and direction?

He and his family had breakfast and went to church in San Nicholas. After church, Pat attended Sunday school, so they left him there and went home as usual. When Sunday school was over, Art would drive to church on his motorcycle and pick him up. Mike usually rode with him perched on the gas tank, but this Sunday, he had a cold and was left at home.

The road to the church through the town of San Nicholas was winding and twisted. Quaint stucco houses with paved sidewalks lined both sides of the road. Riding down the road, Art started to daydream about being able to perform the death-defying jumps with his motorcycle just as he had seen Evel Knevel do the night before.

"How did he get started?" he pondered. Small jumps, of course. He could get started the same way, and there is no better time than the present. Driving down the road on his motorcycle about fifty miles an hour, he reasoned that all he had to do was to drive up one of the driveways which lined the road and jump off the six-inch-high curb.

"Mere child's play," Art thought, *"compared to Evel Knevel's jumps,"* but it would be a start. It would be a starting place for bigger and better jumps. It was now or never. He headed the motorcycle towards one of the driveways. He misjudged the driveway ramp and hit the curb and was now flying through the air in an uncontrolled manner.

"Oh my God, help me!" he screamed frantically. He came crashing down on the concrete pavement, and the bike was on top of him. He was sliding along the ground face down, being propelled by the momentum of the 300 lb. motorcycle. With the motorcycle on his back, he was traveling at fifty miles per hour.

Soon he came to a grinding halt. Stunned, he managed to get the bike off of him and picked himself up off the ground. Looking around, he discovered that he was in someone's front yard. The people were standing there in shock, looking at him in astonishment. What had gotten into him? Had he seriously lost his sense of looking through things and the ability to make fair judgments? Who takes such risks in the middle of a street with houses on both sides? He felt so stupid at that moment; it was hard for him to put it into words. Embarrassed, he didn't know what to say to them. The bike was banged up, and the front wheel was bent, but the motor was still running. He jumped on what was left of the bike and headed home. Somehow, he managed to make it.

Joy was standing in the doorway when he walked through.

"Oh, my God!" Joy exclaimed. *"What happened? You look like you've been through a meat grinder!"* She panicked and couldn't register what had just happened.

His clothes were ripped and shredded, and his arms and legs were lacerated. Every inch of his body was covered with blood. She got him into the car and rushed to the Company hospital. His wounds were washed and bandaged. He was now in great pain; every inch of his body hurt, and he couldn't even bend his legs to sit in the car. His physical pain overshadowed the mental anguish he was suffering. His ego was bruised.

He realized that he didn't have any of the skills and abilities that Evel Knevel had. El Temible, or now maybe El Stupido, he couldn't even jump off a six-inch curb. What was more mentally draining was, he didn't know how he was going to explain his injuries to his friends and coworkers without them thinking that he was a complete idiot.

Art overestimated his abilities and failed, but at least he tried. He knew that he had to try again. If he survived this, he'd probably be in more pain than he was after that stupid motorcycle accident. *"Good God, if you're listening to me, I'd rather have that pain than die now,"* Art thought, as the dragster was hurling along upside-down, scraping the ground.

A month later, on a Saturday morning at 7 a.m., the sun and the Aruban chickens had been up for almost an hour, but not him. It was the perfect time for sleeping and dreaming. *"Ring! Ring! Ring!"* he was awakened from his sleep by the loud ringing of the phone. Who could it be at this hour of the morning?

"Hi, Art! It's Walt. Sorry to wake you, but we have quite a serious problem with the new jet fuel storage tanks. Can you come to the plant now?" His tone had a sense of urgency, and he could feel it through the phone.

"Sure, Walt. I'll be there in 15 minutes," he said without a second thought. There was no point in saying no as Walt was the manager in charge of the project, and Art would have to look into it now or later ultimately.

"Good, meet you at the tanks." He said approvingly.

Walt was the manager of the construction division and was the supervisor of the project engineering section of Lago Oil Company, and Art was the recognized technical expert for solving strange engineering problems. They had just finished the construction of two huge storage tanks for jet fuel. Each tank cost over one million dollars to build.

The tanks were 150 feet in diameter and 64 feet high and were designed to hold 8,500,000 gallons of jet fuel each. The tanks were inspected by the refinery inspectors and turned over to the refinery for filling on Friday. When Art got to the plant, he saw Walt and a group of the other supervisors and operators standing around talking while occasionally looking up into the air.

"What's the problem, Walt?" he inquired as he approached him.

"Look up at the top of tank 501," Walt said frantically.

He looked up and was shocked. The steel top of the tank was undulating like a balloon filled with water. One to three-foot-high ripples could be seen moving across the top of the tank. He couldn't believe that this was happening. The steel roof was moving up and down just like it was made of rubber. Walt and the others were worried that the entire tank would split, dumping 8 million gallons of volatile jet fuel into the refinery. Art was worried too.

"What's causing it, Walt?" he asked, unable to come up with logical reasoning for this bizarre emergency. He tried to keep his calm and brainstorm ideas about what could be done to prevent this tank from splitting. His experience and technical knowledge allowed him to envision this would be a highly disastrous blast and would have highly intoxicating after-effects.

"I don't know; Walt said I don't have the foggiest idea. That's why I called you." He did not want to give up in such a situation but rather be a source of motivation and encouragement for Art to exercise his technical abilities and come up with a solution as soon as possible.

"Tell me what happened to the tank since yesterday," Art asked so that he could have some background knowledge of what had happened and make a well-informed decision.

"Well, the operators began filling the tank yesterday morning. About 5 a.m. this morning, they noticed some fuel running down the side of the tank. Realizing that the level gauges weren't working and that fuel was overflowing out of the top of the tank, they then opened the drain valves to lower the fuel level. About a half-hour later, they noticed the rippling in the roof, and they called him. That's all he knew. Got any idea?" Walt asked.

"Yes, it could be that the vacuum vents were installed improperly." Art replied insightfully.

"No," he said, "it can't be. They were inspected yesterday," retorted Walt.

"I still think there's something wrong with them." he

insisted, *"because that was a very likely place for the root problem to originate,"* insisted Art.

"Where are you going?" Walt asked in an inquiring tone.

"Up to the roof to check them out. Come with me," said Art in a hopeful tone

"Are you crazy?" "It's too risky. The tank could rupture," he replied hastily. He was in a frenzy, unable to think of the next most practical step to sort this out.

"If we don't do something quick, it will rupture for sure," Art said to create a sense of urgency as Walt felt in no position to see this through and reach any logical conclusion.

"But, but!" he muttered hesitatingly.

"But what?" Art retorted. Art knew they had very little time and couldn't afford to waste it like this. The clock was ticking, and if they didn't do something immediately to tackle the situation, they would be sitting regretting their complacently and inability to take decisive action.

"But, nothing," Art said, giving up. He knew that Walt had called him because of his sound technical knowledge, and he couldn't negate him or his way of solving this

emergency situation since he was in charge right now.

"Alright, if you're afraid to go, I'll go myself," he said impatiently. He couldn't take in the pressure for too long. He had to assume responsibility and take charge before it was too late.

Off Art went. He climbed the stairway to the top of the tank. Standing at the edge of the roof, he looked across at the vents. They were about 75 feet away from him. He saw and felt the undulating motion of the roof. It looked like swells of huge waves moving across the surface of the ocean before they broke. Suddenly, he was afraid. He started to think about the consequences.

What if the roof ruptures while he's crawling across it? He wouldn't have a chance. But, if he didn't do something, the whole tank could rupture and dump 8 million gallons of fuel into the refinery. It could catch fire and become a major catastrophe. It could destroy the entire refinery and wipe out all of Sero Colorado.

It's only a matter of time. If he turned back now, Walt would know he's afraid. Why did he get himself into this? He shouldn't have come up here in the first place, but somebody had to do something, and he's the only one who wanted to do anything.

"*Dear God, help me and protect me*!" he murmured to himself as he said a little prayer. He started to crawl across the rippling roof, praying all the time. It seemed like an eternity had passed before he finally reached the vents. He examined them, but they looked okay. Shit! What could it be? Boy, he's going to look stupid in front of everybody. There's got to be something wrong with these vents, but what? It can't be anything else. There has to be a problem with these vents. In desperation, he then reached up inside one of the vents.

He felt something. What is it? He didn't think there's supposed to be anything in there. He managed to grab hold of something and quickly pulled it out. Suddenly, the air started to rush into the now unplugged vent. The roof moved violently up and down about three feet like a giant trampoline.

Oh, God, this is it, the roof's going to split, help me! He held onto the vent to prevent being thrown off the roof. After a few seconds, the movements subsided, and the roof came to rest. He breathed a great sigh of relief.

"Thank God! Thank you very much." he was shaking as he got up and walked to the edge of the roof. Looking down, he saw Walt talking with Roy, the refinery manager who had just arrived.

Art yelled to Walt, *"Walt, I solved the problem."* he was shouting because he couldn't believe he had taken up the responsibility to go so up close to the vent and expose himself to so much danger.

"I know. I can see that," Walt yelled back.

"I was just about to come up there to help you, but I had to explain the situation to Roy first." He said casually, giving himself the benefit of the doubt.

"Sure you were," he said to himself. He very well knew how much of a coward his manager was, and he would never risk his life to troubleshoot a problem like this. His facial expressions had shown that he had chickened out the moment he proposed this idea even.

"Was it the roof vents, as we suspected?" Walt asked.

"Yes," he answered, holding up a large piece of cardboard in his hand.

"Somebody left this cardboard packing inside the vents," he said, frustrated at why his manager would never listen to what he had to say in the first instance.

"I knew it had to be a problem with the vents," Walt said.

"Sure you did, Walt, the only thing you knew was that you didn't know what the problem was," he muttered to himself. At that moment, it was infuriating to see how conveniently Walt was trying to come into the limelight.

"Good job Walt! I knew I put the right man in charge," Roy said.

"Right, man! Shit!" Art said to himself.

"Boy, am I a fool? I risked my life to prevent a catastrophe when everybody else refused to do anything, and Walt gets all the credit." Art thought furiously. His head was splitting with what just transpired before his eyes. Was he insane to have taken the onus of solving the problem despite it being life-threatening? Did he not deserve to be acknowledged and appreciated for his efforts?

At that moment, he reflected on the saying, 'Fools rush in where wise men fear to go.' Now he had a new insight into its meaning. Fools are those well-meaning people who often risk themselves, act quickly in an emergency, and sometimes save the day. Still, wise men are those people who, being afraid to take risks, often ponder long and hard about what should be done and often do nothing, but yet, they get the credit for the work of the fool. Guess that's why they're known as wise men. He hated the fact that there was no trace of work ethic practiced in such a situation, and the entire credit would just fall on the shoulders of the "wise man" who had just been a bystander all this time.

My Dad

It was December of 1973, and Art had rushed home to New Jersey because Art's father was dying of cancer.

Art's dad called him with a voice thick with something he couldn't place his finger on. *"Art, will you still be here when I wake up tomorrow morning?"* he finally said. It felt like he had wanting to ask him this for a long time.

"Sure, Dad, of course, I'll be here. I'm not going anywhere. You have a good night's sleep," he replied with a reassuring tone. He suddenly missed his dad. It felt like ages ago when they last had a heart-to-heart discussion.

"Good night, Art. See you in the morning." He said again.

"Good night Dad."

Art's dad was sick, very sick. He was now a mere shadow of the man he was nine months ago before cancer struck him. Unfortunately, he hadn't seen him much since he got sick since he was working 3,000 miles away in Aruba. But now he's home, and he wanted to do everything he could for him. He remembers having a happy childhood because of his dad.

He was always there to support him and let him know that it was okay to make mistakes. Art wanted to be with him now and hopefully be with him forever someday. He left Joy and the kids at home in Aruba to come there as quickly as possible, to be with his father. His mom had called yesterday and said he looked like he was taking a turn for the worse. He remembered how, when he was a little boy, his Dad would sit still awake all night whenever he got sick to keep him safe from harm.

He remembered the comfort it gave him to know that his dad was there watching him and keeping him company throughout the night. Now, he wished he could only give him back some of the comforts he gave him as a child. He was a kind, gentle, trusting man who would give you the shirt off his back. He was always giving a handout to the downtrodden or less fortunate people in life. His benefactors included the struggling jobless and the poor, the nuns, the priest, as well as the winos and bumps desperate for a meal. No one who ever asked was refused. Art's mom would often call him a sucker, but he gave it his all. It was his nature. Maybe he trusted some people too much. Maybe some took advantage of him, but he thought it was better to give all the benefit of the doubt rather than risk not helping someone who was genuinely needy of a handout.

Maybe he trusted people too quickly, and perhaps some people took advantage of him, and Art got that trait from his father. Art's dad was the breadwinner and the provider for the family, but his mom was the boss. He was easy going and forgiving, but his mom insisted that he be the disciplinarian.

When Art was naughty, his mom would say, *"Arthur, when your father comes home, he's going to spank you."* But, under his own volition, he never would. If he was really bad, she would call him up at work and insist that he come home during his afternoon break to spank him. When he got home, she would order him to spank him. He would then chase Art around the dining room table.

Around and around they would run until his Dad caught him, or until he managed to make a break for it and escape to the safety of the bathroom where he would lock the door and sit in solitude until his Dad had to go back to work. He was always confident that by the time he would return home in the evening, things would have blown over, and he would safely escape punishment.

When he did manage to catch Art in the dining room, however, he would spank him hard with his hand across his backside or, if the punishment warranted it, he would use his belt. He would say that it was going to hurt him more than Art and Art believed it really did.

His Dad managed the family restaurant for his parents until they died, and then, he and his uncle became partners and ran the business. He had wanted to be a lawyer but chose to drop out of college in his senior year to manage the restaurant and care for Art's grandfather when he was seriously injured in a car accident. When he was a little boy, his dad would take Art to the restaurant in the mornings with him. He had the whole restaurant to himself to run wild in, to play with the cash register, and to build forts with the tables and chairs.

As a teenager, he would often go there with his friends. Meals were always free to his friends, whether he was with them or not. Art's father also loved racing, any kind. But his particular passion was horse racing. Every morning, he would read the Morning Telegraph (a horse racing paper) from cover to cover. He knew horses, and he was a good handicapper.

After breakfast, he would pick his favorite horses for the races that day. If he couldn't get to the local track for a few races during his afternoon break, he would place his bets with a local bookie. He never bet big money, usually, only $2 per race, but if he got a special tip from a jockey or trainer friend of his and thought the horse had a particularly good chance, he might up his bet to as much as $20. This happened only on rare occasions.

He was wise and knew that it was much easier to lose than it was to win. When he bet even a small amount, he had the thrill of rooting for his horse to win and the comfort of knowing that he wouldn't lose very much if the horse lost.

He didn't win very much either, but he got great pleasure from it. His friends came from all walks of life, rich and poor. Among them were actors, singers, lawyers, judges, senators, gamblers, ballplayers, priests, bums, and even a few criminals. Art was incredibly proud of his Dad. Even in this sickly state, his Dad never once cried in front of his family. His smiling face gave him hope; it taught Art his biggest life's lesson-that no matter what's going on in your life, either good or bad, never lose hope, keep smiling, keep fighting, and someday you'll survive even the greatest of battles.

Now, he's all alone with only his mom and him by the side. Art knew that it was all he ever wanted - for his family to be there in his last days, to even say goodbye. Cancer has taken its toll on him, and he had been in a lot of pain. Art could see it in his face and his movements. He went through all that pain and fear alone, keeping it inside, never uttering a single word.

He would never admit that he was in pain or that he was seriously ill. He insisted that he would recover and be well someday. Art wished to be like him someday. Even half of what he was. His father's willpower amazed him.

Throughout his treatment, he didn't want us to worry about him. He suffered and prayed in silence and had great faith that God and the Blessed Mother would take care of him.

Art woke up the next morning and checked on him. A smile graced his lips at the sight of his father sleeping peacefully as if the great pain had miraculously been lifted from him. He's not ready yet, but Art knew that his departure from this world is the only way he'll be in peace.

It was Sunday morning, which meant he had to go to church. He prayed with his tears to give his father some peace to be where he deserves to be. When he returned home an hour later, his mom was crying. He knew. Even though they were expecting it, his heart sank to the ground.

"Your dad died in his sleep. He never woke up this morning. At least he won't suffer anymore. He's glad he got to see you before he died," she said. The words were true, but that didn't make his throbbing heart hurt any less. Tears welled up in his eyes, and he stumbled and lost balance. Sliding down the wall, he cried his heart out. My dad was the one person I could always count on to get me out of trouble.

Upside down in his dragster Art cried out.

"I miss you, Dad. Help me now."

Chapter 11
The Great Escape

Art's two-year assignment in Aruba was coming to an end. He had served his time in exile and had avoided being drafted by Exxon's new chemical company. What would be his next job? Would he get an immediate promotion in Florham Park, or would he go back to supervising a group of engineers for a while? The thoughts of his future career life rummaged continuously, and he was quite perplexed. Little did he know what lay ahead of him and where he would be destined to.

He pondered over all of these questions, but the only way to find out was to call the home office in Florham Park. He was anxious, but the curiosity was killing him, and he wanted to know where he would be headed to, from Aruba. With the volatile job market presenting a plethora of challenges, he wanted to be sure of his position.

"Hello. This is Art Dinick. Could I please speak to Don Gard?"

"Mr. Gard has transferred to another division and no longer works in Florham Park. Mr. William Braid has taken over his position as manager of Exxon's Technology Division. Do you wish to speak to him?

"Yes, please put him on the phone." Art didn't know Bill very well, and he had only met him briefly on one occasion several years ago.

"Hi, Bill. It's Art Dinick; as you know, my assignment in Aruba will be up in three weeks, and I'll be returning home to Florham Park. I was wondering if you could tell me what my next assignment will be?" Art asked, not wanting to sound very desperate.

"Well, Dinick, I really don't know you very well, but I heard a lot about you. I've gone over your employment records, and, contrary to everyone else's opinion of you, I think you are overrated. I hope you are not looking down the gun barrel for a promotion as soon as you return." He said with a touch of slight sarcasm in his voice.

Art was shocked. What does he mean overrated? He deserved the promotion he was promised. Holding his tongue, he replied, *"Well, no, not right away."*

This was not the first time that Exxon had disappointed him, and he wasn't surprised that he was yet again refused his right to promotion after returning from Aruba. Although he wasn't told explicitly but subtly, Bill made sure that Art did not set his hopes too high. Managers at Exxon always managed to make you feel undervalued and would always find ways to eat away from your fair share of credit that you deserved.

However, Art was of the nature that he still worked hard at every project that he was assigned and never performed less than his capabilities. He was a man of his words and never wished to gain an advantage without truly deserving it. He was a polished engineer who knew his work well, and he would make every possible effort to solve the problem at hand if it was under his jurisdiction. He was not the kind of person who had a laid back attitude and would do anything to prove his capabilities.

"Good," he said, *"but I really don't have any positions available for someone of your experience. Maybe you could work on some research projects we are doing. We might be able to find someone who needs some assistance in one of their projects."* He said matter-of-factly. It's like it was

unsaid that Art had to go through this ordeal and make his own path.

"Well Bill, as you know from my records, I don't work on long term research projects. I do design, troubleshooting, consulting, and supervise engineering groups, but I don't do research." Art said assertively. He had come this far after a lot of hard work, and he did not want to give away his strengths. He wanted to work in his fields of specialty so that he could work with complete confidence.

"Well then, Dinick, it looks like we don't have any jobs for you here in Florham Park, but George Claypot from our new Chemical Company calls up here every couple of months to ask about you. Maybe he is still interested in you. You know they didn't move to Houston after all. They decided against that move. Why don't you give him a call?" he said as a gesture of goodwill. Maybe, if he couldn't hire him, he could link him to someone credible. We never know his intentions, but this is what he portrayed.

"Well, thanks a lot, Bill. It's good to know that you and Exxon Engineering Co. have put so much effort into planning my career. I guess despite all verbal and published bullshit propaganda in Exxon, it's still every man for himself

and "catch as catch can." Goodbye, Bill, sorry for wasting your time with this phone call. I'll give George a call and see what if anything of my career he can salvage." Art said, hardly taking a breath. He was infuriated at the way Bill was addressing him. All those years of loyalty felt futile. What did he do to deserve this treatment? But he let it go since professional relations are not meant to be taken at heart.

"Don't be so bitter, Dinick; it's just that we don't really need anyone of your qualification at this time." He said nonchalantly. Art couldn't expect Bill to do justice to him, his efforts, and all the time that he had invested at Exxon. He had just recently come to power, and he hadn't personally interacted with Art, either. And the fact that he called him overrated was proof enough that he was egoistic and didn't want to make Art comfortable in the first instance.

"Don't be bitter? Why shouldn't I be bitter? I just spent two years in exile to avoid getting transferred to Exxon's Chemical Company, and now I find that the only job available is with the chemical company that I tried to avoid two years ago." Upset and angry, he slammed the phone down. This is insane. What was the whole point of spending two years in Aruba when he had to meet with the same fate?

However, seeing how things were proceeding, he felt it was high time he took things in his hand and took the steering wheel in his hand.

After calming down, Art called George. "Hi, George. It's Art Dinick. My assignment in Aruba will be over in about three weeks. I was just talking to Bill Braid, and he said that you might still be interested in me." He said in a formal tone, sounding calm and exposed.

"We sure are Art. We need someone of your abilities to run the reactor group. Kivie is running it now, but he is transferring to Big Ed's division. Are you interested?"

"I sure am George! I'll take the job! See you in about three weeks when I get back from Aruba." Art had finally given in to his destiny. If he was destined to work Exxon Chemical, be it so. He had done a lot on his part to escape that torture.

A Night in the Park

While working for George, Art was supervising the Exxon Chemicals reactor design group in Florham Park N.J.

and making troubleshooting consulting for Exxon's Chemical Plants all over the world. He had just finished up a three-week assignment in Tokyo. Next stop Kuala Lumpur, Malaysia. Exxon had a plant in Port Dickson, which was a seaport town and about 60 miles from Kuala Lumpur. The plant was having problems. Combustion in their reactors was bad, and tubes in the reactors were overheating and bursting when the flames impinged on them. He had arranged his itinerary so that he would be able to devote four days of his time working on their problem before reporting to work in Melbourne, Australia, for an urgent job.

Art arrived at Haneda airport in Tokyo at 11:45 a.m. Monday morning for a 12:30 flight to Kuala Lumpur. He was running a little late. The traffic was heavier than he had anticipated. He rushed up to the ticket counter and handed the reservationist his ticket.

"Could I have a window seat in the back of the plane for your 12:30 flight to Kula Lumpur?" Art inquired.

"I'm sorry, sir, but we don't have a 12:30 flight to Kuala Lumpur today. We have only one 11:30 flight, and I'm afraid it has already departed. Our next flight will not be until Thursday." She said with a sympathetic tone.

"But, but my ticket is for a 12:30 flight today." Art stuttered apprehensively.

"I'm very sorry, sir, but someone must have made a mistake when they issued your ticket." She said apologetically.

"But I have to get to Kuala Lumpur. I can't wait for Thursday's flight." Art panicked. All his planning couldn't go down the drain just like that. He had planned every minute of his trip to the minutest detail.

"Well, sir, since there appears to be an error on your ticket, we will assume complete responsibility for it. We can fly you to Bangkok, Thailand, today. We will put you up in a hotel at our expense, of course, and fly you to Kuala Lumpur tomorrow on our 4:00 p.m. flight." said the attendant apologetically.

"Is that the best you can do?" He questioned. He was in a state of panic, and he couldn't help but make out what to do in this situation.

"Yes, sir, it's the best; we try to accommodate our customers to the best of our ability. I have studied all the itineraries and routes that are there, and this is the best that

we can do in the present situation to accommodate you, sir."

"Well, then I guess I will have to take it. Thank you very much for your help." Art gave in to the only option that he had.

Art didn't want to go to Bangkok, but it seems that he had no choice. He couldn't wait for Thursday's flight. His work in Australia couldn't be delayed. He landed in Bangkok at about 6:00 p.m. that night. A gorgeous airline representative escorted him off the airplane and guided him through customs and immigration.

The security guards at the customs booth caught his attention. They were armed with machine guns. It looked as if they were expecting a terrorist attack. The Vietnam War was going strong, and Thailand is nestled next to Laos and Cambodia. He felt a bit uneasy in their presence and was glad the airline representative was there to assist him.

The sun was beginning to set as he boarded the bus for his journey into town. Shacks and dilapidated shanties lined the roadway. Art could see families dressed in rags milling about outside their meager homes. Scantily clad little children and old men and women sat on their doorsteps. As he drove further into the heart of the city, the crowds swelled. Sidewalks and shops were filled with people making their last-minute purchases before heading home for the evening. The streets were crowded with bicycles, motor scooters, and taxi cabs. Directly across from him on the bus sat an elderly gentleman. He was dressed in a blue ship officer's uniform.

He smiled at Art and asked if he had ever been to Bangkok before?

"No! This is my first time." Art replied sheepishly

Have you been here before?" Art asked in return

"Yes," he replied, *"many times."* He replied casually in a conversational tone. It seemed like he wanted to carry on the conversation ahead.

"You are lucky to be here today." The man replied in an amused tone. He had a very welcoming disposition and told Art that the timing of his visit was very apt.

"Why?" he asked curiously.

"Today is a Tai holiday. It is the Festival of Lights. There will be a lot of festivities tonight. The center of the festivities

will be in the park across the street from the hotel where we are going. You can view the festivities from the windows in the hotel." The man told Art in a way that would want him to say more.

It was 7:30 p.m. when Art arrived at the Dusit Thani Hotel. After seeing the run-down condition of many of the buildings on his journey from the airport, he was pleasantly surprised to find that the hotel was a very modern twenty-story high concrete and glass structure. Leading to its entrance was a large circular driveway.

At least fifteen taxi cabs stood waiting to take patrons to the multitude of nightspots for which the city was renowned. After checking in, Art went up to my room for a quick shower. At approximately 8:15 p.m., he returned to the lobby. There were numerous restaurants and night clubs off the lobby. Their Marquees and entranceways were marked with a multitude of glittering and flashing lights. Loud music was emanating from the clubs.

Strip shows were the main and only attraction. Art went into one of the restaurants for a quick bite to eat. He didn't want to waste too much time on a mundane thing like eating alone. He had too much to see and do before my 4:00 p.m.

flight tomorrow. Eating, especially dinner by yourself, is lonely and boring. He rushed through dinner, a well-cooked steak, some fried potatoes, well-cooked vegetables, a glass of wine, and some bottled water. There was nothing uncooked or raw, no sense in taking a chance to get dysentery, which is common to tourists in this part of the world. Art left the hotel lobby and proceeded down the walkway of the hotel towards the park. He was in search of a peaceful, serene spot where he could unwind and find his own comfort zone. The part was the only option that appealed to him at the moment. Approximately ten feet from the hotel door, a taxi driver approached me and asked, "*Can I take you someplace, sir?*

"No, I'm just going across the street to the park." Art replied suspiciously. Why was the taxi driver so enthusiastic about taking him somewhere?

"You shouldn't go there; it's not safe for you, it's too dangerous. It's only for Tai people. You could be beaten up and robbed." He warned.

"I can take you to a nice club that has the most beautiful women in the world. You will be very safe there." The taxi driver insisted, trying to convince Art

"No, that's OK. I'm not interested." Replied Art, wanting to escape the scene as soon as possible

"But I have a friend who has a private club where beautiful women will fulfill your fantasies." He said, pushing the matter a bit too much.

"No, I am really not interested," retorted Art. This time with irritation in his voice. The non-stop insistence of the taxi driver made him sense that something was fishy, and he had no intention whatsoever to get enticed by the offer.

"I know a beautiful woman; she is my wife's sister; she will escort you around the city and will show you a very good time." described the taxi driver in a fascinating way. It was like he was being paid to publicize this.

"No, no, I'm not interested." Art kept on giving the same answer to make it very clear that he was not going to buy into the offer despite repeated insistence.

"But she is very, very beautiful. Here is her picture." He thrust a picture of a young woman with long black hair and slight oriental features into Art's hand. The entire encounter was really eerie, and Art wanted to flee from the situation.

Art returned it and said, *"Yes, she is beautiful, but I am really not interested."* Quickly, he walked away from him. No sooner had he escaped from him then he was approached by another taxi driver. His line was the same, only this time, it was his beautiful cousin who would escort him around the city. He, too, warned him against going into the park. Art also told him that he was not interested in it. Before reaching the entrance to the park, he was approached by three more taxi drivers. All were trying to pawn off various female members of their family on him. He was now having second thoughts about entering the park.

A tinge of fear came over him, and all the possible worst-case scenarios tried to spring up into his mind. He fought it off. Why should he worry? He can handle himself. There probably is nothing to worry about anyway. The taxi drivers were just trying to use fear to convince him that he should spend his money with them. He was going to spend his time and money the way he wanted to.

Anyway, he couldn't get robbed; since he had left his wallet in his hotel room. Night had firmly set in, and stars shone brightly. The park grounds were lit only by the thousands of little bonfires of families cooking their evening meal. The air was filled with pungent and strange odors emanating from the cooking of fish and exotic spices on the open fires. The park was crowded. Thousands of people were there. Every family in Bangkok must have been there. He made his way through the crowds to the edge of the lake. Hundreds of families were gathered on the shore. They were making small paper boats. The boats were laden with flowers, and a small candle was lit in each little boat as it was set afloat on the smooth dark waters of the lake. The hopes and prayers of these people were carried to their God by these small boats.

They sailed smoothly across the lake, and the entire scenario seemed picturesque and calming. It gave him a sense of inner bliss. They seemed peaceful and friendly, nothing to worry about. It was just what he wanted at this moment, to calm his nerves and get some mental peace and clarity of thought to think about his future.

He had been fighting with his thoughts for quite a long time now, and he did not want his emotions to take the better of him. As Art was walking among the crowds, three Tai men approached him. They were in their early twenties. They were fairly well dressed compared to the rest of the people in the park. Lightly tanned skin with slightly oriental features, they were slight of the build as is typical of the Tai people. One of them spoke to him in perfect English.

"Are you American?"

"Yes." Art answered. *"I like your belt."* One of the men said. *"Thank you,"* he replied.

Art was startled by his comment. It was just an ordinary white leather belt, nothing special, except that his dad had given it to him for his birthday. Now all three of them were eyeing it up. Can we have your belt? One of them asked.

"No! I need it." Art replied defiantly. What sort of behavior was this? Who goes around asking for a belt like that? It really weirded Art out, and he couldn't make much sense of the situation.

"You don't need it; you are a rich American tourist. I'm not rich, and I'm not a tourist. I'm here on business. I have a family back home in America that I have to support. The only reason that I am here is that my job requires me to travel. I won't be going home for several weeks, and I need this belt to hold up my pants." Art explained.

He did not want to defy them openly and pick up a fight for no reason. He thought that if he talked to them logically and calmly, they would get his point and not try to poke in his business unnecessarily.

"How about your shoes? You must have another pair of shoes? We would like to have your shoes?" One of the men demanded. This was getting too much. Art was dazzled at their audacity. Who were they to act so obnoxiously and try to intimidate him unnecessarily?

"*Are you crazy*? *I don't have another pair of shoes with me. I need these shoes*." he was starting to worry, but he was not prepared to give them his shoes or belt just yet. So far, they hadn't really tried to use any physical force, they were just feeling him out, and he was feeling them out. Thoughts started to run rampant through his mind.

What made them display such preposterous behavior? What was their motive behind all this nagging and bullying? Maybe they would threaten him. Maybe they would try to use force to take them from him? There were three of them against Art.

Maybe they had knives? No, they wouldn't try anything, they were surrounded by thousands of people, but they were all Tai people. Maybe Tai people would stick together?

Maybe they will all join in and fight to get the rest of Art's clothes? Art didn't like to get pushed around, and he didn't want to give them his belt or shoes out of fear.

All the possibilities went through his mind, and he mentally prepared himself to put up a strong fight if need be. He wasn't going to give in to their bullying because he hadn't done anything wrong. They might take it as a sign of weakness and go for more. The tallest one reached out to grab his belt. Quickly Art grabbed his arm and held it tightly.

"Do you work? Art asked, sighing heavily.

"Yes," one replied while trying to free himself from Art's grip.

"Did you steal your clothes, or did you buy them?" Art asked in a reprimanding manner.

"I steal nothing; I bought them." He was wearing a fancy white dress shirt with ruffles down the front and around the cuffs. Looking directly in his eyes, Art asked, "I like your shirt. Can I have it?"

"No!" He replied. *"It cost me much money; I need it."* He replied, as expected

"Well, I work just like you, and like you, I bought my clothes, and I need them." Art retorted. *"If you cannot give up your belongings because you've earned it yourself, then the same goes for me."* He released his grip on his arm, and the man quickly withdrew it. They looked at each other and conversed in their native tongue. Then they turned to Art and said, *"OK, American; you can keep your belt and shoes."* They then disappeared into the crowd. Art breathed a deep sigh of relief and then quickly left the park to return to the safety of the hotel. Upon reaching the hotel, he couldn't stop thinking about how he had managed to escape those bullies or thieves, whoever they were.

He was lucky that they understood, and if only for a moment, they saw that Art wasn't too different from them. Art didn't have any such privileges that gave them the right to boss over him or take away anything in this way.

With the dawn of a new day, Art was rejuvenated and, once again, was ready to face the Tai world. The fears of the previous night were now put aside and neatly relegated to the deep recesses of his mind. He was now ready to take up a new day with increased vigor and renewed faith. He was not a person who would give up his plans from fear of uncertainty or the unknown. He knew how to protect himself, and he had decided to make the most of his spontaneous trip. Art's plane wasn't leaving until 4:00 p.m., and he wanted to do some sight-seeing.

Thailand's magnificent Buddhist Temples with great gold statues were Art's first choice. With great difficulty, he managed to convince a taxi driver that he wasn't interested in his women. Reluctantly, after numerous unsuccessful attempts to take him to several other destinations where he could collect a commission from the proprietor, he drove Art to the grounds of the Emerald Temple.

The Emerald Temple was composed of approximately nine separate buildings or shrines, each magnificent housing works of Art. Thousands of people roamed about on the temple grounds. Merchants peddling their wares were everywhere. Upon entry to the Temple grounds, Art was accosted by twenty kids, each wanting to serve as his guide and advisor.

Coerced into hiring one, he promptly guided Art to the "best" merchants. Trusting his guide and not being skilled in the Art of negotiation, he was ripped off by several of them when they charged him significantly more for souvenirs and artworks than was being charged by the expensive airport shops. He was sure his guide collected his commission from each unscrupulous merchant. Art also managed to tour the Royal Grand Palace before departing the country.

The remainder of the trip was relatively uneventful. The combustion problem in Malaysia was quickly solved, and his work in Australia was easily accomplished. Thankfully, despite the uncalled for change in plans, Art had managed to attend to his commitments, and he couldn't be more relieved than he was in the moment.

After six weeks of living out of suitcases and dining alone, it was good to get home to his family. Art had missed Joy and the kids immensely and didn't like the constant traveling and long absences from home, but his job required it, and there was nothing short of quitting he could do about it. Art was a family man and a well-grounded personality. He did not consider these business trips as an escape from home and longed to be back amongst his loved ones.

Joy didn't like his absences either, never knowing where he was or when he would be coming home. It had started to take an emotional toll on her, and it was getting harder for her to keep up with this Art's uncertain schedules and spontaneous travel plans. She also resented his racing, as in her opinion, it took too much of his time when he wasn't traveling. The better part of a Saturday or Sunday was spent at the track, and one or two nights a week were spent at the garage working on the race car. She was quite vocal about her feelings, and they frequently quarreled about them. Joy wanted Art to take quality time for her and their children, but it seemed like Art was always caught up in something more important. It was not that he did not want to spend more time with them himself, but he had signed up for so much, and he had so much on his plate that it was getting difficult to juggle everything with all the responsibilities of a businessman, husband, and father.

He was unable to strike that perfect work-life balance that all of us yearn for. Upon his return from each trip, she always had a long list of things around the house and in her car, which required his attention. With each succeeding trip, it seemed the list of items requiring attention would grow. It seemed as if this was her subconscious way of punishing him for going away.

Absence makes the heart grow fonder, however, and she was always glad to see him after each trip. It was like a little reunion that they have every time he would return from a trip. This time was no exception. It was obvious, however, that her unhappiness was growing, and she was becoming more accustomed to living and doing without Art being around when she really needed him. She had grown weary of waiting for him and being there for her.

The Trade-In

Every company, there are usually a few employees that, either because of their work accomplishments or their personal characteristics, stand out from the rest of the workforce. A multinational company like Exxon, which to the outside world, appears conservative, and the reserve is no exception.

In fact, the company is composed of so many of these abnormal or "oddball" employees that it is almost impossible to find a "normal" employee. Over the years, a number of these "characters" had significantly influenced Art's life, and he had affected theirs. Art was not sure who was the most abnormal "character" at Exxon, but Dear God, maybe just maybe it was him.

Dick Dock, as he was known by his fellow engineers, had

a Ph.D. in Chemical Engineering. He weighed 350 lbs. He didn't have a single hair on his head or, for that matter, anywhere on his entire body. He looked just like the Michelin Tire man. Dick loved to eat, and he ate more in one meal than what Art ate during an entire week. He was sloppy; his clothes were always dirty and rumpled. Dick was naive but good-natured, and Art liked him. He was an easy person to joke with or to play a joke on. He liked to kid around with Dick. Once in a while, Art would walk into Dick's office and look at his dirty rumpled appearance. Taking a quarter out of his pocket, he would throw it onto his desk and say, *"here, Dick, walk through the car wash on your way home."*

Dick would look up at him, smile, and say, *"Art, I'm a pretty big fellow. Could I have another quarter so that I could go through twice?"*

Dick was hired by Kivie, but soon after Dick started to work, Kivie transferred to Big Ed's division. He left Dick behind to torment Art and the rest of George's division. One day, Art decided to play a joke on Dick. He told Dick that George thought that his appearance wasn't in keeping with that of the other engineers in the division. He was the only person in the division who was completely bald, and of course, that made him look out of place. *"What can I do to improve my appearance?"* Dick asked.

"*Well, I think you should wear this safety helmet around the office. That way, no one will be able to tell that you don't have any hair on your head,*" suggested Art, trying to hold in his laughter.

"Good idea," Dick said. Art handed him a very old safety helmet that he had found in storage. An old fashion design, it looked like a Smokey the Bear hat. When Dick put it on, he looked comical but, he wore it in the office constantly. He even wore it to lunch, and he wore it on his way out of the office to his car at night.

After a few days, Art began to feel sorry for Dick. Everyone thought that he looked so funny. Art thought he would have realized quickly that it was a joke, but apparently, he didn't. He didn't know how to tell Dick that it was a joke, but he decided he had better be blunt about it.

"Dick, take off that silly looking helmet I gave you. It was a joke. I'm sorry, George doesn't really care that you're bald. No one cares that you are completely bald."

"No, I won't take it off, I like it," Dick retorted, and he refused to remove it.

One day, about a week later, George called Art into his office. *"Art, why is Dick always wearing that silly looking safety helmet around the office? He looks really stupid. No one else wears a safety helmet in the office or at lunch."*

"I know, George, I played a joke on Dick. I told him to wear it, but a couple of days ago, I told him that it was a joke, but he refuses to remove it."

"Well, Art, you got him to wear that silly thing, so you get him to stop wearing it. Now!"

"Okay, George, I'll see what I can do," Art said and went off to find Dick.

"Dick, you have to remove that stupid looking helmet. George doesn't want you wearing it around the office."

"No!" he replied firmly.

"Please, Dick, you have to take it off."

"No!" Art didn't know what to do. He left his office to think about it. Shortly, Art returned. *"Dick, if you take off the helmet, I'll buy your lunch for you."* Said Art. He knew Dick

would never miss an opportunity for free food.

"It's a deal," Dick said, and off popped the helmet, out came Art's wallet. That day Dick gorged himself at lunch at Art's expense. He doesn't know who played a joke on who? Dick's work wasn't always up to par with the other engineers in the division, and sometimes he really couldn't hold his own.

At times he was positively brilliant, but at other times, he acted like a complete idiot and couldn't seem to do anything right. Dick had some strange habits which pissed off a lot of people. Every day at lunch, Dick would get three scoops of ice cream for one of his desserts. The ice cream scooper was kept in a bucket of water next to the freezer, which housed the ice cream containers. If someone wanted ice cream, they would take the scooper out of the bucket, scoop the ice cream into their dish and return the scooper to the water bucket for the next person to use, but not Dick.

After taking his three scoops of ice cream, Dick would lick the ice cream scooper before returning it to the bucket. This unsanitary habit upset a lot of people, and they complained to the cafeteria manager. The cafeteria manager, however, decided that he couldn't accept hearsay evidence and had to catch Dick in the act himself before he could take any action. One day he hid behind the ice cream freezer and laid in waiting for Dick to commit his crime. When he saw Dick lick the ice cream scooper, he jumped out from behind the ice cream freezer and yelled out, *"I got you! I caught you! You have to stop licking the scooper! It's against all the sanitary codes!"* He then dragged Dick off to George's office for an official reprimand. George reprimanded Dick, and Dick stopped licking the ice cream scooper. Once in a great while, however, Dick just couldn't resist the urge and would give the scooper a quick and almost unperceivable lick before dropping it into the bucket.

Eventually, a power struggle emerged between George's division and Big Ed's division over the issue of who had control over the design of the ethylene reactors. Art's group had been doing the design and troubleshooting of these reactors for years, but now, Ed wanted to take that function over in his division. George refused to give up that function. Once a year, there was a meeting which was attended by all the company's managers and several of its higher-level technical people from Exxon's plants all over the world. The meeting this year was in Sweden. At one of the official lunches, Art was seated at a table with Big Ed, Kivie, and Ellis Songe, a manager from Exxon's plant in Baton Rouge. Ellis was aware of the struggle between George's division and Ed's division over who was to have responsibility for the design of the ethylene reactors. Ellis knew that Art was not about to give up this function without a fight and decided he would have some fun.

"Well, Ed," Ellis said. *"Our plant will be needing a new reactor this year, but I'm confused, who should I ask to design it?"*

"My division, of course," Ed said, "we're now responsible for that function."

"No way," Art said. *"You don't have anyone in your division who can design a reactor. My group and I have always designed those reactors, and I will continue to design them in George's division."*

"No, you won't," Ed said. "You'll only design the parts of the reactor we ask you to."

"No, I won't, I'm not going to be your bat boy and jump at your beck and call. I'll design the entire reactor or nothing at all." Ellis had now gotten the response he wanted. He had

gotten both Ed and Art agitated. He just sat back and smiled while he enjoyed the ensuing argument between Ed and Art.

Monday morning, back in the office in New Jersey, George called Art into his office. *"Art, we're transferring you to Ed's division today."*

"*Why? Why now*?" said Art defiantly

"Well, Art, Ed didn't like the way you opposed him and stood up to him at the meeting in Sweden. He thinks you're too arrogant, and he wants to be able to control you, so, in order to do that, he's decided to take you into his division."

"Do I have to go?" Art asked.

"No," George replied.

"What if I stay in your division?" asked Art

"Well," he said, *"we won't be designing any more ethylene reactors."*

"*Why did you finally give into him, George*?" "Because this morning I was pressured from Headquarters," George answered.

Art didn't want to work for Ed; he wanted to work for George. George had done a lot for him, and he really liked him, but he really had no choice. All his expertise was in the design of ethylene reactors.

"Well then, I guess I have no choice but to transfer to Ed's division. I guess Ed won. He got everything he wanted."

"No he didn't, he didn't really win," George said.

"What do you mean, 'he didn't really win'?

"Well, I only agreed that he could have you if he took Dick Dock too. You know, Art, I have been looking for a way to get rid of Dick Dock for months, and now, I've finally found it. I put together this package deal for you and Dick. I'm really going to miss you, but now Ed will be stuck with Dick. He'll have all the headaches now. I'm not sure who's getting the best of who."

Art wasn't sure either. Did George finally agree to the transfer because he really got a lot of pressure from Headquarters? Or, did he finally find an easy way to get rid of Dick by sacrificing him? This was really a perplexing situation for Art, and his judgment seemed to be blurred by the series of events that transpired before him. Why was he being sacrificed at the cost of Dick? Why did Art have to bear the brunt of someone's incompetence and inability to perform well? Time was to tell.

Chapter 12
Engineer Characters

J. B

He stood six feet tall and weighed 220 pounds. At 24 years of age, his hair was starting to thin, and his waistline was beginning to show signs of enjoying too many good meals. He was a foodie, and food was something that reached his heart. A glimmer in his big blue eyes could be seen through his gold-framed, wire-rimmed glasses. His Mona Lisa smile was both enchanting and mysterious.

A jovial manner almost masked his insecurity. The conservative attitudes and values which he exhibited were almost certainly the product of his childhood development in an upper class extremely conservative WASP neighborhood in Baltimore, Maryland.

It was 1966, and J.B., fresh out of graduate school, had just begun his engineering career with Exxon in Florham Park N.J. At that time, Art was a veteran engineer with six months' experience. Being somewhat shy and introverted, J.B. kept to himself and rarely spoke to anyone. He would rarely voice his opinion at the lunch table and quietly listened to whatever discussion was being done. His only acknowledgment was the nodding of the head in approval. His personality piqued the curiosity of everyone around him, and they would keep experimenting with tips and techniques to get him to say something or express his opinion on any recent affairs or a trending topic.

The thing with such people is that they bottle up all their energies within themselves and are unable to take part in any social gathering actively. More than often, they are viewed with intrigue, and people are always looking for a way to open them up. It challenged Art and his fellow colleagues to draw him out of his protective shell. They would always stir up a topic and try to tag him in so that they could get to know what kind of a person he was.

One day, the subject of golf was the topic of conversation at the lunch table. J. B., as usual, wasn't participating in the conversation. Art happened to mention that he played a round of golf last week with John, his next-door neighbor, and managed to shoot 100. This somehow triggered something in J.B.'s mind, and he momentarily poked his head out of his shell and said that he could shoot consistently in the low 70's. Boom! Finally, they had something that they knew interested in him. Art and J. B's mutual passion for golf would maybe take them somewhere, Art thought to himself. Sports is one thing that can get people of far-fetched personalities to come together as there is nothing much like the heartfelt bond one feels when they can challenge each other on the playing field.

Normally, Art's buddies at lunch would have challenged this proclamation. However, it was such a rare experience to have J. B. participate in a conversation that they didn't want him to retreat. They tried to elicit further conversation from J B by ganging up on Art. They wanted to capitalize on this opportunity and get him to continue taking part in discussions so that J B would feel a part of their team.

"Why don't you challenge J.B. to a match," Dubie suggested. All of the colleagues hooted and made noise to show their agreement and approval. Everyone had gotten on J.B s side and ganged up against Art.

"No, I don't think I want to." Art replied sheepishly without showing much enthusiasm.

"Why not is J.B. too good for you?" Fred questioned. All the colleagues were trying to create a hype around this challenge and pump up J.B. to actually challenge Art for a match of golf and see who would win the match.

"No," Art replied assertively. He wouldn't give in to the pressure that easily.

"Then, why not?" Burg piped up. He wanted to spice this up, and he left no stone unturned in trying to do so.

"J.B will give you a handicap of 2 strokes per hole." Won't you J.B.?

"Uh, Uh, Yes," J.B. hesitatingly replied.

"No, that's okay, I don't want to play J.B.," Art replied, trying to act all naïve when he was getting around what his colleagues were trying to do.

"Why not? Why don't you want to play J.B.? One of the colleagues provoked Art. Are you afraid of losing? Don't you have the guts to challenge someone to come and test your skills? Maybe you can't shoot anywhere near a 100," prompted Dubie and then giggling later. Dubie had successfully lit the fire on Art's side by challenging his golfing skills, and he was not going to let this pass.

"Sure I can; I can shoot 100." They were really putting the pressure on Art. He did not want to boast about his golf skills, but he did not want to come off as any less either. If they were to challenge him, he was going to accept it head-on and prove his mettle.

"Okay, I'll play J.B." Art finally gave in to the peer pressure, knowing that he was the one who was going to win this game. He was confident that nobody could beat him with the handicap JB was going to give him. And although all his colleagues seemed to side with J.B., he would show them who the real player was.

"How much money are you going to put up?" Dubie, now really getting into the spirit of a challenge match, questioned. This was an apt opportunity for everyone to have some fun.

"Money! How about 10 dollars?" Art quoted a reasonable price, to stay on the safe side.

"Uh, ten is fine with me," J.B. replied.

Since the match was to be scheduled after work and there wouldn't be time to play 18 holes, the game was set up at the local 9-hole public golf course. It was a rundown course about 5 miles from work, but it was cheap, and they could get starting times very easily. It was decided that the game would be played with partners. Art's partner would be his neighbor John Kohler. J.B.'s partner was going to be Chuck, a fellow engineer. Both Chuck and John could shoot in the low 90s, and therefore they were evenly matched. Word got around work about the big golf match.

Everyone was looking forward to the match because it would change the tone for everyone at work and break the monotony. Also, this match got more than the needed attention because J.B. had finally voiced his opinion on something, and it wasn't something unusual.

When they showed up at the tee for the first hole, they had an entourage of 20 hecklers from work. For some reason, they had decided that their mission that afternoon was to make Art lose the match to J.B. It was all in good spirit as they wanted to raise the spirits of J.B. and help him gain some confidence to face his colleagues with some pride.

"One stroke for Dinick," Burg shouted.

"No, that's a practice swing. I wasn't even trying to hit the ball." Art challenged the decision. *"I was only warming up, and it's obvious by the shot that I wasn't ready."*

"Yes, you were," Irve shouted.

"It sure looked like you were trying to hit the ball to me," Les shouted. It was as if everyone was ganging up against Art. Little did Art know that they were all doing this for J.B.'s self-confidence, and he continued to put up a strong demeanor.

"*No, I wasn't. I didn't even come close.*" Art retaliated. He was determined not to let his practice shot be considered as part of the game.

"That's because it was a really bad swing," Don said.

"Yes definitely, one stroke for Dinick," Boyde said. Towing in with the majority so that the decision would be taken in favor of J.B.

"Dinick is no match for you, J.B.," Fred said in an attempt to cheer up J.B. spirits.

"Yea," seconded Dubie. And so it went.

With them keeping score, Art didn't have a chance. By the 6th hole, Art had 60 strokes by their account and 45 on his own. He finally conceded to J.B. The match was indeed being played in goodwill and a friendly spirit, and there were no hard feelings. The most positive and uplifting aspect of the game was that the ice was finally broken with J.B., and they would hopefully see him participating in future team discussions and activities. John and Art went off to the local bar to lick their wounds only to be joined by their entourage of hecklers who wouldn't let them suffer in peace. J.B. was pleased with his victory and his newfound friends. It was just what was needed to crack open his shell.

He had finally gathered the guts and social confidence to let out his personality and mingle freely. In fact, this ice-breaking activity seemed to have become such a big hit that all the colleagues, including Art, noticed a drastic difference in his behavior and body language. Not only was he now volunteering to speak up, but he was also thoroughly enjoying himself. The introvert J.B. had finally spoken up.

La Grand Charles

Art couldn't believe his eyes, an elf, a real live elf, slightly larger than he expected, but none the less he has to be an elf. He even has a mischievous twinkle in his eye as he flits about the office. Those were the thoughts that rushed through Art's mind twelve years ago, the first time he saw Charles. He wasn't really an elf, but he was just as mischievous. Slight of build and less than five and a half feet tall, he was extremely light on his feet. A Frenchman by birth, he was a little more pompous and a little more nationalistic than most. In his own words, if you were not French by birth, you were a barbarian.

He had a great flair for the theatrical. His manner of speech and everything he did was done in grand theatrical fashion. He never wore his overcoat but always draped it over his shoulder like the early French noblemen's cape. His mannerisms exuded pompousness, and he would leave no chance to exhibit his dramatic side.

Over the years of working with Charles, Art developed an understanding of him and a relationship with him that has confused and bewildered their peers and company management. It was like a love-hate relationship. In 1976 a new ethylene plant was being constructed at Exxon Chemical's plant site in Koeln, Germany. Charles and Art shared the responsibility for supervising the contractor's design and field construction for the cracking reactors. They were to share the role of startup advisor to the plant operators for these cracking reactors with his friend Jacques Boutillier.

Jacque was also a Frenchman by birth, but he, however, thought and acted more like an American than a Frenchman. He was not nearly as pompous or nationalistic as Charles. He was also not afraid to ask for advice when he thought it was needed. He believed that it was necessary to work as a team and admit to not knowing something rather than facing the consequences of ill-informed decisions.

Charles would rather die than publicly ask a question, even if the answer could save his life or his job. Much too proud to let the world know or even suspect that he didn't know something, he would often let his guard down when in private with ~~me~~ Art and probe in a roundabout manner to get the needed advice or answers. His ego was sky-high, and he would make every possible effort to have the upper hand in matters of business and also in personal life.

His high-fi standards couldn't bear to see someone rise up the ranks and secure a position above him. He wanted to be the cynosure of all eyes and made sure that he always came off as the most intellectual and knowledgeable person in the room. Not to forget to mention that he considered himself to be the most sought-for engineer at Exxon in Europe until a recent event proved otherwise.

Charles was working out of Exxon's office in Brussels, Belgium, and Art was working out of their office in New Jersey. Jacques was stationed in Germany at the construction site. Jacques, concerned about a potential problem with the combustion stability in the reactors, sent a telex to Art asking for his advice on the problem. As a courtesy, a copy of the telex was also sent to Charles in Belgium. Art answered the telex and made a recommendation for a modification to the burners for the reactors.

As a courtesy, a copy of his reply was sent to Charles. When Charles saw his recommendation, his pride was injured because Jacques solicited Art's advice and not his. There, there Charles considered this to a direct attack on his credibility and position in the company. In his mind, how was Art being given so much importance, and why? Momentarily infuriated, he sent a telex to Jacques with copies to every company manager he could think of. In his telex, he stated that:

"Dinick knows nothing about this complicated burner design problem. He only pretends to know. His theories are crazy. Only I have the knowledge and the ability to solve this

problem. Burner design is an Art, not rigorous science, as Dinick has tried to make it a science. The solution cannot be calculated; you have to solve it with finesse and feeling, the feeling only I have developed through years of experience in burner design." It was clear from his telex that he was mentally hurt and was out to show his importance. His only agenda behind this reply was to make Jacques and the other company manager's acknowledged his presence and make him feel like the more important person.

He went on to recommend a design modification that was diametrically opposed to Art's recommendation. When Art got his telex, he was upset that Charles told the company management that he was wrong when he wasn't. Art was sure about his technical competence and his ability to troubleshoot solutions to technical emergencies, as he had proved time and again in the past. Only to see someone else take the credit of his genius and spontaneous thinking.

Art quickly shot back a telex stating that Charle's proposed solution was totally wrong. Engineering calculations could definitely solve the problem, and if he could not understand the calculations, he should get out of the engineering design business and get into the business of designing women's clothing. His special talents could then be put to better use. Art sent a copy of his telex to all the company managers who had received a copy of Charles telex. Telexes with arguments and counter-arguments for their respective combustion theories and expressed or implied charges and counter-charges of engineering incompetence went flying back and forth between them. The matter blew way out of proportion, and instead of thinking of a solution to the problem at hand, the attention was being untimely diverted to this unruly, non-productive banter between two employees trying to outdue each other. Someone had to intervene and put an end to this pointless discussion, which was putting more important matters in hindsight.

It became a game of 'one-upmanship' between both of them. Neither Art, not Charles was ready to give up their stance and were ready to back up their claim till the end. A game to see who could come up with the biggest and best put down and the best supporting argument for their respective theories. To Charles and Art, it soon became a game, a game of harmless sibling rivalry. Through all their telexes, they were converging on a compromise course of action based approximately on 80 percent of Art's engineering calculations and 20 percent on Charles's feelings for burner design. Company management, however, was upset. They didn't understand their sibling rivalry, the relationship between Charles and Art, or their mutual respect of each other's abilities. Afraid of an all-out confrontation between them that would jeopardize the startup of the plant, they arranged a meeting between Charles and Art with instructions to iron out their differences.

Otherwise, both of their careers would be in jeopardy. The management had had enough of this commotion, and there were not ready to cause any harm to the company's agenda in light of the 'so-called' sibling rivalry. Both parties needed to sit down and reach a middle ground based on mutual cooperation and respect and not indulge in any such unhealthy banter in the future.

The meeting was to take place in Koeln, Germany, several months before the plant's scheduled startup. Both Charles and Art insisted on their respective management that there was no bad blood or serious problems between them, but no one believed. The management arranged the date and place for the meeting. At the appointed time, Charles and Art met in Jacques's office in Germany.

Several of the company's managers were present at the meeting. When Art walked through the door, Charles greeted him in a rather unexpected and gratifying way. *"Hello, my little pussy cat! I am so glad to see you."*

"Hello, my little frog!" Art answered. *"I am glad to see you too."* The way these two rivals greeted each other seemed like none of the fiery, impulsive words that were shot out from either of their telexes. The Exxon Managers were shocked and perplexed. They expected a violent confrontation. It actually seemed like a game of sibling rivalry, where one was just adamant about proving the other one wrong and wouldn't get to rest until they had succeeded in their mission.

"You know, Dinick, these crazy managers do not understand us. I must admit, when I first received a copy of your telex to Jacques, I acted a little hastily." Confessed Charles. *"But you know that I have no such hard feelings towards you, and I completely trust your competence and ability to perform to the best of your abilities."*

"Yes, Charles, you did act a little hastily." Art said, taking

advantage of Charle's confession.

"And, I guess I was a little hard on you too in my reply, telex." Said Art humbly, not wanting matters to blow out of proportions unnecessarily, they were now summoned to sort out matters.

"But of course you were, my little pussy cat," he said, *"but I understand these things, and of course, we have now worked out a better solution to combustion problem in the cracking reactor. So, for our career sake, let us show these crazy managers who do not understand us that there are no hard feelings and that we have made up,"* chuckled Charles.

What seemed like an inconsequential thing to him had actually gotten the other managers all pepped and concerned, and here they were addressing each other with nicknames and acting as if nothing had ever happened between them.

With that, Charles walked across the room and threw both his arms around Art and kissed him on both cheeks as only Frenchman do in the movies. He then picked up a felt-tipped marking pen from Jacques's desk, and on Art's briefcase in bold letters, he scrolled the words, LOVE CHARLES. Now, whenever they meet, especially at large meetings, they stop whatever they are doing, rush up to each other, and throw their arms about each other.

They then exchange the greeting, *"My little pussy cat, it's so good to see you!"* and Art replies, *"My little frog, it's so good to see you!"* Kisses on both cheeks in a traditional French fashion are then exchanged.

Later that night, after their reconciliation meeting, while they were walking down the streets of Koeln, Germany, en route to dinner at the most expensive and best restaurant in town, French, of course, to celebrate the official ironing out of their differences, Charles, with his coat thrown over his shoulder, turned to Art. The mischievous twinkle in his eye was brighter than ever. He threw his hands and arms out in an uplifting fashion to the heavens and said to Art, *"You know, Dinick, I think someday I shall be God."*

"I don't think so, Charles," Art said. *"You know that job is already taken."*

"Perhaps you're right, Dinick. I know I could never really be God, but maybe God will give me a special title and prepare a special place for me." He said with over-confidence. However, the deep-rooted belief that he had in

himself was really inspiring.

"Maybe he will, Charles. Maybe he will."

Sam

Sam was a fellow engineer, but unlike the rest of the engineers at Exxon Chemicals, he was destined to someday join the ranks of Exxon management. Art had developed a new type of cracking reactor, but before they could commercialize it, however, the design had to be tested. In order to test the concept, Art designed a test unit to fit into one of the existing reactors in their plant in Stenungsund, Sweden.

When the construction was completed, Big Ed, Art's manager, decided that he had to go to Sweden to help start the test unit up. Art was supposed to advise the Swedes on operating the new reactor and making the initial adjustments. As usual, he was summoned to travel on an ad hoc basis for work reasons. This was the very reason Joy had resented, but he had found no way to escape his work commitments.

In addition, Art was to take data on the unit to enable them to determine how successful it was. Sam, a fellow engineer, who had only been with the company for seven years, was chosen to go along to assist him. He was to help him adjust the reactor during start-up and take data. Sunday afternoon, the cab came to Art's house to take him to the airport. Art was dressed in his blue polyester comfort suit he purchased on sale from the Sears Men's Store. Polyester comfort suits were popular in the early '70s but were quickly losing popularity with the fashion set. The cab then stopped to pick Sam up at his house, since it was on the way to JFK airport.

Dressed in an old pair of jeans with a hole in the left knee and an old grey sweater which had a hole in the elbow of the right arm, Sam's hair was ruffled, and he hadn't shaved all weekend. He was wearing a pair of old brown scuffed penny loafers, and he wasn't wearing any socks. To say that Sam looked like a bum was being kind.

"Hi, Sam! I see you're wearing your working clothes."

"Yeah," he replied, *"I like to be comfortable when I travel."*

"Well, I guess that's okay. I guess it saves packing space in your suitcase if you wear your working clothes."

"Yeah," Sam said. When they finally got to Sweden the next morning after a two-hour layover in Copenhagen, they checked into the hotel to shower and shave before reporting to work.

"Meet you in the lobby in an hour," Sam said.

"Okay," and he went off to his room. After washing up, Art donned his working clothes, an old pair of jeans, an old windbreaker, and a scuffed well-worn pair of safety boots. Startups are usually very messy and dirty. There are hydrocarbon leaks, wet paint, and greasy valves, and other dirty equipment. After dressing, Art went down to the lobby. He was early, so he sat down to wait for Sam. After about five minutes, Sam showed up. To his surprise, he was shaved, his hair was neatly combed, and he was decked out in a three-piece, light tan, custom-tailored, $300 wool suit. Art was shocked by his neat appearance.

"Sam!" "What the hell are you dressed like that for?" This is a startup. It's dirty, messy work. You'll ruin your good suit."

"I know it's a start-up," Sam said, *"but there's no need to get dirty. I've got it all figured out. You do all the messy work, and I'll do all the supervising."*

Art knew then that Sam had the right stuff to be a manager someday. Managers get you to do the dirty work while they sit around and look good. Isn't that what all managers do?

It's like they were born to boss over their subordinates. However, there was no time to fight over this petty issue, and Art had no option but to join hands with Sam and sort out the startup issue as soon as possible. They successfully started the new test reactor. Art did all the real work while Sam stood around, looking like a supervisor. His $300.00 custom-tailored suit came through unscathed. To be fair, however, Sam did make a few good suggestions, and they made a good team.

That's all that matters in the end. Art has had even worse experiences in the past when he has had to do the dirty work himself without the company or supervision of any of his boses and not get credit in the end as well. At least, Sam assisted Art throughout the course of the project and was there to advise and guide Art as and when needed.

During the ensuing years, Art frequently ran into Sam while working in Europe. Just like the song 'April in Paris', it was April, and they really were in Paris for the weekend. After spending Saturday afternoon sight-seeing, Sam and Art decided to meet Bjorn, a friend of theirs from Sweden, and his wife Inga at the Club Lido (the world-famous Parisian night club) for dinner and a show that evening.

Art was driving down the Champs de Elysee that evening in his Renault while Sam was looking for a parking spot not too far from the Lido.

"The city sure is crowded tonight. There's no place to park," Art said.

"Sure there is if you know where to look," Sam said.

"You see that green Peugeot over there," Sam said. *"Just park in front of it."*

"Are you sure?" Art asked.

"It doesn't look like you're allowed to park on that side of the street."

"Don't worry," Sam said. *"Just park there, it's alright. I know Paris very well. After all, I've been living in France for the past six months. Don't you see all those cars parked on that side of the street? 5,000 Frenchman can't be wrong."*

"Well, okay," Art said, as he parked the car in the choice spot that Sam had recommended. They met Bjorn and his wife outside the Lido, and after tipping the maitre'd 100 Francs, and got a very good table. They ordered dinner and the mandatory two bottles of champagne. The Maitre'd come

over to their table. "*Would you gentlemen mind participating in 'zee show?*" he asked.

"*What do we have to do?*" Art asked.

"*I cannot tell you until you agree to participate, but I can assure you it will not harm you. What do you say?*"

"*Well, sure, I will,*" Art said. "*I will too,*" Sam piped in.

Bjorn declined since he preferred to stay at the table with his wife, Inge. Art and Sam were then whisked off to the backstage to the dressing room of Francoise, the magician, the star performer. After swearing them to secrecy, Francoise's assistant removed their jackets, ties, shirts, and socks.

He then redressed them in such a manner that from their outward appearance, everything seemed normal even though it wasn't. They were then escorted back to their table. Bjorn and Inge were none the wiser and could not detect anything different in their dress. When the show started, Francoise mesmerized the audience with floating card tricks, disappearing rabbits and ducks, and other terrific illusions. At the proper moment in the show, Francoise asked for volunteers from the audience to come up on stage.

Sam and Art were, of course, chosen. On stage, Sam and Art clowned around with Francoise, and under the illusion of magic, Francoise Z'Grande proceeded to remove their shirts, ties, and socks with lightning-quick speed. The audience was fascinated and impressed, and they received a great round of applause.

When the show was over, Bjorn was full of questions as to how he did it. "Magic," they said, and refused to tell him anymore even though he questioned them relentlessly. Art and Sam said good night to Bjorn and Inge at about 1 a.m. and went off to retrieve their car.

Walking down the Champs de Elysee, Art was shocked. On the entire street, there was only one car, their car, and on the windshield, tucked neatly under the windshield wipers was not one, but two parking tickets for $100 each.

Art turned to Sam and said, *"Sam, you were right. 5000 Frenchman weren't wrong. It seems they knew when to move their car. What should I do with the tickets?" "Give them to me,"* Sam said, *"I'll take care of them."* Art handed the tickets over to Sam. *"Are you going to pay them,"* he asked. *"Of course not, don't worry,"* he said as he tore them up, crumpled them into a ball, and tossed into the street.

"Don't worry? What do you mean, don't worry? What if they track us down through the rental car agency?" "Well," he said, *"I'm not the slightest bit worried about that." "Why?"* Art asked. *"Because,"* he said, *"why should I be? The car is registered in your name."*This now confirmed to Art that Sam was destoned to be an Exxon Manager.

Chapter 13
Tourist

History always fascinated Art, and when working outside of the United States, he would take every available opportunity to sightsee historical sights. He had heard that Chateau Gaillard, which was the ruins of the 12th-century castle that belonged to King Richard the Lion-Hearted, was located on a mountain along the River Seine banks near the town of Les Angeles. It was a small town between Notre Dame de Gravenchon, the quaint little town where he was working in France, and the city of Paris.

One Saturday morning, Art got into his trusty Peugeot and headed out to find what remained of King Richard's Castle. After about an hour and a half drive through the countryside, he got to the little town of Les- Angles. He looked for signs that would give him directions to the castle but couldn't find any. He then asked several people how to get there. None of them spoke English, but with great difficulty, through the use of a combination of hand signals and body language, he managed to make his destination known. An old Frenchman who was working in his garden by the side of the road pointed to the top of a large hill as he said, " Le Chateau, Le Chateau." He now knew in which direction to head but still had to find a path to the top of the hill and the castle. After searching in vain for over an hour and asking many more people, all of whom gave him the same type of response, pointing to the top of the hill. As there were no signs or roads to it, he concluded that King Richard's Castle was not a popular tourist attraction, and not many people had been interested in seeing the castle ruins.

It appeared that the only way to get there would be to climb up the mountainside. So, he parked his car and started his ascent up the rather steep grass-covered hillside. After about 15 minutes of climbing, he slipped on the wet grass and managed to slide almost all the way back down the hill on his backside, ripping his pants and cutting his hand in the process. Undaunted by the setback, he was determined to reach the castle ruins, which, obviously, had not been explored by many tourists because of the great difficulty in reaching it.

Chateau-Gaillard was a leading-edge example of military architecture in historical times. It was built in record time by Richard – the Lion Heart on the high cliffs. The great meander dominated this in the River Seine.

Art was filled with visions of King Richard leading the Crusades and defending his fortress against invading armies who attempted to capture it. Also known by the name of 'Richard Coeur de Lion, King Richard was portrayed as a noble and brave warrior. He imagined the difficulty and frustration experienced by the invading armies who climbed this hill in an attempt to besiege the castle.

After two more falls, he managed to reach the precipice of the hill. With great anticipation, he awaited gazing upon the castle, which was built in 1196 and located on this desolate, almost impregnable mountain. Some of the most breath-taking views can be seen in the Dordogne by the fortress, which has the historical importance of being the French and English battlefield. Despite being protected by double walls, ditches, and a sheer drop of 150 meters, Richard held the Chateau de Beynac for a decade.

Art eagerly looked over the precipice with great expectations and, to his horror, was greeted by the sight of an ice cream cart vendor and hundreds of tourists. With great disappointment, he discovered that a well-paved access road was located on the opposite side of the mountain about 5 miles from where he started his difficult ascent. Art was upset and pissed with himself that he didn't find the access road. He was also disappointed at finding all the tourists who had made a leisurely trip in the comfort of their air-conditioned tour buses to the fortress of solitude.

In physical pain from his three falls, he paid the five Francs admission fee to the castle and toured the ruins with the other tourists. Art came to the realization that tourists are everywhere and we sometimes are merely just a tourist in life too. Some of us just have a harder time getting to our destination than others.

How Far Do You Go

Art had recently developed a design for a new type of cracking reactor to produce ethylene gas. Ethylene is used to make polyethylene plastics (the stuff garbage bags are made of). In order to test this new concept, a test reactor was built in Exxon's plant in Baton Rouge, Louisana. His buddy, Chuck Nogy, had finished his assignment in Japan and was now stationed in Baton Rouge. One of his responsibilities was to follow the test reactor's operation and ensure that it was functioning as it was supposed to. Art had spent two weeks in the plant when the test unit was commissioned. However, since it appeared to be functioning correctly, he had returned home to Florham Park N.J. to undertake the design of a new reactor for a plant in Texas utilizing this same new concept. One day in July 1976, while sitting at his desk working on the design, the phone rang. It was Chuck.

"Art, we have a serious problem with the new test unit. The tubes in the reactor are distorting, and I am afraid they may rupture. Is there anything that can be done to correct the distortion and prevent the failure?" (This reactor had 80 high alloy stainless steel tubes in which liquid hydrocarbon is heated to 2000 degrees as it cracks to produce the ethylene gas. Each of the tubes was 60 feet long. Large burners heated them in the reactor.)

"I think I might be able to correct the problem, Chuck, but I'll have to see the reactor first," replied Art hastily.

Rushing home, he quickly packed and said goodbye to Joy and the kids. Although she didn't like it, she was now accustomed to him dashing off to all parts of the world at a moment's notice. After all, what could she do? Fighting his way through traffic, he made it to the airport in time to catch the 7:30 p.m. flight to Baton Rouge. Early the next morning, after a restless night, he met Chuck in the plant, and they inspected the reactor. Art then concluded that the distortion could be corrected by adjusting the supports which hold up the tubes.

It was a simple procedure and could be done by the plant maintenance crew. The only hitch was that the supports were enclosed in a weather protection enclosure on top of the reactor, which had almost no ventilation. The only access to the support was by climbing over hot effluent pipes from the reactor.

Chuck and Art met with Mack Gregory, the plant's operations and maintenance department manager, and informed him of the situation. *"Well, Art, I would like to help you boys out but, it's against plant policy to do that kind of work on a unit that is in operation."*

"But Mack, the only way this adjustment can be made correctly is when the reactor is hot. It can't be adjusted properly when it's cold. If it's not fixed soon, the reactor will fail, "Art pleaded.

"Sorry, Art, but there is nothing I can do. I guess we'll just have to shut her down before she explodes," smirked Mack.

"But Mack, if you shut her down, the company will consider the design a failure. None of our other plants will ever want a reactor like this one."

"Sorry, boys, but that's not my problem. My problem is the operation and safety of this plant, and we can't jeopardize that for some crazy design you boys in technology have come up with," retorted Mack with disdain. Why was he acting this way? His behavior came off as very weird and peculiar to Art, but then he realized he worked at Exxon Chemicals.

Art offered to adjust the supports himself, but he wouldn't hear of it. He was just too adamant not to provide help or support of any sort, and that was clear by the way he was behaving.

"No, absolutely not, it's against plant policy, and besides, it's too hot in that area for anyone to work."

Feeling frustrated and helpless, Art went out to the reactor and looked it over again while Chuck went off to make some calculations. Something had to be done soon. At this rate of distortion, the tubes would rupture within a week. When they failed, his design would be history, bad history, a wasted effort. No one would ever try it again. He climbed up to the enclosure on top of the reactor and peered into its dark cavernous area. It was a nightmare, a maze of hot pipes and steel beams.

He could easily understand why no one in their right mind would want to work there. He couldn't let his design die an ignominious death. He knew it was a good design. He had spent too much time developing it. It was like his child, and he had to save it. The sentimental value that was attached to this design was something that Art could not put into words.

He had spent several months and sleepless nights to come up with this grate new design, and he wouldn’t let it breathe its last breath like this. He had to do something to sustain it and keep it going. Art convinced himself that he could safely get in there and make the necessary adjustments.

It was hot in there, and it would be very uncomfortable, but he could do it. The maintenance people would never find out about it, it was an operating unit, and they never went into an operating reactor, let alone, way up on top of one. It takes too much effort to get up here. He climbed into the enclosure and worked his way along the steel beams over the hot pipes. It was hotter in here than he expected. Ventilation was poor, very poor. It was difficult to breathe.

The hot, muggy 100 degrees July weather outside the enclosure wasn't helping matters either. Art started to adjust the supports. The hot pipes were scorching the leather soles of his boots. He had to keep jumping from beam to beam to prevent his feet from being burned.

It was extremely uncomfortable, but he was almost finished. Suddenly without warning, he was hit with a blast of hot air. It took his breath away and seemed to sear the lining of his throat and lungs. He started to gasp for air. He couldn't breathe. He felt like he was going to faint. *"Dear God, no, help me, help me get out of here,"* he heaved to himself.

"If I blackout, it will be all over for me. No one even knows that I'm here. No one will be able to rescue me in time," Art started to panic. He grabbed onto an overhead electrical conduit and held on for dear life. He was beginning to lose consciousness. His world was beginning to spin. It was suffocating in there, and he was gasping for some fresh air. He had taken an enormous risk by getting down into this

dungeon of darkness, and now only he could help and save himself. He felt he couldn't last much longer. It was like impending doom was dawning upon him, and his end was drawing near. Summoning every last bit of energy available in his body and suddenly gifted with a miraculous surge of adrenaline, he swung from the conduit onto a beam adjacent to the entryway.

He flung his body through the opening in the enclosure. Gasping for air, he came crashing down on the hard steel grating of the access platform, which surrounded the enclosure's entryway. Thank God, Art had escaped. He lay motionless on the grating, trying to recover enough strength to get up. In about twenty minutes, still weak and feeling light-headed, he managed to regain enough strength to sit up.

His throat was still irritated, but he was now breathing normally. It was like; he was granted another chance in life. Chuck came rushing up the access stairs. "*Art! Art! Where have you been? I've been looking all over for you. You won't believe it, but somehow the reactor tubes straightened themselves out. It's like a miracle. The design is saved.*"

"Yea, Chuck, God must have answered my prayers." He really did, he was alive." He survived that one."

Art breathed a sigh of relief. It was a time for rejoicing. The project that he was so invested in had been saved from getting devastated.

A Time for Action

The reactors in Exxon's chemical plant in Germany were severely fouling and had to be cleaned every week. It cost the company millions of dollars in lost production. La Grand Charles had been sent to Koln, Germany, to study the problem and develop a solution. He had spent about two months there but wasn't making any progress. Headquarters was losing patience with the Technology Department as a solution was not forthcoming.

One day Big Ed called Art into his office. *"Art, you have to go to Germany next week."* As always, there would be an emergency, and Art would be sent over to manage the situation as he was one of the most technically sound people at Exxon Chemicals.

"Why?" asked Art in a not-so-surprised tone. Travelling felt like part of his job description now. But it was his right to inquire what was the reason for this sudden trip.

"Because Charles is going on vacation, and you have to

relieve him while he is on vacation." He replied casually.

"But why do I have to relieve Charles?" objected Art. It was not his responsibility to take care of Charle's matters while he was busy 'vacationing.' It was outrageous and downright unfair even to expect that from Art.

"Because Headquarters in Brussels wants someone to follow up on Charles' studies and take the data for him while he is on vacation." He replied, losing his patience now. It was, and order, and he expected Art to comply with it without further questions.

"No way! I'm not going to take data for Charles and follow up on his studies. He hasn't made any progress. Why should I follow his course of action? If I go, I'll determine for myself what to do, and I'll do what I think is necessary, not what Charles thinks is necessary," replied Art sternly and adamantly. He had enough of being exploited and see others take credit for his work. Everyone had their way and pace of working, and he couldn't just pick up from where Charles left off and expect to adapt his style of working.

"Art, why do you have to give me such grief? Why can't you just follow orders and play the game to keep

Headquarters happy? Why do you have to always rock the boat?" Big Ed reprimanded him.

"Because sometimes the boat needs rocking." Sighed Art. He knew that Exxon's management was too full of their power and status and would use their influence to exploit employees under them.

Monday at 8 a.m. Art's plane landed at the Bohn Airport in Germany. He rented a car and arrived at the plant in Koeln by 9:30 a.m. He met Charles and was informed that a meeting was scheduled at 11:30 a.m. with Otto Viser, the plant manager, and all of his department managers.

"I will explain the problem and the status of my studies in detail to everyone at the meeting," Charles said. *"I will also explain what data you are to take in my absence. I will leave for vacation immediately after the meeting, and when I return, I will solve the problem."* He said in a carefree manner as if he was doing a favor by even holding this meeting.

"Okay, Charles, cut the bullshit, have you found out anything about the cause of the problem?" Art interrupted, losing his calm about the situation at hand.

"No, but this is a very complicated problem and requires a lot of studies," Charles said.

"You have been studying this thing for over two months, Charles, how much more time will you need?" Art questioned his judgment. It was a direct attack on his reliability.

"Maybe two to three months more," he replied. *"Why don't you go to the hotel now, and rest up before the meeting,"* Charles suggested.

"No, I think I will go to the plant and look around. I'll check out some of the data in the control room," replied Art, assertively. Since he had to handle matters while Charles would be on vacation, Art wanted to be well-prepared with as much information as possible for the meeting that would help him take a stand and do things his way. He at least deserved to take up things the way it was convenient for him, rather than following someone else's footsteps, who hadn't been able to make any progress for two months.

"That is silly," Charles said. *"You cannot possibly learn anything about this complicated problem in two short hours. You are wasting your time."*

"Well, it's my time to waste," and off he went to the plant control room with Gerd, an engineer from the plant and a good friend of Art's. They went out to the reactors to take a look at them, and then they went into the control room. They then pulled some of the data for the operations from the plant computers. Art quickly looked at the data. It showed something that didn't make any sense.

He made some quick calculations and concluded that some major fouling was occurring in the upper part of the reactor, a part of the reactor that no one was even looking at. Art explained his reasoning to Gerd. He understood his logic and then agreed with him. They then rushed off to the meeting. Otto, the plant's general manager, called the meeting to order and presided over the meeting.

The meeting room with its gray walls was cold and austere looking. They sat around a long oval-shaped mahogany table. Otto at the head, Art sat between Charles and Gerd. Charles got up and in his pompous style and made a lengthy, long-winded presentation. In which he said nothing except that he could not even guess the cause of the problem. He needed more time to dig deeper and reach to the root of the problem. He claimed that further study and more data, lots more data, was required. After hearing enough of his presentation, Art spoke up, *"Bullshit! You have studied the problem for a long time now! It's time for action. We don't need any more studies. There is a major problem in the preheat section of the reactor. It's fouled by some internal deposits.*

The only way we are going to find out what the deposits are is to shut down one of the reactors, cut it open and look inside. We can then get a sample of the foulant and have it analyzed in the laboratory." Dead silence fell over the meeting. A totally different serrano was presented. Charles was just dragging the project for no rhyme or reason and just buying time. The problem solution was right there to identify, but either he was purposefully delaying it to make the problem seem complicated and time-consuming or he was incompetent.

Charles then jumped up. *"You are mad, Dinick! You are mad!"* he shouted. *"You have only been here for two hours, and you pretend to know the solution to this complicated problem! I have been studying this problem for months! I have not seen any indication that the problem is in the preheat section of the reactors. You're wrong!"* He said.

"You know nothing! You are much too impulsive and hasty!" He was taken aback by Art's sudden confrontation, and he was in a state of frenzy and fury when he had to defend himself in front of all the members present in the meeting. Hence, he took the route that outright rejected what Art said.

"No, Charles. I'm not wrong," Art said. "I will stake my reputation and my job on it!"

"We cannot shut down the reactors!" Manford Fuchs, the operations manager, shouted. "We will not be able to supply our customers. It will cost us too much money in lost production!"

"You are losing a lot more by having to clean the reactors every week," Art replied, infuriated. Otto now spoke up, *"Yes, we are losing a lot of money by having to clean the reactors every week. Dinick, are you sure there is a fouling problem in the preheat section? We have not seen any indication of it, and Charles has not uncovered any evidence that indicates the preheat section is fouling."*

"Yes, Otto. I'm sure," replied Art confidently. He had inspected the reactors himself, and there was no denying the fact that this undeniable problem was being overlooked. It

was a matter of culpable negligence on account of Charles and his maintenance team. Charles was not ready to assume responsibility because he knew he had been evading it all this while.

"Well, Dinick, I trust your judgment. I have known you for years and have never known you to be wrong. We will call Headquarters in Brussels to inform them that we will be shutting down the reactor, and then we will have to call Big Ed and his management staff in the New Jersey office to inform them," announced Otto decisively. Since Otto was the head-in-charge, his trust in Art was a moment of pride and honor for him.

His reputation at Exxon was known far and wide, and those who had previously worked with him or known him could vouch for his reliability as an engineer. Nothing could take away from his reliability and sound technical knowledge. Not even a dominating, over-ruling personality like Charles, who was only trying to exert his authority and make the tables turn in his favor.

They called Brussels, and Art explained his analysis to them. The managers there said they didn't like the idea of shutting down the reactor based on his snap analysis and thought Art should study the problem for a few more weeks, but he insisted, and they finally agreed. They then said they would arrange to supply plant customers with materials from Exxon's plant in France. They then called his office in New Jersey to explain the situation to Ed and his managers.

"Dinick, you're crazy! You've only been there for two hours, and you're shutting down a reactor. Study the problem further before making any recommendations," Big Ed commanded.

"You had better be right, or else it would be wise for you to look for a new job in another company when you return. If you're wrong, I won't be able to save your career. Your impulsive decision will have wasted hundreds of thousands of dollars, and the higher-ups will be looking for your blood." Explained Big Ed bluntly.

He was trying to scare Art through authority, but Art was someone who would not budge from his analysis or decision if he thought he was right, no matter what.

"I'm sure I'm right. You know I've never been wrong before, why should I be wrong now?" replied Art with outward confidence but hidden fear. He always did fool-

proof work, and he always had evidence to back up his claims. He never made said anything without being entirely sure about it.

"I know," he said, *"but there is always a first time for everything. Good luck! For your sake and ours', we hope you're right."* Big Ed had given his final statement, and now Art only wished that the odds may be in his favor.

Art's job and reputation were now on the line. He wished that he hadn't stuck his neck out. Maybe, just maybe, he was wrong. What would happen then? He would be publicly shamed and disgraced. His entire career's hard work would be questioned if he would be proved wrong.

He could hardly sleep that night; he prayed hard that he would find the foulant. If his claims were to be proved wrong, he would have to bear the brunt of Charles, Big Ed, and other managers at Exxon as well. Tomorrow was going to be decisive. Tuesday, they shut down a reactor. Art was apprehensive as they started to cut it open. The first cut was at the inlet to the preheat section.

Nothing, absolutely nothing, it looked perfectly normal. The next cut was at the center of the preheat section. Again nothing. It did not look too good for Art. Maybe he was wrong. Maybe Ed was right. All sorts of thoughts started bombarding his already stressed mind. Maybe he should have studied the problem longer. He shouldn't act so quickly and take so many risks. Fuchs and Charles were gloating.

"Give up, Dinick, you were wrong. Everyone makes a mistake sometimes." They insisted.

"No, I'm not wrong, I haven't made a mistake." At his insistence, one more cut was made. This, the final cut was near the outlet of the preheat section. Much to everyone's surprise, this section was severely fouled and corroded. It looked worse than even Art had expected.

Samples of the foulant were taken to the laboratory to be tested for their nature. Within a matter of hours, the source of the contaminant was identified. Art thanked God. He knew he couldn't be wrong in identifying the root of the problem. His years of sound technical knowledge had only been polished over the years, and that is what made him talk with so much confidence. He had an eye for detail, and his claims were rarely wrong. He knew his work well.

If the plant had continued to operate the reactors with the

contaminant in them for another couple of months, the contaminant would have eroded through the reactors. It would have caused an entire plant to shut down. Plant personnel could have been injured, and the company would have lost millions and millions of dollars in lost production while they repaired the reactors, and it would have a domino effect of disastrous events.

Art believed that sometimes someone has to be willing to take a risk, take the bull by the horns, and react quickly. It would have been nice to have his managers in Florham Park support him, but they were too conservative, and they didn't take any risks. They didn't make snap decisions. They move slow and cautiously like a turtle. Art thought that by now, they would have had more confidence in him. But guess he was wrong. Not everybody has a high-risk appetite and can take up things head-on without worrying about failing. However, they said that there was always a first time for Art to be wrong; there is always a first time for everything.

He never had a serious accident in all the hundreds of times he had raced a dragster, but he was sure he was in the midst of one hell of a one now.

A Traffic Ticket

Art was working at Exxon's plant in West Germany, and he was living in the Intercontinental Hotel in the heart of Koeln. Parking in the hotel garage was very inconvenient as it was always very crowded and very expensive. Every night he would park his car in one of the available public parking places on the streets surrounding the hotel. Street parking meters would be dormant overnight but would start operating again at 8 a.m.

Therefore, it was necessary to vacate the parking spot before 8 a.m. or else risk getting a ticket for not having put money in the meter. In the morning, he would eat breakfast at the hotel and walk to his car before 8 a.m. He would then drive downtown on his way to work and pick up his friends Bjorn and Steve K, who was staying at another hotel in Koeln. They would wait on the street corner in front of their hotel for Art to come by and pick them up.

One morning upon arriving at his car, Art discovered that there was a brown Mercedes with a Koeln license plate parked behind him. The Mercedes was blocking him, and so he couldn't drive the car away. He walked back across the street to the hotel and asked the bell captain to announce in the lobby to find out if the car belonged to one of the guests or if it belonged to someone who worked in the hotel. He made the announcement but got no response. Then the bell captain suggested that the car might belong to a construction worker who was working in the building in front of which Art was parked.

He walked back across the street and went into the building to find the owner of the car. As best he could understand from their German responses, no one seemed to know anything about the car. It was getting late, and he knew that Bjorn and Steve would be waiting on the street corner for him. So, he went back to the hotel, and again no help. He then went back to the construction site and went in again. This time, no one seemed to be there.

He was now really frustrated, and his patience limit was being tested. He couldn't just stand there helpless as it was getting late. He had no way of contacting Steve or Bjorn, and he had to get to work for an important meeting. He then remembered Archimedes' famous words, the ancient Greek mathematician, who once said, *"Give me a lever long enough, and I will be able to move the world."*

Well, the Mercedes was a lot smaller than the world, and

he felt that if he had a lever long enough, he could move the Mercedes. He found a piece of construction lumber, which was approximately 10-foot-long and seemed it would make a perfect lever. He started to use it as a giant pry bar to move the Mercedes out of the way. He inserted one end under the frame of the car and pushed up on the other. In this way, he was able to move the car over about two inches each stroke. He had managed to move the car approximately 2 feet when suddenly he noticed that a large gang of construction workers surrounded him.

One man started yelling at him in German. He was holding a large pipe wrenched in his right hand and was making threatening motions with it. Art couldn't understand a word he was shouting. He then shoved Art against the car. He didn't know what to do. Momentarily, Art stood there with his back against the car, and his arms hung motionless at his sides. Art had no defense against his large pipe wrench. The guy then put his huge left hand around his throat and began choking him. Art could hardly breathe, and it felt like he would throw up anytime. Being subjected to this unfair brutality, all of a sudden got him more anxious than anything else. After all, he was only making way for his car. He wasn't stealing or harming someone else's property. Art had enough. With lightning-quick speed, he raised his arms and knocked the guy's hand off his throat. He then quickly grabbed the wrench and struggled with it. He was trying desperately to rip it from his grip. Art was managing to hold onto it, but for how long? Art knew that if he got it free, the man would bash his head in.

Meanwhile, the hotel bell captain who was observing the fight called the police. They arrived in record time and restrained the construction worker from hitting Art with the pipe wrench. It seems that he was the furious owner of the car that Art had moved with his lever. He told the police that he had his car parked in his spot, a spot that was reserved for trucks and construction workers. In order to punish him, he parked his car behind Art's.

He then became enraged when he saw Art moving his car with the wood beam. He thought he had no right to park in "his" spot. The police told him to calm down as there was no damage done. Art had meant no harm to his car. Then they pointed out to Art some obscure sign in German, which was posted on the side of the building proclaiming that only construction workers would be permitted to park there during the week while construction was in progress. The police were quite sympathetic to Art and easily understood that the sign was not clearly posted. They then asked the man politely to move his car. He was still angry and flatly refused. The police then asked him again, and again, he refused.

Now, the policeman was getting a little perturbed and annoyed by the construction worker's unnecessary stubbornness. The matter was resolved, and even the police understood that it was a genuine mistake. The police then carefully inspected the man's r car and told him that they would give him a ticket for having a bald tire if he didn't move his car, but he still refused.

After some discussion in German between the police and the car owner, the police informed Art that the only way the man would agree to move his car now would be if they gave him a ticket for illegal parking. Otherwise, even if they gave him a ticket for the bald tire, they would still have to call a tow truck to move his car, and that might take hours. The police were calm but perplexed and frustrated. They didn't know what to do. It seemed they had no control over the situation.Art was running late for his meeting, and he needed to get going as quickly as possible to pick up Bjorn and Steve, who was standing on the corner, not knowing what was going on. He didn't want a ticket and didn't really deserve one. By the police's own admission, the "no parking" sign was very obscure. It was unjust, but he really had no choice. He had to get to work, so he told the police to give him the ticket. They then issued Art a ticket for illegal parking.

The very pissed off car owner then moved his car. Art thanked the police and then got on his way. The next morning on the way to his car, he passed by the construction site. The brown Mercedes was parked in front of the building, in "his spot." On the windshield tucked neatly under the wipers was a ticket, a ticket for a bald tire. He smiled to himself; justice was now served. Eventually, maybe in a lifetime, justice is served for everyone.

Windy

Just as a rose will wither and die on the vine if it is not nurtured, so too will a relationship between two people. You need to constantly water your relationship like a flower to prevent it from withering. This requires initiative and effort from both sides. Joy and Art had unknowingly become complacent in their marriage. Gradually, they had drifted apart, and the differences seemed to be gnawing away at the bond they once shared. Days turned into weeks and weeks into months, and they didn't seem to make even the tiniest effort to make things work between them. It's easy, very easy, for married couples to start taking each other for granted.

The excitement and passion that they once experienced had all but died several years ago. Boredom had become routine. They did not feel the spark that had kept them together this long. Why do couples have to meet such a fate? Sometimes, the couple is to blame themselves, while at times, it is their life situation that distances them.

With each passing day, they were slowly but imperceivably growing further apart. It was a sad state of affairs to see them being so indifferent to each other's presence, feelings, and emotions. But, guess it was too late to go back. Traveling around the world for work, Art was frequently away from home. The trips had become too frequent and came unannounced, which left Joy with no option but to embrace her solitude. Art was oblivious to

Joy's emotional needs, and he always chose work over her. Gone were the days when Joy used to openly express how much she needed him to be there in the moment. However, the lifestyle that Art had chosen for himself came at the cost of his marriage. Little did he know that in the quest for professional growth and success, he was leaving behind a beautiful part of his life, which he should cherish forever. It's not that Art did not miss his wife and children back home while he was on his work trips, but life had not left him with any other option.

Joy, resenting his lifestyle, was getting more accustomed to each succeeding day to live without him, and she started to withdraw from the world. It felt like she had given in to her destiny and made no efforts whatsoever to make things go in her favor. Things needed some stirring, and neither Art nor Joy was in the mental state to make any efforts. Maybe they had left their personal space long back, and the rift that had settled between them was too much to bridge now. Her unhappiness was infecting all their family members and friends.

It was toxic and contagious. She was becoming unsympathetic and uncompassionate towards her other relationships as well. It seemed like someone had sucked out the very energy from her, and nothing in life excited her the way it used to. She now appeared to care for no one except herself and seldom did anything for anyone. She acted as if the world owed her a living. She took from life and rarely gave anything back in return. She was developing all the characteristics that were foreign to Art.

Was she the Joy that Art had married? She seemed to have turned into this alien person who was far away from the person that Joy was initially. What had life done to her? Did she deserve to be treated this way? Or did her friends and family deserve better? Life is undoubtedly a complicated mesh of feelings and emotions and nothing, and sometimes you just seem to surrender your weapons in the face of challenges that life throws at you.

They were bickering like two old maids who had lived their entire lives together. Small irritations festered and erupted into large open wounds, and they did nothing to heal them. It was like they had become desensitized to their negative emotions and just moved on even if the fight turned ugly. They just left it behind just like they had moved on, leaving their bond behind. They were now living separate lives under a common roof. They merely existed together in a platonic relationship for the sake of the kids. They shared nothing except living accommodations. They never went anywhere or did anything together.

Quality family time seemed to be a thing of the past, and whatever time they got on their hands, they preferred to spend it on their own. They had no desire to create any more memories together. The essence of their relationship had faded away with time. However feeble they may have been at times, Art's attempts to salvage what little remained of their relationship were fruitless. They had gone too far down on their separate paths.

Joy had given up. She just wasn't interested in reviving their dying relationship. She refused to do anything with him. She wouldn't even share weekend outings with him and the kids. He would often ask her to come with him and the kids to the park, zoo, or another place of interest, but she would continually refuse. She always had an excuse, "I'm too tired. I have to put up with the kids all week while you're at work or traveling around the world.

You take them out today. I don't want to go. I just feel like staying at home by myself." She would say dejectedly.

Life had taken a toll on her, and she was done trying to fix things that had long been broken. If only Art had realized this before and taken up things with his wife, they wouldn't have been in this situation now. He let their relationship slip away from their hands like grains of sand.

Art was unhappy but didn't know what to do. Resigned to accept his marital situation, he rationalized to himself that their relationship or lack of involvement was normal. That's the way married life is supposed to be after twelve years of marriage, isn't it? There was nothing he should or could do. Maybe this is what their marriage was destined to.

They had spent some of the most beautiful years of their life, and he didn't want to let go of the memories by ending this on a bad note. So he just let it be. He took each day as it came, and since Joy had become used to her solitude, Art did not find her interfering in his life or creating any hindrances whatsoever. Work already dominated the majority of his life, and he had just gotten used to that.

"Hey, Art! Can you come to my office for a minute? I want to ask you a few questions about your design specification for the test reactor we're going to build in Sweden." Sam called out..

"Sure, Sam, what do you want to know?" replied Art in a helping tone.

"Art, I don't really understand why you used these orifices to distribute the hydrocarbon gas flow."

"Well, Sam, the reason I used..."

"Hi, Sam!" a sweet, nectar-filled voice interrupted their conversation.

"Hi, Windy!" replied Sam casually.

"Excuse me for interrupting your meeting, but Ed's marked his comments on a copy of your report, and he wants to see you about them this afternoon if you're available." She replied promptly.

"Tell Ed that any time this afternoon after 2 p.m. is okay with me."

"Thank you, Sam!"

That was the first time Art saw Windy. Her resemblance to Tony was uncanny, and the sight of her revived fond memories of his long lost Tony. She was tall, slender, and incredibly sexy looking. She was wearing a black skirt and sweater, which hugged her shapely figure and clearly showed that she had all the right parts in all the right places. She had a flattering figure with accentuated curves that made her look all the more appealing. Her long blonde hair hung midway down her back and swished in the breeze as she walked briskly down the hall. Knee-high black leather boots graced her well-shaped legs and added just the right finishing touch. She carried herself gracefully and turned heads wherever she went. Her personality had a magnetic aura to it that instantly attracted Art, and he felt like he was in love all over again.

About five months later, He got transferred to Ed's department. George's department was located on the second floor, while Ed's offices were located on the third floor of Exxon's office building in New Jersey. He frequently saw Windy in the halls as she went from office to office, delivering Ed's messages. Their interchanges were limited to a casual nod of recognition. Art knew almost nothing of her personal life, and they rarely ever held a conversation. Yet, there was something about her personality that made Art curious to get to know her more.

The Meeting Place was a bar and restaurant in Madison, a quaint little town about a half-mile from their office. It was the place for meeting new friends and socializing with old acquaintances. Bob and Sam, the bartenders, knew everyone by name. At 9:00 o'clock, Jimmy would sit down at his piano and play old favorites for dancing or just listening.

Every Friday night and sometimes on Wednesdays after work, the engineers and secretaries would go to the Meeting Place for a few hours of social drinking and conversation. The place was usually very crowded, and they were always packed tightly together. It was a good break from the monotony of the day to day routine, and Art and his colleagues loved socializing there. After all, everyone needs a platform and some time to de-stress.

On one of these occasions, quite by accident, Art wound up sitting at the bar next to Windy. They started to make small talk about the insignificant, meaningless, and non-controversial things in life, like the weather and their favorite movies and television shows. But somehow, as the night wore on, their conversation drifted to the utmost secretive areas of their private lives. They discovered a remarkable commonality in interests as well as in their marital situations.

Art learned that she had married her childhood sweetheart, John, but had recently gotten divorced from him.

One day, soon after their wedding bells stopped ringing, she woke up from her dream world of wine and roses infatuation. Over their morning coffee, she was hit squarely in the face with the stark reality that she and John had nothing in common. Boredom soon took a firm hold of their relationship or lack of relationship.

Now, after only two years of marriage and an amicable divorce, they had gone their separate ways. Such is the reality of life. That sometimes, you are blinded by something temporary and when you realize it's too late. However, sometimes life gives us a perfect chance to start afresh, and that is when we need to make the right decisions.

Windy and Art talked until about 10 p.m. that night, and then as friends, they went their separate ways. On Monday at work, Art saw her in the hall. She greeted him with a friendly smile and the usual casual nod of recognition. She seemed a bit distant in light of the conversation and secrets they shared on Friday night, and he didn't know what to make of it. On Wednesday, however, she popped into his office.

"Hi, Art. Everybody's going to Meeting Place after work tonight. Are you going?"

"Well, no. I wasn't planning to go."

"Why not?" she asked.

"Well, I have to work on the race car tonight to get it ready for Sunday's race."

"Oh, too bad," she said.

"Are you going?" Art asked.

"Well, no. I don't think I will; I have some shopping to do." She replied nonchalantly.

"Shopping?" "You can do that any time, you don't have to do that tonight. Why don't you go? If I go, will you?"

"Well, maybe, yes, I'll go."

"Okay, then I'll go for a while too."

"Good," she replied, *"I'll see you there."*

They met at The Meeting Place after work and spent most of the night talking to each other. They discovered more common interests. They were quite similar in most of their likes, dislikes, attitudes, and even temperament. During the next month, every Friday night after work, they met at the Meeting Place. They spent most of the night talking to each other, but once in a while, when Jimmy would play a number that they really liked, they would dance. It was a pleasant coincidence that they could hang out so casually and dance to their favorite song. Something that most couples crave for. It seemed things were going in Art's favor.

One beautiful spring Saturday morning in May, about two months after their first conversation in the Meeting Place, Art rode his motorcycle over to her house. After some coaxing, he convinced her to go for a motorcycle ride with him. They spent a pleasant afternoon talking and riding down the peaceful tree-lined winding country roads. They even stopped for a quiet romantic lunch in a quaint little mom and pop restaurant that only had three tables.

It seemed like a dream to both of them since both of them had broken off from their soulmates. However, it was sheer coincidence or a game of destiny that crossed each other's paths and found so much in common to talk about. Sharing this exclusive time was quite uplifting, and something definitely unique from their normal routine. Both were loving it.

In all the year's Art had owned a motorcycle, he could never get Joy to go for a ride with me. She just wasn't interested. Windy was a friend with whom he could talk freely and share good times with. They really enjoyed each other's company and started seeing each other more frequently. She was someone to share experiences with, to exchange secrets of life with, but it was only a friendship, as they hadn't even shared a kiss. However, these newly brewing emotions were quite pleasantly overwhelming, and he did not want this to end. He had never thought that he could find love in a best friend.

Chris, the Greek, as he was fondly known, had immigrated to this country from Greece five years ago. Though he spoke with a heavy accent, he had an excellent command of the English language. Streetwise, in the ways of the world, he paid an American woman who was vacationing in Greece to marry him when he was denied a visa to this country. Once granted a visa and work permit by virtue of this arranged marriage to an American citizen, he settled his account with her and obtained the agreed to divorce. He was an entrepreneur and had a million ways to make a fast buck.

He was always working on one deal or another. This huge burly, rough-looking 250-pound man was generous to a fault and had a heart of gold. For his friends, no favor was too big or task too difficult for him. Chris was Art's friend. When problems between Joy and Art would get out of hand, Art would camp out over Chris's apartment until things at home settled down. Art had a key and could come and go as he pleased.

Chris spent most of his evenings in the City (New York) over his girlfriend's apartment and, therefore, Art usually had his apartment all to himself. It would be a relieving break from Joy, and he wouldn't be creating a hindrance for anyone else as well. In times like these, he really valued this solitude and would love to de-stress away from the stresses of life, especially the mood fluctuations and bickering of Joy.

It was a warm, summer, Friday night in June, and their usual Friday night gathering at the meeting place was coming to an end as their friends started heading home for the night. *"Good night, Art. I'll see you at work Monday, I guess,"* Windy said.

"Yeah," replied Art meekly.

"Where are you going now?" Windy asked.

"I don't know. Probably over Chris's for a while," he

answered.

"Where are you going?" "Oh, just home to feed my dog," Windy replied.

"It's still early. Why don't you come over Chris's? He'll probably be there with his girlfriend, Anna. She's very nice. You'll really like her."

"Well, okay," she replied, *"but I don't know the way. How do I get there?"*

"Just follow me in your car. I'll drive very slow so you won't get lost."

When they got to Chris's apartment, he wasn't there, but since Art had the keys to his apartment, getting in wasn't a big deal. He turned on the stereo, and they sat on the living room couch.

While they talked and listened to music, she reached out and held his hand. After a while, he put his arm around her. She moved closer and, to his surprise, kissed him. It was a long slow romantic kiss.

He couldn't ever remember feeling as wonderful before. He was completely awestruck and mesmerized by the bold step she had taken, and he had never thought that they would ever kiss. He did not want to cross the line and make her uncomfortable because he loved her presence. He thoroughly enjoyed her company because he could unapologetically be himself in her presence. Slowly, he had started to develop feelings for her, and he would be lying if he said he wasn't attracted to her.

He was now holding and kissing this beautiful woman with whom he shared so many interests.

They started to make love. He felt something that he had never felt before. It was a warmth from within, a special closeness, a sharing of mind and body. He knew her; he knew her secrets and all her thoughts.

When he looked into her eyes, he saw everything he ever dreamed of.. A feeling of great peace and satisfaction fell over them as if there were only the two of them in the whole world. A feeling that was almost impossible to put into words. A warm, feeling filled him inside out, and he felt he was transported to heaven on earth when they made love. It it felt like the reunion of two souls. This feeling was something that he would remember all his life.

Suddenly they were startled and brought back to reality by a loud tapping on the bedroom window. *"What was that?"* she asked.

"I don't know." He looked down at his wristwatch.

"Holy shit! It's 1:30 in the morning. We've been in here for over three hours." He went over to the window and looked out. He saw Chris and his girlfriend sitting on the curb of the sidewalk. Damn, this was one of the most embarrassing moments for Art, and he couldn't believe how time had passed by. They quickly dressed and went to the front door to let them in.

"What's up?" He asked Chris, trying to act casual as if nothing had happened. Obviously, he was really ashamed, and he did not want to create an awkward situation in front of his girlfriend.

"You lost your key?" Asked Art in an interrogative tone.

"No," he replied as he smiled and looked at Art. "You must have been having a really good time here."

Embarrassed, Art tried to act casual as if nothing had happened. "What do you mean?"

"I started banging on the door over two hours ago to let you know we were here. We didn't want to come in and surprise you," he said.

"Thank you, that was nice of you. I'm really sorry, but we didn't hear from you. The stereo must have been too loud. You really didn't have to wait outside. You could've come in here."

"We were just sitting here talking." Art stammered

"Sure you were, my friend," he said as he smiled at Art. His smirk showed that he had gotten the gist of the situation, and he purposefully didn't come in because he didn't want to embarrass Art by catching him off guard in action. It was obviously unplanned on Art's behalf too, and he just lost track of time. Chris was smart and considerate enough not to intercept someone's personal time like this. Even though it was his own apartment, Art really owed him. They then all sat down and had a cup of coffee and chatted for a while. At 3:00 a.m. He walked Windy out to her car, and they kissed good night.

September came, and Joy and Art decided to go their separate ways. They agreed that their marriage was beyond salvaging and that they should get a divorce. There was nothing left to save anymore. It would just be like being in a relationship for the sake of being in one. They had grown weary of one another, and even though they may not have parted ways physically, Joy had left the relationship long back.

They divided up their possessions equally. She got the fragile china, and he got the unbreakable plastic dishware. She got the crystal, and he got the peanut butter glasses with the beautiful flowers on them. She got the fine wooden dining room furniture, and he got the mar resistant kitchen table with the durable vinyl chairs. She got the new larger car with the large uneconomical engine, and he got the old smaller car that got much better gas mileage. She would stay in the house with the kids, and he could move out. Art moved out of their house and split his time and possessions between Chris's apartment and Windy's house. After a few weeks, however, Joy had a change of heart. She realized that since she still wasn't happy, it wasn't right for Art to be happy either.

To Joy, the grass was always greener on the other side of the fence, and she always wanted most what she couldn't have. She didn't want Art when she had him, but now that he wasn't available, she wanted him, or at least she didn't want any other woman to have him. She formulated her battle plan based on her natural instincts. Her strategy was to attack Art in his wallet.

After all, she reasoned, if he didn't have any money, no woman would want him. What woman in her right mind would want a penniless man? She knew how to sabotage all his efforts to embark on a new journey of life, and she was adamant about making it as difficult as she could for him. Yes, she was the same person Art had loved, but time had brought such a distance between them that she was out to exact vengeance. Joy and her merry band of lawyers now started harassing him and making ridiculous demands. She would call him at all hours of the day and night and talk to him on the phone for long periods of time, telling him of her problems or making threats. One Sunday afternoon, the phone rang, and Windy answered it.

"Put Art on," Joy demanded in her usual nasty manner.

"Hi, Joy. What's the problem today?" He asked.

"The problem is I've had it. I'm fed up. Get your ass over

here Saturday morning and take these damn kids. I'm leaving. I don't want them anymore. I'm stuck with taking care of these kids while you're out having a good time playing around. Well, I've had it. You take them. I'm going to California and make a life for myself."

Joy had become frustrated and angered; she and her lawyers weren't making any progress. Her emotions were now getting the best of her. She was striking out at anything in her path, even the innocent kids. Maybe she was sexually frustrated as well. Just knowing the fact that Art had an active sex life while she was stuck with the kids was infuriating her.

How could Art just leave her to take care of all the responsibilities? After all, they were both their children. She wasn't solely responsible for caring for them. Her maximum limit had been reached.

"You can't," he said. He was trying to keep his calm. He had become used to Joy's sudden panic attacks and outbursts of emotions. He knew this was just a phase, and it would pass by, or at least he hoped so.

"You don't know what you're doing!" said Art in a

manner to put his foot down.

"I can't," she replied. *"Just watch me, buster!"* she replied frantically. She was out of her senses, and right now, she would do anything to make Art's life a living hell.

"Do you really want to give up the kids?" asked Art patiently. There was no point in yelling back at her as it would only worsen matters.

"You're damned right, I do. Why should I waste my life raising them? They're your responsibility. You raise them." She yelled at him in a highly irritable voice.

"What about the house?" he asked.

"I don't want it; it's just a hassle. Just give me some extra cash," she demanded.

"How much?"

"I don't know right now, you'll hear from my lawyer. He'll tell you how much," she replied in her now typical nasty tone.

"Sure, I'll take the kids. You know I've always wanted them, only I can't take them on Saturday. I am going to my brother's wedding in Florida. We already have plane

reservations, and we're leaving for Florida on Wednesday. I won't be back until the middle of the following week. Why don't you think about it, Joy, and we'll talk some more about it when I get back. You can make sure that this is what you really want."

Art really did exercise all of the patience that he could muster. It was evident that he did not want to blow their divorce and child custody out of proportions. And since he already had plans, he did not want to blow them off due to Joy's random tantrums and mood swings. He was playing it safe.

"I'm sure this is what I really want," she said.

"You get your ass over here next Wednesday, and be sure to get here before the kids get out of school. I'll be gone by then." Wednesday came, and Joy, true to her word, had packed her most cherished possessions in her car and headed off for parts unknown.

She had turned into this badass woman who did not give a care in the world about what people thought. She was determined to take the high road and not regret it one bit. She had finally decided to live for herself, and no power on this planet could stop her from doing so. However, in the process, she had grown insensitive and desensitized to a lot of feelings and emotions that she previously felt very deeply.

Windy moved into the house with Art to help him take care of 7-year-old Mike and 12-year-old Pat. She soon settled into the mother role. The way she effortlessly took over the responsibilities really made a special place in Art's heart. He has never thought that Windy would be so welcoming to his kids as well. It felt like a dream come true. It was as if he was finally getting what he deserved. After three or four weeks, things settled down to a normal routine, and Art and Windy were living quite happily together as a family.

They did everything together as a family; the kids and Art were happy. Genuinely happy. It was as if this was meant to be as everything fell into place like a jigsaw puzzle. However, as they say, happiness is short-lived, and you need to be careful of the evil eye, lest it takes away all your happiness.

The peace and tranquility of their new family life were short-lived, however. One day out of the clear blue, just like a bad penny, Joy returned and demanded that he give her back the house and kids. What on earth was even that irrational demand? It was solely her decision to walk out on her kids. And she was the one who decided to give up on the house as well in return for some extra money. She was completely turning back on her words.

"No way! You gave them up. The kids are living with me. I want them, and you can't have them back. We had an agreement." Art refused outrightly. This outraged him to the extent that he would do anything not to reverse this decision.

"Well, I changed my mind," she said.

"Well, you can't. You can't have them or the house."

"We'll see about that," she snapped.

"You'll be hearing from my lawyer," she said as she stormed off in her usual nasty style. Joy had really turned into this ugly version of herself, whom, if she met a few years earlier, would have completely despised her. Not only had she become a selfish, self-centered person, but she also bought turmoil in the lives of those associated closely with her.

Art quickly contacted Peter, his lawyer. Sadly, he informed him that it was almost impossible for a father to get custody of his children in New Jersey. In his entire career as a lawyer, he had not heard of any case where custody was awarded to the father.

"But, she gave them to him, she didn't want them. She deserted them." Art argued. It was her own decision, and now she couldn't just back out of it because it did not work out for her.

She had turned the kid's lives topsy turvy. She was not thinking about them. Their parents were busy fighting legal and custody cases. Nobody asked the kids what they wanted. It was indeed a sad state of affairs.

Peter retorted. *"It won't make any difference to the court that she told you she didn't want them or that she took off and left the children with you. You really don't have much of a chance of gaining custody. Any extremely slim chance that he might have will be destroyed as long as Windy was living in the same house with him and his kids. The judge is very old fashioned and would frown on him living with an unmarried woman in the same house as the children. It won't matter how happy or how well adjusted the children are or how much they liked her. I know how good Windy is with the kids, but if you want to pursue this custody battle, she will have to move back to her own house."*

It was 'catch 22'. Art loved Windy and would have married her in an instant, but he couldn't because he wasn't yet divorced from Joy. He couldn't get a final divorce from Joy until the question of custody of the children was settled. Windy and Art discussed the situation, and she too thought it would be best if she moved back to her own house until the custody question was settled. So, much to Art's displeasure and sadness, Windy moved. Art's mother left her home in Ventnor to come to his rescue and help him take care of the children.

Court day came, the day before Thanksgiving. Just like his lawyer had warned him, he didn't have a chance before the "hanging" judge. The judge ordered Art to move out of the house immediately that very afternoon and return custody of the children to Joy. In rendering his decision, the judge proclaimed, *"In our society, I believe that children belong with their natural mother. I don't believe their place is with their father. From time eternal, children have been raised by their mother, and I am not about to change that tradition. Case closed."*

That was it. Plain and simple. No argument to the

contrary, allowed. He didn't want to hear it. He didn't care that she really didn't want them and had deserted them. He didn't care that the kids were now well adjusted and happy and that they wanted to live with Art. He didn't care how much he loved them. He didn't care about anything except his perception of the role of a father and mother from 'time eternal.' They moved out of the house that afternoon as ordered. His mom made the long lonely drive back to her home in Ventnor City. Sadly, he said his goodbyes to the boys and moved back into Chris's apartment. They didn't have much to be thankful for that Thanksgiving.

Round one was over, and Art was beaten, but he was determined that he could stage a comeback and beat the system. He became obsessed with the custody battle for his children and his financial struggle with Joy and her lawyers. They were going for his jugglers. They wouldn't be satisfied until he was financially destitute. It occupied every spare moment of his time. Nervous and irritable, Art was constantly on edge and quick to temper.

Being frustrated and helpless made Art difficult to live with. His attitude and temperament took its toll on Windy, and their relationship suffered. As time passed and their once strong relationship grew weaker and all but died. He spent less and less time at Windy's house and more and more time in the solitude of Chris's apartment.

His struggle for custody was all for naught, however. He ultimately lost not only the custody battle but severely hurt his relationship with Windy. Just as the seemingly unending darkness of the blackest night is vanquished by the golden rays of the sun's light, at the dawn of a new day, so too sometimes is the ignorance and confusion which causes turmoil in our lives.

Joy woke up one day, and the stark reality suddenly dawned on her that there was only so much money and property to divide between them. Their accumulated wealth wasn't growing, and in fact, it was shrinking rapidly. The more her lawyers charged for their harassment services, the less there would be left in the pot to divide between them, and ultimately, the smaller her share would be.

She was a bit startled by this sad realization that the only ones making out well in the divorce battle she was waging were her lawyers. Their fees had already reached $30,000.00 and were growing by the minute. Every time she picked up the phone to talk to their sympathetic ears, it cost her money, every letter they wrote, every phone call they made, every deposition they took, and every interrogatory they requested cost her money.

Having seen the light, she realized that half a loaf of bread on the table was far better than getting a whole loaf and having it eaten by the dogs before getting it home. So, she called off her merry band of lawyers and accepted Art's offer for a truce and peace. Although they would still pursue a divorce, they agreed to continue it amicably. Art decided to drop his suit for custody in exchange for her promise of free and unencumbered visitation rights. They could now begin to develop a long-needed friendship. Time heals all wounds. Finally, both of them had realized that no matter what, negotiations held out in the light of mutual respect would be far more uplifting for their relationship and individually as well. They realized that theu had to chjoose was best for the children. After all, it was not the children's fault that they had to see their parents fighting like this. It would scar them emotionally and mentally for life.

Chapter 14
The Race

"Are you going to go to the races today?" Windy asked.

"Yes, why don't you come with me?"

"No, I don't want to. I don't like the races, and I don't like to see you race. Why don't you give it up? It's dangerous, you could kill yourself," Windy said.

"I can't give it up. I have to race. I won't get hurt, I've been doing it for too many years, and I have never gotten seriously hurt." He replied passionately. His love for racing knew no bounds, and he could never give it up for anything in this world.

"How about coming to Church with me before I go to the races?" He asked.

"Okay, I'll go to Church with you, but not to the races," Windy replied, giving up trying to convince him to stop racing.

"How about dinner tonight?"

"No," she replied, *"let's not rush it, let's go slow. We just spent the night together, and we had a good time, and that was a big step for me."*

"Well, then, how about next Friday night?" Art asked.

"Well, maybe," she replied, *"I'll think about it. I'll talk to you during the week and let you know."* Art loved her very much, but the custody battle with Joy had strained their relationship to the point where Windy had become cold and distant during the past couple of months.

In her mind, she was convinced the relationship was over. She was afraid of getting hurt by getting too close again and only have it fail once more. She loved him, and he loved her, but their personalities and temperaments now clashed. They both were extremely independent and wanted their way. They both thought they knew all the answers, and the subconscious power struggle was too much for them to handle. They had dated several times during the past months, but she didn't want to get close again. Art did, however, so their dates usually ended up in an argument. Frequently she put artificial constraints or made unreasonable demands on their relationship. In an attempt to satisfy herself that their relationship could not work, she often looked for something to start an argument over. Last night was an exception. Art didn't push her, and he didn't act too eagerly either. He let things unfold naturally, slowly and painfully, he had learned she couldn't be pushed. She had to move at her own pace and decide whether or not she wanted to make love. She couldn't be coaxed. It was tearing him apart inside that he couldn't patch up their relationship and make everything better. He felt helpless.

She was in control of their destiny, and he could do nothing other than giving her room. Today, things were looking a little better than they had in a long time. Maybe, just maybe, they still had a chance, but Art knew it would be a long slow process. There was nothing he could do to speed things up. Like the song says, Cei-sara', Sara,' whatever will be will be. The future is not ours to see.

They went to church together, but they hardly talked that morning. Art was feeling kind of hurt that she wouldn't commit to going out again.

"Are you sure you don't want to -come to the races with me? Chris and his girlfriend are going to be there today."

"No, I don't want to come, I'm going out with my girlfriend, but, good luck today and be careful," she said. *"Be really careful."* They kissed goodbye, and he drove off to pick up Pat and meet his partner, Bill, at the garage where they kept the race car.

Pat always went to the races with Art. Even though by New Jersey law, he was too young to be allowed in the pits, they still always managed to sneak him in. They got to the garage a little late. Bill and their friend Johnny had already loaded the race car into a trailer. They then *hook*ed the trailer up to the truck. The atmosphere was all pepped up for the grand race tonight.

Everyone had settled and were ready for the races. His passion for racing was something that he nurtured in his heart knew no bounds. Every time while preparing for a race, he would be excited beyond measure and would always try his level best to be well-rested before the race. Over the years, he had bagged enough experience to learn from his past mistakes and not repeat them again.

"You're late, must have had a good night last night?" John asked with a smirk.

"Yeah, it was good," Art replied with a smile as he got into the truck.

"How good?" John probed.

"Good enough," replied Art in a way to push the topic aside.

They got to the race track and unloaded the race car from the trailer. John fueled the car while Bill and Art checked the tire pressures. They then took it through tech and safety inspection. After the car received a clean bill of health from the scrutinizing eyes of the tech inspector, Art made a practice run. The car was quick and handled well, which set adrenaline rushing through Art's veins. He hadn't stopped his racing for anyone, and he would not do it in the future as well. Come, what may!

It was now time for the first round of racing. He donned his Nomex racing jacket and gloves, put on his helmet, and climbed into the cockpit of the dragster. It was a snug fit, not enough room to maneuver his arms to fasten the safety harness. Bill strapped him in the safety harnesses and lap belt. Art started the motor, and it roared to life like awakening a sleeping dragon. He drove the car into the burnout area behind the starting lines. The air was filled with smoke and the stench of exhaust fumes and burnt rubber. John poured the water on the track surface in front of the rear tires. Art revved the motor up to 7,000 rpm and released the clutch. The huge rear slicks spun furiously in the burnout water, emitting great clouds of smoke as the car shot across the starting line, heating the tires and improving their traction. The spinning tires laid down a long patch of black sticky rubber. A slam on the brakes and the car came to a screeching halt 300 ft in front of the starting line. As Art backed up the car, Bill guided him into the staging lights.

The car was staged carefully to get a starting advantage, the rear tires resting on the sticky patch of rubber laid down during the burnout. Glancing to his right, he watched as the black dragster in the right lane slowly crept into the staging lights and revved his engine. He was apprehensive and keyed up just as he was hundreds of times before.

"I can't be distracted by my competitor. Now I have to concentrate only on the starting lights." Murmured Art to himself.

He was trying to motivate himself as much as he could so that he could clear his mind and concentrate only on the track and controls of the car to do everything perfectly to win. To be passionate about something meant to beat all odds and emerge victorious, come what may.

Revving the motor to 7,000 rpm, Art pressed hard on the brakes to prevent the car from creeping forward. *"Dear God, please keep me safe during this run."* The starting lights came down. First amber, second amber, and then on the last amber, with lightning-quick reflexes, he released the brake and the clutch.

Art could feel the sweat drops trickling down his forehead. The car launched forward across the starting line like a rocket, and he was on his way thundering down the track, the finish line only a scant eight seconds away from launch. Soon, all too soon, the race would be over.

Dirt. Sparks. Darkness, light. Darkness. Sparks. Darkness everywhere. "*I've rolled over three times, but I'm still alive. When will it stop? I can't die now.*" Art murmured in panic. *"Dear God, You've got to help me! I touched the lives of a lot of people, although not always for the best, but I did help a few people and made a lot of friends along the way. Some might even say the world is a better place because of me. Maybe some things didn't always turn out the way I wanted them to, but I tried my best! You can't say I didn't try! Judge me not on what I did, but on my efforts and my intentions. I know I made some bad choices and mistakes, and I'm sorry for all the wrong and stupid things I've done and the pain I've caused. Maybe I should have devoted more time to my family rather than racing. Maybe I should have stopped racing after my friends were killed in their race cars. I shouldn't have let my custody battle with Joy destroy my relationship with Windy. I shouldn't have let work take its toll on my marriage with Joy. If I didn't take all the troubleshooting trips in foreign countries and stayed home more, maybe our marriage wouldn't have been so strained. I wasn't always the master of my destiny, was I? Give me another chance!"* Art was in desperate condition. He could hardly breathe, and he was sweating profusely. His heartbeat was at an all-time high, and he didn't know what to do. All he wished for was a breath of fresh air, something that would feel refreshing and invigorating.

Sparks. Sparks. Dirt. Darkness. Darkness, everywhere. Light, light, there's light. The car's stopped rolling, it's right side up! I'm still alive! It's a miracle. Thank you, dear God! I'm alive. Oh no! Oh no! The car's on fire! Flames are everywhere! I've got to get out of here before the gas tank explodes. I've got to get out before I burn up. Oh no! I'm strapped in. I can't get the safety harness unbuckled, and the flames are too hot. I'm strapped in, and I can't get out. Oh, God! I know you didn't save me from this crash only to have me burn up here. I've got to unbuckle the harness. Nobody is coming to help me. I've got to reach that buckle. It's hot, and it's burning my hand.

I'm being engulfed in flames! *Jesus, help me! Blessed Mother, help me!*

I've got it; I've got the buckle, it's unbuckled. I've got to get out of the cockpit before the car explodes. Flames, flames everywhere. *I'm out. Thank God! I'm out.* His attempt to keep himself calm was very necessary; otherwise, if he panicked, his body would just give in to the flames.

Oh no! I'm on fire. My clothes are on fire! I'm soaked with gasoline. Nobody is here to help me! I've got to get the flames out. I'm burning up. What do I do now? I'll roll on the ground! Maybe that'll get the flames out.

Art could hear the crowd yelling and shouting, *"he's on fire, he's on fire! Get the fire extinguishers! Somebody get over the fence to help him! Somebody help him, he's burning up! Somebody put the fire in the race car out before it explodes.*" Nothing was happening, he was burning up, but no one was helping him. He heard someone yell.

"Somebody squirt the fire extinguishers on him." It was important to take action at the moment; otherwise, anything could have happened.

Someone else replied in panic, *"I can't, the pin's stuck in the fire exchanger."* Someone else yelled, "Give it to me!"

"Now! I've got it! Hurry! I can't spray him from here! I can't spray him from the other side of the fence! Somebody get over the fence to him! Somebody get over the fence quick!"

Then, out of the corner of his eye, he saw something amazing with one mighty leap, 250 lb. Chris jumped over the 7-foot-high fence, which separated him from the crowd.

"Give me the fire extinguisher!" Chris yelled. "I've got it! I've got it! I've put the fires out!"

"Come on! Somebody get over here quick, he needs help!"

Now, some of the people in the crowd and some of the other racers were surrounding him.

"Art, how do you feel?" Andy Boye asked.

"I'm okay, and I feel okay. Please help me up." Art said in a slow pitch. He was still in denial that he had just been saved from a wildfire.

"No, Art. You're not okay. You're hurt, you have to sit here and let the emergency crew work on you." Said Chris and Andy, trying to calm him down and make him realize that he had serious burns on his body.

"Why? I'm okay. I'm okay." He said casually

"No, you're not, Art. You're hurt."

"No, Andy, I'm okay."

"No, Art. You're badly burned."

"No, no, I'm not."

"Yes, you are Art."

The surge of adrenalin in his body staved off the pain temporarily.

"How's the car, Andy?" Don't worry about the car now. But I want to know. Well, if you must know, it's destroyed. You're lucky to be alive."

"Looked to me like the left rear tire blew. No one can control a dragster at that speed when one of those big tires let go. We thought you were a goner when the car rolled over three times. In all my years of racing, I never heard of anyone surviving a crash like that." Andy said. He told Art to be super thankful to be alive right now because he has just escaped death.

The emergency crew and ambulance finally arrived. They started pouring water saline solution all over Art's legs and hands. *"I'm alright,"* he insisted.

"No, you're hurt," the paramedic said. "I've got to cut your pants away."

"Why?" "We've got to see your legs," she insisted. With a pair of scissors, she cut away his charred pants and boots. To his shock and great disbelief, great gobs of skin peeled away with them. He felt a sharp pain rise up his legs as his surge of adrenalin subsided. The reality finally started to settle in that the situation was indeed very serious. Art was badly

burned, severe second and third-degree burns on his legs, and first and second degree burns all over the rest of his body. He started to feel intense pain. They put him into the ambulance and rushed him off to the hospital. He was in agony, but he was alive.

Art could see the flashbacks in his mind's eye of the car toppling over and going up in flames. How had he thought he would survive this insanely outrageous fire. He didn't have the least bit idea of what he was putting himself into. When the car first rolled over, he was in pitch darkness. In mere seconds that seemed like an eternity, his entire life flashed before him and he saw how the perceived good and wrong choiced choices he made in his life fit together like the pieces of a puzzle. Everything nowemade perfect sence.

His prayers were all about forgiveness, for ever being a source of hurt or pain to anybody intentionally or unintentionally. That moment made him realize how short life is to bear grudges or even keep any animosity in your heart. At that moment, it was like the whole world came crashing down, and all he wanted was to get another chance at life.

If only he got a chance to go back in time and rectify his

mistakes, he wouldn't waste it for anything. He pondered again if he could have changed things should he have, and did he really have the freedom to do that or was it determined by fate. Would his life have been totally different, and would it have been better or maybe worse?

Now that you have read my story, I ask you. If you could, would you have changed something in your life? If you did, life would certainly be different today, but would you be better, or would you have a completely different set of problems. Would you have the same children, grandchildren, and friends? Would life be better than what it is now? Did you really have the ability to make different choices, or were some of them determined by fate?

"Thank God I am alive. I know somehow I will recover from this. I've got another chance."

He wondered if Windy or Joy will even care that he's hurt so badly? Joy will, he knew she would. Without a second thought, his heart told him that Joy was the one who could see his pain and care for him genuinely. It was like all these emotions and feelings were swarming up in his heart, and he couldn't help but ruminate on all his relationships and everything that he held close to his heart.

He felt the urge to have someone to go to, who really cared for him and would wish well for him with all their heart. Joy was once a person that he had shared some of the most intimate moments of his life. Even though they might have gone their separate ways, there are some things that never change. They had two children, and that bond of being parents was unbreakable.

Choices

As Fate Would Have It

About The Book

This true story is about a man in his mid-thirties who is in a race car crash, and death was imminent. At that moment between life and death, the past and present merge, and time stands still. In just a few brief seconds, he relives his entire life. This story chronicles his experiences and decisions he made in his life from childhood through adult life.

As an engineer for EXXON oil company, he had to choose between traveling for the company on emergency trouble shooting trips or staying at home with his family. He also would have had to reduced his hectic racing schedule. The choices he made severely impacted his family He wonders if the choices he made were determined by fate or did he have the ability to change them.

This book is based on the author Art DiNick's personal life experience, which left a huge impact on his life and almost changed everything. After 30 years of wait, he has finally penned down the story. So, grab your copy today to read about how he got a second chance at life! and ponder the impact of the choices you made in life.

Made in the USA
Middletown, DE
28 March 2023

27804267R00305